THE WRITING RETREAT

THE WRITING RETREAT

A Novel

JULIA BARTZ

THORNDIKE PRESS
A part of Gale, a Cengage Company

Copyright © 2023 by Julia Bartz Inc.
Thorndike Press, a part of Gale, a Cengage Company.

Thorndike Press® Large Print Basic.
The text of this Large Print edition is unabridged.
Other aspects of the book may vary from the original edition.
Set in 16 pt. Plantin.

**LIBRARY OF CONGRESS CIP DATA ON FILE.
CATALOGUING IN PUBLICATION FOR THIS BOOK
IS AVAILABLE FROM THE LIBRARY OF CONGRESS.**

ISBN-13: 979-8-88578-705-5 (hardcover alk. paper)

Published in 2023 by arrangement with Emily Bestler Books/Atria Books, a Division of Simon & Schuster, Inc.

Printed in Mexico
Print Number: 1   Print Year: 2023

For Andi, my blood and soul sister, who's always up for a scary movie.

■ ■ ■ ■

PART ONE:
THE CITY

■ ■ ■ ■

CHAPTER 1

Fuck her.

These were the words that got me down the subway steps. I was going to Ursula's book party, and if Wren was there, too, well, she could just go fuck herself.

But my fingers were shaking in the moment before I gripped the subway pole. So much for bravado. And I had to admit: this wild, frenetic energy coursing through me wasn't rage, exactly. It was more like abject terror.

Friday night commuters filled the sweaty subway car. I stood over two seated girls who were maybe in high school, their mascara-laden eyes darting, hands pulling nervously at hair. One leaned in and said something into the other's ear. She nodded sagely, and they regarded each other with smirks.

The interaction jabbed like a penknife in the ribs. Their shared world. Their undeniable certainty that they were a team. It reminded me of early days with Wren, holding hands as we rode out to Bushwick, wearing cheap pleather leggings, swigging from a shared plastic bottle of vodka and soda.

Stop. I curled my fist in my pocket, digging my fingernails into my palm. I couldn't show up like this, with soft, pathetic yearning in my eyes. Wren and I were no longer best friends. Or friends at all. And that was fine. I was thirty years old. It didn't make sense that I was still so broken up about a goddamn friendship.

The doors slid open. I followed a small stream of people out, throwing a final glance back at the teen girls. One stared directly at me, her gaze both curious and hostile.

Pete was waiting for me in the hotel lobby, a mishmash of leather couches, gleaming wood surfaces, and golden chandeliers.

"Alex, hello!" He jumped up, then stuck his hands in his pockets and grinned. "Don't tell anyone, but I'm definitely not cool enough to be here."

I'd been more relieved than I'd let on that Pete, my one work friend, had agreed to come to the book party. Seeing him in his smudged glasses, loose jeans, and non-ironic running shoes caused my heart rate to slow.

"Careful." I smiled, shrugging off my heavy coat. "They can smell your fear."

He chattered as we walked towards the basement steps and I tried to focus on his words. Pete and I had only started hanging out outside work recently, and while part of me enjoyed his unselfconsciously affable personality, another part was bereft. I could almost hear Wren's amused voice: *Really? This* nerd is your new bestie?

At the top of the stairs, two women blew past us, waves of flowery perfume streaming off their fur-trimmed coats. I felt like I was in a dream as I followed Pete down the steps, studying the back of his head as he kept half turning to explain something ridiculous his boss had done that day.

At the bottom a hallway stretched in both directions. From the right came the sounds of laughter and clinking glasses, undercut by some kind of buzzing electronic music. A mirror ran down the hallway, a thin strip cutting us off below the shoulders. I looked like a disembodied ghoul: pale skin marked with red blotches from the cold, eyes teary from the wind, dark hair staticky from my hat. I tried to bend my mouth into a smile. I'd redone my makeup before leaving work,

11

adding extra eyeliner and lipstick, but I worried it only made me look false and weird.

We strode towards the music. A marquis sign with pressed-in letters greeted us at the open doorway: URSULA'S BOOK RELEASE!! WELCOME BITCHES!!!!!

Beyond was a wall of people. It looked like a living thing, blinking and shimmering and pushing various tentacles towards the bar. My stomach plummeted. I'd never been afraid of crowds before. In fact, I'd always thrown myself in — at dance parties, sweaty basement shows, art galleries so packed that you knew someone was going to knock over a sculpture.

But now I was afraid. More than that: on the verge of a panic attack.

"Yikes." Pete considered. "I can literally feel my social anxiety rising."

The words made me smile. "Me too."

"What do you think?" Pete studied me. I knew that if for whatever reason I wanted to leave, he'd take it in stride. He'd probably offer an alternative: a beer, a snack nearby.

But I had to do this. True, I hadn't seen Wren since that awful day — her birthday, nearly a year ago now. Sure, I'd stalked her social media, watching as her beauty editor job had earned her a blue check mark. I'd seen her style change, her dark bangs go blunt instead of choppy, her growing proclivity for designer jackets. I couldn't comprehend seeing her in person; it'd be like confronting a ghost who'd come back to life.

"Let's make for the bar." I said it grimly and Pete laughed.

"Here we go!" We plunged into the crowd. Pete slithered up to the bar, leaving me a few steps behind. It was sweltering and loud, guests shout-talking to be heard over the music, slurping drinks like it was 2:00 a.m. instead of early evening. I glanced surreptitiously around. My breath caught in my throat as I saw the back of her sleek dark bob. But she turned and no — it wasn't her. I forced myself to take a deep breath. Maybe she wouldn't come; maybe she was out of town or something. Wouldn't that be hilarious, all that panic for nothing?

"Jesus." Pete returned with two beers. "These cost twelve dollars each! I thought that was the whole point of book parties — free booze!"

"Thanks. I'll Venmo you." I took the glass gratefully and gulped.

"Hmm." Pete squinted at the crowd like a shipman searching the horizon. "Maybe let's go over there where it's more chill." I followed him into the main room with the stage. We made it to the back wall and both leaned against it with relief. The tightness in my chest eased.

"That's Ursula, right?" Pete gestured with his glass.

"That's her." She stood near the stage, holding court with a semicircle of admirers.

"How'd you meet her again?"

"A writing group. A long time ago." Seeing her in the flesh — tortoiseshell glasses and animal-print dress against pale tattooed skin and hot-pink hair — made me relax further. It was a bit sad that the fear of seeing Wren had made me forget about the point of this whole event: to celebrate Ursula's success.

I'd met Ursula through Wren, actually, shortly after meeting Wren at work. An image reared up: Wren in her signature vintage black rabbit fur coat and red lipstick. She'd been assigned to train me as an assistant, though she'd been working at the educational publishing company only a few months longer than me. That first morning with Wren, I'd known — instantly — what becoming friends meant: secret dance parties in abandoned warehouses, madcap dates ending with kisses in forlorn alleys, boozy brunches laughing over the night before. It was as clear as if someone had whispered it into my ear. Wren was a ticket into the life I'd envisioned in my fantasies, staring out of the window of Mom's broken-down hatchback as we raced over gray plains to get far away from her last disastrous boyfriend. Wren was the tornado that could pick me up and put me down in the midst of a luscious, Technicolor dream-world.

But first I had to impress her. In an uncharacteristic burst of luck, it had happened before I could even make a plan. Leaning over my desk to help me log in, she'd seen the book I'd set down: *Polar Star,* the most recent Roza Vallo. I'd already read it, of course, having put a hold on it at the library before it had even come out. But the past few months of job hunting had been demoralizing, and I'd splurged on the gorgeous hardcover during a particularly low day.

"You like Roza Vallo?" Wren stared askance. I knew her skepticism stemmed from my uncool professional outfit: slacks and a pale blue button-up shirt. She loomed over me, a tall girl who wore platforms because she didn't give a fuck about towering over everyone else.

"She's my favorite author." I calculated

15

and continued: "She's a big inspiration for me. For my writing, I mean."

Wren's ruby lips curved. "Me too." She leaned in, eyes narrowing. "I kind of love your eyebrows. Where do you get them done?"

I fought not to touch them self-consciously. Was she referring to my inexpert plucking? "I do them myself."

"Nice." She yawned. "Lord, I'm hungover. Let's get lunch."

Though it was barely eleven, we'd soon found ourselves slurping spicy noodles while talking nonstop about our current writing projects. We were both working on novels, and both extremely serious about them. That afternoon I sent my first email to her, containing a link to a Roza Vallo article that explored the feminist themes underpinning her novels' use of period blood. I also boldly joked about my boss's cleavage. She responded almost immediately, and we started a spate of witty exchanges that I spent much more time and energy on than my actual job.

Two months later Wren had asked me to join her writing group, since their third person had dropped out. There I'd met Ursula. She was nearly ten years older than us and had a calm self-confidence that I could only dream of. At this point I'd been blatantly copying Wren — which meant spending whole days at Goodwill, looking for clothes she might admire. But Ursula was her own person. She had her own neon-colored, clashing style and wrote intensely personal pieces about being Chinese American, queer, and a fat activist. She was so different from Wren and yet was the one person Wren ever seemed in awe of.

The music switched off, and Pete's next question rang too loud in my ear. "How long have you known her?"

I blinked before realizing he was talking about Ursula, not Wren. "I guess about eight years?" The crowd from the bar oozed into the main room.

"Huh. Back before she was famous."

"Yep." Even back then I'd known Ursula would find success. I'd always thought her essays were good enough to be published in the New York Times, so it wasn't a surprise when one actually was. After her Modern Love piece came out, she got snatched up by an agent and editor who fast-tracked her first book of essays. That had been three years ago; she was now publishing her second.

"You recognize anyone?" Pete scanned the crowd.

I forced myself to look. Hordes of hip people, many of them young, early twenties, purposefully plain with severely shorn hair and no makeup. That level of confidence — at such a young age! — amazed me. I couldn't leave my apartment without a full face of makeup.

"Not really," I was saying, but then I heard it — a familiar laugh. About ten feet away stood Ridhi, one of Wren's choice friends. I shifted so that I was partially hidden by Pete.

"Hi, everyone!" a female voice crackled over a loudspeaker. "We're going to start!" The crowd shuffled and I saw with relief that Ridhi and her group were moving ahead. My stomach dropped as I recognized several others with her, including another of Wren's good friends, Craig. He wore a slim olive suit and was murmuring into Ridhi's ear with a wide grin.

"Welcome, everyone." Ursula's agent, Melody, had a commanding voice and everyone quieted down immediately. As she introduced Ursula, I kept an eye on the crew. Watching them gave me an unexpectedly powerful ache. The friend breakup with Wren hadn't just been between the two of us; I'd lost all our mutual friends too.

I should've known; it was unthinkable now

that I hadn't. After all, the night of Wren's birthday had ended in arcs of blood, splattering black in the moonlight.

People were applauding. I shook myself and clapped along as Ursula strode across the stage in iridescent platform boots. "Guys, seriously, thank you so much for being here." Her low voice was often sardonic, but now it was resonant with sincerity. "You are all amazing people and sometimes I have to pinch myself that I have such an incredible support network." As Ursula continued speaking, I took another gulp of beer, realizing it was almost gone. I hadn't eaten since lunch, and the alcohol was making me woozy in the overheated room.

"Okay!" Ursula raised her glass. "I know at book parties you're supposed to read an excerpt and blah blah blah, but why don't we skip that boring part tonight and just party?" She laughed at the ensuing wolf whistles. "Awesome. Let's go ahead and mingle, then! Oh, and buy a book or three!" Amidst cheers, Ursula left the stage and the crowd dispersed, many making for the bar. I watched Wren's crew join the signing line, still oblivious to my presence. If Wren was here, she'd be with them. So she wasn't here. She must be traveling, at a photo shoot, doing something she was probably already posting about. And, no, I wasn't going to immediately check. The confirmation made me relieved but also unexpectedly disappointed.

"This is wild," I told Pete, attempting to distract myself as we joined the back of the signing line. "Ursula's last reading was in the basement of a bookstore in Greenpoint with bottles of Two-Buck Chuck."

"At least they had free alcohol." Pete held up his own empty glass. "Want another IPA?"

"Sure." Finally, I could relax. This called for at least another drink, maybe more.

Ursula's publicist strode down the line with a stack of books. I bought two copies, one for Pete. The smooth, weighty hardcover showed a picture of Ursula on a vintage red-velvet couch. She sat cross-legged in ripped denim overalls, gazing unabashedly into the camera. A hungry, wolfish feeling reared up in my gut. What would it feel like to hold your own book in your hands for the first time? For it to be a physical object, a thing that people paid for?

I glanced up, feeling eyes on me. The crew was staring at me, surprised and faintly disgusted, like I was a racoon that had wandered into their living room. Only Craig was looking at someone else —

Wren. He was looking at Wren.

The world blurred, and for a moment it was just me and her. There was something glinting in her eyes, a reflection of the pain and loss that I so keenly felt. A sob rose up in my throat at the realization that she felt it, too, that she did miss me, that she, too, wanted nothing more than for us to grasp each other in a tight, desperate hug, pulled back together like two powerful magnets.

But then a wall came down. The pain shifted into something else, something darker: revulsion.

Don't touch me. I'd been drunk that night but could still remember her voice with perfect clarity. How she'd hissed the words from between clenched teeth. How literally moments later she'd been lying in a spreading pool of blood.

I felt frozen, unable to look away. Wren turned and said something to Craig. He laughed and looked relieved. The others moved inward towards her, though Ridhi glowered at me a few seconds longer.

The beer gurgled in my stomach. I turned and raced towards the bathroom, making it to a stall just in time. Yellow liquid frothed in the bowl. I sat on my knees and wiped my mouth. I was still clutching the books.

Slowly, I stood and flushed the toilet. At

the sink a pretty girl washed her hands and avoided looking at me. She must have heard my retches. I wanted to burst into tears but I kept them firmly down.

What had I expected? For Wren to smile and ask if I wanted to be friends again?

We were over. Forever. I knew that now.

A text pinged. Hey where are you? Can't find you. Pete. Leaning against the sink, I wrote back with shaky fingers. I just saw someone I didn't want to run into. Mind if we leave?

Sure! came the instant reply. Sounds like we need to get you another drink.

CHAPTER 2

My phone rang, a tinny guitar riff that made me grit my teeth. I rolled over in bed and groaned. I had a headache, the type that felt like hot metal spikes through my skull. I silenced the ringtone, noting the string of text messages from Pete.

3:00 a.m.: Let me know you got home safe

4:00 a.m.: Alex??? You okay?????

7:00 a.m.: Please call me when you see this, I'm serious

Memories from the night before poured in. Guzzling more beers at a pub down the street and feeling good, better than I had in days, weeks, months? Pete and I chatting with the bartender, an actual Irish dude who'd given us shot after shot of whiskey. Making eyes at him, even though he couldn't have been more than twenty-two, and him grinning back at me as he poured, as if telling me he knew what I wanted and he wanted it too.

But then somehow Pete and I had ended up in a cab, furiously making out. We'd gone to his apartment, which was in Manhattan, stumbling straight to his bed, suddenly naked.

The next part was blurrier, but I knew that we'd had sex. Afterwards, I'd freaked out and left, wasted but determined to get home.

I pulled my phone closer and typed. Hey Pete. I'm okay. Thanks for checking in.

He started writing back, then stopped.

I moaned, burying my face in my damp, sweaty pillow. The one friend I'd managed to make after my excommunication from Wren's coterie, and now I'd ruined that too. How was I going to be able to go back to work? How was I going to be able to look him in the face after forcing him to call me those names? *Slut. Cunt. Whore.*

I emailed my boss, Sharon, letting her know I'd woken up with a fever — untrue but close — and pulled myself out of bed to crack the windows. The radiators in the apartment were always tropical in the wintertime, no matter how far I turned them down. I stumbled to the bathroom and stepped into the shower, letting the water strip my greasy skin.

You like that, don't you? Pete's voice in my

ear as he thrust into me from behind. *You like that, you little . . .*

"Stop," I said out loud. When I got out of the shower, I felt a little better, though my stomach still roiled. I made ginger tea and settled onto the couch, grateful that my roommate was over at her boyfriend's. I had a voicemail notification from the night before: Ursula.

"Al!" Her voice was barely audible over thudding music. "Where are you? We're out at Simone's! Right by you. Anyway, I'm with some people . . ." Her words melted into mutterings as she spoke to someone else. "They're telling me you were at the book party but bounced? And that you and Wren still aren't talking? What is this, middle school?" Craig's laughter in the background. "Anyhow, I want you here, so you should come immediately. Also, I have to tell you something cool: I just found out from Melody, my agent . . . say hi, Melody!" A warm *"Hiiiii."* "Get this: Melody knows Roza Vallo's agent! Isn't that amazing? I'm trying to finagle a visit to Blackbriar . . . oh, okay. I have to go; they're telling me I have to go. Call me or text me, okay?" More sounds of music, laughter, screams, then nothing.

I smiled, remembering nights out at Simone's, a dirty dive that turned into a dance

25

party after midnight. It would get hot and sweaty and disgusting, but we didn't care, because we were more often than not absolutely sloshed. Wren and I would find ourselves there if the earlier parts of the night had been a bust, meaning we hadn't yet met cute boys. There were always boys there, reliably attractive, though maybe that was due to the hours of drinking beforehand.

I called Ursula back.

"Hey." Her voice was subdued, a marked contrast to the voicemail.

"Hey." I stretched out my legs. "Just got your voicemail."

"Voicemail?" She chuckled. "Oh my god, yeah. We were at Simone's and I really wanted you there. Where were you?"

"Yeah, I'm sorry. I got wasted and ended up making bad decisions with a coworker." I blew out my breath, attempting to sound breezy. "Anyway, I wanted to call and say congratulations! I am so proud of —"

"Hold up, who's this guy? They said they saw you there with someone."

" 'They'? You got the full report from Wren?" The thought gave me a flash of unease.

"Well, Craig." She coughed and said a soft thank-you, presumably to her girlfriend

Phoebe, then sipped something. The sound buzzed and crackled. "Missed you last night."

"I'm really sorry." Shame washed over me. "I wanted to see you, obviously, and celebrate with you. But then I saw Wren and kind of freaked out."

"Okay." She sighed. "So this is really still a thing? Because of what went down at her birthday? I don't get it. That was an accident. Horrific, yes. But an accident."

"It was." Which wasn't exactly true. I pushed the growing panic down into my core.

"And you guys were so close. I mean, I've grown apart from people before. It happens. But you guys were like sisters."

"Yeah. It was pretty unexpected." The recurring ache reared up in my chest, all the way to my throat. I swallowed, driving it back down. I didn't want to think about this, much less talk about it.

"I told Wren you guys should get a third-party person and sit down and talk about it," Ursula went on musingly. "Maybe couples counselors do that. Or I could even do it if you wanted."

"You told her that?" I asked, my curiosity piqued. "What'd she say?"

Ursula paused. "You know what? I do not

remember."

"Listen." I forced a smile. "Enough about our drama. Really, it's fine and we will both survive. I want to know about you: living in LA, book events . . . I'm really excited to read your book, by the way!"

"Yeah, let me know what you think. I feel like they rushed it and I had to write the last two essays in, like, a day." She snorted. "Things are good. Some podcasts and interviews and whatnot coming up, which still make me feel awkward. But I guess that's the writer life. I actually wanted to ask you: How's your writing going?"

"Good," I lied, bright.

"Did you apply for that fellowship I sent you a few months ago?"

"I did," I lied again. The shame returned, heavy and damp. Another topic to make me feel horrible about myself. Then, to change the subject: "Also, wait, you were talking about Roza Vallo last night? Your agent knows her?"

"Yes! I had no idea!" She chuckled. "Apparently she — Roza's agent — was one of Melody's mentors. So of course I had to ask Melody if she's ever been to Roza's estate. Sadly, no. But, hey, that's only two connections away. I feel like we can make it happen."

"Totally." It had been a running joke between the three of us: how to meet our shared favorite author, the famously reclusive Roza Vallo.

"That retreat must be starting soon," Ursula went on.

"Next month." I'd kept track of it, following the news articles as they popped up on literary sites and in the arts sections of major outlets. Wren and I had both applied, sending in our best, most polished short stories. Somehow we'd been convinced that at least one of us would get in.

Two years ago, Roza Vallo — our guru, imagined mentor, and patron saint — had come out with a shocking announcement. She was going to hold a monthlong writing retreat at her home, Blackbriar Estate, for four up-and-coming female writers who were under thirty. She wanted to foster and cultivate the next big names. Simply getting picked would mean instant fame. Wren and I had promised that whichever of us got in — hopefully both, but we didn't want to be too presumptuous — would help raise up the other.

Of course, neither of us had been chosen. Thousands must have applied. And the reading period had lasted so long that, by the time the winners were picked, both of us had aged out of the under-thirty condition.

I'd been so curious to see who the chosen ones were, but that information had been kept from the public. I'd read on a Roza Vallo subreddit that the winners had had to sign NDAs promising not to tell anyone they'd gotten in. Some commentors guessed it was because they'd be approached by news outlets promising payment for pictures or video inside the estate. Honestly, it had been a relief not to know. It was exhausting enough to stalk one person on social media — meaning Wren, embarrassing but true — let alone four more.

"We'll find a way to meet Roza," Ursula said. "Don't worry."

"Someday. Hey, when do you go back to LA?" I felt like death, but I'd conquer it in order to see Ursula. "Want to get lunch or something? I took the day off."

"I'd love to, but Phoebe and I are heading to the airport soon. It was a really quick trip. Let's make plans the next time I'm here, okay?"

"Sounds good."

After we hung up, I made myself a piece of toast and turned on some mindless reality TV. My mind drifted back to Roza. What would she do if she were in my position?

She would've fucked Pete without a second thought. No shame or regret at all. And before, at the party, she would've gone right up to Wren, called her on her attitude, and maybe even slapped her sharp cheek.

I pulled up Roza's recent *New York Times Magazine* interview, intent on infusing her signature badass energy into my tepid life. I'd even used the main picture — Roza lounging on stone steps in a floor-length sequined gown — as my current lock screen. Roza stared directly at the camera, her expression a little amused, maybe even teasing.

Roza didn't do many interviews, so this was a big deal. It had come out six months before, after the contest had closed.

Who is Roza Vallo?

"People think I'm a witch." Vallo says it lightly as she picks up her stoneware mug of peppermint tea. We're in Blackbriar Estate, her famed home in the Adirondacks of New York. The mansion has been renovated to re-create the home originally built in 1881 by oil tycoon Horace Hamilton. Driving up to the circular drive to view the imposing Victorian mansion reminded me of approaching Daphne du Maurier's Manderley or even Shirley Jackson's Hill

House. There's a sense of unease beyond the stonework and sun-blocked windows.

Vallo had answered the front door herself, barefoot in a floaty black dress. She's in her midfifties, but — like many wealthy, well-kempt women — she could easily pass for a decade younger. Now we sit in the library, a stunning repository of more than 10,000 books.

When I ask if she's a good witch or a bad witch, she laughs.

"Bad." She swings back her long auburn tresses. Her voice contains just a hint of her Hungarian heritage, a slight emphasis on the consonants. "Is there really any other kind?"

Vallo has cultivated this witchy, mythical existence around herself, starting at 19 when her first novel, "Devil's Tongue," was published. The prose is lyrical and lush, and it's astounding to remember it was written by a teen. Perhaps even more surprising is the depth and complexity of the story itself, which I believe holds important clues to unlocking the mysteries of Vallo. (Spoilers ahead.) The plot begins with 12-year-old Kata, whose best friend Eliza has just died. The reasons for her death are murky but somehow related to an early sex scene between Eliza and her male teacher. After the funeral, as Kata tearfully contemplates her best friend's open coffin and the grown-ups settle payment with the funeral director in the back, Eliza wakes up. She climbs out of the coffin and beckons Kata to follow her outside.

The problem: Eliza is still dead. But as she begins to decompose, she and Kata share a few more days together, stunned by this occurrence, talking and holding each other and, eventually, sexually exploring together. They also discover what's keeping Eliza alive: an elderly woman at the edge of town is actually a witch who wants Eliza's essence for herself. Eliza is convinced that if they kill the woman she'll come fully back to life, so she and a reluctant Kata make plans to murder her in her sleep.

But the plan doesn't work. In a last-ditch attempt, Kata tries to cast another spell with the witch's spell books. Eliza's soul enters the body of a hunter in the woods nearby. Kata and Eliza continue their love affair in Eliza's new form. Eventually, Kata catches Eliza casting another spell to jump into Kata's body. She must decide whether to save herself by destroying Eliza or to sacrifice herself for her friend's existence.

Vallo wrote the book while her own best

friend, Mila, was dying of stomach cancer.

"I couldn't believe it when she got sick." Vallo picks at a sugar-dusted molasses cookie. "She was so tough. Always the one who wanted to rebel. She loved stealing lipstick from the store. Teasing boys. But I think it's because she felt safe. Secure. Her father was a rich man, a lawyer." Though Vallo and Mila were neighbors in Budapest, and both Jewish, they came from vastly different economic backgrounds. Vallo's father worked in a factory while her mother was a seamstress. The family struggled under Soviet rule and the ongoing economic depression.

"They were older," Vallo says of her parents. "My mother had me at forty, which I think was an accident. And they were always financially struggling. They worked a lot and expected me to take care of myself, even when I was very young. So I'd entertain myself with books. There was a used bookstore nearby they took me to and there was such a variety to choose from. Nancy Drew, Dostoyevsky; I read it all. And when I got a little older, I would steal from my mother's purse and buy books myself." She leans forward, conspiratorial. "That's when I was able to get what I really liked. The pulp. Mystery, horror.

And to my delight, these were the books that had the most sex in them. Hurray! Real sex, I mean, not those stupid romance books with soft embraces in the moonlight." She rolls her eyes. "That didn't appeal to me at all."

Vallo's known for the "real sex" in her books. "Devil's Tongue" is considered an early queer classic, with explicit sex scenes that later caused the Hungarian government to censor it.

Vallo has always remained private about her relationships, but has been romantically linked to men and women. However, she has always denied a sexual relationship with Mila.

"I'm so sick of talking about that fucking book," Vallo says suddenly. She smiles. "You want to talk about 'Lady X,' don't you? The flop? Everyone does."

Vallo published her second book six years after "Devil's Tongue," when she was 25. The book — a more subtle haunted house story about a poor Hungarian family mirroring Vallo's own — was widely ignored. Her "Devil's Tongue" fans were disappointed and called the book tedious and slow. For a time, it seemed Vallo was a one-hit wonder.

Then came the dreamlike "Lion's Rose"

four years later, in 1993. Critics hailed it as a return to form. The novel concerns a female gardener who is dying of AIDS. She finds a flower that can give her everlasting life — but only if she stays in the garden. Vallo's two latest books, "Polar Star" and "Maiden Pink," are formed around similar themes: changing bodies, the constant whisper of death, the thrill and brutality in sexuality, the intimate connections between women. "Polar Star" (2002) is a quieter and sweeter book, despite its disturbing premise: two elderly women who own a bed-and-breakfast invite one's young niece to join them in their annual ritual of killing and dismembering a male guest.

The lags between Vallo's books have expanded; her next, "Maiden Pink," didn't come out until 2014. This story centers on a college student who becomes drawn to her professor, a woman with a seemingly supernatural connection to a long-dead poetess. At once a sexually charged love story and an over-the-top murder mystery, like most of Vallo's books it's hard to put down.

As Vallo prepares to welcome four unnamed young female writers into her estate for a monthlong writing retreat this winter, one could wonder whether her focus has shifted. Is she going to become a mentor, outwardly facing and fostering talent, instead of disappearing back into her reclusive writer's life?

"Oh no." She winks. "I'm always working on something new."

A text popped up from Sharon, my boss. Where is the Madison proposal???? I need it for the meeting!!!

Shit. I'd totally forgotten about the all-hands-on-deck meeting for one of my projects. Somehow I always managed to block out my work life the second I walked out the glass front doors. I never would've expected that I'd be at the same publishing company for six years, having risen up the ranks from bleakly underpaid editorial assistant to bleakly underpaid associate editor. Wren had pushed me to pursue another career even as she'd left to become the beauty editor at a tiny media startup that had, against all odds, succeeded.

Now Wren was making bank and traveling and wearing designer clothes, all while I was stuck at a failing publisher under a domineering supervisor.

I wanted to ignore Sharon, who'd been freely using my personal cell since I'd stupidly given her my number at a conference in Ohio. But I couldn't, if only because I didn't want to let down the other members of the team. So I texted back the location of the files while I felt Roza watching over my shoulder, disgusted at how quickly I responded to Sharon's demands.

I stared at the ceiling, half listening to the English accent–tinged confessions coming from the TV. Ursula's innocent question came back to me: *How's your writing going?*

The truth was, since everything with Wren, I hadn't written a word.

That afternoon I ventured out for a bagel sandwich. The cold outside was a shocking, cleansing blast. A text dinged as I gave my order at the deli counter, inhaling the scent of garlic and coffee. I sat at one of the tiny metal tables and pulled out my phone. It was from Ursula.

Random: Which story did you send to the Roza contest? Was it the one about the two girls in the woods?

I'd shared that story in our writing group, many years ago.

No, I wrote back. I sent a newer one. It had been a bit of a Roza knockoff; maybe that's why they hadn't chosen it. I added: Why?

But in response, she just sent a smiley face.

I opened up Instagram with my fake account and, before I could stop myself, went to Wren's profile. She'd blocked my personal account, so I'd started this other one to keep tabs. The most recent picture was of her from the night before, holding up a drink next to Ursula in the dark bar, glowing in the flash of the camera. *Celebrating another incredible book from one of my oldest friends.* Her head tilted slightly to the right; she knew all her best angles. At this point she had 32K followers.

When Wren and I had met, I wasn't even on Instagram. I'd joined solely to connect with her. I'd sent my first DM to her — someone had posted the original cover for *Devil's Tongue.*

Wren had not only responded but brought up *Devil's Tongue* the next day.

We'd been in Madison Square Park, our new lunchtime spot. I remembered we were eating sushi and I was trying not to look like an idiot struggling with my chopsticks. Wren, in one of her storytelling moods, shared how she'd read *Devil's Tongue* in junior high after one of the other cheerleaders gave it to her. ("Wait, you were a *cheerleader*?" "Al, there were thirty people in my grade; of course I was a cheerleader.") Wren had read it secretly, under the covers with a flashlight, but her born-again Christian mother had still found it tangled in her bedsheets. This was the first time I heard about the many cruel and unusual punishments Wren's mother had inflicted upon her, starting with locking her in a closet at three years old. This time her mother grounded her for two weeks and refused to serve her dinner. Wren would still have to show up for the meal and just watch her mom and dad and three siblings eat. Luckily, Wren's friends at school brought her food — mostly cupcakes and chips — and she'd gorge on them after everyone else had gone to bed.

After hearing Wren's story, I'd been speechless. As we watched a nearby man try to get a fat squirrel to eat out of his hand, I tried to come up with something to say. *Damn. I thought* I *had it bad.* But when I finally decided on "I'm so sorry," she shrugged and even laughed. "My mom was and is a total cunt. How about your parents?"

So I told her. That my dad had left when I was eight and we'd never seen or heard from him again, at least to my knowledge. That Mom had dragged us from city to city, oftentimes to meet up with an "old friend" who always inevitably turned out to be male. That we'd stay with him or at a cheap weekly rental, and Mom would get a job at a drugstore or grocery store. And that just as I'd start to get comfortable at a new school, she'd get fed up with her boyfriend and would haul us to the next town, until it seemed easier to stop trying to make friends altogether.

"That sucks." Wren's voice was both soft and matter-of-fact.

And it had, but at least there hadn't been any out-and-out abuse. While I never did much to be punished for, I had the feeling then that Mom wouldn't have noticed even if I had tried to rebel: stayed out all night and come back stinking of whiskey and cigarette smoke.

"Did any of the guys try to do anything to you?" Wren asked.

Thankfully, no. I'd kept my distance, knowing that my very existence was likely an annoyance to them. I tried to be as neat and quiet as possible. Even hearing them having loud sex was weirdly comforting, knowing that they weren't thinking of me, that I wasn't getting in the way.

"Who gave you a copy of *Devil's Tongue*?" Wren asked, popping her last piece of sashimi into her mouth. The squirrel man had succeeded in his quest. The woman sitting on the other side of his bench watched him, faintly grossed out. I already knew that most New Yorkers did their best to avoid touching squirrels, pigeons, and other city creatures.

"It was this woman at Barnes & Noble." We'd just moved from Minneapolis to a suburb of Chicago to stay with Mom's friend John, one of the nicer ones who would occasionally ask how I was doing. It was the summer before seventh grade, and while Mom worked, I spent most of my time at a mall where she would drop me off in the mornings. I'd hang out for hours in a stuffed leather chair by a window, reading. Leanne, one of the employees, couldn't have been more than eighteen or nineteen, but she seemed so much older when she started chatting with me, impressed by my reading speed. She didn't seem annoyed that I never bought anything, and she actually started bringing me recommendations after she found out I liked sci-fi and horror. One of those was *Devil's Tongue.*

"Nice." Wren smirked at me, squeezing my arm. "You should dedicate your first book to her!"

"Order forty-two!" The yell jolted me out of my reveries. I went to the counter to pick up the paper bag. My phone pinged again as I left. I pulled it out immediately, wondering if it'd be another cryptic text from Ursula.

But instead it was from Sharon: But where are the Madison P&Ls?? They're not in the folder!!!!!!

With a heavy sigh, I wrote back. By the time I got home, I'd forgotten all about Ursula's question.

CHAPTER 3

Ursula called me with the news on Monday morning. I was en route to work, after having taken Friday off too. It was time to face Pete. But I still stopped to get coffee so that I wouldn't have to chance seeing him in the kitchen. As I waited in line, an image arose: him looking up at me with a drunken smirk on his face, fondling my breasts.

I squeezed my eyes shut, weathering the shame. Pete hadn't texted or emailed at all while I was out, which was unusual. Or not so unusual, considering what had happened.

A text popped up from Ursula: CALL ME ASAP! URGENT!!!!! I got my coffee and slipped into a miraculously open seat at the window.

She picked up on the first ring. "Al!"

"Urs!" I tried to sound enthusiastic. "What's up?"

"I have some news for you." Her voice was loud, and I could hear the murmur of traffic. "Are you sitting down?"

"I am." My foot began to jiggle in anticipation. "Why? What's going on?" Several possibilities arose: Did she want me to interview her for something? Was she coming back to New York for some reason?

"So get this: my agent Melody was having drinks with Roza's agent this week and she told Melody that one of the women going to the retreat dropped out."

"Oh, wow." The idea seemed absurd: How could anyone drop out, barring a surprise terminal disease? Even then?

"Yeah, so Melody told her that her favorite client, meaning me, knows plenty of talented young writers if they didn't want to go back to the drawing board. And she said yes, and I sent your story and she loved it."

"Wait, *what*?" The words weren't computing. The information was coming too fast.

"To fast-forward to the end, you're going to a monthlong writing retreat with Roza Vallo." She coughed. "Also, you owe me for life."

I pressed a hand to my clavicle. "Urs. You're not fucking with me?"

She laughed. "You think I'd fuck with you about this?"

"Oh my god." Wonder and excitement burst like fireworks in my chest. "This is unbelievable. How . . ."

"I sent your story about the two girls in the woods." Ursula sounded pleased with herself. "The one you gave us in writing group. It was always my favorite. And I guess she liked it too."

"Roza's agent?"

"Roza."

"Roza read it?" It was like finding out a mythical creature, a goddess, had come down to earth to choose me. I expanded past the wooden counter and the people sipping and chattering around me, stretching in all temporal directions: My twelve-year-old self, reading *Devil's Tongue* in a tucked away corner of Barnes & Noble. My future self, sitting across from Roza as she meted out tough criticism but also little jewels of praise.

"Yeah." Ursula murmured to someone, then came back. "All right. So you know the retreat is coming up fast. Like, two weeks."

"Whoa." I leaned forward onto the counter. "My boss is going to freak out. She'll never let me go."

"Then quit. This is literally a once-in-a-lifetime opportunity."

"Okay." I squared my shoulders. "No, you're right."

"Damn right I'm right."

"But just . . . are you *sure*?" I couldn't do this — feel this hope, this exhilaration — if it was going to be snatched away from me. "Like, this has all been confirmed? Or . . ."

"It's all done. Check your email — you should be hearing from her people today. Apparently you have to sign some NDA thing . . . She has strict policies, privacy things. But once you sign, you should be good to go."

"And they know I'm thirty? Wasn't everyone supposed to be under thirty?"

"Yeah." She sounded thoughtful. "I mentioned that because I didn't want it to come back to bite us in the ass. But they didn't care. I get the feeling the whole thing has dragged on and they just want to move forward."

"Okay. Wow. I can't . . ." Tears filled my eyes and spilled over. "I can't thank you enough. I don't even know what to say."

"Well." Ursula's voice rose an octave. "There is one more thing I have to tell you."

"Sure." I wiped the tears away, not caring if my mascara was all over my face. I wanted to curl up on the tile floor and blubber and scream. This was happening. After so much pain and disappointment, something — the best possible thing — was actually happening.

"I gave two stories to my agent. One from you and one from Wren. Because . . ." She sighed. "You both helped me become a better writer. I wouldn't have kept going with those early essays if you hadn't both pushed me. And I respect both of your writing so much. I couldn't just choose one of you for this."

"Okay." The words barely touched me.

"So anyway . . . they picked both of you. You're both going."

My trachea constricted. I could barely eke out: "What?"

"Yeah. So I know that might be a little weird for you."

" 'A little weird'?" The words burst out, so loud the woman next to me gave me a wary glance. I turned away. "She ruined my life."

Of course Wren was going to take this triumph from me. *Of course.*

Ursula didn't respond. After a moment I exhaled. She'd done so much for me. Much more than she'd needed to.

"Look, I'm sorry." I forced myself to sound calm. "I know I sound dramatic."

"I mean, I don't want to sound harsh, but yes." Ursula was now using her Tough but

48

Kind Voice, which I'd mostly heard her use on Wren when she was being crabby. "I'm sorry, but you need to get over it and move on, Al. This is an incredible opportunity. And I picked you both because I believe in you both. So go to the retreat, ignore Wren, charm Roza, and write your ass off. Enough of this petty shit. Okay?"

"Okay." I said it in a small voice. Now I'd gone and made Ursula mad, on top of everything else.

"Look." Her voice was softer. "It's just a month. You're going to be so busy writing and connecting with Roza that you won't even have the time to think about Wren. Just focus on you and know that, after this, you'll never have to see each other again. How does that sound?"

"Yes." I straightened up. "I can do that."

"Good." Her voice was cheerful again. "This is a huge opportunity, lady. And you deserve it. You're an amazing writer."

The words continued to ring in my ears after I hung up. I stared at my coffee, lost in the swirls of steam rising from the open cup, feeling stunned.

You're an amazing writer.

A mixture of horror and despair filled my gut. I'd kept it a secret. Ursula didn't know that I'd failed to write anything post-Wren.

I'd tried. Early on, I'd wake up early and prop my computer on my lap and stare at a blank screen, willing any phrase or fragment to rise. But at those times my mind went completely and stubbornly blank, like a white expanse of snow. I switched to a notebook and pen, hoping that would kick-start the words, but all I could do was write *I don't know what to write about* and doodle childlike pictures of flowers and cats.

So I'd given up. I figured I'd get back into it at some point, but with the weeks and months passing, it began to seem less and less likely.

And then, as I sat there, the true reality hit, clubbing me in the back of the head.

I was going to Roza Vallo's monthlong writing retreat with a killer case of writer's block.

CHAPTER 4

Two weeks later I was on a train speeding north out of the city. It was a Friday afternoon and the car was nearly full. A skinny teen with giant headphones was slumped next to me. My sunglasses shielded me from the pale winter sunlight and I watched the dull landscape — gray buildings, empty lots — speed by.

I was on my way to Roza's. I was actually on my way to Roza Fucking Vallo's.

Time had broken down after that phone call with Ursula. Just as she'd predicted, I'd received the email that afternoon and had immediately responded: *I'm so thrilled for the opportunity!* I'd received an NDA, which I signed without reading it. Since then, my body had been filled with a low-grade buzz, like an electric fence just waiting for someone to test it.

Telling Sharon had been surprisingly satisfying. She'd almost lost her cool, her

51

voice rising to a squeak. "Really? Next month? When the Bogman-Briggs is supposed to transmit?" But she couldn't touch me. I was using all my vacation and sick days at once. And I'd already asked the other editors to cover me. In the end, she'd sent me out of her office with a disgusted shake of her head.

I pulled my copy of *Maiden Pink,* Roza's most recent book, from my leather tote. I'd slipped it in at the last minute, wondering if it would be gauche to ask Roza to sign it. I'd bought it at the Brooklyn Book Festival at a rare Roza appearance six years before, but the event had devolved so quickly into chaos that she hadn't stayed behind to sign anything.

The memory of the event had remained with me, in apparently minute detail, to take out and marvel at every so often like a cherished photo. It had just been so incredibly satisfying to experience the display of Roza's power.

Wren had somehow gotten us into the sold-out event, which was held in St. Ann's, a majestic church in Brooklyn Heights. Both of us were delighted that the profane Roza was being interviewed in God's house. But the church didn't have air-conditioning and it had been hot and humid despite the large, whirring fans. Roza was late. All of us packed into the old wooden pews fussed like colicky babies.

"This is ridiculous." Wren fanned herself with a program. "If she doesn't come out in five minutes, we're leaving."

"I'm sure it'll start soon." We were both hungover from the night before, but one of us had to remain calm. And there was a reason we needed to stay: when I got my book signed, I was planning to mention that I was also of Hungarian descent, a small but important tie between us. Roza would meet dozens if not hundreds of people that day — but maybe, just maybe, she'd remember me. And if I lived in a pocket of Roza Vallo's brain, however small, I sensed it would bolster my own existence.

Three people strode onstage and the sweltering audience went silent. There was a female book editor from the *New Yorker,* a young male author who'd won all the awards that year, and Roza, gorgeous and casual in torn jeans and a black tank top. She wore her russet hair long and loose, and her unexpected thick-framed glasses balanced nicely with her red lips. She was laughing at something the editor had said. Her musical voice, picked up by the small mic attached to her neckline, bounced around the space like a bell.

"Well." Asha, the editor and moderator, exhaled and grinned. "This is something, isn't it? Everyone, let's welcome Roza Vallo and Jett Butler to the stage."

During the rapturous applause, I looked around, realizing how many men there were in the audience. Probably there to see Jett, who'd gotten a high-six-figure deal for his first book and had been called the next Hemingway.

Asha introduced Roza and Jett in contrast: established versus new, overtly feminist versus a more terse and traditionally masculine approach. They watched her with modest smiles. While Asha perched on the edge of her seat, Roza and Jett looked completely at ease. Jett grabbed the water bottle waiting by his feet and took a large swig, tucking his longish blond hair behind his ear. Roza was still, watching Asha with a beatific expression.

"So where do we even begin?" Asha fingered the tiny notebook in her lap. "You've both come out with new works this year: *Maiden Pink* and *Mr. Mustang*. Both brilliant."

"Why, thank you," Jett said in a low, smooth voice, prompting a few chuckles. He glanced at Roza like a daring child.

"Jett, let's start with you. How does it feel? You're twenty-six years old and you've been nominated for a National Book Award. What was your reaction to that?"

"My reaction was: Finally!" he intoned with a slight Southern drawl. "Just kidding. Um, I don't know, really. 'Surreal' is such a clichéd word, but that's how it felt."

"You started it at quite a young age, right?" Asha asked.

"Yes, in college, actually. But it took six years to get it right. Thousands of hours. And actually that's important." He held up his pointer finger. "A lot of people were mad about the advance. But when you break it down by labor, it's really pennies on the hour."

"You went to Duke?" Roza's sudden question, honeyed with her light accent, was like a hitch in the script. Asha and Jett both glanced at her. "Good school."

"Yep." He nodded. "I was blessed by the good Lord above to get a full ride."

Roza's eyebrows shot up. "Ahh. So you began this beautiful novel at Duke."

"Thank you for calling it that." He grinned, flirting. "Some thought I was a little young to consider myself a novelist."

"Oh, no, Jett." Now her brows knit. "When I started writing *Devil's Tongue,* I was sixteen years old. Don't let anyone ever tell you you're too young."

"Thank you." He crossed his arms, enjoying the attention.

"How did you support yourself there?" Roza cocked her head. "Apart from the full ride, how did you pay for food, rent?"

Jett glanced at Asha, who looked slightly perturbed but seemed to be letting Roza take over.

"Odd jobs, mostly." Jett shrugged. "Things that would tire my body but not my brain."

"Odd jobs." Roza beamed like a parent viewing her child's straight As. "Wonderful. And after school, you moved to New York?"

"I stuck around Raleigh for a while first."

"Girlfriend?" she asked knowingly.

He chuckled. "Well, yes. I was with someone. But I also didn't have the money to move at that point."

"Who was this girlfriend?" Roza asked.

"Whoa," he laughed, turning to Asha. "This is getting personal."

"Jett," Roza said before Asha could answer, "these lovely people all trooped here in the scorching heat because they wanted to learn about us. Isn't that the whole point of author events? To get a glimpse into the life and mind of the person who's been whispering into your brain for the last ten hours?" Roza turned to the crowd. "You would all like to hear about Jett's college girlfriend, right?"

We cheered. The tenor of the hot room had shifted. A new eagerness swelled, a sharpening of the senses, like we were a crowd at a coliseum watching a brave but ultimately doomed gladiator stride out into the ring. Somehow we knew even then she was out for blood.

"Sooo." Roza's intonation rose and fell. "What was she like? What was her name?"

Jett glanced at Asha with pleading eyes. Catching his gaze, she cleared her throat. "Roza, I have a lot of questions for us to get to today —"

"June." Jett said it suddenly, almost involuntarily, stopping Asha short.

"June and Jett." Roza pressed a hand to her chest. "My god, that is adorable. What was her major?"

"She was — is — a writer, too. We met in freshman seminar." He'd resigned himself; he was going along with it, confused but regaining his cockiness. "She's a fantastic writer," he added generously.

"Is she published?"

"Not yet. She will be."

"Was she on scholarship too?"

"Oh, yes." Jett liked his women self-made,

just like him. "And she waitressed."

"June the writer-waitress. How long were you together?"

"Uh . . . about four years, I guess. Most of college and then a bit after." His brows furrowed with a new thought. "Why, is she here? Do you know her?"

"I don't. I just find writer relationships fascinating." Roza leaned forward. "I was with a writer, once. We were always butting heads, each of us convinced that we were the real genius. Did you ever feel that way?"

"Not at all." He said it vehemently. "She was always better than me."

"And yet you're published and she's not."

"Yeah." He scratched his chin thoughtfully. "I'm not sure what happened. We lost touch after we broke up. I don't know where she's at with her work."

"That must be hard for her." Roza steepled her fingers. "Her ex getting a big fancy book deal, moving on to bigger and better things."

"As much as I'm enjoying this stroll down memory lane, should we actually get to the book?" Jett grinned wryly at Asha.

"Good idea. Let's get to the book, Jett." Roza's voice went down an octave. "Let's talk about the book that June wrote."

Jett's eyes widened, then narrowed. His

thin lips stretched into a humorless smile. "What?"

"Maybe that's an overstatement. You worked on it too. But it was her idea, her story."

Roza was half smiling, as if to soften the blow of her words.

Now a stunned Asha asked: "What?"

"I know you had to pay her off to keep her mouth shut, but it was so little compared to the advance; she just didn't know." Roza wrinkled her nose. "And the book was so much of her. Because she's a car mechanic, Jett, not a waitress. Right? But that would raise some questions if you made that known, wouldn't it?"

"That's not true." Jett waved his arms. "I don't like speaking badly of anyone, but June was — is — I mean, she's a little crazy —"

"Oh, yes?" Roza whipped out her phone and scrolled through it. "She contacted me last week. I wasn't going to bring it up like this — it's really none of my business — but when you told us that sob story, Jett, how you worked so, so hard, I guess it was just a little too much for me."

"It's not true. Can you stop this?" Jett beseeched Asha. "She's making this up. I don't know where she's getting this —"

"She has a recording of you both talking about it." Roza held up her phone. "The deal you made. She needed that money at the time. Her shop doesn't pay a lot, you know. But she didn't think it was fair, you making all that money and getting so much acclaim. Did you know, Jett, that most people have only one good story in them? And you took hers."

Jett jumped up. "Stop. Just stop." A knot pulsed in his neck.

Roza bit her lip, eyes on the screen. "And she tried and tried to get in touch with you but you just didn't want to talk to her, did you? You blocked her, in fact. And so she had to turn to alternative plans. None of the reporters believed her. Your editor and agent ignored her. I guess you could say I was her last chance. That she was grasping at straws." Roza looked up at Jett. "She's still working in that shitty garage in Raleigh. And she's too depressed to write."

The crowd murmured, shock and glee and horror pulsing like little eddies of current. At some point Wren had grabbed my arm, her nails digging into my flesh.

Even from this far back I could see Jett's hands shake. "Okay, you are actually fucking crazy." He turned to the moderator. "What the hell, Asha? How could you let her do this to me in front of . . . ?" He gestured to us and turned. His foot connected with his water bottle, which skittered over the side of the stage. He collected himself and strode off.

Asha appeared to be frozen in her chair, staring after Jett. Finally she turned and mouthed something to someone offstage.

"Let this be a lesson to everyone." Roza stood and faced us, hands on hips like a TED speaker. "If you're going to do stupid shit, do it well. Don't be lazy enough to get caught so easily. Try a little harder. Otherwise you don't deserve any of it. Okay?" She looked at Asha. "That's all for today, I think." She turned and sauntered offstage. Asha jumped up and followed.

The crowd billowed into confused, excited chatter. Beside me, Wren let out a shriek of delighted laughter.

We hadn't gotten our books signed that day. But as the event and the revelation exploded online, causing Jett's publisher to cancel the second half of his two-book deal, we agreed that being there to witness a show of Roza's vengeance had been more than enough.

CHAPTER 5

The shout from the conductor startled me out of a half sleep.

We were approaching the station. The floppy-haired boy next to me was long gone, the car nearly empty. The train slowed with a juddering whine. A fuzzy, electronic voice repeated: "This is . . . [inaudible]."

If I'd been sleeping more deeply, I would've missed the stop altogether. Rushing to pull my suitcase from the rack, I found myself waiting behind the only other person disembarking. She was short, with blond hair spilling out the bottom of a bright orange ski cap. Could she be going to Roza's too? The train steps were steep and both of us stumbled, righting ourselves on the pavement. Outside, the wind slapped our faces. She turned and squinted at me.

"Are you by any chance going to Roza Vallo's?" Her words were fast and choppy, like she was rushing to get them out before she sprinted away.

"I am!" I'd managed to remain somewhat calm on the train, but now excitement and fear lit up my entire body. I stuck out my hand. "I'm Alex."

"Poppy." Her little hand squeezed surprisingly hard. "Oh my god, are you just like *dying*?"

I laughed at her openness. Her animated face and Valley girl intonation were so different from what I would've expected at a Roza Vallo retreat.

"Yes, absolutely." I grinned. "I can't believe it's actually happening."

"Girl, me neither!" Her warm brown eyes widened. "I've been driving everyone I know nuts. I've just been freaking out about it. Oh, should we find the car? It's probably down there." She continued to chatter as we crossed the icy terrain, across the platform and down the stairs. Below, in the small lot, a black car waited, steam rising from the tailpipe.

"Oh thank Jesus. I'm so effing cold." She beelined for the car and I hurried to keep up. A man climbed out as we neared.

"Afternoon, ladies." He had a flat upstate accent and a full, white-flecked beard. We greeted him and jumped into the back of the car. Inside, it was deliciously warm and smelled like fake vanilla. An air freshener shaped like a cookie hung from the rearview mirror, along with a rosary.

"I'm Joe," he called.

"Hi, Joe. I'm Poppy. This is Alex." She grinned at me, eyes crinkling. There were faint lines around her eyes and mouth; I had the feeling that she smiled a *lot.*

"Poppy! Haven't heard that name before." Joe pulled smoothly out of the lot.

"It's Scottish." She shrugged.

"Scotland, huh?" Joe said. "I've always wanted to go there."

"It's great. Really violent, though. People are constantly getting into fights. Once I saw two men walk out of a church and punch each other."

Joe and I laughed and Poppy leaned back, pleased. "Do you work for Roza, Joe?"

"Sometimes. Not directly. I just work for the cab service up here." He glanced back at us in his rearview mirror.

"You from here?" I asked.

"Born and raised." He dipped his head. "It's a nice area. Pretty isolated, though. Guessing that's why Ms. Vallo likes it."

"Have you interacted a lot with her?" Poppy asked.

"Nah, she keeps to herself when she's here. Her staff — I think her name's Yana, the one who calls — they set up the transportation when people come in from the city."

"How long has she been up here?" Poppy leaned forward, grabbing onto the back of his seat with pink-painted nails. She was definitely trying to get some kind of inside scoop.

"I think she bought the estate in 2000? Took a few years for her to fix it up. The place had really gone to shit." He coughed. "Pardon my French."

Poppy noticed me watching her. "I'm super obsessed with Roza." She rolled her eyes. "And Blackbriar. I'm such a sucker for haunted houses."

"Oh, yeah. I totally get it." For the past few weeks I'd been focusing so much on the reality of spending a month with Roza and Wren that I hadn't even thought about the estate. Of course, I knew all about it. After I'd read *Devil's Tongue* at twelve, I'd done a deep dive into Roza on a library computer the first week of school. She'd fixed up Blackbriar just a few years before then, and several magazines and papers had covered the transformation. It only made sense that one of her houses was the site of unsolved murders.

"You know the story, right?" Poppy asked me.

"Of course. Daphne and Horace."

"And Lamia." She grinned like I'd passed a test. But anyone who was more than a casual fan of Roza's knew the story, which was itself like something out of one of her novels.

Oil baron Horace Hamilton built Blackbriar Estate in the late nineteenth century. A lifelong bachelor, he fell for a waitress in town, Daphne Wolfe. Daphne caused a stir, first by her much younger status, then when she started a séance group. The spiritualist community at that time considered Daphne a powerful channeler, initially through automatic writings, then drawings and paintings. The trouble started when Daphne claimed to have connected with a powerful female demoness named Lamia. Daphne told her group that Lamia wanted to channel a "great commission" through her art.

The others in the group became disturbed by Lamia and left. Horace forbade Daphne to welcome a dark spirit into the house. After a huge snowstorm, the staff returned to find Daphne and Horace dead. Horace had been eviscerated in bed. And Daphne was in the basement, her body burned beyond recognition.

Most assumed that Daphne, caught in the throes of a psychotic break, had killed Horace in his sleep and then lit herself on fire. But, mysteriously, the rest of the basement was completely untouched, including three completed paintings nearby.

"So you grew up here," Poppy said. "You heard all the stories about Blackbriar?"

"Oh, sure." He chuckled. "We used to dare each other to spend a night inside. The doors were locked but people went in through a broken window in the back."

"Oh my god. You stayed there?" Poppy's eyes sparkled with interest.

"Nope, not me. I was way too scared." He considered. "My cousin did once. He ended up falling down the basement stairs and breaking his ankle. Everyone said it was the curse."

"The curse?" I repeated.

"That female demon, whatever her name was. People said she's still there." He cleared his throat. "You couldn't pay me to stay there, to be honest. I don't know if I believe in demons or whatever, but there's definitely some odd energy in that house."

"Uh-oh." Poppy sounded gleeful. "I guess we'll have to let you know."

The houses and buildings abated and eventually we were surrounded by unending woods. I used the time for some deep breathing. Every mile we were getting closer and closer. Every minute that passed meant one fewer minute before seeing Roza — which was overwhelmingly exciting — and Wren — incredibly horrifying. It was so strange to balance the two, and they both revved up my system, causing a fluttering in my chest.

"The cell service is cutting out," Poppy announced. "Is that normal?"

"Unfortunately, yes." He glanced back at us. "Real spotty up here."

The undulating line of woods opened up briefly to showcase several long gray buildings. A figure stood at the mailbox by the road — a woman whose strands of loose gray hair flew out from beneath a furry hunter's cap. I nudged Poppy and she looked over. The woman raised a hand, her plain face solemn but kind.

Poppy waved cheerfully back. "Who's that?"

"That's a nun, believe it or not," Joe said. "That nunnery's been there for two hundred years."

"I love it!" Poppy watched out the back window. "How many live there?"

"There are only about ten of them now, I think. Ten nuns in that big place. But they live here all year round. Have a few cows and chickens. Make some real tasty jams that they sell out by the road sometimes."

"Aww, that's cute." Poppy returned to her phone.

"They're pretty cut off from the world, aren't they?" I asked.

"They have interns in the summer." Joe's dark eyes alighted on mine in the rearview mirror. "College kids who help out with the gardens. But in the winter they're alone, far as I know." He cleared his throat. "They're actually the closest people to Blackbriar."

"How far are we?" A new flush of excitement and fear filled my chest.

"Not far. About fifteen miles."

"Whoa." Poppy glanced at me. "So we're going to be super isolated."

"Pretty much," Joe said. "Especially if there's big storms. Last winter the people who live out here got snowed in twice."

"So when you say 'snowed in,' what does that mean, exactly?" Poppy asked.

"Well, it didn't used to be this bad. Maybe a few snowfalls here and there. But last year and the year before, there were some big storms. It took a few days for the snowplows to come all the way out. Until then, they were stuck."

"Yikes." Poppy bit her lip. "What if the

power goes out?"

"Most places have backup generators. Don't worry. I'm sure the house has a couple."

We moved on to happier topics, and ten minutes later, we slowed to turn onto a bumpy gravel path. *We're here.* Every cell in my body crackled with new energy.

"Is this it?" I tried to sound calm.

"Sure is," Joe responded.

Breathe. Breathe. Breathe.

"Oh my god." Poppy's hand shot out and found mine. Hers was bony and cold, a skeleton's grip. We wound through a long, curving path with some potholes that made us fly up in our seats. Poppy giggled nervously.

"You'd think a millionaire would fix her driveway," Joe muttered. As if in answer, the gravel turned into cement, and we smoothly transitioned out of the trees to an open space.

Of course I'd seen pictures, but in real life it was even more impressive than I'd expected. The Victorian fortress towered over us, magnificent and proud. The doorway was flanked by two turrets, and snow-cloaked ivy climbed up the gray stone walls. There were so many windows, all milky white with the pale setting sun. It unsettled me, like looking at eyes rolled up into a head.

"Wow," Poppy breathed.

"Beautiful, huh?" Joe sounded proud, as if taking ownership in the sight.

My unease faded, and now I felt only joy. This was it. This was Roza Vallo's mansion. This was real. This was happening. I quivered with anticipation as we pulled into the circular drive and stopped at the front steps.

"Well, girls, this is our stop." Joe opened his door and the cold swept into the warm space.

Poppy was still staring at the house.

"Ready?" I asked.

She turned and there was a peculiar look — uncertainty? apprehension? — on her face.

But then she smiled. "Yeah! Let's do it."

Joe had already taken both our suitcases from the trunk, and now he rubbed his gloved hands, as if eager to go.

"Oh, wait, can I — should we give you a —" I plunged my hand into my purse.

"No need, it's all taken care of." It was strange seeing Joe head-on after the forty-five minutes in the car. He was similarly taking stock of me, his expression serious. "You two be careful, okay?" He reached out and I shook his hand.

"Thank you, Joe! You're the best!" Poppy cried, wheeling her suitcase to the front steps. I followed, glancing back to see Joe already pulling around the drive.

"Okay, girl." Poppy grinned, her hand hovering over the circular doorbell. "Ready?"

For a second I couldn't breathe, but I nodded and Poppy pushed. A deep thrum came from inside the house, like a purr or a growl. My fingers tightened on my suitcase's handle as the door slowly creaked open.

CHAPTER 6

A woman poked her head out, her expression impassive, as if faintly annoyed we'd appeared on her doorstep. She was maybe in her late forties, with pale skin, delicate lines ringing melancholy sea-gray eyes, and bleached hair pulled tightly into a bun.

"Uh, hi," Poppy said after the woman remained silent. "Is this . . . we're here for the retreat." She glanced at me. "I mean, obviously."

"Okay." The woman squinted and pulled open the door. "Come in." She had an accent, something Slavic. Now she motioned impatiently for us to pull our suitcases inside. She wore a cherry-red velour tracksuit that hugged her curves. Poppy widened her eyes at me — *WTF?* — and I shrugged, hiding a smile. The woman reminded me of an imperious countess I'd been seated next to at an immersive dinner theater in college.

The second we let go of our bags, our host grasped them and took off. Her glutes swayed and the pink soles of her gym shoes flashed. Poppy hesitated and then rushed after her. I hurried after them both, my wet boots squeaking on the marble floor.

We zoomed through the entryway into a large front hall that rose at least fifty feet above us. An enormous marble staircase swept down from a second-floor landing. Large paintings filled the walls — to the left, abstract shapes, to the right, looming figures. A chandelier hung suspended over the staircase, casting light with hundreds of electric candles.

The space was grand, majestic, and a stream of giddiness filled my veins. I was here. I was in Blackbriar. I wanted to go back and tell my younger self, reading *Devil's Tongue* in Barnes & Noble: *Keep going. Despite all the bullshit, magical things are coming to you.*

The woman veered off to the right, past a marble table topped with a vase of orange flowers. We followed her down a long hall lined with plush Moroccan rugs and marble statues, lit by stained glass wall sconces. Paintings dotted the velvety green walls. My eyes were trained on one that appeared to show a dead cow lying in a field when I slammed into Poppy.

"Oof!" she muttered while I cried, "Sorry!"

Poppy had stopped because our hostess had stopped. Still clutching our suitcases, the woman gestured with her chin at a nearby doorway. Through it, female laughter and the sounds of clinking glasses could be faintly heard.

"You go in there, with the other girls," she said. "Okay?"

"Yes, thank you *so* much, and one quick question." Poppy held up her phone. "What's the Wi-Fi password? I'm not getting any reception."

The woman watched her with barely hidden disdain. "No password." She motioned to us. "Coats." We obligingly slipped off our coats and handed them to her. She pointed to our hats and we gave them to her too. Somehow she managed to take hold of everything and rolled on, disappearing down the long hall.

"No password?" Poppy's forehead crinkled beneath her freed crown of golden hair. She frowned at her phone screen. "But I'm not seeing any networks."

"If everyone else is in there, they can probably tell us." I was amazed at the calm in my voice. At the sounds of other women, my heart had started thudding, throwing itself against my chest like a caged animal. *Wren.*

"Yeah, okay, you're right." Poppy slipped her phone into her purse. "Let's do it." She squared her shoulders and went inside.

We both softly exclaimed as we entered the library, which, from my research, I'd always thought was the most spectacular room. *Roza Vallo's famed library. Ten thousand tomes.* As a child — maybe still now — this would've been my fantasy: to be surrounded by so many books. The shelves stretched up to the high ceiling, more books than anyone could read in a lifetime. At the far end, windows shone pale light on an assortment of plush couches and chairs grouped around a massive stone fireplace. A table nearby was heaped with platters of cheese, meats, fruit, and about five bottles of wine. One woman's back was to us as she loaded her plate. Another appeared to be lying on a couch, but all I could see was a striped, socked foot resting on the arm.

"Hi!" Poppy called as we approached.

The woman by the food turned and the other's head popped up.

My heart slowed. No Wren.

It was funny: I hadn't even considered the other women who would be at the retreat.

Who they would be, what our group would feel like.

I plastered a smile on my face. First impressions were important — and especially if Wren was going to arrive after me, it'd be helpful to have a head start in getting everyone on my side.

"Heyyy!" The girl on the couch had a mischievous grin and freckles sprinkled over sharp, fox-like features. Her short blond hair was tinged with a faded green dye, which added to the overall elvish effect. She lifted her glass, and her loose, falling sleeve revealed colorful tattoos that glowed against her pale skin. "Welcome, friends! Come get some motherfucking wine!"

"Um, *yes*. That's exactly what I need." Poppy strolled towards the table. "How are you, it's so good to meet you! I'm Poppy!"

The woman by the food wore red cat-eye glasses and her box braids were twisted into a high bun. "Good to meet you too. I'm Keira. She/her." A serene smile lit her face. She wore all black: chunky sweater, jeans, and a cashmere scarf.

"Taylor." The tattooed girl waved from the couch. "She/her. Sorry, y'all, I'd get up, but this is the most comfortable I've been in years." Her voice held a faint Southern drawl.

"I'm Alex. She/her." I felt a brief flush of relief to be able to say my pronouns easily. Sharon had asked us to start using them at work six months before when introducing ourselves in author meetings. It had struck me as ironic that Sharon was at all concerned about being "woke" when she'd only ever hired BIPOC people at the assistant level.

To be fair, I'd only ever thought about race — particularly, being white — within the last few years. It had made me realize that my whole life, I'd existed in mostly white spaces. Growing up in suburbs around the Midwest, my schools and neighborhoods had been glaringly white. College classes had been the same. In New York, Ursula had been my first close nonwhite friend, and she'd only expressed thoughts on race to me within her essays. I remembered reading about a racist comment directed at her on the subway and feeling shocked. Publishing was mostly white — ditto my neighborhood, East Williamsburg.

Even now, it appeared that Keira was the only woman of color in the group. That was surprising. Or . . . not?

"Oh. Yeah." Poppy looked stricken. "Sorry. Preferred pronouns. She . . . how do you say it?"

"She/her." Taylor evaluated her, then smiled kindly. "You can just say pronouns. They're not preferred, they just are, you know? Thanks for sharing."

"Sure." Poppy accepted a glass of wine from Keira, cheeks pink.

"Want one?" Keira asked me.

"I'd love one, thanks." The wine was a dark maroon, the type that always reminded me of blood. I shook off the morbid connection. Wine would be nice, would cool down my insecurities. I just had to be sure to eat too. I dropped some crackers and cheese on a small crystal plate.

"Poppy — that's a cool name." Taylor settled back onto the couch, sitting cross-legged. I sat beside her.

"Thanks, I know, it's kind of different, right?" Poppy plopped onto a chair near Keira, nibbling on a strawberry. "Irish."

"I thought you said it was Scottish?" I asked.

"Oh my god, yeah, sorry." She chuckled, rolling her eyes. "It's such a mishmash that I usually just pick one country to tell people. Just to make it easier."

"I get it," Taylor said. "I'm the same: ancestors from all over Europe." She studied me. "Where's your family from, Alex? You look kind of French to me."

"Oh, wow, really?" I giggled nervously. "I don't consider myself particularly chic." I'd spent a comical amount of time that morning trying to figure out what to wear, and I still felt somewhat frumpy in my jeans and polka-dotted sweater.

"Take the compliment." Taylor grinned.

"Thank you. Um, I'm German and Hungarian." Mom had been born in Budapest after the war but during the Soviet occupation. Her parents — both Holocaust survivors — had died when she was in her twenties, and she rarely spoke about her past. I'd had to glean details when she was slightly drunk and in a chatty mood.

"Hungarian like Roza." Taylor tipped her glass at me. "That's a nice connection."

"Where in Germany?" Keira asked.

"I don't know, actually. It's my dad's side. And he's not really in my life." I wondered if it was too much to share, but Keira gave me a sympathetic glance. "But it's fine," I went on. "Do you have ties to Germany?"

"I studied in Berlin for a while." She smiled.

"Keira, where's your family from originally?" Poppy asked, chewing.

"Senegal."

"I'm guessing they didn't come here by choice," Taylor said.

80

I froze, cracker halfway to my mouth.

"Nope." Keira's voice was mild.

"Sorry." Taylor sighed. "I just hate talking around that shit. Pretending slavery never happened. I deal with that enough in my hometown."

Keira shrugged. "Hey, at least I wasn't the only one here asked where I'm from — where I'm *really* from. Even in LA, I get that a lot."

"So you're in LA?" I asked Keira, wanting to move us onto a safer topic. Did Taylor really have to bring up slavery, especially with Keira being the only Black person in the room?

"Yep. Just flew in this morning." She popped an olive into her mouth.

"What do you do?" I asked.

"Hold up." Taylor clapped her hands. "Since we're all here, how about we save time and go around and do a little intro? Where we live, what we do, all that fun stuff."

Since we're all here. They didn't know Wren was coming. And maybe — chance of chances — she wasn't? It was hard if not impossible to believe Wren's fangirl adoration of Roza had waned. But her life was different now. Maybe another trip or opportunity had come up that she couldn't turn down. I felt a twinge of hope in my chest.

"Good suggestion from the teacher." Keira smirked, pushing up her glasses.

"Why, thank you. I'll start." Taylor straightened. "So, yes, I'm a middle school teacher, so if I try to organize things and it's annoying, well, I have no idea what to tell you." Poppy and I chuckled. Taylor had a theatrical, kinetic way of talking and moving, and I could totally see her keeping kids' attention in front of a classroom. "I'm in Austin." She cocked her head. "Let's see, let's see, what else. I have a cat named Orson and a girlfriend named Kitty. We're open — me and Kitty, not me and the cat. We love Roza — me, Kitty, *and* Orson. I think that's good for now. Poppy?"

"Okay." Poppy set down her glass and brushed back her honey-colored hair. "I'm Poppy, as you know. I live in Atlanta — born and raised. And I work in PR."

Atlanta: a large metropolitan area. It was interesting that she'd seemed so confused by the pronouns — but maybe she'd just been flustered?

"PR!" Taylor snapped her fingers. "Of course! I can feel the pep!"

"Aww, thank you, girl. I have a boyfriend named Jack . . . Did I miss anything?"

"I'm curious to see what kind of stuff you write." Taylor crossed her arms. "You seem somewhat straitlaced to me. No offense, of course."

Poppy laughed. "I get it. I don't know if I'm as dark as Roza. But I'm pretty dark. Is that enough?"

"Absolutely." Taylor turned her gaze on me like a flashlight's beam. "Alex, you're up."

I felt naked with everyone's eyes on me. "So I'm in Brooklyn." I cleared my throat and forced a grin.

"Short trip," Keira remarked.

"I know. I'm lucky." I hesitated. Should I share that I was a late addition to the group? But if Wren didn't end up coming, what would be the point? The hope, the feeling that I might've made it home free, gave me a sudden giddy rush of confidence. "As for my job, I think I can proudly say I'm in the most exciting field here." I paused for dramatic effect. "That field is academic publishing."

"Hey!" Taylor cried. "Come on, be proud! We're both educating the future!"

"I guess." I rolled my eyes.

"Partner?" Taylor asked. "Dating anyone?"

A quick image of Pete, which I pushed away.

"Nothing serious." I said it brightly, hoping it didn't sound too pathetic. It was rough to be the only single one in a group. *Oh, no one likes you? What's wrong with you?*

"Playing coy, huh." Taylor tapped at her lips. "We'll get some more intel from you later. Keira, did you finish sharing? Job?"

"I write." She smiled.

"Full-time?" Taylor pressed her hand to her chest. "Are you one of the last unicorns?"

"Well, I write all sorts of things. Press releases, wellness articles, corporate handbooks." She shrugged. "The corporate stuff is not super fun. But that's how it goes."

"Until now." Taylor hopped up to refill her glass. "I mean, this is Roza Vallo. Anyone connected with her is going to have no trouble getting published. We're golden."

Keira smiled. "I hope so."

"Partner?" I asked, conscious of using a non-gendered term.

She shook her head. "I broke up with someone recently. He and I were together for three years. So just being consciously single for now."

I felt a brief sense of relief that I wasn't in fact the only single one. And Keira somehow made it seem preferred. I imagined her lighting candles in her room, reading a book, enjoying her own company. Why couldn't I be more like that?

"So, have you guys met Roza yet?" Poppy frowned. "Can I say 'guys'?"

"I'm fine with it." Taylor glanced at Keira. "And not yet."

"We met Ian," Keira continued. "Her editor, or one of her editors. He said she hadn't gotten here yet. She's flying in from Europe."

"We also met Yana." Taylor said her name with a surprisingly good accent. "Our Russian friend."

"She made me think of a czarina from a community theater play," I said, and Taylor laughed.

"Right? She's awesome. She does not give a fuck." Taylor ran her hand through her short hair. "Sorry, peeps, I swear a lot. And because you're not nine years old, I don't have to hold back!"

"Oh, hey, another question: Did you guys figure out the Wi-Fi?" Poppy pulled out her phone.

"I asked earlier too." Keira raised an eyebrow at Taylor.

"And?" Poppy blinked.

"No Wi-Fi," Taylor said.

"What?" I asked. "But there's no service here, either."

"Yup." Taylor seemed satisfied by our shock. "We're completely and utterly cut off."

"But I told Jack I'd call him tonight." Poppy pressed her lips together.

"There's a phone in the study," Keira told her. "A landline. I called my mom earlier. I can show you where it is."

"I guess this explains why Roza doesn't use social media?" Taylor shrugged.

"It's fine. I could use a break." Poppy pressed a palm to her cheek. "It's so surreal, talking about Roza, knowing I'll meet her."

"Hang out with her," Taylor amended. "For a whole month!"

"How'd you get off of school?" I asked.

"What?" She glanced at me.

"Yeah." Had I misunderstood? "Aren't you a teacher?"

"Oh, yes." She grinned. I noticed her canines, which were slightly vampiric, descending noticeably below her other teeth. "I took the semester off. It was hard because I love those fuckers, but there was just no way around it. I'll go back for the summer session."

"None of us have kids, right?" Keira asked. "And no one's married. Interesting."

"Shit." Taylor closed her eyes. "I literally

forget that there are people out there in their twenties who have kids. It just seems way too young for me. All the parents at my school are in their forties. Some are even in their fifties."

"Austin, Atlanta, LA, Brooklyn," Keira noted. "All big, progressive cities. Which makes sense, I guess, considering that we're all attracted to Roza's work."

Should I tell them I was thirty? I felt a throb of unease to be holding something back from the others. But it wasn't a huge deal, was it?

The second glass of wine was making me slightly woozy, and I leaned back, giving in, allowing myself to relax and be carried along in the casual chatter. I couldn't remember the last time I'd smiled and laughed so much.

It just felt so nice to belong.

CHAPTER 7

"Do you want to see our rooms?" Taylor wiggled her eyebrows.

Over the past hour, the wine and excitement had quickly cemented our little group.

"What?" Poppy slammed her hands on the arms of her chair. "You saw them?"

"Yes, we did," Taylor sang. "Yana had us haul up our suitcases."

Poppy was already standing. "Can we go see?"

"Easy, tiger." Taylor chuckled. "Let's see if we can remember the way. K, you remember how to get to them?"

"Vaguely." At some point Keira had undone her bun and she was twisting a loose braid around her finger.

"It'll be an adventure." I felt practically giddy. It was the golden hour and amber rays poured into the room, transforming the thousands of books to dusty gold blocks. Compared to the dingy, fluorescent hallways of work and the cracked white walls of my apartment, this place felt real and solid: the plush rug beneath me, the heavy wineglass weighing down my hand, the fire and waning sun warming my face.

"Let's pour one for the road." Taylor tipped wine from a newly opened bottle into Poppy's and my glasses — Keira declined — then jumped to her feet. "Follow me, children!" In the hall, she whipped around to face us and held her glass high. "Our tour today begins here," she began in a trilling English accent, "in the Hall of Unusual Acquisitions. One of Roza Vallo's earliest works was a touching portrait her father got her on her fifth birthday. Heartwarming, don't you think?" She pointed to the picture of the dead cow in the field.

"Gorgeous!" Poppy cried.

"Okay, everyone, we have much to see. Come along!" Taylor turned on a heel and marched down the hall toward the front entrance, continuing to theatrically opine while waving her free hand. Keira shook her head, chuckling.

"And here we come to the grand hall!" Taylor ushered us in, arranging imaginary glasses. "This hall was constructed in 1601 —"

"Um, I think it was 1856," Poppy called.

Taylor glared so long and intensely that Poppy and I collapsed into giggles against each other.

"Ahem. As I was saying, this house was built by Horace Hamilton in 1856. Here's a portrait of him and his young wife, Daphne."

I'd glimpsed the large painting on the way in. Now I recognized it from articles I'd read. Daphne had a long nose and wide jaw that made her pretty in a solid, farm-girl-type way. But her expression was unsure, questioning. She stood next to a seated Horace, a large man with a salt-and-pepper beard and a bulbous forehead.

"And here's just Daphne." Taylor pointed to the next painting. Daphne sat behind a table, white lace covering her face like a wedding veil. It was hard to believe it was the same person. This Daphne had dark makeup around her eyes and her lips were crimson. She wore a high-necked black dress that flashed with beads or sequins. Her eyes were closed and she was writing on a pad of paper on the table. She looked contained but also intensely alive, as if an electric current were running through her.

"These are amazing," Poppy breathed.

"Are they originals?" Keira squinted.

"No," Taylor said. "They're pretty new.

Roza had them painted from photos." She gestured with her chin. "But those over there are the real deal."

We crossed to the other side of the hall where the two mammoth abstract paintings hung. The canvases were dark and blue-tinged, as if from the depths of a cave. Organic shapes and shadows filled the frame. Close up you could see the detailed work: emerald, ruby, and burnt umber objects like feathers and amoebas.

"Beautiful." Poppy's nose was almost touching the canvas. "And creepy."

"It's perfect for Roza," I said. "The whole story about Daphne, I mean. The same dark, disturbing vibe as her books."

Taylor narrowed her eyes at something that looked like a twisted, blackened human organ. "Maybe she's channeling Daphne's demoness too." Straightening, she looked at us. "Ready to see the bedrooms?"

The landing gave an even more impressive view of the hall and chandelier. The front of the house was dark and sunless. So if the sun was setting in the library's windows, that meant the hall faced the south. There was something about this house that made me feel like I needed to orient myself. Taylor led us towards the left, down another hallway. The indigo-and-gold-patterned wallpaper glinted in the light from the wall sconces, which were nymphs staring determinedly ahead.

"How do we know which room is ours?" Poppy asked as we approached the doors.

Taylor winked. "You'll see."

"This is me," Keira said as we came to the first door on the left. "The green room." Poppy and I stopped in the doorway, taking it all in. An enormous four-poster bed took up much of the left side of the room, which was draped with velvety green bedding and pillows. It matched the emerald wallpaper, which showed an intricate leaf motif. A chandelier shone soft light over the room, its golden boughs intertwining in an intricate wreath. There was a large oak dresser near the bed and a wardrobe across the room, next to a stone fireplace.

We exclaimed as we went in, almost shyly. I studied the oil painting over the fireplace, which showed a shadowed naked woman standing next to a deer in the woods. Towards the back of the room, in front of one of the two windows, sat a sleek desk with a padded leather chair. It was the only modern piece of furniture in the room. I wandered closer, seeing that it was neatly covered with notebooks and other office supplies, either black or gilt-colored. Keira's laptop sat in the center, and on top was a black jewelry box.

"Now this." Taylor grabbed the box. "This is a welcome gift."

"Oooh," Poppy cried. "What is it?"

Keira watched, her expression inscrutable, as Taylor lifted out a long golden chain. Poppy studied the charm at the end of the necklace and I leaned in to see. It was the head of a lion with diamond eyes. I instinctively reached out and Taylor dropped it in my hand.

"Wow, this is heavy." I raised and lowered the necklace. "Definitely real gold."

"You an appraiser?" Taylor asked, eyebrow raised.

"Just an appreciator." No need to get into my family history. I glanced at Keira. "So this was in the room when you came in?"

"Yep." Keira folded her arms. "Wrapped up with my name on it."

"You know, that probably makes up for a month or two of lost income." Taylor nudged her. "If push comes to shove."

Keira playfully elbowed her back. "Like I'd sell a necklace Roza Vallo gave me." I handed it to her and she slipped it on. "It's actually my style, something I'd buy. If I could afford it."

"Did you get one too?" I asked Taylor.

"I'll show you." She strode to the door. "Follow me!"

Taylor's room was much the same as Keira's, only decorated in shades of blue. Above the fireplace was a painting of a boat on a stormy sea. While Keira's room had been pristine, Taylor's bed, chair, and desk were already covered with clothes and notebooks. Taylor swiped the box from the bed and brought it over.

"Aww." Poppy cupped the small, golden figure at the end of the chain. It was a rabbit, again with diamond eyes.

"Less intimidating." Taylor smirked. "But more bizarre. Which I'm into." She slipped it over her neck. "We have to wear these to dinner, don't we?"

"Absolutely." Poppy was already at the door.

The room next to Taylor's held Poppy's suitcase. This room was done in hues of red and blush. Poppy beelined right to the desk, picked up the gold-wrapped box, and tore it open.

"Huh." She wrinkled her nose.

"What is it?" Taylor bounded over and hooted. "No way!"

It was a pig. I reached out to touch its curly tail with the tip of a finger.

Keira studied it over my shoulder. "It's cute."

"Is this some kind of message?" Poppy laughed, but her eyes narrowed.

"That you're adorable?" Taylor took the chain and slipped it around Poppy's neck. She looked down and her pursed lips made us laugh.

She chuckled too. "It is cute."

"So random," I said.

"Let's go." Taylor hip bumped me. "I want to see what Alex got."

There was just one room left across the hall. Relief bubbled up, a cool fountain in my chest. Wren wasn't coming. Either they'd decided to ask only me or she'd had to decline, as unthinkable as that seemed.

But as we walked into the orange-hued room, I froze.

Instead of the giant four-poster bed, there were two smaller ones, side by side.

"Shit." The word popped out. There were also two desks, pushed up against each other, each getting half of the window.

Not only was Wren still coming . . . we were going to be roomies.

Suddenly the room felt stuffy and stifling. My breath lodged in my throat and I forced myself to inhale.

"This is odd." Taylor picked up the

wrapped present on the left desk. "This is for Alex."

Poppy was already holding the other. "This one says . . . 'Wren'?"

Keira remained at the doorway, watching me as if suddenly suspicious. I wanted to run, I wanted to race down the stairs and burst outside and plunge my burning face into a snowbank.

Roomies. Beads of sweat ran down my back. My chest tightened and black spots danced at the edges of my vision.

"Hey, you okay?" Taylor asked.

"I'm fine, I just feel a little dizzy." I tried to laugh but the spots became blotches, growing from my periphery and covering up my vision. I was going to pass out. Clutching at my chest, I squeezed my eyes shut.

"Let's sit her down." Taylor's voice sounded far away. Gentle hands took my arms and walked me to a chair.

"Put your head between your legs. Just take a few breaths. It's okay." Keira's voice was soothing, and I did as told. There were low murmurs, and then someone lifted my hair and pressed a damp washcloth to the back of my neck. Slowly I came back to my body, realizing that I was squeezing someone's hand. I sat up. Keira kneeled beside me, her hand in mine.

Taylor was sitting cross-legged on the floor in front of me. "You okay?"

"Yeah. Sorry. I don't know what that was." I tried to laugh but it came out shaky. "That's never happened to me before. I just got really light-headed."

Liar. It had happened on the subway a few times, especially in the months after the incident with Wren. Keira and Taylor exchanged glances.

"Panic attack," I said with resignation.

Poppy came out of the bathroom, where she'd re-wetted the washcloth. Their solemn faces sparked a sharp anger at myself. I'd just met these people, and already I was showing myself to be the unstable one. The words spewed out, powered by a hopeless fury. "So I should probably just tell you guys. I wasn't one of the original people who was picked for this. Someone dropped out, so my friend whose agent knows Roza's agent sent some of my stories. They accepted me but they also accepted Wren. She and I used to be close. Well, best friends. We had a huge falling-out a year ago." I motioned to the beds. "And now apparently we're going to be staying in the same room together."

"Damn," Taylor muttered.

"What happened?" Poppy kneeled next to Taylor. "With the falling-out?"

That was the question, wasn't it? The answer lived in different layers, like a pyramid with deep hidden chambers. I decided to start with the easiest story. "Well, we were best friends for a long time. Eight years. And then she just kind of dumped me." That was true, at least. "I didn't take it very well, to say the least."

"That sucks," Taylor proclaimed. "I hate when shit like that happens."

"Yeah. She moved out suddenly, and then we had a confrontation at a bar . . ." I crossed my arms. "It was bad."

The arc of black blood gleaming in the fairy lights.

They watched me, waiting. I might as well tell them this part; Wren probably would anyway. "I tried to talk to her on the back patio and she ended up falling backwards off a step, onto concrete. She fell on her wineglass. There was blood everywhere. Someone called an ambulance and they took her to a hospital. It turned out she'd cut a tendon in her hand and needed all this surgery."

"That's awful." Keira bit her lip. "But it sounds like an accident. Did she blame you for it?"

98

A flash of Wren's face, her lips twisted in disgust. *Don't touch me.*

Which had only made me angrier.

"I don't know." I pushed the dark thoughts away. "But she — and all our friends, actually — stopped talking to me after that."

"I'm sorry, girl." Poppy scooted forward and patted my knee.

"That shit is worse than a breakup," Taylor declared.

"Friend breakups are way worse," Poppy agreed. "I went through something like that in college."

"People change, and not always for the better." Taylor gazed up at me. "Was there a guy involved?"

"Kind of," I said, relieved that Taylor was building the story, however inaccurate. Because there had been a guy, a few months later. I'd watched the relationship quickly progress on social media. Even taking pictures with a guy was unusual for Wren, but this dude was photogenic: tall, blond, partial to slim suits. I told myself it was just good for her brand, expecting the relationship to implode, as they all did. But a year later they were still together.

"I knew it." Taylor gave a definitive nod. "Some women are so competitive. She probably thought you were going to try to steal him or something."

"Yeah." I felt guilty letting this narrative take hold, but it seemed too complicated to correct her. "You know what? I hate talking about this. I don't want to turn anyone against her or anything. But I wanted to be honest."

"Hey." Poppy clasped her hands. "I just had the best idea. Why don't you take my room? I'll stay in here with . . . what's her name?"

"Wren."

"Of course it is." Taylor's low, dry voice made all of us, even me, laugh.

"That's sweet of you." I shook my head. "But I don't want to make you give up your own room."

"Oh, it's fine. I'd actually like it. I get scared on my own." Poppy jumped up, smirking. "Which I know is super ironic, based on what I read and write."

"Great." Taylor jumped up and went to my suitcase. "Let's make the switch."

"Are you sure?" A giant wave of relief crashed down on me as Poppy confirmed. As she and Taylor walked out, I leaned back in the plush chair and sighed.

Keira observed me, her face calculating. I felt a flutter of fear — did she think I was being dramatic, or petty? — but then she smiled.

"Should we check out your gift?" She went to the desk and brought back the box. I opened it, feeling ashamed, though I wasn't sure why. I hadn't done anything wrong. If Wren had arrived before me, she surely would have told everyone about our history. And I hadn't even gone into detail.

Because if you had, they would know. About that night, and about the other night. What happened before.

I shoved the thought away, lifting out the necklace. Dangling at the bottom was a heavy gold spider.

"It's beautiful." Keira pulled it closer, touching the diamond eyes.

"It's gorgeous. Even though normally I'm scared of spiders." I laughed uneasily. Maybe it was the unearthliness of being there at Blackbriar, but it felt like a message or a clue.

Keira smiled. "Maybe this will keep them away."

CHAPTER 8

Dinner with Roza was at 7:30 p.m. sharp, Ian the editor had told Taylor and Keira. After my freakout, everyone decided to use the extra hour to unpack. I told myself it wasn't my fault, that I hadn't ruined the festive mood. But I still felt embarrassed as I lay back on the bed, gazing at the wallpaper. Thick vines of red flowers twisted on a pink wallpaper background, but from even a few feet away they looked like fat intestines sliding down the wall.

Suddenly, someone was knocking at the door. I sat up with a gasp. The room was pitch-black and I struggled to find the lamp on the bedside table.

"Hey there, sleepyhead," Taylor cried as I pulled open the door. She wore a tight patterned blazer and slacks. Behind her, Poppy and Keira waited in dresses and bright lipstick. Their new necklaces glittered from their chests.

"What time is it?" I muttered.

"Seven twenty-five," Keira said.

"Shit," I muttered. I hadn't meant to fall asleep, but I must've passed out immediately.

"Hey." Taylor leaned in. "You get ready and we'll tell everyone you're coming. Okay?"

Once they left, I ran to my suitcase, picking hopelessly through my clothes. I hadn't even thought to bring cute dresses. I cursed my lack of foresight and pulled on a sweater and dark jeans. I swiped on more makeup and hurried out, my ankle boots squeaking on the marble staircase.

Where was I going? I found myself turning automatically to the left, towards the library.

"Whoa!" I stopped short to avoid crashing into Yana. She'd been waiting for me.

"Wrong way." She walked past me, unsmiling. Now she wore a chic blue sweater dress and thin leather flats. The backs of her bare ankles were red and she took quick steps. I tried to think of something to say as I followed. But my abrupt awakening from a wine-addled sleep, combined with the winding, luxurious hallways, left me reeling.

A delicious scent wafted towards us. It grew stronger until we entered the dining room, centered on a long wooden table laden with china, glasses, flickering taper candles, and plates of appetizers. It looked like a dinner party photo from a home decorating magazine, complete with chatting, elegant attendees.

At one end of the table, a man with slicked-back hair gestured with a too-full wineglass, shouting a triumphant punch line. Taylor, Poppy, and Keira, all sitting on the far side of the table, burst into guffaws. The head of the table — presumably where Roza would be — was empty. Yana gestured towards an empty place setting nearest the man.

The next seat was taken by Wren. I forced myself to look at her. The back of her glossy head shone above her thin shoulders. She'd always had excellent posture.

As if in a trance, I stepped up to the table. In the split second before she noticed me, I took in every detail of her profile. While I'd seen her briefly, horrifyingly, at Ursula's book reading, I was now able to study her closely. Her eyebrows were heavier and she wore a nude lipstick instead of her usual trademark red. Her bangs were shorter and more piecey. But otherwise she looked the same as she had a year ago, when we'd been living together. Or maybe even younger, as if she'd been siphoning my life force, using it to plump her cheeks while I grew more listless and depressed.

She was grinning but not laughing. Then she noticed me and her smile drained. She righted herself and curved her lips politely. Her hazel eyes shone.

"Hi, Al," she said quietly as I sat beside her. The low, familiar voice stunned me. In my dreamlike state, sitting in Roza Vallo's dining room, it felt as though I'd slipped into an alternate universe, one in which Wren and I were still best friends.

Something on her neck sparkled: a gold necklace against her green silk dress. I squinted to make out the creature resting against the slight swell of her breasts.

It was a coiled snake.

"Alex!" Taylor raised her glass. "You made it!" Her eyes gleamed from the wine.

"Hi." I was still standing over my chair. In a kind of daze, I realized I'd left my spider necklace upstairs. Yana pulled my chair out roughly, and as I sat she pushed it in too fast. My knees buckled and I fell onto the cushion heavily. It took me a moment before I could look at Wren again, but when I did, she was sipping her wine, ignoring me.

"Well, hello there." The male editor had a clipped English accent. He was probably in his late forties, handsome in an unseemly kind of way. Someone who'd hang out at clubs buying drinks for twentysomething girls. "I'm Ian, Roza's editor and, dare I say, friend. Pleasure." He turned back to the rest of the table. "So this is the full crew, yeah?"

"We need a team name or something." Poppy giggled.

I was about a foot away from Wren, so close I could smell her familiar perfume: roses, incense, and smoke. Smooth dark hairs glistened on her arms. Wren was Egyptian on her mother's side, and she'd told me that in junior high the cool girls had followed her around one day, lumbering and wailing in guttural tones. They tossed a note onto her desk that afternoon, a crude drawing of a woolly mammoth. She started shaving her arms that night. She didn't stop until college.

It was shocking that even someone as perfect-looking as Wren had those stories. But we all had those stories, didn't we? Horrific taunts, the trials of female adolescence. Growing up, I'd been ridiculed for my acne, my nose, my weight, my breasts . . .

Ian poured wine into my glass and I jerked. He was talking again, telling another story.

"Is Roza here yet?" I said it softly, almost to myself, but Wren heard.

"She is. She just had to take a call."

The whole table stopped to listen.

"She's upstairs," Ian added. "She'll be down shortly, don't worry, love."

"We were joking this is all an elaborate setup." Taylor gestured at Ian. "He's actually a serial killer who lured us here."

"Because, as you know, I *hate* women." He grinned.

"So, Ian." Poppy leaned forward. "Can you tell us more about this retreat?"

"Ladies." He raised his hands, like a conductor. "Believe me when I say I know absolutely nothing. Roza's in charge of all that. To be honest, I'm just here because I happened to be in New York for the week and I never miss a chance to visit Blackbriar."

Yana and another woman appeared carrying steaming plates. The other woman had kind, lined eyes and dark hair threaded with silver.

"Specifically because of this woman." Ian pressed his hands together. "Chitra Patel. One of the finest chefs in the state if not the country."

"Oh, here we go." She had an English accent as well, though it was softer, more lyrical. "We all know you're a charmer, love; no need to lay it on so thick."

"Just wait." Ian fluttered his fingers. "Take a bite and tell me I'm wrong."

The plates held filet mignon and small heaps of creamy risotto, salty mushrooms, garlicky brussels sprouts. We set to the food quickly, with exclamations: "Oh my god." "This is incredible." "Chitra's specialty: neo–comfort food. You girls really are in for a treat."

"So, Miss Wren." Taylor sat back, appraising her. "You said you had a photo shoot this morning?"

"I did." Wren swallowed, a delicate pulse at her throat.

"That is so effing cool." Poppy stabbed at her mushrooms.

"It was a lipstick shoot at a sewage treatment plant." She rolled her eyes. "My bosses think they're so cutting-edge."

"Did it smell?" Taylor looked horrified.

Wren raised an eyebrow. "You mean I *don't* reek? I guess the stench is just permanently in my nostrils now. But, hey, anything for a good picture."

Everyone chuckled. Her charisma was starting to unfurl, its vines wrapping around the table. It caused anxiety deep in my belly. But as she moved to a story about a photo shoot in the reptile house of the Bronx Zoo, when a Komodo dragon had escaped and eaten several designer shoes, I tried to push it down. This month wasn't about Wren, and it wasn't about who people liked more. It was about Roza.

Then the word "fiancé" caught my ear.

"What does he think about your intrepid adventures?" Ian pointed at Wren's left hand. It had been in her lap for most of dinner, but she'd just used it to gesture.

"Evan?" She stared at her hand, flat on the table. The gigantic diamond sparkled. "He's fine with it. I think he likes getting a break from me."

Wren was *engaged*? I was floored. When had that happened? She hadn't posted about it on social media.

"Wait, show us!" Taylor cried. Wren obligingly flashed her hand. I looked to be polite, even though my stomach churned. Wren glanced at me and quickly away.

"Girl." Poppy gasped and leaned forward. "That rock is ob-*scene*!"

"I keep forgetting about it." Wren laughed a little, her eyes lowered. "Evan loves it when someone asks me about it and I'm, like, what?"

"What's he like?" Poppy watched Wren

dreamily, swirling her wine. "What does he do?"

"He's in finance." She shrugged and the hand disappeared back under the table. "And a musician, in his off time. He's . . . I don't know; he's a good guy."

"When?" I croaked.

Everyone looked at me.

"When's the wedding?" I managed to say. It would be strange to ask my original question of when they'd gotten engaged.

Her eyes flickered away. "We're not sure yet. Maybe in the fall."

"Cheers!" Ian jumped up to smash his glass against hers, which led to a table-wide clinking. Taylor pounded the last of her wine and threw up an arm, almost punching Yana, who was bending over her to fill her water glass.

"I'm really starting to think you've got Roza tied up in the basement or something, Ian." Taylor leaned back, giving Yana space.

"She just likes to make an entrance." Ian rolled his eyes.

"What's she like?" Poppy asked.

"Well, sweetheart, what would you like to know?" His tipsy grin turned into a leer as his eyes dipped down at her cleavage.

Wren and I shared a disgusted glance.

Stricken, we both looked away.

The shared look, the shared thought — *Ugh, what a dick* — had happened so automatically, like a missing note that had to be filled in.

I chanced a look. Wren was now concentrating hard on Poppy.

"I mean, everything," Poppy said gamely. "Do you have any crazy stories?"

"Crazy stories? There's plenty of those." He leaned back, his eyes screwed up as if peering into the past. "There was this one time in Barcelona —"

"Oh no you don't." Suddenly she was entering the room, she was striding towards us, she was seating herself with a heavy sigh. "I get to tell that story, Ian; you always fuck it up."

She perched on her chair, primly positioning her napkin in her lap, the scent of a dark jasmine perfume wafting over the table. The energy in the room ran to her like a current; it was impossible to look away. It wasn't her outfit, or that she'd in any way dressed up for us. In fact, she wore a gray sweatshirt, and her hair was still damp from a shower. But something clung to her that made the rest of us in our finery — even Wren — look silly and childish, like teens in sparkly dresses trying to sneak into a bar.

Time slowed; I felt frozen in place.

It was Roza. My high priestess, my guiding light since age twelve.

Roza in the flesh.

"Hello, girls." Her long, full lips pulled into a smile. She raised a glass, which Yana had already filled, and took us in. "Welcome to Blackbriar. I'm so pleased you're here."

CHAPTER 9

The next few minutes passed in a blur. We introduced ourselves as Roza listened in a queenly way, sipping her wine and completely ignoring the steaming plate of food before her.

I ended up going last, and I stumbled through my little spiel. Name, where I'm from, what I'm doing when I'm not writing (*ha*). After, there came a pause.

"Where's your necklace?" Roza's brow furrowed.

"Oh." My face warmed. "I was rushing to get ready and I totally forgot to wear it."

"You forgot to wear it?" She said it lightly, but her expression was suddenly grim.

"I'm sorry." I glanced around the table. Poppy, Wren, and Taylor stared down at their plates while Ian and Keira watched Roza. "I mean . . . I didn't know we were supposed to."

"You come to *my home.*" Roza suddenly

leaned forward, her accent growing stronger as she said the words slowly, empathically. "And you receive *my gift.* And you don't stop to think that perhaps it would be a good idea to show your appreciation by wearing it?"

My mouth opened and closed. I felt stricken. Was this actually happening?

"Nothing?" She narrowed her eyes, then sighed and looked down. "Well, Alex dear. I think we know exactly how seriously you're taking this opportunity." She picked up a brussels sprout with her fingers and popped it into her mouth. "You can leave," she said, chewing.

"What?" I gawped stupidly.

"Goodbye." She waved a hand.

I thought suddenly of the book festival, how the mood in the church had shifted so rapidly. The atmosphere in the dining room, so light a seccond ago, was now heavy with shock and dread.

"Roza." Ian smiled, appeasing. "Come on, love. You don't really mean that."

She stared not at him but at me, her green eyes blazing. I wanted to crawl under the table or flee upstairs to my room, where I could lock out whatever this brutal punishment was.

But I forced myself to stare back at her.

There were tears gathering behind my eyes but I refused to let them well up.

The silence stretched out, interminable. I stopped breathing and my heart thundered.

Then Roza threw her head back and laughed. The mood pitched again, this time to confusion and relief. Uneasy smiles formed on Taylor's and Poppy's faces. Ian groaned and rubbed his temples. Wren continued to gaze at her plate while Keira stared at Roza, her face filled with distrust.

"My darling!" Roza wiped at her eyes. "You're so serious!" She finally calmed down and exhaled with an *Ohhhh.* "You really think I would kick you out for not wearing a stupid necklace? Jesus. You must think I'm an absolute monster."

"Um, no." My voice was shaking and I steeled myself. "Of course not."

Ian raised his hands. "Ladies, I should've warned you all. Roza likes to play little tricks sometimes. You really can't take half the things she says seriously." He shook his finger at her. "These beautiful, talented women don't know you yet, dear. You're going to make them want to run off before the damn retreat begins."

"Ian, shut up." As if my humiliation had revved her appetite, she picked up her knife and fork and dug into her steak. "They're not children." She looked up at me, chewing and considering. "Alex, darling. Can you forgive me? Maybe I was too cruel."

"No, it's totally fine." I managed a chuckle. The relief was like cool water down a parched throat. But it also left me feeling unsettled and upset. How could she do that: treat me like a dog she raised her hand to, just to see if it would flinch? Keira caught my eye, her forehead lined with concern.

"By the way." Roza motioned to me with her fork. "Alex, I absolutely loved your story. I almost missed a flight reading it. You're incredibly talented and I'm so delighted you're here."

The words warmed me and I tried to force myself to relax as Roza and Ian started bantering about Roza devastating a potential suitor Ian had sent her way in Rome. Maybe I was overreacting. Roza was known for being unpredictable, and most definitely not for being a kindly, caring, Mother Goose–type mentor.

Roza Vallo wasn't nice. And that's how she'd gotten where she was.

Maybe I could learn something from her.

When Roza pushed her half-eaten plate away, Yana was immediately there to collect it.

"So." Roza pulled something out of her

pocket: a mother-of-pearl inlaid cigarette case. She popped it open and brought out a thin, hand-rolled cigarette. "Let's talk."

An air of expectation arose as Chitra appeared, setting down small, delicate cups of espresso and trays of truffles and fruit.

"I know I was being a bitch before, but I really am glad you liked the necklaces." Roza jutted out her chin as she lit her cigarette with a silver lighter. "They're twenty-two-karat, so be gentle with them."

"They're beautiful," Poppy said earnestly.

"Where'd you get them?" Wren asked, touching hers.

"India." Roza blew out a thin stream of smoke. The scent of weed, piney and pungent, suffused the dining room. She handed the joint to Poppy, who took it uncertainly. "A long time ago. I knew I'd need them someday. And the set of five worked out perfectly."

"How'd you choose who got which animal?" Taylor studied her charm, holding it up in the candlelight.

Roza shrugged. "I just had a feeling."

"Really?" Taylor smiled, flirting. "A rabbit? Is this a commentary on my sex life?"

"Regeneration," Roza said playfully. "Like a phoenix, my dear, only cuter."

"And the pig?" Poppy held back a cough

and handed the joint to Taylor.

"Pigs are a sign of luck," Roza said.

"Snake?" Wren asked.

"Knowledge, of course." Roza stared at me. "What was yours?"

I cleared my throat. "A spider."

"Resourcefulness," she said sagely.

"Are you making this up?" Ian asked.

"Of course!" she cried, and we all laughed.

Roza took a sip of her espresso and set it down on the saucer with a jangle. "Okay, let's get down to business. Before I'm too stoned to think."

Keira passed the joint to Ian without taking any.

"That's strong," Taylor remarked, her eyes pink.

"It's time for me to tell you what we're really doing here," Roza said.

Taylor and Keira caught eyes. Poppy propped her chin on her hand expectantly. I managed not to look at Wren but could feel her shift uncomfortably in her seat.

"This isn't going to be an easy-breezy, hang-out, write-whenever-you-feel-like-it kind of retreat." Roza picked up a truffle from one of the trays, chewed it, and swallowed. "This is going to be a little more intense."

"I like intense," Taylor said, still flirting.

"Good." Roza leaned back in her seat, pulling in a knee and setting her heel on the end of her chair. Her jeans had a large tear and skin showed through like a bone poking through flesh.

Ian held the joint out to me. Sitting with my enemy and my idol, my brain spewing morbid nonsense: the perfect time to get high! I pretended to inhale, then passed it to Wren. She kept her eyes on it as she took it. Her nails were bare and her cuticles were ragged. This, more than anything so far that night, took me aback. Wren loved her nails and was never without a fresh manicure.

"Question: How do we all feel about the publishing industry?" Roza asked.

"It sucks!" Taylor called through cupped palms.

"It does suck." Roza took the joint from Wren, who I was almost certain had taken a faux puff like me. "I got lucky, I published in the seventies. They were open to radical stuff from nobodies back then. You could push the boundaries and they'd take a chance on you. Now you basically have to be running your own brand before they give you the time of day."

The weed really *was* strong; even with the small amount I'd accidentally inhaled, I could feel it.

"You have to be so slick these days," Roza mused. "Not just with all that social media nonsense. But also a highly sellable manuscript that will appeal to the masses." She rolled her eyes. "It's absolutely disgusting. Right, Ian, darling?"

He shrugged, watching her with amusement.

"So. Because I was lucky, I want to pass some of that luck along to you." She gazed solemnly at each of us in turn. "I believe that you are the most talented young female writers in America. And because of that, this isn't going to be a normal retreat. You're not going to fool around with the first chapter of something that you've been working on for three years. No, we're going to start fresh."

"What does that mean?" Poppy asked.

"What it means, darling, is that during this month of February, over twenty-eight days, you are going to write a completely new novel."

"What?" Taylor snorted. "That's not possible."

"Oh, no?" Roza's voice sharpened. "Are you that lazy, dear? In a month when you have absolutely nothing to do but write?"

I'd stiffened, hunching over my plate. Terror tornadoed in my chest. I'd already been nervous about writing, period. Now I was going to have to write an entire fucking novel?

"So." Roza smiled. "I'm sure you have questions. Ask away."

"How long?" Keira asked. Her face was perfectly neutral. "I mean, what's the word length you're expecting?"

"Good question, dear. This new work will have to be at least eighty-one thousand words. So that means you will need to write at least three thousand new words every day. Twelve double-spaced pages. You can do that in a day, easy. And you even get today off to settle in."

"How will you know?" Taylor was now leaning forward, her arms on the table. "I mean, that we make it to three thousand"

"This is how." Roza used her fingers to mimic legs walking downward. "Every day, you will take your laptop, and you will go down to the study, and you will print out your work from that day. Then you will walk back up" — here the fingers rose — "and you will slip the pages underneath my door. No later than midnight, please." The hand dropped and she cleared her throat. "Every morning by eight a.m. there will be copies of the excerpts in the dining room. You will read your colleagues' works by two p.m., when we will meet in the library to discuss during a two-hour seminar. Please have notes on the others' works to share."

The new realization was settling in: not only would we have to write a book.

We'd have to help edit four others.

"Every day at four p.m., I will meet with one of you to go more in depth; I'll share the order tomorrow at our first group meeting. Let's see . . ." She held a finger to her chin. "Oh, yes. We will meet for cocktails in the parlor every evening at six thirty, with dinner to follow at seven thirty. Please be prompt; lateness will not be tolerated. She considered. "Breakfast and lunch will be a buffet laid out for you in the dining room; you can eat when you please. And you are also welcome to visit the kitchen at any time, day or night. More questions?"

"What if we want to — or need to — edit what we've already written?" Keira asked.

"You'll have to just keep going." Roza shrugged. "So unless you're a gambler, you'll probably want to have some kind of outline. You'll be able to go back and edit at your leisure after the retreat. Well, except for the winner. That person will just have a month or two, if we want to get it out by fall."

" 'Winner'?" Poppy repeated as Keira

echoed: " 'Get it out'?"

"Oh, yes." Roza's eyes danced. "Did I forget that? Whichever novel is the best, Ian here will publish it. I'll write a nice introduction. And you'll also get an advance. I believe it was" — Roza glanced at Ian — "one million, wasn't it?"

Taylor whistled.

Ian nodded, smug. "And the book tour."

"Right. And we'll go on tour together." Roza sighed. "I'm finishing up my own blasted book, so I'll be working right along with you."

Wren, silent up until now, let out a sudden laugh.

"Yes, dear," Roza said patiently, as if she'd raised her hand.

"I'm sorry, I just . . ." Wren's eyes flashed. "I'm just processing this. And wondering . . ."

"Yes, dear," Roza said again.

"Well, okay." Wren straightened. "I'm wondering why. It feels like we're being forced to compete against each other, like a reality show or something."

"Oh!" Roza turned to Ian, eyebrows raised. "What an interesting way to see it. Here I thought we were being so generous."

"I don't want to seem ungrateful." Wren shook her head. "I guess . . . I don't know. I

123

just wish we could all work together. Instead of having winners and losers. It's just what we've been dealing with forever."

Wow. Wren didn't take shit from anyone — that was a core personality trait, one I'd envied since the first day I'd met her and overheard her talking back to her supervisor. But I still wouldn't have expected her to question Roza.

Even though . . . she definitely had a point.

Roza was gazing at her with a frown. We held our collective breath.

But then Roza smiled. "Here's the reason I'm not giving all of you a personal grant, darling. It's because I'm not in the business of dispensing handouts."

Wren watched her, giving a slow nod.

"And there's another reason too," Roza went on. "I've found that the best work comes when the stakes are raised. When there's an element of stress. That's when the survival instinct kicks in. And that makes for the most raw and vivid work."

"Okay." Wren said it woodenly.

"After all" — Roza fiddled with her lighter — "I'm not running a spa, darling. You didn't think a retreat with me was going to be a nice, relaxing time, did you?"

Wren blinked. "Well, no, but —"

"You knew this was a writing retreat,"

Roza pointed out. "That writing would be involved. Just think of this as an added bonus. A one-in-five chance to win a million dollars." She raised her hands. "And even if you don't win, you'll have a novel! One that a group of brilliant writers will have helped you create. It will be your best work yet. And, of course, you'll have me as your champion." Roza tapped the lighter twice. "I don't plan on leaving anyone out in the cold. Unless you leave first. I can't support someone who gives up so easily. Understood?"

Wren bobbed her head, chastened. "I do."

"What if we fall behind?" Taylor asked suddenly.

Roza widened her eyes. "Don't fall behind. If you fail to make your daily word count" — she shrugged — "then you'll be asked to leave the next day."

The table was silent. We stared at Roza, waiting for her to burst out laughing. *You're all so serious!*

"Anything else?" she asked instead.

"Any restrictions regarding the content?" Keira's tone verged on casual.

"Up to you." Roza pushed back her chair. "Of course, you know what I like, based on what got you here. But if you want to try sci-fi or whatever, that's up to you. I lied about the day off; please come up with a one-paragraph proposal by our first meeting tomorrow. No need to share beyond the midpoint unless you'd like to. Print out copies for everyone; we'll discuss them at two."

"Oh god." Poppy looked stricken. "That's fast."

"That's the game, darling." Roza stood, picking up her glass.

"What if you don't like it?" I asked. "The story idea."

Roza studied me. "Then you'll have to come up with something else."

Being the focus of her gaze was like nothing else I'd ever experienced: like being pinned down as she cracked open my skull, staring impassively, considering the slimy things inside.

Then she grinned and it was friendly, almost jaunty. The switch jarred me.

"So, my dear." Her voice was light. "Make it something I like."

Chapter 10

After dinner, we returned to our rooms. The earlier camaraderie at dinner had dissipated and we were silent as we climbed the marble staircase.

Halfway up the stairs, Taylor broke the silence. "Well, fuck."

"Guess the party's over." Keira pursed her lips. "That was fast."

"Do you guys have ideas yet?" Poppy's large eyes were veined with red. "Because I am freaking the eff out."

Keira squeezed her arm. "Don't worry. We'll figure it out. I was thinking of trying some freewriting. Seeing what comes up."

"That's a good idea," Taylor said.

"What time is it?" I asked.

Only Wren wore a watch. "Ten thirty," she said without looking at me.

I felt a curious remove from the situation. It was like all the stress of the past two hours had completely shut me down. Seeing Wren and finding out she was engaged. Roza messing with me in front of everyone. And now having to come up with an entire novel idea when I hadn't been able to write anything over the past year.

I hadn't expected it to be easy. But maybe not quite so punishing?

Still, the stakes were admittedly high. As Roza had said, I now had a one-in-five chance of a million-dollar publishing deal. The idea of that much money didn't even compute.

But it would certainly mean I could quit my job. And even if I didn't win, I'd still have a new novel, one that Roza had helped me write. Any way this shook out, I'd end up in a place infinitely better than where I'd started from.

If I could keep up, of course.

It was a relief to shut my door. I took a hot shower and blasted myself with cold at the end, trying to shake the drowsiness from the heavy dinner, wine, and weed. The night was not over yet. Wrapped in a heavy robe that hung on the back of the bathroom door, I settled at the desk and opened my laptop. It was time to get to work.

An hour later I moaned and pressed my forehead onto the desk. I'd come up with a list of ideas, and they were all awful. Worse than awful: boring.

I knew what it felt like to have a good idea. The concept would trigger something, a little ember deep down in the belly. You'd have to be careful not to hold it too tightly. But you could feel it — the expansive glow of all the possibilities.

But these ideas were dead. Inert. I was digging around in the mud but finding nothing.

I imagined Wren bent over the paper, her lips curled into a sneer as she read my synopsis. From the beginning of our writing group, Wren had been harsh. Her written notes would litter my pages like little bombs: *Boring. Get rid of this. She would never do this in a million years.* Ursula would call her Sweeney Todd for her ruthless cuts.

I jumped up and slammed the laptop closed. I needed a break. I needed to calm down. An idea would come; I just had to be patient.

Something I'd done, back when I could actually string words together, was to always have a mug of tea on my desk. In the rhythm of writing, it was helpful to be able to pause and sip and consider before jumping back in. Maybe that would help.

Roza had told us to feel free to use the

kitchen. There had to be tea there, right? I slipped into clothes and pulled open the door. Light shone from the cracks beneath everyone's closed doors. They were off to the races and probably significantly further along than me.

Someone had turned the hallway lights off, and I grabbed my phone to use the flashlight. The marble statues cast sharp shadows in its beam. A chill tickled my lower spine. I felt like I was in a video game, walking down this dark and opulent hall, waiting for something horrific to pounce.

I headed to the landing, marveling at how unnerved I was. For someone who loved horror books and movies, I was way too easily spooked. At the top of the stairs, I hesitated. Something was pricking at me. A noise. I stood still. There it was. The faintest of sounds, but they were somehow clear.

Faraway whimpers, like someone was being hurt.

They were coming from the other side of the landing. I crept towards them, passing a hall that went straight back, towards the rear of the house. The sounds came not from down there but from the other wing, across from our rooms. There was a beat of silence, and then it rose up again: a sharp yelping.

I slipped down the hall, chest tight, feet

sinking into the plush rugs. This was a double of our own hallway, also flanked by paintings and punctuated by statues.

The cries were louder now, rhythmic and obviously sexual. *Oh.* I slowed, but then I continued. The hall ended in a red-painted door. I touched the wood and leaned in. It had to be Roza. Was she alone? The now guttural grunts seemed somewhat exaggerated for a masturbation session, but who was I to judge?

But she wasn't alone. Somehow I knew there was someone else there.

The visual reared up in my mind: Roza writhing, bucking, crying out as a silent, shadowy figure — Ian? — held down her hips, his tongue moving against her, unrelenting, dominating.

Now her groans escalated, quickening, amplifying. I remained frozen at the door, eyes wide, a pulsing in my own groin. It felt like there was something in the sounds, a code to crack. Because they contained passion and pleasure, sure. But there was also something else. A knowing smile at the edge, somehow tinged with disdain. Maybe even hate.

She came with a keening wail.

Then there was silence. Maybe she'd killed Ian, crushed his head in between her thighs as ecstasy flooded through her. Maybe she was sitting up, examining the mixture of skull and brain, still breathing hard but calming every second.

Ugh. What a mess.

The image was so visceral that terror leapt into my throat. I backed away from the door, then jumped as something cold poked into my thigh.

It was a statue of a rearing horse; I'd bumped into one of its hooves.

I turned and fled back to the safety of my room, trying to shake the disturbing images from my mind.

I woke early the next day. I'd forgotten to close the drapes, and bright sunlight beamed straight into my crusty eyes. I slipped out of the bed and goose bumps pebbled my arms from the chilly air. As I got ready, I thought about the night before. After scurrying back to my room, I'd crawled under the covers and watched calming downloaded shows on my phone until I'd fallen asleep.

In the sunlight, I felt embarrassed about my overreaction. So Roza was sleeping with Ian: So what? It was a little surprising — he'd seemed like a bit of a creep — but they obviously went back a long time.

More shaming, though, was that I'd snuck up to her door in the first place. What on earth had made me act like a curious, horny twelve-year-old boy? I was lucky no one had caught me.

Wrapped in fluffy towels, I sat at the desk. The sky was a bright, cloudless blue. A sparkling layer of snow covered the backyard. I envisioned throwing my laptop through the window, shattering the glass, watching it land with a *poof* in a snowy pile.

The first writing group session was at two. It was currently 8:30. I had to come up with a novel idea by the afternoon and then write 3,000 of its opening words.

Back home, that would be impossible. But we were living by Roza's rules now. And after a full night of sleep, I felt oddly confident. The right idea was there, just slightly beyond my reach. I got ready, grabbed a notebook and pen — how awful would it be for that idea to burst into being and then slip away before I could catch it? — and headed downstairs.

Scents of savory breakfast foods filled my nostrils as I neared the dining room.

"Morning!" Taylor was at the table, green/blond hair mussed from sleep, still in pajamas. I noticed she'd slipped her rabbit necklace on and it clashed with her plaid top. Her laptop was open next to her.

"Morning."

She motioned to the buffet. "Grab some food. It's delicious."

"Don't mind if I do." I pulled the top off the first tray to find a half-eaten pan of breakfast potatoes glistening with oil and rosemary. "I could get used to this." I didn't usually eat a big breakfast, but now I loaded up my plate.

"How's it going?" I sat two chairs down. "You still working on your idea?"

"Oh, no." She picked up a piece of toast, revealing vines of purple flowers that climbed up her wrist. "I came up with that pretty quickly, thank god. I'm trying to get a head start on the daily word count. Three thousand is no joke."

"Seriously." My stomach filled with dread.

"You?" She gestured at my notebook.

I paused, chewing. "Can I tell you a secret?"

"Of course." She grinned, eyes wide and waiting.

"I've had writer's block this whole last year." I felt a rush of relief saying it out loud.

"Damn." Her eyes softened with concern. "You poor thing. Because of Wren?"

"What?" The name made my shoulders tighten.

"Didn't you say you had that friend breakup a year ago?"

"Yeah." Taylor was more perceptive than I'd taken her for. "We did."

"It has to be connected, right?"

"Probably." I swallowed a mouthful of eggs. "I haven't totally psychoanalyzed it yet."

Taylor watched me thoughtfully as we ate. "Hey." She pushed her plate away and closed her laptop. "Keira's in the library. When you're done, why don't we go see her? Maybe being around all those books will spark some ideas."

I agreed, and fifteen minutes later Taylor was leading us confidently to the library. I wondered if she'd further explored the house that morning; she seemed to know her way around.

"Have you seen Ian at all?" I asked, wondering if he and Roza were still entangled in bed.

"Nope. But his car wasn't in the drive this morning." Taylor nudged me. "Why, you have a thing for older English gentlemen?"

I chuckled. "He's not my type. Just curious who's all here."

"Just us, Roza, Chitra, and my favorite person . . . Yana."

We entered a hallway lined with windows

that showed the backyard. Something bright caught my eyes. Two figures in puffy coats and bright knit ski caps were marching over the snow, heading towards the woods.

"Oh," I said. Taylor turned back, followed my eyes.

"Poppy and Wren," she said. "They mentioned they were taking a break and going for a walk this morning."

"Cool." I said it too loud. Why not? Poppy was rooming with Wren, and Wren could be infinitely charming, especially to a cute twentysomething like Poppy. It wasn't like Poppy and I had fallen into an intense, immediate friendship the day before while traveling together. But I still felt a tiny sting of betrayal.

The library looked even more majestic in the sunlight. Keira sat in one of the overstuffed chairs by the fireplace, a stack of books on the floor beside her.

"K!" Taylor strutted towards her. "Miss me?"

Keira looked up, smiling and adjusting her glasses. "So much." Today her braids were down, pulled over her shoulder. Again she wore all black: leggings, a loose button-up shirt, and patent leather lace-up oxfords.

"Hey." I waved, feeling a flush of self-consciousness in Keira's put-together presence. Sure, Taylor was in her pj's, but her hair and tattoos made it seem punk. I'd dressed quickly in jeans and a gray sweater that now felt vaguely mom-like.

"Hey, Alex." She turned her smile to me. "How'd you sleep?"

"Pretty well. How about you?"

"Not great." Keira stared at the ground and fingered the lion charm on her necklace. "I had a nightmare."

"About what?" Taylor settled on the couch.

Keira finally looked up. "Don't remember. Just left me feeling disturbed."

"I'm sure it's the house. Definitely haunted." Taylor yawned and pointed to the stack of books. "What are you researching?"

"Well, speaking of this house . . . I was looking into Daphne."

"That's a great idea for a novel," I said, impressed.

"You want it? Take it. Unfortunately, it's not clicking for me." She tossed a book onto the stack and rubbed her eyes. "I need to get more coffee. And maybe take a stroll around Blackbriar, since it might be my last day here."

"It won't." Taylor jumped up and held out her hand. "C'mon, I'll walk with you and we'll brainstorm."

"You have the time to brainstorm?" Keira raised an eyebrow.

Taylor grinned. "I'm at almost two thousand five hundred."

"I hate you." They laughed and I forced myself to smile. Fear stirred in my belly. Wren and Poppy must be doing well, too, if they were taking the time to go for a walk.

I really needed to figure something out. Fast.

"Coffee?" Taylor asked me.

"I might stay and look at these books. If you're cool with that, Keira."

"Of course." They walked out together, chatting and laughing. When had they become so friendly?

Whatever. I had a plot to figure out. I settled into Keira's seat and grabbed the first book on the pile. The cover showed a black-and-white photograph of Daphne draped in a lace shawl, her dark-rimmed eyes closed as she scribbled on a pad. It was the same photo that was now a painting in the front hall. The book's title was *Daphne Wolfe: Feminist, Artist, Spiritualist.* I paged through the first chapter.

We have little information on Daphne's early life. She grew up in a humble home, her father a factory worker, her mother a washerwoman. She had three siblings, and her younger sister, Grace, died of a burst appendix at twelve years old. Scholars believe that this was the beginning of Daphne's interest in the occult, which only came to public light after she married Horace and had the means and respectability to host seances at their estate.

I flipped to another section.

Horace was a lifelong avowed bachelor. It surprised everyone when, in his fifties, he fell for a village waitress half his age. He was by all accounts a handsome and charismatic man, and his friends questioned the sudden decision to get married to someone who was "lower-class." Later, people in town spoke of Daphne as having bewitched him, especially after her spiritualist activities became known.

And there were Daphne and Horace standing together, the other photo replicated in the front hall. A few pages on, Daphne stood before a fireplace with two women. One stared at the camera, her chin proudly raised, her hands clasped in front of her ruffled dress. The other, who looked younger, smiled shyly, her head bowed above her high neckline. The caption read:

Daphne, Florence, and Abigail, founding members of the Blackbriar Spiritualist Society.

I glanced at the paragraph next to the photo.

Daphne became close with two other members of high society, Florence Binninger and Abigail Williams, who were also interested in spiritualism. For three years, they met weekly and called themselves the Blackbriar Spiritualist Society. During these meetings, the women attempted to channel spirits through automatic writing and drawing, a practice that supported Daphne's burgeoning artistic skills. Eventually, Daphne claimed to connect with a female demon named Lamia who asked Daphne to channel a "Great Commission" that would bring knowledge and wisdom to humankind. Daphne took this commission on, even though Florence and Abigail tried to dissuade her, believing that it would cause her to go mad.

Daphne prepared herself for six months in advance, engaging in hours of meditation and eating only bland, vegetarian food. She kept most of this information from Horace, who was often traveling for his business. Daphne chose a two-week period when he would be gone to begin channeling Lamia's works. During this time, she sent all the servants away from the house. In just three days, Daphne finished the first large-scale works of the commission: The World in Between I *and* II *(pp. 62–63). Afterwards, she took to her bed for several weeks to recover.*

I flipped to the next page. The pictures were small and poorly reproduced, but they showed the two enormous abstract paintings in the front hall.

Three months after the first series, while Daphne was preparing herself for the second round, Horace's company went bankrupt. He became depressed and ordered Daphne to stop her work. She humored him but secretly finished the second series, titled The Doorway, *in a four-day span. Unfortunately, Horace found the paintings and burned them in a bonfire. It's unclear whether he believed they were evil or if he was just punishing Daphne. Sadly, we have no record of these paintings. Daphne hid the* World in Between *works in the basement, ensuring their survival.*

Daphne prepared for the third channel-

ing in secret as Horace threatened to divorce her if she continued. But what happened on the eve of this transmission will never be known. A blizzard approached and Horace sent the servants home to their families. The storm dropped eight feet of snow in forty-eight hours, which made it impossible to reach the house for nearly a week. When the servants returned, they found a horrific and mystifying sight. Horace lay in his bed, disembowled. Daphne was at the foot of the basement stairs, her body a charred skeleton. Apart from her burned body, the rest of the basement was untouched. The World in Between *paintings had been removed from their hiding place and leaned against the wall several feet from the corpse.*

No paintings from the third part of the commission, if completed, were ever found.

CHAPTER 11

I was the first to arrive in the library. Someone — presumably Yana — had set up a large rectangular table in front of the windows. I sat and spread out my papers and notebook, attempting to quell the sharp spikes of panic in my chest. There was a coffee carafe on the buffet table but it was probably a bad idea in my already frazzled state.

After hours of attempts, I'd finally settled on what seemed like the least horrible idea.

Unfortunately, someone in the group might find it a bit familiar.

"What's up!" Taylor loped in, dressed in a colorful sweatshirt and red leggings, with Keira close behind.

"Hi, guys." To my surprise, Taylor sat far away, at the opposite end of the table, and Keira settled next to her. Why had they chosen to sit so far from me?

We all turned at the sounds from the

doorway.

"I was, like, what are you even talking about?" Poppy was saying as she and Wren swept into the room. "Have you never heard of a press kit before?"

"That is the most absurd request I have heard in my entire life." Wren could make statements like these sound sarcastic, but it was clear that she was determined to win Poppy over. From Poppy's adoring gaze, it seemed like she'd already succeeded.

"Are y'all ready for this?" Taylor grinned, tapping a drumbeat on the table.

"We'll see." Avoiding eye contact with me, Wren sat across from Taylor. She wore what had to be a designer cashmere sweatsuit in teal, and her dark hair was pulled into a bun. Poppy settled across from Keira, looking cute in a nubby pink sweater. Now they were all clustered around the far end of the table. What the hell? An empty chair separated Poppy and me. I was the outlier, the little trail of the comet, flying off into oblivion.

"How was the walk?" Taylor asked Wren and Poppy. "Run into any wild animals?"

Their chatter and laughter filled my ears and suddenly I was back in middle school, sitting on a bench during recess, pretending to be absorbed in my book. The other kids didn't care enough to make fun of me or even feel bad for me. They didn't see me at all.

What did people on reality shows say? *I'm not here to make friends.* And that was true. But I still felt a nudge of shame. Should I move closer to Poppy?

Why should I? The thought contained a fiery petulance. After all, I'd been the first person in the goddamn room.

Roza strode in, coughing and paging through a notebook, reading glasses perched on her nose. Her hair was loose, and she wore a red sweater, slouchy jeans, and fur-lined slippers. She walked closer and I expected her to sit at the head of the table by the others. But she swerved and settled by me instead.

She looked up with consternation. "Move closer, please? I don't want to shout." The others obediently got up, moving to our end of the table. I felt a low buzz of relief and, yes, smugness.

"So." Roza pulled off her glasses with an expectant smile. "How'd it go?"

We looked at each other in silence.

"Great!" Taylor finally shouted, and we all laughed.

"Good." Roza smirked. "Don't be nervous, girls. The worst I can do is rip it to shreds, right?" She squeezed my forearm, and the sudden intimacy made me jump. "Just kidding. I know this is the hardest part. But I'm confident that after this meeting you'll walk away excited to get down to business."

I felt a flush of hopefulness. Maybe it wouldn't be too bad.

"Keira?" Roza gestured. "Pass out your synopsis, dear. I'll read it aloud and then we'll provide feedback."

Keira did so, her lips pressed in a grim smile. It comforted me that even she, with all her poise, had struggled to come up with something.

The synopsis described a young woman who had gone through her recently deceased mother's things and found a letter her mother had written decades before but never sent. The letter indicated that her mother had almost left her family to reunite with a woman who'd been doing mysterious research on Goree Island, a former slave-trading hub off the coast of Senegal. The protagonist decided to track down the woman and find out more about her, the research, and the secrets her mother had kept from her.

"Well." Roza slammed down the paper. "I'll start. I think it's brilliant. Anyone else?"

Keira's face softened with relief as Poppy and then Taylor both echoed the sentiment.

"Just don't make it too heart-warming," Roza said. "Make it difficult, okay? All right. That was easy. Let's move on to the next. Taylor?"

Taylor offered to read it herself, which impressed me. Her idea concerned an American woman in France who met a female bartender who promised to lead her on an unauthorized tour of the catacombs beneath the city. While at first they enjoyed their time — "Ahem, lots of sex" — they eventually came across a masked group performing a sacrificial ritual. The rest of the story involved them trying to get away from the group, who wanted to kill them.

"Oh my god, how does it end?" Poppy's eyes were wide.

Taylor shrugged. "Betrayal. The bartender was part of the cult all along."

"I knew it!" Roza banged a hand on the table and we all laughed.

After a few more questions and suggestions from Roza, we moved on to Poppy. ("Ladies, we'll be done quite early today if everyone's ideas are as good as these two.") Poppy's proposal was about a young woman who traveled to the Cayman Islands, where she got caught up with a group convinced they could access God in a certain remote cave.

"Islands and cults!" Roza raised her hands. "It seems we have a theme."

Something about the story pulled at me, a thread of recognition. I felt like I'd heard of this story before, though I couldn't remember where.

But no story was completely new. Maybe I was thinking of another book, maybe even something Poppy was using for inspiration.

Wren went next and she read in a clear, precise voice. Her story concerned an actress invited to work with a famous director she'd admired since childhood. When the actress arrived on the remote set, she was unsettled to find that the group comprised only her, one other male actor, and a skeleton crew. As they filmed, the project got more bizarre, until the actress wondered if the director had gone mad — and if she was in mortal danger.

"Another small-group setting." Roza sat back, folding her arms.

"Maybe because of this retreat?" Taylor suggested.

"Could be." Roza tapped one red-tipped nail against her bicep. "Poppy? What do you think?"

"I love it." Poppy grinned at Wren. "I

think it sounds super intriguing."

"Keira, how about you?"

"I like it too." Keira gazed at Wren. "I would definitely read it."

Wren nodded graciously, then her eyes went back to Roza.

"Alex?" Roza's green eyes fixed on me.

"I think it sounds cool." And I did. Wren had her issues, but coming up with creative ideas wasn't one of them. When we'd stopped talking, I knew she'd been finishing her novel. While stalking her social media, I'd waited for the post that would reveal she'd gotten an agent, then a book deal. But, so far, no news. It had made me relieved; at least there was one thing Wren wanted that she hadn't yet gotten.

Roza crossed her arms. "Well, I think it has promise, Wren. I really do. But actors are not my favorites. It's not just that they're shallow and selfish. That's fine. In fact, that can be a good thing. But the problem is that, as protagonists, they're often boring."

"My protagonist won't be boring." Wren's expression darkened.

"I mean, we have to give a shit about her, don't we? This starlet who's jetting off to some remote location to work with a famous director? I'm sorry, but . . . puke." Roza sniffed. "Make her a failure. Make this the last chance she has to get a job before she throws herself out a window. Okay?"

"Okay," Wren echoed.

Roza sat back suddenly, her chair scraping the wooden floor. Her good mood was gone and now she seemed borderline annoyed. "Girls, please work hard to make your work compelling. If I have to read boring shit every day, I'm not going to be able to make it, believe me."

Everyone shifted, uncomfortable. Roza's rapidly switching moods were giving us all whiplash.

"Alex." Roza grinned at me. "You're up."

My chest squeezed in fear. Roza had given Wren a hard time, and her idea had actually been good. What was she going to do with mine?

"The End of the End." I cleared my throat, but to my embarrassment, my voice continued to waver, strained. "Rebecca and Elyse have been best friends for ten years, since they were sixteen. After both their first loves break their hearts in high school, they band together to punish them. They continue this cycle through their teens and into their twenties; whenever a man hurts one of them, they make it their mission to destroy him. They both get jobs out of college at the same publisher. Rebecca is soon pro-

moted. She falls for her new boss, who is married, and who quickly dumps her. Rebecca knows that revealing any of this to Elyse will make him a target. However, Elyse knows her better than anyone. Elyse takes the secret affair as a betrayal and decides to punish both of them. Rebecca must stop her before it's too late. She knows what Elyse is capable of . . . at least she thought she did. It turns out that all this time Elyse has been holding back. Unfortunately for Rebecca, that's no longer the case."

Roza sat back and let out a long sigh. The room was silent. Outside, flakes of snow had begun to gently fall. The sun descended in the sky, casting a silvery veil over the landscape.

"No," Roza said.

I blinked. "No?"

"I'm sorry, Alex." Roza shook her head. "It's not going to work. It's too similar to *Devil's Tongue.* Only it's less interesting, because they're adults." She sighed. "Even the names. Elyse? As in, *Devil's* Eliza?"

I froze, horrified at my mistake. I could sense the others looking down, not wanting to witness my humiliation, as if it were a disease they could catch.

"You know, if you were writing dime-store

pulp, this could work," Roza went on. "It could be sexy. But I expect more from you. And frankly, I'm tired of stories where women fight over men."

"Okay." My face grew warm and I knew it was candy-apple red.

"Any other thoughts?" Roza looked around.

"I actually like it," Keira said. I glanced at her, grateful. "Having female characters who fight over men doesn't dictate whether a story is feminist or not. Alex's story actually subverts the idea, because the women gain control by punishing their exes. It subverts it again when Rebecca actually falls for someone. Ultimately, it's about the futility of self-protection in heterosexual relationships within a patriarchal society."

"Oh my. How very clever." Roza chuckled. "Anyone else?"

Silence. No one — besides Keira — wanted to disagree with Roza.

"I appreciate your thoughts, Keira dear, but I think we can do better." Roza tilted her head, studying me. "Did you have any other ideas, Alex?"

It was all I could do to keep the tears of embarrassment and frustration tamped down.

"A lot," I managed to say. "All of them

terrible."

Everyone chuckled weakly. Roza smiled.

"What about Daphne?" Taylor said. "Weren't you looking at those books in the library?"

"Like, historical fiction?" Wren's voice held distaste.

"Some history, but a whole lot of fiction too." Taylor straightened, excited. "Because no one really knows how Daphne and Horace died. How it all went down, I mean."

"Well." Roza's lips curved into a warm smile. "Perhaps Alex will be the one to solve the mystery."

"How so?" I choked out, still panicking.

Roza tapped her head. "The writer's mind is a channel, dear. When we open, glorious truths can flow in. Rather like Daphne channeling her demoness, wouldn't you say?"

And that was it. The conversation moved on, and Roza was now reminding us of her instructions — 3,000 words printed out by midnight and placed under her door — and it had been decided that I was going to write about Daphne.

My entire body felt icy to the point where I had to clench my teeth to stop them from chattering. It felt like I'd fallen into a void, that the scene was continuing to go on around me, but that I'd suddenly become absent. A dark, blurry shape.

Everyone started getting up, so I got up too.

Then Roza's hand snaked out and clenched my forearm. "We're going to meet today, dear. For our one-on-one."

I tried to focus on her face. "Yes. Okay. That sounds great."

"Come up to my room at four. We'll discuss further." Her emerald eyes filled my vision like bright, bottomless pools of poison.

CHAPTER 12

I knocked at the red door an hour later. After we'd finished the group session, I'd spent the next half hour in my room, panic-reading the stack of books about Daphne.

I'd finally given up. Wren was right: it was basically historical fiction. Something I'd never been interested in writing. Maybe it was a lifeline: Daphne's story was captivating, and I was surprised no one had novelized it before. But as with Keira, it didn't speak to me.

At Roza's door, I tried to steady myself, taking a few deep breaths. If I could just fake it through this meeting, I could go back to my room. I could figure out how to force myself to do this, even if it felt like I was writing in a language I didn't know, even if it felt like torture.

But I had the feeling that faking anything in front of Roza wouldn't be easy.

Roza pulled open the door. "Hello, dear!"

She leaned in and gave me an air-kiss, as if we hadn't just seen each other in the library. "Come in." She ushered me inside and I followed her through a short hall that opened up into an expansive suite. To the left, there was an enormous stone fireplace with a roaring fire, flanked by an oxblood leather couch and several velvet chairs resting on an oriental rug. To the right was a large canopy bed, its red covers mussed and unmade. Polished black furniture including two huge wardrobes completed the space.

The painting above the fireplace caught my attention and I walked closer. I could tell whose it was by the style: scratched images in black and red, almost human, almost body part–like but too abstract to completely make out.

"That's Daphne's," I said.

Roza was bent over a gilded bar cart. "It is." She strode over and handed me a sherry glass. "One of her sketches."

"Interesting." I took a sip and it burned — not wine, but some kind of fiery liquor.

"It's Unicum." She beamed. "Hungarian liqueur."

"I've heard of it. I'm actually Hungarian too." I tried to smile back. "On my mom's side."

"Oh yes? Wonderful. Have a seat."

156

I sank onto the couch and Roza sat in a chair across from me. Her cheekbones looked sharp as arrows in the warm light. "What's going on, Alex?"

"Oh." I forced a casual tone. "I don't know. Not much."

She stared at me, expressionless, until I looked down.

"You're clearly flailing." Carefully, she set her glass on the coffee table. "I wasn't expecting this from you, dear."

My breath disappeared and my lungs crumpled. Tears filled my eyes, and to my horror they spilled over onto my cheeks. "Damnit," I muttered, wiping them away. Roza jumped up and came over, pressing a delicate silk handkerchief into my hands. I took it but felt guilty and disgusting using it to wipe up my tears and snot.

"What's the matter?" She settled next to me, a warm palm on my shoulder. Her jasmine perfume enclosed me.

I chanced a look, and for once there was soft compassion in her eyes.

I couldn't lie to her. I might as well be honest.

"I have writer's block," I said. "I haven't written anything in a year."

"Ah." She exhaled. "That's what it is."

"I probably shouldn't have even come," I

went on. "But how could I not? You're my favorite writer. I've been obsessed with you since I was twelve. So when this all happened, it was just so magical that it felt like it was meant to be, you know?"

"What happened a year ago?" She rested an arm along the back of the couch. "What caused the writer's block?"

I opened and closed my mouth, unsure of how to answer.

"Something to do with Wren?" She raised her eyebrows.

I sniffed, relieved that she'd guessed. "How'd you know?"

"I'm a writer, dear. I can sense these unspoken tensions." She smiled. "Also, Taylor may have mentioned it."

"Oh." I could see that; Taylor didn't seem like the best keeper of secrets. "Well, yes, it was that. Wren and I were best friends for a long time, and then we had a falling-out." I felt nothing as I spoke the words. The liquor had relaxed my body and made the flames of the fire sway and undulate.

"Well." Roza crossed her legs. "There must be more to the story than that."

It struck me, distantly, that this was what Roza really wanted. She liked stories, particularly those that were dark and off-putting. She wanted to gaze at them directly, to hold them in her palms like newborn kittens covered with caul.

By telling her, it felt like giving her something, or entering into a kind of pact. With a sliding feeling of resignation, I launched into the story: how I'd seen her at a party after she'd moved out. How I'd been so drunkenly determined to talk to her. How she'd jerked away from me in disgust — *Don't touch me* — and I'd reached out again and she'd fallen back over that step, wobbling in her stilettos. How I'd just stood there, frozen, watching her crash to the ground, blood suddenly spurting from her hand in pulses.

"And then what?" Roza asked. She appeared unimpressed.

"That was basically it." My glass was empty and I cradled it in my hands. "I mean, everyone blocked me. I managed to find out she didn't lose her hand — it was her right hand, so that would've been awful. More than awful. And she almost did. She severed some tendons and had to have a bunch of surgeries."

"Alex." Roza lowered her chin. "There's something you're not telling me."

The words wormed through my brain, now vibrating from the liquor. Roza stood and brought back the bottle, refilling my glass. I took a tiny sip. She was patient as I considered. This part of the story was in the basement. This part was under lock and key.

And I'd kept it hidden for so long. Who could I tell? Ursula, maybe, but I hadn't wanted to drag her into it. I hadn't wanted her to see the shame that buzzed around me like flies.

Roza waited. It was like it had been destined, for the truth to come out here.

"Wren and I went out a lot together." My voice suddenly felt unused, croaky, and I cleared my throat. "We drank a lot. We were probably alcoholics, to be honest. I mean, everyone in their twenties in New York is, right? So we'd go out and we'd want to meet guys. And we usually did. But if we came back alone together, we often slept in my bed. I don't know when it started. At some point Wren just climbed in and said she needed to cuddle. She wasn't a physically affectionate person, so it was kind of surprising. She'd spoon me and stroke my hair." A smile jumped to my lips. "She used to drunkenly call me her soul mate. She was kind of kidding but kind of not. And it felt . . . I don't know. I knew what she meant."

Roza nodded, leaf-green eyes blazing.

"So." I looked down. "At some point,

maybe a year before everything ended, she started kissing me. Only in those situations — drunk, in my bed, like three in the morning. And it was a little confusing, but she made it seem like it was the same as the cuddling." Something tightened in my chest like a closed fist; I'd never told anyone about this aspect of our friendship. "So that went on for a few months — you know, every once in a while; it wasn't a lot. And then I started seeing this guy, Nick. It was pretty casual, but he was just an over-the-top person, giving me flowers and things like that. Wren said she didn't like him and would just constantly make fun of him. I never thought she might be jealous. But then one night out he and I argued — because of something he'd said to Wren, actually, that had offended her. So she and I went back home alone. She took a shower. And then she crawled into my bed. But this time . . . she was naked."

It came back to me: the scent of Wren's expensive shampoo, the smoothness of her limbs, the surprising swell of her uncovered breasts against my shoulder blades. "She made me turn around and she started kissing me, and then she started touching me. I tried to stop her but she told me to relax. And then . . ." I felt suddenly feverish. "She

161

went down on me."

Wren had always said she was one hundred percent straight, that she liked male bodies and smells and energies too much to explore anyone else. How, then, had she been so good, so practiced, her tongue sliding in a perfect repetitive movement, her fingers knowing exactly what to do? Even now, retelling the story, it felt like a random sex dream I'd had.

"How was it?" Roza sat back and crossed her arms.

"It was good." One of the strongest orgasms I'd ever had, in fact.

"And did you pleasure her?"

I shook my head. Afterwards, we'd kissed and I'd tasted myself on her tongue. I'd slipped my hand between her legs, feeling like I should reciprocate, even if I didn't really know what I was doing. But she'd pushed my hand away, saying she was tired. "She didn't want me to."

"And then what happened?" Roza asked. In my liquor-hazed state, the memories were almost too full in their realness. I stared at the patterned rug on the floor, not seeing it.

"Well, when I woke up the next morning, she wasn't there." The dread flooded my belly, the same trepidation I'd felt walking around the empty apartment. "I texted her and she didn't answer. She came home late that night and . . . I don't know, I could tell something was off. She was on the phone and went into her room and slammed the door. I thought she'd come out at some point because it was Sunday night and we usually watched a movie together. But she didn't. And after that . . ." I shrugged. "We didn't talk about it. It was like it hadn't happened. She kept acting cold but I figured we'd move past it at some point. But then two weeks later she announced she was moving out. It shocked me. I thought she was joking at first. But no."

Roza gave a sharp nod, as if she were a doctor whose diagnosis had been confirmed. "She projected her guilt and shame onto you. You became first irritating, then repulsive. She told herself that it had to be you, that it was your fault."

"Yeah." I rubbed my eyes. "Maybe that's true."

We were quiet, staring at the fire, which crackled and spit.

"You know what?" Roza said. "People who don't know pain — deep pain — are bad writers. Wouldn't you agree?"

"I don't know. I guess that makes sense." I'd expected my confession would make me feel relieved. But instead I just felt sad and exhausted.

"If there's one thing I've learned," Roza went on, "it's that the worst conditions are the most conducive to the best work. I wrote my first book sitting next to my dying friend, who was literally rotting away. The smell . . ." She closed her eyes. "All of it was horrific. And every day I brought a little notebook with me and the words just poured out. My anger and helplessness connected me to something, a powerful and primal energy. And the only corridor to it was through utter despondency, utter desperation."

I nodded, setting the empty glass on the table. The pep talk was only making me more miserable.

"Darling." Roza was suddenly gripping both of my hands. "Wren did you a favor. She gave you a gift. She killed you, in a sense — because of her fears, her confusion about how she felt. She had to make you dead to her. It was the only way she could survive, going back to her buttoned-up little life." Roza's eyes narrowed. "Do you understand?"

"Yes," I said, but the words weren't quite making sense. What had Wren felt towards me? What had I felt for her, for that matter?

It had burned out so quickly: a match struck, bright and brilliant before crumpling into a dark, bent piece of nothingness.

"So," Roza went on, squeezing my hands. "Now you're dead, trapped in the underworld. You feel empty, stuck. And you know what? It's actually the most powerful place to be. You need only reach out to the pain and grab it, use it. But if you don't?" Her expression turned mournful. "Well, then you stay dead. And in effect she'll be killing you twice. I don't know if you can come back from that, dear. I really don't."

I stared into her eyes, mesmerized. A tiny speck of hope, no larger than a piece of dust, floated through my mind.

Maybe Roza had the answer. Maybe this pain wasn't for nothing. Maybe I just needed to mold it into something beautiful.

After a moment she let go of my hands, patted them, and sat back. "My goodness. It's going to be time for cocktails soon. Why don't you go freshen up." She got to her feet, then waited expectantly, looking down at me.

Startled, I stood and followed her to the red door.

"Tell me one more thing." Roza paused, her hand on the doorknob. "At the bar that night . . . when you tried to talk to her.

When she practically spit at you." Her voice was mild but in the dim light of the entranceway, her eyes glowed like a cat's. "Did you . . . ?"

Did you push her?

The answer had not only been locked in the basement, but buried deep under the floor. I hadn't brought it out and looked at it properly since that night.

Don't touch me. Wren had jerked back from me, already much too close to the step, her pencil-thin heels only inches away. And I registered the step, didn't I? I knew what would happen. And yet a deep rage reared, bubbling up into my right arm. Something took over my body, something primitive, lashing out from a place of complete powerlessness.

I'd reached out again, my thumb pressing firmly into her upper arm, my fingers curling loosely, of no real use when she started to fall backwards.

I'd instantly regretted it. The horror at the sight of her blood was connected to the horror at myself, that I was capable of such violence.

I'd waited for the message from Wren, directly or through a disgusted friend. That it was my fault, I'd done it, I'd pushed her. But no one ever said anything. It was more like they just edged away from me, feeling rather than knowing there was something rotten in my core.

I'd been ready to take the small, secret act to my grave.

But now, returning Roza's clear gaze, I nodded.

With a satisfied smile, she opened the door. Maybe I was dazed from the Unicum, or reeling from the relief in spilling an unshareable secret — but in that moment, Roza looked resplendent, radiant, a gleaming angel descended from on high. "Good luck, my little spider." She squeezed my shoulder as I passed through, then shut the door behind me.

Back in my room, I sat at the desk, watching the sun lowering in the sky. My brain still buzzed, my mind moving through dark, tangled currents.

Roza had seen the ugliest side of me, one that I myself was afraid to look at. More than that, she *wanted* to see it. She drew it out of me.

I couldn't leave. Not when my idol was the only one who truly accepted me.

Roza had given me the key. *You need only reach out to the pain and grab it, use it.* I remembered my story, the one Ursula had sent to Roza, about two little girls in a thick and tangled wood, wandering into a different time, a different place. Turning at the sound of something lurching towards them in the dark.

It hadn't been made up. It was a real experience. A traumatizing event that led to my best work so far: the short story that had given me entrance to Blackbriar.

I imagined Daphne, eyes blank, scribbling away at a canvas, paint spotting her nude, gaunt body like blood.

I opened the laptop and the screen sprang to life. I opened my latest Word doc, the one I'd saved as *The Great Commission.* Not a bad title, even though the document was currently blank. Slowly, and then with increasing speed, I started to type.

■ ■ ■ ■

PART TWO:
THE ESTATE

■ ■ ■ ■

Excerpt from *The Great Commission*

Daphne met her first ghost when she was twelve years old.

She and her younger sister Grace slept in the tiny room at the back of the apartment. Normally if she woke at night, having to use the chamber pot, she'd be comforted by the noise of the city that continued, albeit in a subdued state, outside: a carriage clacking by on the street below, two drunks yelling at each other, their voices enraged warbles.

But this night, something was different. When Daphne woke it was completely silent.

Even Grace, who normally snored like a horse, was still, turned away, her spine pressed into Daphne's back. The tiny window was covered by a piece of thick burlap, making the room pitch-black. Daphne sleepily wondered what had woken her up.

Then she heard it.

Footsteps in the hall, unnaturally loud, as if someone was walking in steel-toed boots. They were slow, careful. Daphne knew the sounds of her father and brothers — all slight men who walked with a chipper shuffle. Had someone gotten into their home?

The footsteps stopped — directly in front of the door.

The remnants of sleep scattered as terror bloomed in Daphne's chest. Who was standing there? But nothing happened. She must have dreamed it, or it had just been the random sounds of the old wooden building.

Then: a sharp creak. The innocuous sound made her suck in her breath.

The doorknob was turning.

Daphne clutched the blankets to her throat, listening to the unending squeal. Finally the door began to open, with a sick brushing sound across the wood floor.

Daphne's heart thudded. Could one of her brothers be playing a joke on her?

Sit up. Turn on the light.

But she couldn't. That in itself flooded her with fear.

The footsteps entered the dark room. Daphne felt by turns nauseous and terrified as they made their way towards her, the floorboards groaning underneath the weight.

Scream! Cry out! Do anything!

But still she lay there, fingers cramped around the covers, head turned towards the horrific sounds like a flower trained on

172

the sun.

It came closer. Fifteen feet away. Ten feet. Five.

Then, by the side of the bed, it stopped. Daphne stared at the blackness where it stood, straining with wide eyes. She could feel it, solid and real. She could sense its stare.

But nothing else happened, and the longer she stared, the more she started to doubt herself. It was dead silent — no breath but her own. Could she have imagined it? Maybe it was the remainders of a nightmare, still spinning through her wakefulness?

More time passed. Incrementally, Daphne's body began to relax. Finally, she was able to unclamp her fingers from the covers. The dark room was still impenetrable, but she was no longer certain that a creature stood above her. In fact, the longer she lay there, the more she started to feel ridiculous. A crow cawed outside. The sound broke the spell. Soon it would be dawn. She reached out an unsteady hand, fingers finding the matches on the crate. Half sitting, she swept a match and held it to the wick of the oil lamp, which whooshed into reassuring light.

But in the very same instant that the light

gave her a flush of calm, she saw it.

Horror crashed over her like a tidal wave.

It was still there.

Not it: *she.* The lamplight showed muddy and decaying flesh, topped by bulbous red eyes. It was hard to tell her age, given the state of decomposition. Her breasts were two gelatinous mountains, chunky and melting, only one wizened nipple still attached.

The rank smell of rotting organs unleashed itself over Daphne.

The woman's nose had fallen off, but her gummy mouth was wide in a silent scream.

Blank panic overtook Daphne and she screamed too.

CHAPTER 13

"Darling." Roza flung down the piece of paper. "No. Listen, I don't want to be an asshole. But this is the most important page of the entire book. Do you understand?"

Wren scribbled dutifully in her notebook, her expression stony.

We were back in the library for the second afternoon meeting. The night before, still slightly drunk on Unicum, I'd madly written 3,000 words, lost in the throes of inspiration. When I'd stopped, I'd realized I'd completely missed dinner. I'd thrown open my door to find a covered tray right outside. I'd printed the pages, slipped them under Roza's door, and then feasted on the meal while poring over the books I'd brought up from the library.

I hadn't felt this — the sparkling sense of inspiration — for a long time. The energy felt volatile, almost sexual. It filled every cell, making them glow in the dark. It had been hard to get to sleep after that. I'd kept a notebook on the nightstand and kept reaching over to turn on the light, half sitting up so I could jot down a new idea.

The conversation with Roza had been like a spell, psychically connecting me with Daphne. Or, more accurately: her loneliness, her difficulties, her fears. The one connection Daphne had relied on — Grace — had been ripped away from her. That loss had later caused her to wade into ghostly realms, even though she knew how terrifying they could be.

So: the muse had landed on me, stung me like a bee. After writing and brainstorming most of the night, I now felt exhausted.

But I also felt fucking great.

"This is the problem with a lot of writers today." Roza sat back in her chair. She was wearing the same outfit as the day before, as if she'd been too lazy to change. "They want to ease you into it. But it's boring. Why do I care? This girl, she seems like kind of a sap, to be honest. She was just dumped by her boyfriend, and she's depressed, sitting in the airport, waiting for her flight. I don't care about someone who's depressed. I care about someone who wants something. What does she want?"

Wren cleared her throat, considering.

176

"See?" Roza whipped off her glasses and pointed at her. "That's the problem, dear. That has to be utterly foremost in your mind. If you don't know —"

"I do know." Wren frowned. "She wants to be successful. In her career and in her love life."

"Successful." Roza raised her hands. "What does that mean? Does she want to be famous?"

"Yes."

"Why?"

Wren looked exasperated. "She's an actress. That's her passion."

Roza squeezed her eyes shut. The rest of us sat silent and tense. Poppy's arms were crossed and she stared down at her lap as if wishing she were anywhere else. Taylor's eyes were wide, as if the interaction between Wren and Roza were a particularly intense tennis match. Keira watched Roza, her expression guarded. I wondered what she was thinking.

As for me, I did feel for Wren, now the subject of Roza's prickliness. I knew how awful and destabilizing it was.

At the same time, I couldn't help but feel a burst of glee.

Wren was always so confident in her perfection. Seeing her questioned and criticized — by Roza, no less — was like watching a powerful dictator get taken to task.

"So here is my question." Roza leaned forward. "Why is acting her passion? Does she need other people to tell her how wonderful she is? Does she feel empty inside? Or is she an artist? Does she want to bring beauty to an ugly world? Is she willing to sacrifice herself for it?"

Wren opened her mouth and Roza held up a finger.

"Don't answer." Roza's voice softened. "Think about it. Think hard. Because it can only be one thing. And it needs to drive every single act of the protagonist for the rest of the book. To the point where it harms them. Where they find themselves making outrageous choices. Okay?"

Wren nodded.

"Alex." Roza whirled over to me. She held up a sheath of papers. "Why don't you walk us through your beginning."

I was the last in the group to go, and I briefly explained the first few scenes. The writing energy hummed through me. Even if Roza told me everything was shit, I wouldn't care. I was untouchable.

"Beautiful work, darling." Roza began gathering her papers. "Sets just the right tone. I love this decaying woman popping up at night. I know that feeling. Don't we all?"

I laughed, accidentally making eye contact with Wren. She was glaring at me. She looked away quickly, but I felt the sting, as if she'd launched a tiny grenade into my lap.

Roza dismissed us, leaving quickly as if she had somewhere important to be.

And she did. She, too, was working on a new book. I wondered if we'd get to hear about it at some point. Taylor had asked for details, but she'd remained coy.

Taylor and Keira chatted at the table while Poppy raced back up to her room to prepare before her first solo meeting with Roza. I caught up with Wren at the doorway.

"Hey." I touched her arm and she jumped. "Can we talk for a minute?"

She gazed at me. There it was: that vague disgust I remembered so well. But this time I had Big Writing Energy, and it shielded me and kept me calm.

My admission to Roza the night before had changed something. It was true that I hadn't shoved Wren backwards with both hands. But there *had* been some intention behind my touch. A part of me wanted to hurt her, punish her, make her suffer.

Thus, I could no longer continue to see myself as the victim. And this realization actually offered me a chance for redemption. This was my opportunity to be the bigger person. To make things bearable, if not right, between us so that we could both get through this month and focus on what was really important. That hateful look she'd given me was a clear sign that we were currently far from that place.

But Wren remained silent, pausing so long that I wondered if she'd say no.

"Sure," she said finally. "The parlor?"

"Sounds good." I hadn't yet been in the parlor, but Wren led us there assuredly. It was on the same side of the building, though closer to the front hall. The room was decorated in deep forest greens, and the heads of various animals dotted the walls. I recalled a black-and-white photograph in one of the books. This room had originally been decorated by Horace, an avid hunter. It smelled slightly musty and meaty, like old jerky. I wondered if these were the same animals Horace had killed or if Roza had bought all new ones.

"Wow." I stopped beneath the giant, shaggy face of a buffalo. "Creepy."

"Right?" Wren went towards the empty stone fireplace and settled into a leather chair. She was wearing more designer loungewear today, a sportier look in purple, and she played with the string on her hoodie.

At least today I'd made more of an effort with my appearance, putting on lipstick and a necklace and wearing a loose denim shirt. It gave me a bit more confidence. But the shirt was thin and it was colder in there than the library; I shivered as I dropped into a chair across from her.

"So." She said the word with faux brightness. "What did you want to talk about?"

It struck me suddenly that this was actually a horrible time for this conversation. She'd just been criticized by Roza in front of all of us. I felt a flicker of fear.

"Well —" I started but she cut me off.

"Because I have something I wanted to talk about too." She let go of the cord and started twisting her diamond ring instead. Almost like she wanted me to notice it.

"Okay. Totally. Did you want to go first?" I still felt hopeful. We weren't back in Brooklyn; we were here in Roza's castle. We could get past things. We could be adults.

"Okay. Totally." She was mocking me.

My stomach dropped. This was the worst of all of Wren's moods: when she acted like a thirteen-year-old mean girl.

"Look, I know you've been talking shit about me to the other girls" — she brushed back her bangs and crossed one long leg over the other — "and I'm pretty sure you've told Roza too. And I'd really appreciate it if you'd keep your paranoid conspiracy theories to yourself."

" 'Paranoid conspiracy theories,' " I repeated. Had Poppy revealed what I'd told the group the first afternoon? She must have. It hurt like a small needle prick.

"Right." Now Wren wore a quizzical look, like a child wondering what would happen after she pulled all the legs off a spider.

"Okay." The hope faded and a dull anger started to roil from below. "So tell me. What exactly are these 'conspiracy theories' I've been spreading around?"

Wren scoffed. "That I ruined your life. Which is pretty rich, considering what you did to me." She raised her right palm towards me. The signal for *Stop*. A thin knot of scar tissue ran down the center.

I blushed; I couldn't help it. Suddenly I was back to that place of uncertainty and shame. But Wren couldn't have known my intention in that one tiny move on the steps. If she had, *everyone* would've known about it.

"All because you couldn't just leave it

alone," she went on. "You couldn't just move on. You had to show up at that party and make a huge fucking scene."

I exhaled. She didn't know of my anger; she just knew of my desperation to talk to her.

"Leave what alone?" I forced my voice to sound calm. "And I didn't tell anyone you ruined my life, by the way."

"Good. Because I didn't. We just grew apart. And I actually didn't go around telling all our friends not to talk to you anymore. People just did what they wanted to do."

"Okay. But, Wren" — I leaned forward — "we were best friends for *eight years.* We lived together. It doesn't all just suddenly end one day."

"Sometimes it does." She shrugged. "It happens all the time."

"Really? And is that usually before or after one friend eats out the other?"

She froze. Her nostrils flared. This was the part we weren't supposed to talk about. I felt a sudden pleasure in going there, in forcing her to listen to the words. "Look, it was your idea. And yet you treated me like a leper afterwards. Like I'd done something horrible to you."

"Alex." She rubbed her eyes. "Jesus. I was

wasted. It wasn't a big deal. But you took it as a big deal and that was the problem." I scoffed but she shook her head. "No, honestly, that's how I knew it was a mistake. I thought you could handle it — I mean, my friends and I hooked up in college all the time. But it just made it clear how broken things were between us."

"Broken?" It felt like my throat was closing up.

"Yeah." She shrugged. "We were so codependent. And that was one thing. But I guess I hadn't realized that you had feelings for me. And, listen, I'm sorry, but I did *not* have those feelings for you."

Humiliation surged and, to my horror, tears suddenly blurred my vision.

"I'm sorry." She didn't sound sorry.

"I mean . . . wow." I angrily wiped the tears away. "Your narcissism truly knows no bounds, Wren. Thinking everyone's always in love with you." I got to my feet. "And I did love you. As a *friend.* What we did — what *you* did — was confusing but ultimately it wasn't something that should've ended our friendship."

She stared up at me, silent and blank. There was nothing there: no kindness, no care.

"But you *ruined* it," I went on, a sob

wracking my throat. "Like it meant nothing to you."

"Al." Her voice was soft and steely. "We need to put it behind us. We're not friends anymore, and that's okay. But can you stop going around telling people about what happened? I'm not comfortable with it."

Anything for Wren's comfort.

I scoffed, shaking my head. "You know, I was trying to be nice to you today. I really wanted us to have a truce or something. But you're showing me that the best we can do is just ignore each other."

"Agreed." She lifted her hands in exasperation. "That's all I want."

"Fine."

"Are we done here?" She stood.

I nodded. My whole body felt wooden, dead.

She turned and left. The animal heads and I watched her go.

CHAPTER 14

As I left the parlor, the flat, heavy feeling in my chest began melting into anger. The rage radiated like a burn. Of course Wren would dismiss what had happened. Of course she would make me feel like the irrational and pathetic one.

This had always been a part of our friendship, the darkest part. When Wren got into one of her moods and there was no one else there to pick at, she'd take it out on me. Why did my room smell? Why was I such a bitch to the guys I dated? Why was I still at a job I despised? Why was I so boring?

My teeth were clenched and I rubbed my jaw as I approached the kitchen. I wasn't Wren's punching bag any more. I didn't have to deal with this shit. I had bigger things to worry about, anyway. I'd get a snack and go upstairs and keep banging out my new book.

Because I was going to beat her, goddamnit. I was going to win.

Chitra was in the kitchen, stirring something at the stove. "Hello, love." She turned and grinned.

"Oh, sorry. I didn't know you were in here." I stopped short in the doorway.

"Come in, come in." She waved a hand. "Just starting to get dinner on. Sit down. You here for a snack?"

"Yeah, but I can wait —"

"What kind would you like? Sweet or savory?" Chitra's English accent and bustling, grandmotherly air — though she couldn't have been more than a youngish sixty — relaxed me as I dropped onto a stool at the huge marble butcher block.

"Savory would be great." I hoped she didn't notice my reddened eyes.

"Okay, then." She pulled a few plastic-covered containers from the fridge. "How's the writing going?"

"Good." That was true, at least.

"Glad to hear it." She moved with a fluid grace. "You girls have a lot to get done. I don't know how you're doing it."

"Well, *I* don't know how you make such delicious meals." I cleared my throat. "I didn't get to tell you but the food last night was incredible. Someone brought a plate to me."

187

"Roza's idea." Chitra winked. "She didn't want anyone to interrupt you."

"How long have you known Roza?"

"Oh, long time now. Met her almost twenty years ago. She came into my café." Chitra's voice held a smile. "I had no idea who she was. But after she ate she asked to see me. Invited me to come and be her personal chef."

"Wow. Just like that. And you said yes?"

"Oh, no." She scoffed. "I grew up in London; never thought I'd leave. But my café burned down less than a year later. The insurance was shit, so I reached out to her. And I've been working for her ever since."

"Your café — it was like the food you've been making for us?"

"Somewhat." She smiled, and there was a sad or wry twist to her mouth. "My specialty was Anglo-Indian. Roza wanted that for a while. But now she prefers more traditionally American dishes. Which is fine. I can do that."

I wondered if her chipper tone was covering a different feeling. But maybe I was reading too much into it.

"You travel with her?" I asked.

"Depends. If she's somewhere for a bit of time, I do. But when she's running around, doing interviews and such, I go back home for a few weeks." She walked over with a plate. "In fact, I'm going home at the end of the month. Get to see my daughter."

"Wow." It was a cheese plate dotted with artistic smears of jams and honey. "This is beautiful. Thank you so much."

"Of course." She smoothed back her salt-and-pepper hair. "Where's home for you?" She leaned against the butcher block, crossing her arms.

"All over, really. But I spent the most time in the Midwest. Now I'm in Brooklyn."

"Your mum and dad there?" Her mahogany eyes were quick and curious.

"My mom is. My dad — he's not a part of my life."

"Oh, I'm sorry, love." Her expression shifted, becoming so concerned that I suddenly wanted to launch myself into her arms.

"That's okay." I tried to smile. "It was a long time ago."

Someone cleared her throat at the doorway. Yana stood there, watching us with a cold expression. I wondered how much she'd heard.

Chitra straightened up and went back to the stove. "Need something?"

"Miss Roza would like tea." Yana's voice was flat.

"Absolutely." Chitra swiftly pulled a teapot out of a cabinet. The cozy warmth of the kitchen was gone, replaced with an icy awkwardness. I stood, picking up my plate.

"Alex," Yana said.

For some reason it chilled me to hear her say my name, as if she'd put me on some kind of list.

"Yes?" I forced myself to smile.

Yana glanced at Chitra's back. "You should not be bothering Miss Chitra when she's working."

"She's not bothering me," Chitra called in a singsong without turning around.

"She is very busy," Yana went on, ignoring her. "And Miss Roza will be unhappy if she is not able to get her work done."

Chitra muttered something I couldn't make out.

"Sure. I'll remember that. Sorry." I walked to the door. At the last minute Yana stepped aside to let me pass.

Upstairs, Keira's door was closed. In the past two days she'd spent most of her time writing in her room. Wren and Poppy's door was closed too. I pressed my left temple against the wood. Inside, Poppy was exclaiming something and Wren was laughing. Really laughing, that raucous head throw that made you feel like the most hilarious person in the world.

How could she act like that — like nothing had happened, like nothing was wrong?

But Wren did this. With most people, if you pissed her off, she was done and she moved on immediately. I'd returned home to our apartment more than once to find a guy waiting on the steps with a hangdog expression, desperate to talk to her. And once she'd shown me a text conversation, dozens of unanswered gray lines on her phone screen from a female friend trying to make amends.

It had made me uncomfortable, but I'd tried to be empathetic. Wren had some undeniable issues because of her childhood. I did too. It was a silent understanding between us. And even when Wren had exploded at me, she'd always calmed down and apologized. She'd bring me gifts: bagels, books, earrings. I was the one she cared about, the one she couldn't throw away.

Until she had.

Speaking with Chitra had cheered me, but now I was back to the listless, mourning torpor.

"Hey."

I jerked away from the door. Taylor watched from her doorway. An amused half

191

smile lit up her face. "You okay there, tiger?"

"Yeah. I'm fine." I continued towards her with the plate and she ushered me inside, shutting the door.

"Sorry." I grimaced. "You must think I'm such a creep."

"Well, you're a creep with cheese, so you're okay in my book." Taylor grabbed the plate and danced to her bed. She wore flannel-lined jeans with the cuffs rolled up and a black sweatshirt. The rabbit necklace swung back and forth across the white words LET ME LIVE. "I'm assuming you're willing to share?"

"Yeah, of course." I followed her and perched on the bed. She'd already dived into the double-crème Brie. Suddenly, I wasn't hungry anymore.

"You get any intel?" Taylor asked, spraying a few crumbs.

"Intel?"

"I'm referring to the extremely obvious eavesdropping I just witnessed."

"Oh." I felt drained. After a moment I moved further onto Taylor's bed. "Is it okay if I sit here?"

"Of course!" She scooted down so she and the plate were next to me.

"I didn't hear anything." I leaned against the headboard. "I think I just zoned out for a sec. Wren and I had kind of a fight downstairs. So to hear her laughing with Poppy like nothing happened . . ."

"You had a fight?" Her sky blue eyes widened, though her chewing didn't slow. "About what?"

I hesitated, unsure of whether I wanted to tell Taylor the full story.

"Just everything that went down." I rolled my eyes. "She was mad I told you guys about it."

"Seriously?" Taylor muttered. "You're not allowed to talk about your own life?"

"Guess not." I plucked a grape. "At least, according to her."

"Listen." Taylor gestured with a cracker. "Don't let her get in your head, okay? I know people like that. They make you think they're great as long as they need you. And as soon as they don't — like when Wren met this guy — then they drop you. Simple as that."

It wasn't as simple as that. Wren hadn't even met Evan before moving out. But I just nodded. It was the easier narrative. Better to keep it that way.

"Thanks for listening," I said. "But let's talk about something else. How're you? How's your writing going?"

"Oof. Don't ask." She set down the plate

and sighed.

"Oh, no." I knew that feeling. I'd had it for an entire year.

"Yeah." She stared at the bed, her eyes narrowed. "I brought, like, half a manuscript to this thing too. Thought I'd be able to finish it. And now I get to start all over with something brand-new."

"That sucks." It felt refreshing to talk about something other than my issues. "Your new idea is so great, though. I love the setting: the catacombs of Paris. I saw a documentary about them once. They're so eerie. And they're just there, right underneath everything going on in the city."

"I know." She grinned. "I actually visited them."

I faux gasped. "With a bartender who turned out to be part of a killer cult?"

"Not exactly." Taylor laughed, pushing up her sleeves. "But it was with a beautiful woman. It was actually really romantic. At first. After we hooked up down there, we got lost and for a half hour I thought we'd never find our way out."

"That's my worst fear." I crossed my arms. "Getting stuck underground like that. No one knowing you're there."

"Yeah. Well, we made it out." She wiggled her eyebrows. "Or did we?"

"Oh, so you're a ghost, huh?"

"Check." She held out her arm and I playfully poked it. Again I noticed her tattoos: intricately inked purple flowers against a mass of leaves and fronds.

"What kind of flowers are those?" I asked.

"Wolfsbane." She twisted her arm so I could fully see. "One of the most deadly plants on earth. This is the vine species."

"It's beautiful."

She jumped up and went to the dresser. "Want to see the real deal?" She returned with a silver necklace. At the end hung a small glass vial that contained a sprig of dried purple flowers.

"Whoa." I took the vial. The small glass stopper had a hole connecting it to the sterling chain. "Is this a murder weapon?"

She chuckled. "More like a good-luck charm."

"That's ironic."

"Someone gave it to me."

"Your girlfriend?"

"Yeah." She smiled softly. "It was something that connected us; we found out we were both into wolfsbane. I'd read about it when I was young; some people said it could turn you into a werewolf. That was a fantasy of mine."

"To be a werewolf?"

"Yeah. Or something like that — some supernatural creature. I already felt like an outsider. I grew up in an extremely conservative area and stayed closeted for a long time. I wished for some secret power, something to make my alienation make sense."

"I get it." I handed it back. "I felt like an outsider, too."

She continued to gaze at me, studying me.

"What?" I finally asked, feeling awkward.

"Nothing." She smiled. "Just looking at you."

My stomach flipped. I smiled back and tried to hold her gaze, but it was too powerful. I looked down.

"You know, I should get going." I slid off the bed. "I need to write more before dinner. But it was really nice talking to you."

"Same. Hey, take this." She held up the plate. "You might need some sustenance."

And the tension was gone. But her flirtatious look — and maybe I'd made it up? — had made me feel something sharp. I couldn't tell if it was excitement or fear.

"Sure thing." I grabbed the plate, avoiding eye contact and hating myself for it. Could I be more of a coward?

"Hey, Alex?"

I paused at the door.

Taylor's hands were clasped behind her head. "Some friendly words of advice: Don't let Wren fuck with you, okay? You're the real deal. She's a stuck-up little influencer princess."

The words caused a small avalanche of relief in my chest. This vote of confidence, even from someone who didn't know either of us very well, felt reassuring.

"Don't worry." I tried to sound breezy. "I'm fully planning on kicking her pompous ass and winning this thing."

She broke into a grin. "That's the spirit."

Excerpt from *The Great Commission*

The first official meeting of the Blackbriar Spiritualist Society took place on a bleak, rainy night.

Abigail and Florence arrived at the same time, their carriage horses pounding up the path and neighing with nervous delight. Daphne ran down the stairs, nearly tripping before catching herself on the banister. At the door, Mrs. Linders was letting them in.

"Daphne!" Abigail pulled her into a hug. Daphne was initially shocked by the familiarity, but then she let herself melt into it. After Horace's coldness, the embrace felt so affectionate and sisterly that it made her think of Grace. The brief reminder of her dead sister made Daphne square her shoulders as she stepped back. This is why she was here. For too long she'd blocked the spirits that wished to show themselves to her.

She knew the risks of opening herself back up again. From that first time in her bedroom, when she'd seen the rotting woman, she had learned what soon became common sense. Spirits could come in all forms, depending on how conscious and awake they'd been in life. Knowing they were blocked from moving to the next world, many were able to retain a preferred form. Daphne had encountered children, young adults, and the elderly. Some tried to communicate with her, some didn't. The worst, however, were those poor souls who didn't realize they were dead. These stayed connected to their decomposing physical form. They were the ones who, over time, became monsters Daphne feared to see.

However, reaching Grace would be worth the chance of running into them.

"Good evening, darling." Florence gave her air kisses, enveloping her in a flowery halo of cologne. She was trying to retain her usual cool, but a wide grin revealed her giddiness.

"Come in, come in! The room's all set up!" Daphne brought them into the library, their buttoned shoes clicking against the marble floor. Horace had forbidden them to use the parlor, which had too much of a masculine air, anyway.

"Oh." Florence's dubious tone sent a shiver down Daphne's back. What had she done wrong? "Hmm. I'm not at all sure about this room, ladies. The energy seems off to me."

"Flo." Behind Florence, Abigail shot

Daphne an amused look. "That's nonsense and you know it. Just because you've run one or two of these before . . ."

"One or two! Darling, I'll have you know that when I was living in London, I took part in *twelve* seances —"

"And we are so lucky to have your expertise." Daphne knew how to soothe the fractious older woman even though she hadn't known her very long. To her relief, Florence did seem to calm herself, especially once she spotted the tray of cordials.

An hour later, they were ready to begin. They sat at a low table in front of the fire, settling on pillows on the floor, which all felt very Bohemian. They clasped hands. Daphne noticed that Abigail's hand was very warm, while Florence's was cold, despite the summer air drifting in from the windows. The table was covered with a white lace shawl that Florence had brought, along with several candles. A pad of paper and a pencil waited in front of Florence.

"Okay, girls." Florence's pale eyelids fluttered. "Now close your eyes."

Abigail squeezed Daphne's hand, and she squeezed back.

"O great spirits," Florence intoned. "We ask you to bless us with your presence tonight."

She went silent and Daphne's mind wandered. Despite the atmosphere from the candles, it didn't feel particularly different here than at other times of the day. She stifled a yawn. With all the preparations, she was now somewhat exhausted.

"We implore you to visit us, spirits." Florence cleared her throat. "Are there any who would like to speak with us tonight?"

"Yes."

It took a moment for Daphne to realize that she'd just spoken aloud. Her eyelids flipped open. Abigail was looking at her, but she quickly closed her eyes. Florence's eyes were still closed, but a slight smile played on her thin lips.

"Welcome," Florence said. "What is your name?"

"Dennis." Daphne felt cold uncertainty wash over her. She'd seen spirits before, but they'd never spoken through her like this.

"Dennis, we welcome you to our table," Florence went on. "What would you like to tell us?"

Daphne waited. No words came. Maybe he was gone? Maybe —

Suddenly, Daphne's hands whipped away from Abigail and Florence's, clawing at the table. Abigail quickly moved the pad and pencil in front of her. Daphne clutched it and scribbled.

Panic bubbled up in her chest. Her arms and hands were no longer connected to her body but were acting of their own accord. She finished one page and flipped to the next. She tried to stop — she couldn't.

Jaw clenched, she looked up at the other two, pleading with them to help her. Abigail's hands covered her lips. Florence's mouth hung open.

Daphne flipped another page.

"Daphne, are you —" Abigail began to rise.

"Stop!" Florence bellowed. "Don't break the circle. Let her finish."

"But is she —"

And then, as quickly as it had begun, it was over. Daphne's hands were once again her own. She clasped them in her lap, as if forcing them to behave. Her heart still pounded, but there was something else too. Now that it was over — and she knew that at least for the night, it was — the panic was beginning to shift into pure exhilaration.

She laughed aloud. "My goodness!"

Florence pulled the papers to her. She read one or two lines, and her eyes returned to Daphne. They held something Daphne wouldn't have expected: fear.

"Well, my darling." Florence set the papers down again. "I've never seen anyone contacted so quickly." Now there was admiration in her expression. She beamed at Daphne. "It looks like you're a natural."

CHAPTER 15

The parlor had been transformed for cocktail hour. A fire roared in the stone fireplace and taper candles flickered on the central coffee table. A makeshift bar had been set up by the window. Yana stood next to it in a tight mint-colored jumpsuit, glowering at no one in particular.

I could feel Wren's presence on the far side of the room. It was like having a crush, when you could track them at all times without looking at them. I glanced over. Near the window, she and Poppy leaned towards each other, tittering like teenagers.

"Hi." I approached Yana at the bar. Her ponytail was so tight, it pulled back her forehead, but she still managed to lower her drawn-on brows in a glare. "Um, could I have some red wine, please?"

Without answering, she picked up a glass and poured.

"Thanks," I said, but she was already back

to ignoring me. Her commitment to inhospitality made me smile as I made my way to Taylor and Keira, who were sitting on the leather couch. They were discussing someone with great intensity. It took me a few minutes to realize it was a character from Keira's book.

Roza arrived fashionably late, despite her stern warning about being on time. She'd changed into a long, dramatic maroon dress and she trilled hellos as she swept into the room.

"The writing's going well?" Taylor asked, straightening.

"Very well, my dears." Roza received a glass from Yana and plopped into a velvet chair. Poppy and Wren came over and we listened to Roza hold court. She was in a fantastic mood. For once, I didn't feel like I needed to impress her, or anyone. I knew she liked what I was working on, and that was all that mattered.

Drinks rolled into dinner, which rolled into after-dinner drinks back in the parlor. By this time we were full, stuffed with food and wine, but when Roza poured the familiar Unicum into small glasses, no one refused.

"Well." Roza settled herself into the same chair, tucking her bare feet underneath her.

"Tonight we will play our first game."

The wine had made me feel almost obscenely relaxed, but now I tensed up. I was not a game person. It tended to bring out my insecurities, especially when I had to do something like perform. Wren had often pushed charades at parties when she was drunk and restless.

"Awesome." Taylor rubbed her hands together. She, Keira, and I had returned to our same spots on the couch, while Poppy and Wren were on the love seat. Wren and I had successfully ignored each other throughout dinner, sitting as far away from each other as possible.

"It's not for the faint of heart." Roza's eyes glinted. "It's a parlor game from Japan. Hyakumonogatari Kaidankai, or A Gathering of One Hundred Supernatural Tales. Beautiful name, isn't it? There will be one winner, who will get to have a nightcap with me."

A slight edge entered the room. Taylor started twisting the golden rabbit at the end of the chain. She'd continued to wear her necklace over the past two days, though it looked discordant against her loose sweatshirts.

"This will take creativity and nerves," Roza went on. "And it will go like this. You will tell a ghost story. You can make it up completely or tell one that happened to you or someone you know. We will guess whether or not it was 'real,' at least to the person who experienced it. I trust that you will all be honest. If we guess wrong, you will get to carry a candle in the next phase. If we are right, you will have to go in darkness."

"What's the next phase?" Keira asked, pushing up her red glasses.

Roza just smiled. "You'll see, darling. Of those who complete the task, I'll choose the best story."

Ghost stories: they reminded me of long-ago sleepovers, whispered tales in the dark, the delicious fear that would climb up your spine as you snuggled in your sleeping bag.

Still, I felt nervous. Normally I'd tell my best story — the story of going into the woods with my best friend and what we'd seen there. But I'd turned that into an actual story and Ursula had sent it to Roza, who'd said she loved it. So that one was out . . .

"Who would like to go first?" Roza set her drink on her knee. "Trust me, it's better to go earlier rather than later."

"I'll go," Wren said. She glanced at me. "But Alex has heard it."

"Good point." Roza gestured at me.

"Alex, you sit this one out. Okay?"

"Sure." Wren's confidence had given me a tingle of nervousness.

"So I was a kid," Wren started. "Nine years old. And at the time my family was living across from this giant forest."

The words took a second to sink in. Wren had grown up in Manhattan. Central Park wasn't giant, at least compared to natural forests. So she must be making this story up.

"I used to be friends with this girl down the street named Christina," Wren went on. "She had this beautiful long, wavy hair that went all the way down to her butt. I was so jealous of it."

I stiffened, staring at Wren with amazement. This was *my* story. Wren was telling my story as if it was hers. I looked at Roza, but she was smiling, just taking it in.

"On the Fourth of July one year, her parents were having a barbecue. She and I got bored and decided to go for a walk. We hung out in the woods all the time, but we'd never gone at night before. We weren't allowed to. But with the party happening and with the adults getting tipsy and setting off fireworks, we didn't think anyone would notice. So we grabbed a flashlight and took off."

208

Roza had to know, didn't she? She'd said she liked my story. But then again, was it so hard to believe that she'd never actually read it? That she'd just said that because she wanted to make me feel better after humiliating me in front of the group the first night?

"There was a large path; I think it used to be a tractor path," Wren went on. "One that we always followed. But somehow we found ourselves on this little trail. And the strangest part was that we couldn't hear the fireworks anymore. We couldn't see the flashes. The woods were completely silent. We said how weird it was, that there weren't even any crickets. I had this feeling that we were on a movie set, that everything was fake. The trail opened up, and we were relieved, because we thought we were back on the main path. But then it just stopped. We were in a small clearing. It was a warm night and we were just wearing tank tops and shorts. But in this clearing, it was cold."

A dark fury gripped my spine. How dare she? She was telling my story, in almost my exact words. And with every sentence it was like she was stealing it: my memory. My experience. Using me, taking from me, as she'd always done.

I wanted to run at her, covering her

mouth, tackling her to the floor.

But I couldn't. Because then I'd be the crazy one.

"And then," Wren continued, her eyes wide, "when we turned around and decided to go back, we couldn't find the path."

Poppy gasped and then laughed at her reaction.

"We walked around the whole perimeter of the clearing, but the path was gone. And we were just starting to freak out when we heard something. It was Christina's mom calling to us, and we heard sounds like she was walking towards us. We went in that direction and started yelling for her. I remember we were clinging to each other, we were so relieved. But then the sound of her voice came from further away. It got fainter and fainter. We just stood there. And Christina turned to me, and I'll never forget what she said. She whispered: *'I think it's trying to trick us.'* "

"Whoa," Taylor muttered, impressed.

Just get through it. I locked my arms against my chest. Wren was baiting me, just waiting for me to freak out in front of Roza. It wasn't going to happen.

"We backed away from where the sounds had been coming from and went to the other side of the clearing. Christina was saying we should just walk out through the trees. But I thought that we'd definitely be lost. We had no idea where we were. And the trees and brush around the clearing was super thick, like it was trapping us in. And then" — Wren paused for dramatic effect — "we saw something."

"What?" Poppy whispered.

"It was big." Wren tucked back her hair with both hands. "And it was right at the edge of the clearing. We saw the leaves shake. And there was this *smell* . . . it's hard to even describe. Halfway between wet dog —"

And something rotting.

"And something rotting. I saw these two shiny circles, these orbs way up in the trees. Eyes. And this heavy, sighing sound. Without even looking at each other, Christina and I plunged into the trees. We flat-out *ran.* I banged my shoulder against a tree, which was excruciating, but I kept going. After a few minutes, we slowed down to see if it was coming after us. And that's when we heard . . ."

"The monster?" Taylor asked, chewing on a nail.

"The fireworks." Wren smiled. "It took some time, but we followed the sound and finally reached the main path. It was the most relieved I've ever felt in my life. By the time we got back, we were both bruised and bleeding, just totally cut up. Christina's mom sobered up fast when she saw us. She helped us clean our scratches. Christina told her what happened, and her mom just kept saying that we shouldn't have gone into the woods at night."

"What did your parents say?" Poppy asked, hushed.

Wren had asked me the same thing.

"I never told them." Wren shook her head sadly. "They wouldn't have believed me. Especially my mom."

"What the fuck!" The words burst out. Everyone looked at me, confused. Except for Wren. She just watched me coolly.

"What is *wrong* with you?" I cried. "Do you really think that's okay?" I struggled to lower my voice but I couldn't. All the disbelief and rage poured out like toxic sludge.

"What's okay?" Taylor glanced back and forth between us.

"That's *my* story." I said it through gritted teeth. "It happened to *me*. I wrote a short story about it. Which Wren read."

"It's a game." Wren blinked, innocent. "Roza said we could tell a story that happened to us or someone we know."

"But I'm sitting right here," I cried. "You can't *do* that. You can't just take whatever you want." My hands were curled into claws, and I forced them under my thighs. The rage was back, coursing through my body. I wanted to throttle her, then rip off her skull and throw it into the fire.

"Aw, man." Taylor sighed. "Now we know it's a true story. We can't guess whether Wren made it up just now."

"Are you okay?" Keira asked me. Her look of concern chastened me.

"Yeah, I'm sorry, it's just . . . I don't think that was fair." My shoulders hunched forward. Great. Now everyone thought I was some lunatic who couldn't handle a stupid game.

Roza had been silent, watchful. But now she shrugged. "Wren didn't do anything I said she couldn't do, dear."

"Well, it's a great story." Taylor patted my arm. "So that really happened to you?"

"Yes. I still have a scar from those branches."

"Well." Roza stood, took a taper candle off the table, and handed it to Wren. "You'll get to take a candle, dear, since we never got a chance to vote."

Wren stood to accept it with that smug, infuriating smile.

213

"So now, you'll go into the basement," Roza went on. "Look for a table with a hand mirror and five candles. Your job is to look in the mirror and blow out one candle."

"Where's the basement?" Wren asked uneasily.

"Yana will show you." Roza indicated Yana, who stood in the doorway. Had she been there the whole time?

After Wren left, I stood. "I think I'm going to go upstairs." The disgust and unease roiled in my stomach, both at Wren and at Roza for defending her. And most of all myself, for completely losing it. I'd played right into Wren's hands.

"No," Roza said. "You have to finish the game."

"I don't want to play the game." I hated the whininess in my voice. "Plus I don't have a story."

"Then make something up. Or just sit and listen." There was a note of exasperation in Roza's voice. I sat, trying to quell frustrated tears.

Wren came back a few minutes later, giggling and flushed.

"Well, that's terrifying." She set the candle back on the mantel and then plopped down beside Poppy.

Taylor and Keira went next. Taylor shared

a story of seeing her deceased friend in the tiny room of a yacht when she was sixteen; Keira, of spending six months in a haunted apartment. They were guessed to be true but were both revealed to be made up. So both got candles to take downstairs.

"Poppy?" Roza turned to her.

By this time I'd refilled my glass and had silently drunk myself into a haze. The hatred burned in my chest like a tiny furnace.

"Oh, no, I'm going to pass if that's okay." She giggled. "I'm actually really scared of ghosts."

"I have one," I said. Everyone turned to me quickly, as if they'd forgotten I was there.

"Wonderful." Roza smiled.

"Once upon a time there was a girl who had a best friend." The words flowed out easily, from within the orange-blue flames of the furnace. "They did everything together. They played together, they went to bookstores, they played pranks on their families. And then one day one of the girls was kind of a bitch to the other girl, and so the first girl decided to kill her. She did a lot of research to figure out how to make it look natural. And she decided she'd poison her. So she started poisoning her friend's food little by little, and eventually the girl

215

became really sick. And the first girl pretended to take care of her, and sit by her
bedside, but all along she was the one killing her."

The others were watching me, eyes wide.
I felt peaceful and separate, as if I were talking to screens of simulations instead of people.

"That's the end." I took a large swig, feeling satisfied.

"Okay." Roza eyebrows rose. "True or
false?"

"False." Wren looked unamused. "You
obviously just made it up."

"Creepy, though," Taylor said. "I liked it."
Keira and Poppy nodded their assent.

"You made it up," Roza said. "Yes?"

"That's what writers do, don't they? Of
course I fucking made it up."

Taylor and Keira glanced at each other,
seemingly surprised by my sharp words.
Wren hid a smile. She was loving this: me
losing control, me looking like a sulky bitch.

"So, my dear." Roza smiled. "You will
need to go in darkness. Are you ready?"

"Sounds great." I slammed down my glass
and jumped up. Yana was at the doorway,
waiting. She led me down the hall to the
kitchen. In contrast to how the space had
felt earlier that day, with Chitra bustling

around, it now seemed cold and alien.

"Here." Yana opened a door at the back of the room. A stairway descended into darkness.

"Wonderful." I started clomping down the steps. I didn't give a shit if I fell all the way down and broke my neck. Who cared, really? But as I descended into the chilly dampness, the drunken bravado seeped away. Now I just felt embarrassed. Why couldn't I just keep it together? Why did I let Wren wind me up so much?

At the bottom of the stairs I looked back up, expecting to see Yana outlined in the doorway, but she was already gone. I stayed in place until my eyes adjusted to the darkness, breathing in the stale scent of mildew. There, a ways away, I could see a small light flickering. The candles.

I made my way carefully. There was stuff everywhere: cardboard boxes stacked six feet high, lumps of furniture covered by sheets, piles of gilt-framed paintings. No sounds except for something dripping from a distance. Now an unease overtook my humiliation. Away from all the others, something felt off. There was some dark energy at Blackbriar that lived in the walls. It felt connected to the random story that had streamed out of my mouth so easily.

And how had Wren told my story so flaw-lessly? At least she'd had the decency not to share the ending. How I'd gone home that night to hear Mom and Dad fighting up-stairs. That wasn't unusual. What was unusual was the sharp crack and Mom's hoarse cry. Standing outside their bedroom, the smell of rotting filled my nose. It was like I'd brought the creature from the woods back with me to infect our house.

Dad left two weeks later.

There came a sound of something scuf-fling nearby. I paused and the sound went further away. A mouse, or a rat, or whatever else lived in this gigantic maze. The dark-ness squeezed at my ribs. I turned back to see the reassuring circle of light pooling from the stairs.

Finally, after bumping my shin on a low couch, I reached the table. Four candles surrounded an antique golden hand mirror. Only one was still lit.

Two should be lit, since Poppy hadn't gone. Who had blown out more than one? Who had wanted to leave me in complete darkness?

I hesitated, considering. Should I just say I'd blown one out and leave this last one burning? Or would they know?

Whatever. I was over it. I picked up the

hand mirror and stared at myself, drunk and red-eyed and ugly. I gave myself a wide, humorless grin.

Behind me, something moved in the dim gloom.

I whipped around.

In that moment, someone blew the last candle out.

CHAPTER 16

"Okay, guys." I was holding out my hands in the darkness, as if ready to fight. "Not funny. Pretty fucked-up, actually."

No response. I stood rigidly, my shoulders bunched into my neck.

"Okay." I began moving towards the stairs. My other shin slammed into the couch. And then I bumped into a wooden piece of furniture covered in a sheet. This place was like a goddamn obstacle course.

Every step, I expected to be touched: hands pulling my hips, grasping my hair, gripping my neck. But after what felt like an hour, I made it to the stairs. Halfway up I crouched and looked out into the basement. All I could see were shadows and vague outlines.

"Fuck you," I snarled, and ran the rest of the way up.

Back in the light of the kitchen, I felt a pang of humiliation, then anger. They —

whoever they were — had wanted to scare me, to make me look stupid. I stalked back to the parlor. Taylor, Keira, and Roza were chuckling. I noted with grim satisfaction that Wren and Poppy were missing.

"Where are they?" I pointed to the love seat where they'd been sitting.

Everyone stared, displeased, like I was a raccoon who'd wandered into the house.

"What happened?" Taylor asked.

Then the sound of Wren's laughter reached me and she and Poppy strolled in.

"It was you guys." I turned on them. "How did you come down without me hearing?"

"I have no idea what you're talking about." Wren resumed her place on the love seat.

"Wait, what's going on? What happened?" Poppy sat beside her.

"You followed me down to scare me." I put my hands on my hips.

"Hey, sit down." Taylor came over and touched my shoulder. "Tell us what happened."

I explained, watching Wren's placid expression.

"Ah." Roza nodded. "Darling, it can be very drafty down there. I'm sure you just saw a sheet or something moving as the air blew the candle out." She looked pleased with herself. "But this game can really make you see things."

"But . . ." What I'd seen in the mirror hadn't been a fluttering sheet — it had been moving purposefully. But it had been more a motion than anything else.

"That sounds scary as hell," Taylor said. "Want a drink?"

"No," I sighed, feeling drained. "I'm okay."

Wren was looking purposefully away, but Poppy continued to watch me with huge, concerned eyes. A flash of embarrassment blossomed in my chest. I could imagine Wren slipping down to the basement to mess with me. But not Poppy.

"Maybe it was just a draft." I tried to smile. Then a new question formed. "Where's Yana?"

"She went to bed. It's past her bedtime." Roza grinned. "Why, you think she went down to play a trick on you?"

"No . . ." Yana was unfriendly, but I couldn't imagine her sneaking behind boxes, avoiding the mice. "I just . . . I'm sorry."

"Get some rest, darling." Roza stood. "Taylor, I'll declare you the winner of this game. Let's go have a nightcap."

"Sure!" Taylor jumped up. Wren looked

up in surprise and glared at me.

She'd really thought she could use my story to win.

That night I startled awake, facing the door. Someone was walking by in the hall, the footsteps rapid and noisy. Still half-asleep, I turned on my lamp, slipped out of bed. and tiptoed to the door. In the light spilling out from my door, I could just make out someone hurrying along.

Something was wrong.

I followed, trotting down the dark hallway.

"Wait!" I squeaked, keeping my voice down so as not to wake the others. It felt important. This person was in trouble, desperate trouble, and I needed to help.

The figure scuttled along even more quickly, turning out of sight to the landing. I jogged faster, determined to catch up.

But when I reached the landing, no one was there. I walked slowly to the banister. The gray and white marble floor made a beautiful mandala, crossed with moonbeams shining in from the front hall windows. The circular table was almost directly below, topped with a vase of pink roses.

As I studied it, warm arms slipped around my waist. The arms were bare, pearlescent and glowing in the moonlight. Hard nipples pressed like pebbles into my back.

"Finally." The voice was barely a whisper in my ear. Shock and confusion held me in place. A heavy jasmine scent filled my nostrils.

"Roza?" I ventured. I felt blurry, unable to fully understand what was happening, as if I'd been drugged.

The woman chuckled. "Don't you know me?"

"Wren?" I started to turn around, but her arms tightened. I inhaled with surprise.

"You've wanted me for such a long time, haven't you, Al?" There was a smile in her low voice. "Long before that night."

"Wren, what the fuck?" I muttered. I wanted to pull away, but part of me felt oddly cozy in this tight embrace.

"Remember what it felt like?" Her breath was heavy in my ear. "What I did to you?"

"Why?" I asked, suddenly mournful. "Why did you do it?"

"What? You want to hear that I was in love with you?" She scoffed. "I did it because I could. Because you were my little pet and I could do whatever I wanted to you."

"Okay." I shifted but her arms were like a vise.

"I saw the way you looked at me. You wanted to consume me. You wanted to kill me. It was such a fun game, wasn't it?" Her left hand drifted up and her thumb gently stroked my nipple through my tank top. I felt a stirring in my groin.

"Do you want me to stop?" She pinched, gently.

And even though I couldn't believe this was happening, I *didn't* want her to stop.

"No," I sighed.

"And this?" Her other hand lowered, snuck inside the waistband of my pajama pants.

I gasped at the intensity. "Fuck."

"Feels good, doesn't it? Wow. You're already wet, Al." Her fingers circled my clit, gentle and insistent. "You're my good girl, aren't you?" The intensity melted into a new, desperate need. Something began to build, a rumbling of energy from my tail-bone.

"Aren't you?" she asked again.

"I'm not your anything," I managed to say, still swooning.

"But I want you to be. Let's get back together. Wouldn't you like that?" Her voice was low and hypnotic. "I'll win this contest and then we'll have all the money we need."

The words cut through the sudden desire. I shook my head. "You're not going to win. Not with your stupid actress story. *I'm* going to win."

"Al." She chuckled, and now her voice was threatening, tinged with malice. "I always win. You know that." She kissed my neck, grinding her hips against me, bending me over the railing. I clutched at it. The marble floor was so far below.

"Say it." She bit my shoulder hard. "Say I win."

I gasped at the sharp, sweet pain, then laughed. "No."

"Say it." Her fingers swirled faster and I pushed against them, the energy lifting in my belly like a tsunami.

"No," I moaned. "Never."

She pushed me harder, forcing my upper body over the bannister. I dangled, feeling deliciously weak and helpless. I was suddenly scared of the railing breaking under our combined weight, of falling two floors below, but that, too, added to the rising tension: the raw mixture of lust and fear and anger and submission and even hate, all swelling under her firm, swift movements.

Say it. With her other hand she grabbed my hair, cranked my head back.

"Fuck you," I spit out, grinning.

She pulled so hard, I thought my head might pop off like a doll's. My breath was ragged and I couldn't stop making noises, somewhere between a laugh and a whimper.

"Al . . ." Teasing, threatening. "Say it or I'll stop."

She slowed and I didn't want her to. "No, don't."

"Say please."

"Please!"

Her fingers resumed their pace. I was moaning loudly now, caught in a dark energy that seeped into my pores. My whole body was on fire, every cell throbbing, a dam about to burst.

"Say I win." Her voice was a growl.

I couldn't speak. My moans were my true nature, my true self: her toy, her pet.

"Say I win." Her nails dug into my scalp, bright points of pain. The railing creaked.

"Yes," I whispered. The pleasure enveloped me, placental, whole.

"Say it!" The order thundered in my ears. I was there, on the brink, on the edge of a great cliff. I couldn't stop even if I wanted to.

"You win!" I wailed. I'd wake everyone up but I didn't fucking care. "You win! You win!"

The orgasm that engulfed me was like a nuclear explosion, white light filling my vision, an eruption so powerful that I didn't realize I was falling until I was already in the air.

The back of my skull slammed into the round marble table. My vision shattered into a billion stars, a heavenly pattern that disappeared when my body hit the floor. I landed on my back, struggling for breath, bolts of lightning still jerking my arms and legs.

At first, I could see only faint outlines. I felt no pain. Actually, I couldn't feel my body at all. Had I broken my neck?

Then my vision sharpened. There was Wren far above me, leaning on the railing with her elbows. Somehow, in the instant I'd started to come, she'd shoved me over the railing. Now she grinned and waved, like a parent spotting their child onstage. She straightened and stretched. Suddenly done with me, she sauntered away, back where I could no longer see her.

I tried to call her name. All that came out was a weak huff of air.

Black spots began to dance at the edges of my vision. I felt nothing, physically or otherwise. I couldn't move. It was, in a peculiar way, peaceful.

Faintly, brisk footsteps came tapping towards me.

Yana, of all people, came into view, wearing a white velour tracksuit. She peered down at me, scowling.

I mouthed *Help,* but she rolled her eyes.

"What a mess," she muttered, then stood. "I'll come back in the morning."

I tried to scream as she walked off. But of course nothing came out.

CHAPTER 17

"It's a little expected." Roza flung down the piece of paper. "A little boring. I don't feel like I'm really getting a feel for these other characters. Alex, do you understand?"

"Yes." I dutifully scribbled down notes.

We were nearing the end of our daily group meeting. It was day seven of the retreat, and ever since the bizarre basement situation four days ago, I'd thrown myself into the writing, trying my best to ignore Wren. I thought I'd done an admirable job, especially after the sex dream.

It had disturbed me in a deep, visceral way, especially since I'd never had an orgasm in my sleep before. The dream itself had been so lifelike. I could remember every vivid detail, which left me both horrified and aroused.

After Wren and I had hooked up in real life, I'd spent about a day in a confused, liminal space. I'd always considered our friendship purely platonic. I'd been attracted to Wren's energy, sure, and I'd admired her beauty many times. But I'd never felt a physical desire for her — or for any other woman, for that matter. After watching Ursula meet her girlfriend, I'd briefly wondered if I should expand my dating horizons. But I just hadn't been able to imagine myself with a woman.

After what had happened with Wren, though, I'd reconsidered. Perhaps I wasn't able to imagine sex with women simply because I hadn't experienced it before. After all, it wasn't like I went around spontaneously daydreaming about sleeping with men, either. Most of the sex I did have was combined with a lot of alcohol, and it was something I did because it was expected, not because it felt great. What had happened with Wren, though: it *had* felt great.

So maybe my aversion was from being taught early on that being queer was abnormal and undesirable. A bully in one of my grade schools had started a rumor that I was a lesbian, which caused the other girls to jerk away from me when I got too close. And I had a distinct memory as a teen of Mom telling a boyfriend about the "queen" who'd come into the grocery store that day; she flounced around, mimicking him. Even in the shows I watched that had likable gay characters, they were there to provide exoticism or, more commonly, comic relief.

So then the question became: If I set aside this lifelong conditioning, what did I feel? Could Wren and I turn our friendship into something more? I truly didn't know. But the more I sat with it, the more I felt a thin ribbon of excitement. It must mean something that two heretofore self-identified straight female friends had ended up naked in bed together. Maybe there was more to the story for both of us. Maybe our bond was showing us a truth that had been too buried to see.

Unfortunately, Wren had not been interested in exploring that.

Now, across the table from me, Wren kept her eyes on Roza. Her lips shone a perfect rose color. It was impossible to imagine they'd ever kissed down my thighs. I felt a pull deep in my belly and then, with a swelling of sadness and shame, wished the whole tangle of feelings away.

After the meeting, I followed the other girls into the dining room for lunch. They walked two by two, pairing perfectly: the conventionally beautiful Wren and Poppy, a contrast in brunette and blond, Wren in jewel tones and Poppy in pastels. And the über-hip Keira and Taylor, Keira with her stylish red glasses and black jeans, and Taylor with her messy short hair and tattoos.

I trailed behind, the fifth wheel, drab and plain and alone. After that one conversation with Taylor, I thought maybe I could join her and Keira, make us a trio instead of a duo, but Taylor had become more distant. Maybe she had been coming on to me and thought I'd rejected her. Or maybe she was happy enough hanging out with Keira and wasn't thinking about me at all.

I didn't know, and at the end of the day, it didn't matter. What did matter was the writing, and it was going well enough to keep my focus. Even if Roza was calling it boring, I knew, deep down, that she was just trying to push me.

I would've expected that seven days in one house with one small group would've felt claustrophobic. But the story had me in its grip. I didn't even go out and take walks like the others, I just stayed mostly in my room and wrote.

A week into the retreat, we all had our lunch routines. Wren and Poppy picked up sandwiches from the buffet lunch Chitra laid out and headed out: Wren to their room and Poppy to the cold parlor, which she'd inexplicably chosen as her office. Taylor and Keira usually left too, but today sat at the table. Outside, snow was falling in gentle flakes.

"Alex, join us!" Taylor called.

Embarrassingly, I felt a flash of gratitude. Maybe that need to belong would never totally go away.

"Roza was harsh on you today," Taylor said as I sat. "How're you feeling?"

"I'm fine." I shrugged. "I know she's just trying to help me."

"If that's what you want to call it." Keira frowned. "Yesterday in our one-on-one, she wanted to know all about my mommy issues. I had to meditate for a full twenty minutes afterwards to stop feeling gross."

"Therapy with Roza." Taylor laughed. "She'll break you down to build you back up . . . or at least get a good story out of you."

"Exactly." Keira rolled her eyes. "Who's meeting with her today?"

"I am." I picked up an apple slice. "It's our second one-on-one."

"That's right, you were the first to meet with her." Taylor tilted her head. "She got your juices flowing."

The phrase struck me as sexual. "She did."

"What did you talk about last time?"

Taylor asked.

Oh, you know, just about sleeping with Wren and me almost maiming her afterwards.

"Just writing. Writer's block, I mean." I chewed thoughtfully, avoiding eye contact with Taylor. Why did it feel like she was staring into my soul?

"Well, you're lucky you don't have that problem anymore." Keira swept back her braids. "This word count is taking a toll on me."

"Really?" I said. "Your writing is so polished. I assumed it was . . . effortless, I guess."

"Oh, no." She was grim. "Every day's been a struggle. I'm used to writing supershitty first drafts. But I don't want Roza — or any of you guys — to read that. So I write, and go back and edit, and . . ." She rubbed her eyes, pushing up her glasses. "It's a lot."

"It's been a struggle for me too." Taylor tapped her arm. "As you know."

It was surprising to hear. Everyone had been making their word counts, churning out decent writing, and seemed cheerful enough at the meetings, cocktail hours, dinners, and evening drinks. But it seemed that, despite their retreat besties, they were having a tough time. And trying to keep that

235

fact from Roza.

Which was smart. I couldn't see her being empathetic; she'd be more likely to tell you to stop whining. To appreciate the opportunity you'd been given. To use the pain.

"But not you." Taylor grinned at me. "You're just riding the wave, aren't you? Channeling the story. I can tell. It's the best feeling."

"I don't know if I'd go that far," I said. They glanced at each other, and I felt like I had to defend myself.

"You have to remember, I had writer's block for a year," I said. "I think that's why it's all rushing out."

That seemed to satisfy them. As Taylor brought up a plot issue she was trying to solve, I had to force myself to listen. Because the truth of the matter was that Taylor was right. It did feel like I was channeling the story.

Roza had said something similar during our first one-on-one. The words drifted back in her husky voice: *The writer's mind is a channel. When we open, glorious truths can flow in.*

The question then became: What — or who — was I channeling?

At 3:00 p.m. I knocked on the red door.

Roza wrenched it open wearing a flowered robe and looking vaguely annoyed. "Oh, hello, dear. Come in."

"Is now still a good time?" I followed her inside. A tray with a patterned teapot and teacups sat on the coffee table. No Unicum today.

"Yes, darling." She tightened the robe's knot as she led us to the sitting area.

"How are you?" I noticed the laptop open on her desk. "How's your writing?"

"Like shit." She slammed it closed and joined me on the couch. She sat casually and the robe rode up her bare thigh until she pulled it down. It looked like she'd just taken a shower.

"I'm sorry to hear that." It was strange to think of Roza writing books; I couldn't imagine her sitting at her desk, typing, starting, and stopping. I pictured her books springing from her head fully formed, like the children of Greek gods.

She smiled. "But yours seems to be going rather well?"

"Except for the boring characters." I grinned back.

She leaned forward to pour the dark tea, a smirk still tugging at her lips. "I said the plot is boring, dear. And that I wasn't really getting a feel for the characters. I'm only

237

saying these things because I know you can do better."

"But how can I make the plot more interesting if it's preordained?" I felt a flicker of irritation. "It's historical fiction. I have to follow what happened."

"Well, lucky for you, Daphne didn't keep detailed diaries." Roza picked up a sugar cube with tiny tongs and dropped it into her tea. "And even if she did, you have creative license, darling. You can go wherever you'd like."

"Yeah." I poured milk into my own tea, watching it bloom. "For some reason I feel like I have a responsibility to Daphne to get it as right as I can. And, I mean, the story is dramatic enough on its own." I chanced a sip and burned the tip of my tongue.

"Let's focus on the relationships between Daphne, Florence, and Abigail." Roza watched me through the rising steam. "One, a maternal relationship. The other, something else. Not quite sure yet."

"Sisterly," I offered.

Roza raised an eyebrow. "Is that all? Boring."

I laughed. "Point taken."

"Good."

"You know, I didn't even see Florence as maternal," I sighed. "But I guess you're right. She is older. And thinks she's in charge."

"Mothers usually do." Roza paused. "And what's your mother like, dear?"

Here we go. I remembered Keira's complaint and hid a smile. "She's . . . I don't know how to describe her. I always thought she was pretty cold and shut down. But then she got married a few years ago and now she acts like a completely different person."

"In what way?"

"She's . . . I don't know; she's just way more affectionate. He's a little younger and has two teenagers. And . . . yeah, they're just this normal, happy family. They make a huge deal out of Christmas every year — big tree, all these presents, my mom even makes *cookies.* I was lucky if I got anything, growing up. She was Jewish by blood but we didn't celebrate those holidays, either."

"Jewish?" Roza repeated. "From where?"

"Hungary." I'd already told her this. But maybe it was too much to expect she'd remember every detail about my background.

"Your grandparents survived the war?" she asked, her eyes softening.

"They barely made it through the Holocaust. Most of the family died in camps. But my grandparents snuck out over the

239

border. My mom was two." Every time I thought of the story, it filled me with a kind of distant disbelief. That my grandparents and mother had lived through their own horror movie, complete with a dramatic escape.

"When did they come to the US?" Roza asked.

"They spent a couple of years in Paris. They came to the US when my mom was four. She never shared that much about her parents, but she did tell me that they became completely Americanized, speaking only English, making only American meals. They owned a jewelry store in Chicago and they both died when she was in her early twenties."

"How did they die?"

It felt good, maybe more than that, to be the object of Roza's intense focus.

"My grandmother had cancer," I said. "Lymphoma. And my grandfather . . . he got hit by a car two weeks later. My mom thought it was on purpose. A suicide."

Mom had told me this on her father's birthday one year, drunk and maudlin. Those were the times I pushed, when I knew I might be able to get a few more crumbs about our past.

"That makes sense." Roza watched the

ever-present fire.

"The suicide?"

"No." She absentmindedly pulled at a lock of her red hair. "All of it. I could sense that there was a sadness in you. Suffering attaches itself to people."

"Oh." I winced.

"It makes for the best writing, dear." It was bright in the room, the pale daylight streaming in. A few dust motes danced between us. "Everyone suffers, of course. You can't be a person and not suffer. But there are deeper traumas. Generational. They're encoded in your DNA. The Holocaust. Slavery. Genocide. A reminder of the human depths of depravity. You should be grateful for it."

"Grateful?" I echoed.

She smiled. "You have a reaction. Tell me."

"Well . . ." I didn't want to sound petulant, but I also wanted to be honest. "My childhood wasn't the worst, but in a lot of ways it was messed up. My dad disappeared when I was nine. My mom dragged me around from place to place. I never had a real home."

"And now *she* has one. And the happy, stable life you always wanted. With her new kids. Hmm?"

To my horror, tears welled up. How was

Roza so good at making me cry?

"What's the worst part?" she asked softly.

"The worst part?" I sucked in the building mucus. "It's probably that now, whenever I see her — usually I go back around Christmas, now that everyone's celebrating it — she acts like I'm this gross reminder of the past."

"How so?" Roza's brow knit.

"I don't know. She doesn't say anything. It's just how she acts." Last Christmas, I'd walked into the kitchen to see her casually embracing Emma, my stepsister. Her eyes had met mine over the top of Emma's head. For a second she'd looked startled and vaguely disgusted, like I was a gnarly spider that had appeared on the wall.

"It's like she wishes I would disappear." The tears spilled over onto my cheeks. "So I wouldn't remind her of everything. It's like I'm this ugly ghost."

"Oh, darling." Roza jumped up and came back with a silk handkerchief from her desk, as she had last time. And once again I felt bad about blowing into it. But the fabric felt smooth and gentle against my face. *Therapy with Roza, indeed.*

"I understand now." Roza touched my knee. "Why Wren was so important to you. And why her betrayal was so cruel."

"Yeah." I relaxed back against the cushions. "Well, her childhood was bad too. Much worse than mine, actually. Physical abuse, that kind of thing. So it felt like a big deal for us to have each other."

"You need to compare?" Roza asked. "Physical abuse versus emotional neglect? Some might say the neglect is worse. Because it negates your very existence."

"Well." I shrugged, confused. "I don't know. I guess it felt less intentional. Less punishing. But both are bad, right?"

Roza brooded for a minute, gazing down into her lap. Finally she looked up at me. "I'm going to tell you a story, dear. Is that all right?"

"Of course." Anything to stop thinking about Mom.

"It's about my own best friend. Mila." She looked up at me. "She was the one who died when I was writing *Devil's Tongue.* I've talked about her plenty, but something I don't share is that she was half-German. I found out in the sixties, long after the war. One day she just decided to share that her late father had been a Nazi officer. He had become drawn to her Jewish mother and started a relationship with her, protecting her throughout the war." Roza took a thoughtful sip of tea. "Now, my mother's first husband died in a camp. My mother survived because she was beautiful and very lucky. She was an expert seamstress and sewed and fixed uniforms for the officers. And provided other services to them, too, of course. But Mila's mother had been lucky too. Or unlucky, depending on what you think of Stockholm syndrome. Mila's father had made up fake papers for her mother. She was blond, so she could pass as a German. After the war he'd taken her to Berlin, where they'd had Mila. He left the army and went back to being a lawyer. When he died of a heart attack, Mila's mother took her back to Budapest. Anyway. Mila showed me pictures and told me about the atrocities he'd committed. I never even knew if they were real or if she just made them up. But as she spoke, there was a little thrill in her voice. She felt shame but also excitement, even a strange kind of pride."

Roza was quiet until I finally prompted: "That must've been a lot to process."

"Yes. But I processed. And then you know what I decided to do?" She looked up with a smirk. "I decided to punish her. I didn't speak to her for weeks. She would show up outside my house every day just waiting for me to come out and talk to her. And you know, it made me feel so much better. The power imbalance shifting back. It was very cathartic. And I realized it was possible to change things." She set down her cup. "Eventually, I allowed her back into my life. We were friends again. But when she got sick, I realized my punishment hadn't been enough. There was still more reckoning to be done, for the sins of her parents. I don't know who or what decides these things. But it was very clear to me what was happening."

I nodded, unsure of how to respond.

"You want a moral to the story, yes?" Roza reached out and grasped my hand. "Here's one. The moral is that we don't need to worry. The appropriate punishments will be meted out to the appropriate people. Often in this very lifetime."

On one hand I felt honored, being ushered into Roza's confidence like this. On the other, I felt vaguely disappointed. It was like reaching the cave of a guru I'd been searching for for years, hoping for a revelation, and being given a trite affirmation.

Roza let go of my hand and patted it. "Up until now you've given and Wren has taken. It's time to take. How can you use what she's given you? Turn it into something of your own? Step into your power?"

"I don't know." I felt suddenly confused,

unmoored, as if there had been some drug in the tea. I looked down into the milky cup. I wouldn't put it past Roza, but this was my own uncertainty.

Roza was right. I needed to step into my power. I wasn't sure what that meant yet, but something told me it would have to come out on the page.

Roza smiled, like she'd been in my brain to see this tiny silent shift.

"Don't forget that word," she said. " 'Power.' "

Excerpt from *The Great Commission*

"Daphne." Florence's gaze was steady. "You need to listen to me."

Daphne felt a bubble of hilarity rising in her throat and pushed it back down. Imagine: Florence, the middle-aged spinster, telling her to stop just because she was jealous.

"I'm listening." Daphne smiled at Florence, keeping her gaze bland. It was easy; she'd used the blandness as a cover in her previous life. You couldn't imagine the things you'd overhear working at a restaurant: men bragging in detail about their conquests, women complaining about the state of their marriage beds and bodies. And this was from the mouths of wealthy folks.

Before the restaurant, she'd been a barmaid. It had been impossible to escape attention then. She'd kept her dress just loose enough to fall away from her bosom, enduring the leers. That was the way to get tips. It wasn't something she was proud of. It was just survival.

She and her friend Jillian would laugh at the men while counting their pay. Jillian had shown her how to roll the bills and stash them in her bodice, in case someone accosted her on her way back to her miserable boardinghouse room. And it was Jillian who'd saved her from getting fired that one night, after a smelly customer pulled Daphne down and planted a wet kiss on her lips. Daphne reacted immediately, slapping him across the face. Normally the man would've just been thrown out, but he was a dock-master and a big spender at the bar. If not for Jillian cooling down the manager, Daphne would've been sent away without a second thought.

That night Daphne had been so unsettled that Jillian had walked her home through the drizzling rain, holding an umbrella over them the whole way. Daphne invited her in for a hot tea to warm up before she went onward. Somehow, Jillian made the sad little place feel a little more bright and merry. They hung up their wet dresses over the stove and had burrowed under Daphne's covers in their slips. Jillian convinced her to add a dash from her flask to their tea, and then . . .

Blandness. Pleasantries. Masks. It had gotten her hired at the restaurant. And perhaps it had made Horace fall in love with her. A hollow husk of a person, smiling in polite agreement — in their dining room, their parlor, their bed.

But in the world of spiritualism, a husk was a rare and precious thing. A husk could be a channel, could transmit great amounts of energy from one world to the next. And the feeling of power that swelled up — well, the only thing she could compare it to was those secret nights with Jillian.

Daphne had lost Jillian abruptly when her friend got a better-paying job at a café across town. Jillian promised to get Daphne a position there, too, but she disappeared. When Daphne went to visit her one evening, she was told that Jillian had left town with the cook.

Daphne hadn't had a choice about that ending. But now she did. When you had the opportunity to feel this level of energy, intensity — well, she wasn't just going to stop.

Florence was talking and Daphne was nodding, but she didn't really listen until Abigail moved closer and took her arm.

"We're worried about you." Abigail's soft words permeated her thoughts.

"But why?" Daphne asked, perplexed.

"Because . . ." Abigail's sweet, innocent face was pained. "Because you've changed."

From a hollow husk to something more? They were just like everyone else, wanting her to be whatever they most wanted to see, whatever they could control. Now that she was beginning to strengthen, they weren't happy about it.

"We're afraid this 'great commission' will be too much for you," Abigail went on. "You know these things tire you out. And this . . . creature."

"Her name is Lamia," Daphne said curtly.

"Lamia," Abigail echoed obediently. "She seems . . . well . . . angry."

Daphne hid a smile. Of course these women, wealthy from birth and unencumbered by a husband, didn't understand. They pretended to feel upset about the state of society, about the second-class citizenship of women — women with the same pallor of skin, at least. But they didn't know hardship. They'd never gone hungry, or had to kill rats under their beds with a fire poker, or had silently borne a man's weight as he pumped in and out, scraping their insides, making them bleed.

How could they possibly know what anger was?

It's why Lamia had come to her. Her and not them.

"So do you promise to stop?" Abigail's

desperate doe eyes filled with tears.

Oh, good lord. Jillian's remembered voice, amused and disgusted. If she were there, she'd throw her head back and laugh.

"I'm sorry." Daphne made herself look contrite, like a dog who knows she's been naughty. "I promise, I'll stop."

CHAPTER 18

That night I woke suddenly. I turned on my side, drifting through dreams like a boat casting off, until I heard it again.

Footsteps.

Slow and steady, they creaked as they came closer. I had a wild feeling of déjà vu: the dream with Wren. But this was real. I turned on my lamp. Blinking against the light, I listened to the sounds continue past my room. I slipped out of bed and cracked open the door. Someone was at the end of the hall, stepping around the corner.

The déjà vu only got stronger as I followed. Heart pounding, I crept down the hall and turned onto the landing. No one was there. I walked closer towards the banister. The same moonlight poured in through the front windows. I glanced nervously behind me, then forced myself to keep going until my hands grasped the railing.

There. Someone was going down the stairs, almost at the bottom. A figure in leggings and a dark sweatshirt with the hood pulled up. At the bottom they turned down the hall that led to the parlor, library, and kitchen.

It felt like some kind of sign that my dream had started the same way. Or maybe an invitation? Whatever was happening, I needed to find out. I hurried down the steps. In the hall, the figure — it had to be a she — was about twenty feet ahead of me. She passed the parlor, then the library. Her walk was slow and processional.

She entered the kitchen, heading straight to the door to the basement. I slowed by the butcher block as she opened it and flipped on the light. The tip of her nose poked out of her purple hoodie as she started down the stairs.

Wren's sweatshirt — but this figure was too short to be Wren.

Shoving away the fear, I ran to the stairwell.

"Hey." My voice was groggy and I cleared my throat. "Hey, wait."

The figure halted, one hand on the wooden bannister. Her nails were pink. I knew those nails.

"Poppy?" I said.

She turned around slowly.

I braced myself for a horrific sight: her face half–eaten away or her eyes glowing red.

But it was just her. Her large, walnut-colored eyes peered at me. And yet . . . it was like she didn't see me. It was like she was looking through me, like I didn't exist.

"What are you doing?" I ran down a few steps to clutch her arm. It felt reassuringly warm and solid in my grip.

She jerked away, and I gripped her harder to keep her from falling backwards.

"Poppy, it's me," I said. "Wake up."

She shrank away from me. Blinking, she looked around, young and scared.

"Where are we?" she asked in a thick voice.

"The steps to the basement." I shivered from the cold air rushing up past us.

"What?" Her shoulders were hunched.

"I think you're sleepwalking. You were, I mean."

"What?" She squinted, confused like an animal who'd been disturbed in her burrow.

"I followed you down here . . ." Seeing the look of incomprehension, I sighed. "Never mind. Let's just get you back up-stairs, okay?"

"Okay." She followed me closely, and I

felt suddenly protective of her. Gripping Poppy's hand, I led her back upstairs to her room. She went straight to her bed and climbed into it. In the dim moonlight from the windows, I saw Wren's sleeping figure.

I shut the door gently and went back to my room. Something still felt off. Feeling silly, I peeked in the wardrobe, under the bed, and even behind the shower curtain in the bathroom.

Just to be sure.

The last thing I saw before drifting off was Poppy's enormous eyes staring through me like I was a ghost.

CHAPTER 19

"Oh my god." Poppy's mouth hung open, showing a chewed lump of muffin. "Are you serious right now? Like, is this a joke?"

"No joke." I felt suddenly defensive at Poppy's disbelieving stare, as if she was accusing me of making it up. And as Poppy, Keira, and I breakfasted in the cheerful light of day, it did seem rather unlikely.

"You must've been so freaked out." Keira watched me.

"It was pretty creepy." I tried to smile. "And then I felt bad for waking you up. Well, half woke. You were pretty out of it. But I remembered after that you're not supposed to wake a sleepwalker."

"Wow." Poppy looked thoughtful and played with the cord of another of Wren's hoodies. They were apparently exchanging clothes now. "You know what? I used to sleepwalk a lot as a kid. And actually" — her eyes widened — "I think I used to go

256

down to the basement!"

"Yikes." Keira shook her head. "Your poor parents."

"Right?" Poppy raked a hand through her wavy hair. "I haven't thought about this in so long. My parents would hear me on the stairs and find me just standing down there in the dark. It freaked all of us out. They were even going to take me to a specialist because they were worried I'd hurt myself or wander outside or something. But then after a few weeks it just stopped."

"It is scary to think of what could've happened," I said, feeling anxious. "Like, what if you had fallen down the stairs and no one was there?"

"We could lock you inside your room, if you want." Keira said. "There's a key in the desk drawers."

"Good to know. Hopefully it won't get to that point." Poppy jumped up. "I'd better get back to work. But thanks for the support, ladies!" She tugged my ponytail as she walked by. "And thanks for rescuing me, Alex. You're the best."

"Sure." I watched her go, still feeling uneasy. I liked Poppy. Even though she and Wren were close, she'd never been anything other than friendly to me. It was even hard to imagine her telling Wren what I'd said that first day, when — according to Wren — I'd been "talking shit." Then again, part of my initial problem had been naivete, putting my trust in people who would, at some point, betray me.

"Bizarre, huh." Keira's voice broke into my thoughts.

I followed her gaze to the doorway. "You mean Poppy?"

"Yeah." She set down her toast. "She hasn't sleepwalked since she was a kid, and now it starts up again?"

"It was pretty disturbing," I said, "seeing her like that."

"You were up that late? Writing?"

"Oh, no. I woke up. I'm a pretty light sleeper."

"Any dreams?" Keira's gaze was intense. "Last night?"

"In general." She sighed. "I've been sleeping terribly. And having nightmares."

"About what?" I could only remember the sex dream, and I definitely wasn't sharing that.

"I'm not quite sure." She screwed up her eyes. "I just remember flashes. Being outside in the snow. I'm all wet and someone's dragging me by the arms. Then . . . being in this dark place. It's freezing. And there's this smell . . ."

I waited for her to go on, but after trailing off she stared at her plate.

"You okay?" I touched her arm and she jumped.

"Yeah." She smiled without teeth. "I'm fine. I'm just stressed-out, I think."

"It's a lot of pressure." This was one of the few times Keira had opened up to me, one of the few times we'd even been alone together.

"It is." She stood abruptly and went to the window. "There's a storm coming this weekend. Chitra told me yesterday. It's supposed to be pretty big."

Just as quickly as Keira had started opening up to me, she'd closed again. I felt a small tug of disappointment.

"A storm over Valentine's Day, huh?" I turned and looked out the window too. Snow had fallen the night before, and suddenly a branch shook and released a load onto the ground. "You think Roza will want to celebrate? Maybe she'll get us chocolates or something."

"Maybe." Keira looked back at me with a humorless smirk. "Just watch out for razor blades."

The next three days melted into each other, interchangeable and *Groundhog Day*–like.

Write, eat, meet, repeat. The only parts that stood out were our evenings in the parlor. Roza had given up on the games and let us talk. Rather, she talked, sharing tales of her extensive travels, including exploring the Odessa Catacombs in the Ukraine and the Island of the Dolls in Mexico City. Wren and I tolerated each other like two haughty cats, staying out of each other's way. After Roza, Taylor and Wren were the most loquacious, and even I found myself chuckling at some of Wren's more recent travel and work stories. The flickering candlelight and the wine got everyone into a relaxed, almost loopy state. I kept an eye on Keira, but though she remained somewhat reserved, she also seemed serene. I didn't want to ask about her nightmares in front of everyone, but I wondered if they'd stopped.

The day before Valentine's Day, it started to snow harder. At my desk, I watched the swirls of flakes fling themselves against the window. Daphne was about to meet Lamia. For some reason I felt nervous about writing the scene. I didn't want to mess it up.

"Hey!" Taylor leaned in my open door. "You busy?"

"I could use a break." I turned my chair around. "Come on in."

"Chitra just made oatmeal raisin cookies."

She strolled in and handed me one wrapped in a paper towel. "I had a feeling you might want a snack."

"I absolutely do. Thanks." I took it gratefully, my stomach rumbling at the buttery scent. I wondered why Taylor had really stopped by; it was the first time she'd sought me out.

"Almost halfway through the trip." Taylor settled on the floor, her back against the bed. "Can you believe it?"

"Not at all." I took a bite. "It's just flying by."

"How's the writing going?" She pushed back her blond hair. By now the vestiges of the green dye had disappeared.

"Good." I smiled. "Daphne's going to meet Lamia today."

"Oooh. The demoness?"

"Yup."

"Lucky." Taylor grinned.

"I don't know about that." I chuckled.

Taylor played with her gold necklace. She'd continued wearing it every day like a good-luck charm. "So what's your take on Daphne?"

I crossed my legs, leaning sideways against the seat back. "How do you mean?"

"Well." Taylor shrugged. "All the channeling stuff. Was she making it up? Or did she

261

really believe it?"

"It was real. I mean, to Daphne."

"So she was delusional? Or do you believe in Lamia too?"

I laughed. "That's a good question. In the book I play it straight: that Lamia is real, that she exists. That she's not just some figment of Daphne's imagination. And you know, Lamia *is* real in a sense. She was in the Greek myths, this woman who turned into a monster after Hera forced her to eat her own children."

"That's dark," Taylor said.

"Yeah. One of the books I looked at theorized that Daphne must've read about Lamia and connected with her because they were both childless and ostracized. When Daphne channeled Lamia, she was actually tapping into an unconscious and unacceptable part of her own self."

"That's an interesting theory." Taylor tilted her head.

"It is. But . . . I'm not sure if it's the full story. Part of me's satisfied with that explanation, and part of me's not. I don't know if I believe in female demons, necessarily. But you heard what happened to me in the woods. That thing — whatever it is — was *there*."

"So you think there may have been something supernatural going on."

"Maybe." I felt a tinge of embarrassment admitting this.

"Fair enough." Taylor nodded. "I was curious because I've heard that old-timey spiritualism was all just a way for women to gain power. Which is pretty fucked-up. That in order to have a voice they had to pretend to channel someone else's."

"I know." I rolled my eyes. "I can't imagine living back then."

Taylor stared at the ground, brooding. "I'm not convinced all that much has changed."

"No?"

"In some ways it has. I mean, when I was teaching in Austin it made me so relieved that my kids felt comfortable being gay or trans or whatever — and their parents were okay with it! Obviously, that's not true everywhere. But it was awesome. And just so different from what I experienced."

"What were you like in school?" I grinned. "You must've been cute."

"I was awkward as hell." She laughed. "I was also super Christian, if you can believe it."

"Really." I raised an eyebrow. "I was not expecting that."

"Yep. All the way through high school. My

main hang was with my church youth group. We'd go on these camping trips, and we'd sit around the fire and confess our sins. I always thought it was ridiculous that the boys would confess having 'unclean thoughts,' but the girls never did. I was already interested in girls but I just kept it all in and felt extremely guilty."

"That sounds tough." Mom had made my life difficult in a lot of ways, but one thing I could be grateful for was that she'd never shoved any religious rules down my throat.

"And here's the rub." Taylor wrapped her hands around her knees, a faraway look in her eyes. "When I was a senior, it came out that our youth pastor had been sleeping with a junior for at least a year. I remember we were all surprised because she wasn't even that pretty. And then everyone got mad at *her.* Him, too, obviously. He and his wife moved to another state. The age of consent was seventeen, so he hadn't done anything illegal. But this poor girl, Holly, she had to just deal with it. Everyone hated her guts, students *and* parents. She was the ugly whore who had somehow seduced him. And that was the thing that really shook me out of my religious fervor. I woke up and realized I'd been brainwashed. I was like: What the fuck are we doing? Why do we always have to take the blame?"

"That's messed up."

Taylor's face was drawn. She looked different, older, without her ubiquitous smile. "The saddest part is that she died by suicide. It was a year later, her senior year. Her parents found her in her closet. Apparently the online bullying just never stopped."

"Oh, no." My chest squeezed. "That's so sad."

"I know." Taylor cleared her throat. "Speaking of bullying, I actually came in here to tell you something. It's about Wren." She raised her eyes. "I heard her and Roza in the kitchen yesterday. Wren was talking about you."

"What'd she say?"

Taylor sucked on the inside of her cheek. "That you were obsessed with her for years. That she thought about taking out a restraining order on you multiple times. Especially after . . ." She looked down. "Especially after you pushed her off the steps at that party."

I exhaled, feeling suddenly dizzy and confused. So Wren had known my ugly intention on the steps this entire time? Or was she just saying it to Roza to make me look bad, not realizing it was kind of true?

"I know she's lying." Taylor shrugged.

"But you might want to make sure Roza knows."

Oh, Roza knew.

"Thanks for telling me," I said. "I appreciate that. And it feels good to know you have my back."

"No problem." Taylor scrunched her nose. "I hate mean girls."

Excerpt from *The Great Commission*

This had never happened before. Instead of speaking through Daphne, the creature now stood before her: a magnificent woman who had arrived from a distant universe.

She was nearly seven feet tall, her limbs long and muscular. Her body glowed a bright tangerine color and radiated heat. Silky hair flowed over her shoulders and covered her breasts. Her eyes were the most striking: colorless yet somehow full of color, glowing and hypnotic.

Daphne stood frozen and unable to speak. She wasn't terrified but in awe. The thought arose: *Who* are *you*?

And the woman responded inside her mind, the sound exploding like a bomb:

I am —

CHAPTER 20

"Happy Valentine's Day!" Taylor cried as I opened the door. Behind her, Keira blew a noisemaker.

I laughed. Taylor wore Poppy's pink sweater and had pinned paper hearts all over that said things like *Be My Sub, Whats Yr kink*?, and *Let's Fuck*!

I yearned to stay at my desk and continue writing about Daphne's meeting with Lamia. But it was cocktail hour. I knew the rules.

"Where did you get this stuff?" I asked as Keira handed me another noisemaker out of a plastic bag. She was wearing her usual all black but had added hot-pink lipstick.

"I bribed Chitra when she went out for supplies." Taylor wiggled her eyebrows, handing me a Mardi Gras–style necklace made of red plastic hearts. She also wore a headband of hearts that pushed back her short hair.

Odd that Taylor was making such a big deal out of the holiday, which I'd completely forgotten about. But then again, she was a teacher. I could picture her decorating her classroom and handing out valentines — though without the profanity.

"Honestly, it's just easier to go along with it." Keira pushed up her glasses and rubbed her eyes wearily.

"Hey!" Taylor cried. "Guys, life is dreary enough. We have to make our own fun. Right?"

"Sure, why not?" I went back to my desk to turn off the lamp and close my laptop. Outside, the wind was picking up. Snow lashed against the window in shimmering undulations.

"Al, are you wearing that?" Taylor motioned at my jeggings. "Let's jazz it up a little, huh?"

"Yeah, look at me!" Poppy appeared behind Taylor and Keira. She was already wearing a cheap heart-laden necklace, in addition to a scarlet dress and lipstick. Her blond hair settled against her shoulders in perfect waves.

"Did you bring that dress specifically for Valentine's Day?" I asked.

"Ew, no. I totally hate this holiday normally, but we're at Roza Vallo's!" Poppy hopped up and down. "I mean, best Valentine's Day ever, right?"

"Can't argue with that." I pulled off my jeggings, ignoring a twinge of embarrassment that I was changing in front of everyone, and pulled on black pants and a ruby sweater.

"Where's Wren?" Taylor asked Poppy.

"Oh, she's not feeling well." Poppy twisted her mouth in sympathy. "She has a cold."

"Uh-uh." Taylor whirled around. "V-Day is nonnegotiable. I'll meet you bitches down there."

In the parlor, paper heart streamers were draped over various animal heads, giving them a festive air. Red pillar candles flickered from the coffee table. The lights had been dimmed, and it felt much later than 6:30. The side table held different types of cookies — homemade by Chitra, it looked like — and a large crystal punch bowl. Six gleaming goblets waited beside it.

"Wow," I said. "Taylor, did you do all this?"

"With Chitra's help." Taylor went right to the punch and began ladling out glasses of the pink liquid. "Is it a bit much? Perhaps. Could I be going slightly insane after being stuck inside, writing my brains out for two straight weeks? Really, who's to say?"

I took a glass and drifted to the window. The reflection from the fire sparkled in the middle of a pane like an outside apparition. The wind roared, a dull insistence. Suddenly music came on, a jazzy song with a woman singing low and throaty.

The punch was fruity and flavorful but not too sweet. I couldn't even taste the alcohol.

A pitiful cough made me turn. Wren entered the room, sans makeup, looking miserable. I felt a mixture of irritation and amusement. Wren didn't often get sick, but when she did, it was the Worst Illness of All Time. It had amazed me that someone so seemingly strong could fall apart from a mild cold.

She fell dramatically onto the couch. Remembering what Taylor had told me, I felt a wave of dull fury.

How could she have lied to Roza that she'd considered taking out a restraining order against me? That I'd been obsessed with her for years?

Unless . . . had she really believed that? Wren was good at rewriting stories in her mind so as not to have any responsibility. But even for Wren it seemed extreme.

"How are you doing, sickie?" Taylor called,

still ladling.

"Not great." She sniffed. I half expected her to throw a hand over her brow.

Poppy went to her with an extra glass. "You want to taste? It's really good. I don't think it's that strong."

For a second it looked like Wren was going to refuse, staring at the glass suspiciously, but then she grabbed it and took a sip.

"Good evening, ladies." Roza swept in wearing a clinging floor-length black dress. Her hair was pinned back and she looked like a high priestess from the Middle Ages. I tried to tamp down my anger. Wren was not going to make me lose it again in front of Roza.

Behind Roza, Chitra carried two trays of candy — gummy bears and candy hearts — to the table, greeting us affably.

"Chitra, can you stay and hang out?" Taylor asked.

"I wish. But I need to go and finish dinner preparations." She gave Taylor a playful wink.

Roza sat at her normal place in the red chair nearest the fireplace. She accepted the glass from Taylor without looking at her. Taylor plopped into the chair next to her, appearing a bit put out — presumably that

Roza hadn't appreciated or even noticed her creative outfit.

Poppy sat next to Wren on the couch, and Keira and I settled onto the love seat.

"And so we reach the midpoint." Roza grinned. She turned, noticing Taylor's shirt. "Oh, my, what's this?"

Taylor straightened her paper-coated sweater and smiled proudly. Roza gave a little laugh. "Brilliant. How appropriate it is that we get to be together on the traditional day of love." Roza's makeup made her even more striking than usual.

"Does everyone know the true story of Valentine's Day?" Taylor asked in her snooty faux–English teaching voice.

Roza smiled and gestured. "Do tell, darling."

"Well, it started in ancient Rome," Taylor said in her normal voice. "In those days the Romans celebrated a festival called Lupercalia. It fell over a few days in mid-February. And it was pretty kinky." She moved her head from side to side. "The strong, hunky men would sacrifice animals and use the hides to whip the ladies. They thought it bestowed fertility. And" — she gestured with her glass — "they had a fun little lottery where the guys would pull female names to have a . . . *companion,* shall we say, for the rest of the feast."

"A true bacchanalia." Roza beamed.

"But where did the name Valentine come from?" I asked.

"Good question. It was the Catholics. They actually martyred a couple different Valentines. And seeing as how they liked to reclaim pagan holidays, they decided to just go with it." Taylor raised her glass and drained it. "You've got to hand it to them, naming a fun new holiday after people you've murdered is pretty bold."

"Gross," Poppy said.

Taylor jumped up with her empty glass, eyes on the punch bowl.

"That's enough," Roza said sharply. Taylor froze, her mouth slightly agape.

"You don't want more than one glass," Roza said more kindly.

"Why not?" Keira asked, stifling a yawn.

"There's a special Valentine's Day ingredient." Roza pulled up her feet to sit cross-legged. The dark dress fluttered over her lap.

"There is?" Poppy held up her nearly empty glass. Mine was empty, too, with just a pink crystalline drop rolling at the bottom.

"Wait, what?" Keira straightened. "You put something in the punch?"

I looked around; Wren's drink was nearly gone. Keira had the most left, maybe a half inch.

Roza tapped at her empty glass. "Ladies, do you trust me?"

My stomach dipped like I'd been walking on solid ground only to find my foot plunging through air.

"Actually, no." Keira set the glass on the coffee table. Her face was a mask.

"Oh, darling." Roza gazed at her. "You know how much I care for you all. That I would never do anything to hurt you."

"Okay, what's going on?" Poppy asked, sounding uneasy. Wren sniffled into her tissue, looking befuddled.

"But my goal is to make you better." Roza's smile dropped away. "The process is not always enjoyable or easy. In fact, it can — and should — be very painful. I've noticed that as we reach our midpoints, we're all feeling *much* too comfortable. We're not taking risks. We're not pushing ourselves. We need to go deeper. We need to let go."

"So . . ." Keira indicated her glass. "What does that have to do with the punch?"

"Did you drug us?" Taylor asked. In the stunned silence, she let out a laugh. "You drugged us!"

"You make it sound so predatory." Roza rolled her eyes.

The information took a second to sink in. I felt dazed as I set the glass on a side table. Did I feel drugged? I couldn't tell. I felt off, but then again the whole situation felt off. It brought me back to college, to the mantras we all knew. *Don't leave your drink unattended. Don't let a guy buy a drink for you.*

A hysterical thought arose: *Who would've thought my first drugging would be from my feminist heroine?*

"Roza, I'm sorry, but this is not okay." Keira's sharp voice broke through. "It's unethical, not to mention illegal." For once, Keira's careful guard was down. Her face was tight with anger, her hands curled into fists.

"Well, darling." Roza seemed unfazed. "We could discuss the ethical implications, certainly. But it's not illegal. You all signed the paperwork. You agreed to fully participate in this retreat."

" 'Participate'?" Keira scoffed. "Are you serious right now?"

"What's in it?" Taylor asked.

Wren, Poppy, and I turned to her. The three of us were the audience for the time being, stunned and wide-eyed.

"Not a downer, I'm guessing." Taylor

actually grinned. "That doesn't seem like it'd boost our creativity."

"Taylor . . . ," Keira started but Taylor raised a hand.

"I'm sorry, K, but this is fucking awesome." Taylor slapped the arm of her chair. "It's LSD, isn't it? LSD drops?"

Roza nodded. "Yes."

"Wait, *what*?" Keira touched her temples. "You drugged us with *LSD*?"

"I know you're upset now" — Roza smiled softly — "but you will thank me for this."

"You think I'm going to thank you for lacing my *drink*?"

"Keira," Taylor pleaded. "Just —"

"You know, I should've seen this coming," Keira interrupted. "You're Roza Vallo, you're out there, that's your thing, right? But this . . ." She pointed a shaking hand at her glass. "You're using us, Roza. You're using *me*. And that's not okay."

"K, calm down," Taylor pleaded

Keira's eyebrows shot up. "You're honestly telling me to calm down right now?"

Taylor gestured. "No one else is upset."

"Okay, fine." Keira smiled, humorless. "I'm just the angry Black woman, and the rest of you are all just great with this."

"We're not," Wren said in a phlegmy voice. She cleared her throat. "I'm not. This

277

is definitely not okay."

I remembered now: Wren had a fear of drugs because her uncle had overdosed. Our one LSD trip together had been a huge exception.

"I mean, we've all tripped before, haven't we?" Taylor asked.

"I haven't," Poppy said.

"Keira?" Taylor asked.

Keira glared at her. "It doesn't matter if I've tripped before or not. You get that, don't you?"

"Honestly" — Taylor shrugged — "I'm sorry, but I really don't think it's that big a deal."

Keira stood up. "I can't deal with this right now. I'm going upstairs."

"You're going to trip alone?" Taylor asked. "Are you sure?"

"Not like I have a choice." Keira threw up her hands.

"Of course you do! Stay here. We'll all trip together. It's going to be amazing."

Keira shook her head sadly. "I really can't believe you, Taylor."

"Fine. Whatever." Taylor fell back into her chair. "Go upstairs. Try to make yourself throw up. Do what you need to do."

"We'll be down here if you change your mind," Roza spoke up genially.

With a final head shake, Keira swiftly left the room.

The wind picked up and howled, rattling the windowpanes.

"Well," Roza said finally. "That was unfortunate."

"This is fucked-up." Poppy said it quietly, but we all turned to her. I couldn't remember if I'd ever heard her swear before.

"She's right, Roza." Wren swiped at her nose with a tissue. "I did not sign up for this."

"I know my methods are a little unorthodox," Roza said. "But I am truly helping you open your minds. In a safe environment, no less."

"Poppy, you're a newbie." Taylor leaned forward. "That's good to know. Wren, Alex? Have you tripped before?"

"Once," Wren replied.

We'd done it together, five years before, at a massive SoHo loft party. Wren and I lounged on the king-sized bed, on the pile of coats. It felt like a boat drifting through the night, and we laughed at the characters who would sit down and chat with us.

"Once," I echoed when Taylor looked at me.

"Okay, then." Taylor sat in between Poppy and Wren on the couch. "Well, since this is happening, whether we like it or not, let's try to get into a good headspace. Okay?"

"What about Keira?" I asked.

"What about her?" Roza gazed at me.

"I mean . . . I feel bad. She's alone."

"Her choice." Roza shrugged.

But it wasn't *her choice.*

What was there to do? As Taylor had said, this was happening whether we liked it or not.

The next day, when this was all over, I would invite the others into the parlor and we would have a serious discussion. We would go to Roza with our concerns. Maybe we would even rise up against her, take a day off from writing in order to punish her for her disturbing actions. It's not like she would kick *all* of us out.

For now, though, I had to focus. If there was one thing I didn't want to experience, it was a bad LSD trip at Blackbriar. So I tried to breathe, to calm myself. Every minute or so the thought would arise: *Do I feel it now?* It was like pausing at the top of a roller-coaster ride, waiting for the plunge.

And then, at some point, I *was* feeling it. The fire in the fireplace became brighter, alive.

"Do you see that?" Taylor asked, and went

to the window.

I looked at Wren and she was gazing at me. And I knew she was thinking about the loft party, the bed. That same sliding feeling of timelessness arose. I realized Taylor was talking but I hadn't been listening.

It's going to be okay, I tried to transmit to Wren. I wondered if she was more scared than me.

Whoa. When had everyone moved? Taylor was at the buffet table, staring at the candy. Roza was sitting in front of the fire with Wren. Poppy was still on the couch. She looked somewhat perturbed, as if she was trying to remember something.

I got up and looked out the window. The snowflakes sparkled in the light shining out from the parlor, tinged with a neon purple color. For a while I was lost in them, my nose pressed against the glass. The snow went on forever out there.

"Alex." Poppy's hand was on my arm. Her large brown eyes were so dilated that I could've waded into them. "Can you come with me?"

"Sure." I really didn't want to leave the snow, but this seemed important. "What's up?"

"I have to show you something."

"Of course." But as we left I wondered:

281

Why was she asking me instead of Wren?

Wren and Roza were huddled near the fire, as if discussing a secret plan.

"We're going to the bathroom," Poppy announced. Maybe unnecessarily, because no one seemed to notice. Taylor was lying on the couch.

The room felt full suddenly, like the site of a full-blown party: I could hear the glasses clinking, little groups murmuring here and there. As Poppy pulled me along, a realization struck: it was a party that Daphne and Horace had thrown. The linear dimension of time was breaking down, the boundaries thinning. I could hear Horace's voice, loud and deep. A woman laughing flirtatiously in response. Was Daphne here? I couldn't sense her. But then, where was she?

In the hall it was mercifully still, though the party sounds inside the parlor were increasing: there came a shout, resulting laughter, the sound of breaking glass.

"Great party, isn't it?" I said coyly, but Poppy ignored me, marching us down the hall. The paintings were moving and I slowed to gaze at the dead cow in the field. It had raised its head and was mouthing something at me that I strained to understand.

"Come on, Alex." Poppy sounded frustrated. "I have to show you before it's too late."

"Okay, sorry." I allowed myself to be dragged along. We burst into the kitchen. The shiny, flat surfaces felt shockingly severe. There were multiple pots and pans on the stove, burbling merrily. Where was Chitra?

"We're going down." Poppy opened the basement door.

I stopped short. The first few cement steps leading down into the darkness looked ugly and menacing. "Wait — why?"

"I have to show you something. I think I found it." Her voice held both determination and a hint of glee.

"Found what?" The conversation felt increasingly hard to follow. I was Alice in Wonderland, trying earnestly to gather information and getting only mystical riddles in return.

"I'll show you." She switched on the light and started down. When I didn't follow, she tugged at my hand like an insolent child.

"Poppy, this is freaking me out." Her pulling was making me bend forward. "Basements are creepy. Especially this one." I suddenly remembered the candle game, the flash behind me in the mirror, the candle going dark. I'd accepted that it had just been my imagination, simply drafts moving sheets around and blowing candles out. But now, when the worlds were bumping up against each other, it felt possible that something really had been down there.

"Do you want to see it or not?" Poppy hissed. "Hurry up, before Chitra gets back."

Sounds drifted up from the basement — a woman talking, very seriously, her voice echoing. "There's someone down there."

"There might be." Poppy said it grimly. "Come on. You're the only person I can show."

"Why?"

"Because you already know."

"Know what?"

"All of it. You suspect, at least."

It felt slightly embarrassing that I had no idea what she was talking about. Then another thought arose.

"What about Wren?" I asked. Somehow the fact that she was showing me and not Wren caused me to finally start a slow descent. "Isn't she your bestie? You didn't tell her?"

"Of course not," Poppy said.

Halfway down the steps, the woman in the basement's voice switched to a whisper. Daphne? Was she down there, away from the party? The cold rushed up at us and I shivered.

"So what are you showing me?" I asked.

"Proof," Poppy declared.

"Proof of what?"

"Of what she does. That she's not who she claims to be."

We stopped at the bottom of the steps. Poppy bit her bottom lip as she turned on the light. No whispers. I imagined Daphne watching us, hiding behind a stack of boxes. Maybe we looked like ghosts to her. Ghosts decked out in red clothes and shiny heart necklaces.

Poppy let go of my hand. "Over here." She strode towards the left. "It's this wall."

A sound came from the right. A single footstep. Then a brief exhale.

Not Daphne. It was too large. Much larger than Poppy or me.

I froze, struggling to listen. Then came slow, deliberate steps scraping against the cement floor. It was moving away from us.

Poppy was by now out of sight to my left. It sounded like she was moving boxes around and muttering to herself.

"Alex." The whisper came from the right, from deeper in the maze.

I would've expected to be more scared. But as it was, I just felt curious. This creature had tried to communicate with me before, during the ghost story game. But I'd run off before it could speak.

Now I followed it deeper into the basement, past towering stacks of boxes and sheet-covered furniture. The space was a winding labyrinth, lying underneath the house like its unconscious mind. It was pitch-black now, but I somehow knew the way.

A small hand slipped into mine. It was Christina, my best friend with the butt-length hair, and we were again lost in the woods. Only this time we were moving *towards* the creature, not away from it. The cement floor was now a spongy path of rotting leaves. Leaves and branches scraped against my arms and I pushed them away.

Christina was ahead of me, pulling me behind her. I couldn't see her in the dark, but I got a whiff of the vanilla body spray she'd loved. I felt a rush of grief, as if she were dead, even though she was right in front of me.

Christina had been the friend I'd had the longest. When I'd had a real life, a mom and dad and house and neighborhood. After the woods, it had all been ripped away.

"I missed you," I told her, and she squeezed my hand.

We came to the clearing. I couldn't see it but I could sense it. Christina let go of my hand and I gasped.

"Wait, no!" I whispered.

And then gentle hands — many sets of them — took hold of my arms and led me to a couch. A couch in the middle of the clearing! An owl hooted and crickets chirped all around.

"What is happening?" I asked. The moon came out from behind a cloud and I could see: the short, soft-handed creatures were all wearing hoods.

Christina had fled; she was gone, back into the woods. But I felt excited and triumphant. We'd missed the opportunity to behold something incredible all those years before. But now it had brought me here. It was giving me a second chance.

And then she appeared, lit up like a neon sign. Cross-legged, she still rose above me. Her arms and legs were the size of tree trunks; her bare breasts large as basketballs. Her body glowed orange-red like a furnace.

Lamia.

The whispers fell silent. A great and terrible beauty emanated from her, a power so palpable, it surged off her in waves. She could kill me with the flick of a finger. And yet she was conscious of it, her strength and my lack. She felt only love and tenderness for me.

She stood, shrinking down until she was my size, and came closer. Heat poured from her like she was the sun. We stood face-to-face. Her eyes glowed, constantly changing color.

And then I stepped forward and kissed her.

The heat from her lips spread through my body. She grabbed my hips, pulling me towards her, and her touch burned through my skin and muscles and bone. She slipped her hand into my hair, gripping the back of my head.

The hooded creatures that had led me to the couch were back, surrounding me and taking off my clothes. I acquiesced, shifting my hips and lifting up my arms. I was now naked before her. She yanked me back to her, her tongue like a burning coal in my mouth.

And still I kissed her back. I longed to be consumed. There came the distinct thought that I might not survive this encounter. And that would be okay. Wonderful, in fact. She was life and death itself, and both were the same, really, just two sides of the same coin. And what was here in this world, anyway? Betrayal, disappointment, failure. Maybe the next world would burn it all away.

I was encased in flames now, miraculously unharmed. I exhaled as she embraced me. Her bare flesh was smooth and so hot it was cool again. A flat palm caressed my hair. A tongue flicked at my neck. A finger trailed down my breast, over my nipple. Kissing and caressing her back, I squeezed my eyes shut. If I opened them — if I really looked into the depths of her own kaleidoscopic eyes — then it would all be over.

The hushed whispers around us settled into chants. The creatures were watching us, protecting us, worshipping us. The chants undulated like a wave, in time with our strokes. They intensified as our soft touches turned to grasps. I reached between her thighs. She took my hand away.

First, you. The words appeared in my mind, alien sounding, like another language I could somehow understand.

She pulled me onto the couch. She was above me, below me, all around, enclosing me. It was like she had extra limbs, curling me into her like a spider. Her fingers slipped against me, inside me. Everything went red behind my eyes. Time fell away.

And then I was on the verge of orgasm. But I held back. If I let myself go, I'd become hers. The chants had risen to shouts. I undulated my hips and clenched my jaw. Physical release would mean I was signing a contract, bonding myself to her forever. There would be no escape.

Words arose, and I didn't know if they were from her or me:

Wouldn't that be a relief?

When I came, the waves of pleasure seemed to go on forever, washing me clean. Now we floated in a great void. A buzzing hum surrounded us as thickly as wool. Her power had filled me, and until she moved I thought we'd merged into one.

She could've obliterated me if she wanted to. But she'd shown mercy instead.

"Thank you," I breathed, quivering with gratitude, though my voice fell away in the blankness. And then she reached for me and we were melting together, our bodies their own swirling universe, and as I kissed down her glowing belly, all was fated and right.

■ ■ ■ ■

PART THREE:
THE BASEMENT

■ ■ ■ ■

CHAPTER 21

I woke slowly, consciousness seeping in like fog. I moved my legs, feeling my silky sheets catch against fabric. I was still wearing my clothes from the night before.

The quiet felt ominous. I finally sat up, groggy, blinking against sunlight bursting in from the windows. I slipped out of bed and padded to the desk. The wide expanse of the backyard was covered in huge snow-drifts. Beyond, the forest glittered, a spar-kling white layer clinging to every branch and twig.

Slumping in my desk chair, I rubbed my eyes, trying to sort out the night before. The last thing I remembered was being in the basement with Poppy. She'd wanted to show me something. And then I'd happened upon . . . well, Lamia.

Had I fallen asleep in the basement and dreamed it? Or was it possible to have an LSD-induced hallucination that was that intense and realistic? And why didn't I remember going back to my room?

I took a quick shower and headed to the kitchen, suddenly desperate to see other people. The *Twilight Zone*–esque thought came to me as I hopped down the stairs: What if everyone had disappeared? What if I found myself alone at Blackbriar, haunted by an erotic yet terrifying demoness?

"Hey!" Taylor sat at the table, wearing her LET ME LIVE sweatshirt. Her short blond hair was messy enough to resemble a Mohawk. She gave me a lazy grin. "How you feeling?"

"I'm okay." I grabbed some coffee and sat a few seats away. "Pretty out of it. How about you?"

"I'm good." She took a bite of oatmeal and chewed. "Wild night, huh?"

"Yeah. Really wild." I slurped my coffee.

"What was the best part?" she asked.

I shook my head. I didn't want to sound cagey, but I also didn't want to reveal quite how fucked-up I'd been. I imagined Taylor's response: *Wow, you* clearly *needed to get laid, huh*?

First Pete, then the dream with Wren, now this. Why did all my sexual experiences have to leave me feeling confusion and shame?

"It was all kind of a blur." I forced myself

to smile. "In a fun way. How about you?"

"Right on. Yeah, it was fun." Taylor swirled her spoon. "I was tripping balls, man."

"Me too."

"Oh, hey." Taylor's brow knit. "Where did you and Poppy go? Upstairs? You weren't at dinner."

"Yeah." At some point I *had* gone back upstairs. No need to get into the whole complicated story of why Poppy and I had gone into the basement when I didn't know myself.

"Huh." She rubbed her forehead. "Well, I don't know about you, but I have no fucking clue how I'm going to write three thousand words today. But there are no days off in Roza's house."

"God, me neither." The coffee was at least starting to help me feel less hazy. "Have you seen Keira?"

"Yeah." Taylor grimaced. "She's still pissed. Apparently she had a pretty bad trip up alone in her room."

"That's too bad." I made a mental note to go check on her.

Taylor indicated the window. "Did you see the snow? Almost four feet."

"Really? In one night?" I jumped up to look outside. The glittering drifts almost reached the bottom of the pane.

"Yeah. It's been nonstop until now, basically. And it took out the power too. We're running on generators."

"And the phone?" A metallic panic rose in my throat. I tried to push it back down. This anxiety had to be a chemical aftereffect of the drug.

"Down too." She picked up a piece of toast. "Don't worry. It happens all the time up here, apparently. It'll be fixed soon, I'm sure."

"Great." I bobbed my head. It felt necessary — important, even — to pretend that everything was fine.

"Alex." Wren stood in my doorway. I'd been attempting to write for the past hour but no words would come. That feeling of doom had continued, nibbling away at me like tiny fish.

I whirled around, caught off guard. Wren was still in her pajamas, a matching tie-dye sweatshirt and sweatpants. Her forehead was lined, eyes wide with worry.

"What?" I asked, suddenly nervous. Wren and I had ignored each other since our argument. Her coming to me must mean that something was seriously wrong.

"I can't find Poppy." She perched on the edge of my bed.

"Poppy?" I echoed. "You haven't seen her?"

"When I went to bed, she wasn't there. And when I woke up she was still missing. I just checked the whole house and I can't find her."

I realized I was holding my breath and forced an exhale. No reason to panic yet. No reason to think that the hidden thing causing the foreboding was now coming into focus.

"She has to be somewhere," I said. "Did you check the basement? She and I went down there last night."

"You did?" She jumped up. "Let's go look."

Grabbing my phone, I followed Wren down the hall, trying to reason with myself. This unease was simply caused by chemicals, a depletion of dopamine or whatever that the LSD had used up. Poppy was almost certainly curled up in the basement where I'd left her. Wren was freaked out because Poppy was her new little codependent BFF and because she'd also been left jittery by the drug's aftereffects.

Now I regretted wandering away from Poppy, drawn in by my hallucinations. She'd wanted to show me something — but what?

That secret, too, was now tinged with un-ease.

In the kitchen, Chitra was chopping something at a cutting board. "Good morning!" She grinned. "Back from your trip?"

"Yep." Wren glanced at me. Did Chitra know it hadn't been our choice?

"Everything okay?" Chitra looked back and forth between us.

"That's what we're trying to figure out." I opened the basement door.

"Where are you going?" Chitra's sharp tone stopped me.

"We can't find Poppy," I said. "And she and I went down there last night."

"Well, be careful." Chitra turned back to the counter. "I've always said that door should be locked. There's too much junk down there and not enough light. Someone could get hurt."

"Shit," Wren muttered as we started down the stairs.

"Poppy?" I called as we reached the bottom. "Are you down here?" The basement was even more frigid than I remembered. I turned on the light.

"So she went over there." I pointed towards the left. "That wall. And she was pushing boxes around for some reason. And I went this way." I pointed to the right.

"Why?" Wren sounded suspicious.

"I don't know. I was tripping." I shrugged. "I got distracted and wandered off."

"Why did you come down here to begin with?" Her eyes gleamed in the dim light.

"Poppy wanted to show me something."

"What?"

"She didn't say." I turned abruptly. "I'll look over here, where I went. Why don't you go over there, by the wall?"

Using my phone's flashlight to see, I wound through the stacked boxes and furniture. Last night had felt so momentous, operatic, stepping from the cement floor into a magical forest. But now it just looked like any other dusty basement filled with shit. At least it felt slightly warmer over here.

One of the little paths opened up into a wider space. A black leather couch sat in the middle. Was this the "clearing" I'd come across last night?

I remembered holding Christina's hand, how *real* it had felt. The chanting creatures, the demoness . . . had I really just been lying here alone, fucked-up and masturbating?

My shoe kicked something that went skittering across the floor. I went after it, searching amongst shadows until I spotted something glint under the couch.

It was a tube of peppermint lip balm.

"Alex!" Wren's panicked voice tore my attention away.

"Be right there!" Slipping it into my pocket, I hurried towards her.

Wren ran up to me when I reached the stairs. "Oh my god!" She clutched my arms, on the verge of sobbing. "Oh my god, Alex, oh my god." She dragged me away from the stairs, towards the back wall. We wound through more tall stacks of boxes that obscured the view. Something white and fragile blew past. At first I thought it was a piece of cobweb, but then it dissolved. We rounded a covered wardrobe and I halted abruptly.

Half-hidden behind the wardrobe was an open door. Beyond, snow-covered cement steps rose up into sunlight. Flakes drifted in, creating a small hill just inside the doorway.

"Do you see it?" Wren pointed with one shaking finger.

I stepped closer. My heart thrummed so intensely it felt on the verge of exploding.

Yes, I could see it. I pressed my arms against my chest, shaking from cold and fear and shock.

In the snow that covered the cement stairs, there were indentations, shallow but

unmistakable.
   Footprints.

Chapter 22

I turned back to Wren but she was already gone. I heard her pounding up the basement steps, yelling, nearly shrieking.

I sank down into a crouch, feeling suddenly light-headed.

My parents were going to take me to a specialist because they were worried I'd hurt myself or wander outside or something.

Poppy the sleepwalker had sleepwalked outside.

Had she done it while tripping, in a dreamlike state, or after she'd fallen asleep? It could have been either. As I stood there, frigid water seeping into my socks, it struck me that this was the horrible news I'd been dreading ever since I woke up.

My feet sank into the imprints as I climbed the steps, the frosty wind snatching at my clothes and hair.

"Poppy?" I could barely get the strangled word out of my throat. The back lawn was an expanse of white. I forced myself to scan for lumps.

"Alex!" Chitra was calling from inside. "Come back. You'll freeze."

I examined the landscape once more. Nothing. In a daze, I came back inside. Chitra's face was distorted with fear. She pulled me away from the doorway and shut the door.

"No!" I cried, but Chitra held fast to my arm.

"She's not coming back that way, love." Chitra's voice was grim.

"Do you think she's okay?" I asked. The dread had broken into a raging gale, ravaging my insides.

"I don't know." Chitra pulled at me. "But standing here dripping wet isn't going to help. Let's go back up."

When we reached the kitchen, Taylor was just entering the room, Yana and Wren close behind her.

"I need to see." Taylor hurried down the steps but Yana and Wren stayed. Wren's face was blotchy, her eyes red. Yana looked the same as Chitra: lips pressed together, eyes opaque and calculating. She kept smoothing back her tight ponytail.

"This can't be happening," Wren said loudly.

I went to the window and looked out. Had Poppy made it to the trees? If so, her trail was long filled in. The only reason the footprints were still visible was because the concrete steps down to the basement were partially protected from the wind. I felt detached, like we were working on a math problem: If a 98.6-degree human wanders out into subzero temps in a drug-altered state, how long before they slip into unconsciousness?

"We need to go look." Chitra watched Yana as if she were the leader. "Right?"

Yana gave a brief nod and left.

Steps pounded up the basement stairs.

"Okay." Taylor burst in, energized as an action hero. "We need to do a search. We'll get Roza and Keira and then we'll split up the yard."

In the front hall, Yana was bringing out our boots and coats and leaving them in a pile. Chitra and Taylor hurried upstairs to get the other two.

Wren and I sat on the floor to lace up our boots.

"This is so messed up," I muttered.

Wren stared at me, her blue eyes glassy. I'd seen her look like this only once before: when she'd gotten the call about her second cousin. The one who'd gone to bed and never woke up, clutching an empty pill bottle.

"We'll find her." My words sounded false even to me.

Wren gulped. "But what if she's dead?"

If she's outside, then, yeah. But I couldn't say it, nor believe it. Maybe there was a chance. Weren't there stories of people making little igloos for themselves, surviving snowstorms overnight?

Chitra and Taylor came back down the stairs, followed by Keira and Roza. Keira was still in her pajamas — pants and a button-up top covered in stylized English bulldogs. She looked dazed. Roza hurried a few steps behind, fully dressed, her brow knit with worry.

"How long has she been out there?" Roza grabbed her boots.

Wren choked back a sob.

"We don't know," I said. "We just saw those footsteps going outside. Maybe she circled back? The front door?"

"We keep the front door locked," Yana said.

Keira turned to Roza. "Did you call the police?"

"The phone's out." Taylor stood, bundled up and ready to go.

"Radio?" Yana glanced at Roza, who nodded. Yana hurried out.

"What is happening?" Keira muttered. She held her face in her hands, then cried: "You happy, Roza? Is this enough suffering for you?"

Heading to the door, Roza didn't respond.

Three hours later, we sat in the parlor drinking coffee. It felt wrong, too eerily sedate, after the panicked activity of the morning and early afternoon.

We'd searched outside first. The fresh snow was powdery and we sank in up to our knees. It was almost impossible to walk around. We checked around the basement steps, but found nothing: including, thankfully, no human-sized, snow-covered masses.

I'd perked up briefly when Yana — wearing snowshoes she'd somehow come up with — went to check the garage, a separate building from the mansion. But she came back alone. Eventually we went back inside, then searched the house, just in case Poppy had come back and passed out somewhere. We checked every closet, every bathtub, behind every curtain. It had been strange searching rooms I'd never before gone into: extra bedrooms, decorated similarly to ours; another study, outlined in bookshelves.

Yana had offered to search the attic, a

306

space that I hadn't even considered. Taylor took the basement. Both came back grim, covered in dust and spiderwebs.

No Poppy.

Yana had radioed the police and they said they'd be here as soon as they could. Now Wren was crying anguished tears while the rest of us sat stone-faced, staring into our coffee cups. Taylor held a cookie halfway to her mouth, forgotten. Chitra had returned to the kitchen but Yana remained, standing by a window, peering out as if Poppy might suddenly appear. Roza stared into the fire, her eyes rimmed with red. She'd barely said a word the entire day. Keira was glaring at her through smudged lenses.

"This is your fault, you know." Keira's low voice broke the silence.

Roza's eyes flicked to her.

"Keira." Taylor sounded weary.

"No." Keira's eyes blazed. "I'm done keeping things in. I knew something was wrong here. And now look what's happened."

"It was an accident," Roza said softly.

Keira shook her head. "If she hadn't been *drugged,* she wouldn't have wandered outside."

"She might've." The words popped out. Everyone turned to me. "I mean," I went on, feeling slightly embarrassed, "I'm just thinking about that night she sleepwalked into the basement. Maybe she sleepwalked outside."

"That's right." Taylor gazed at me thoughtfully. "You followed her into the basement that night. And . . ." She cocked her head. "Were you with her last night, too?"

"Yeah." Everyone was now watching me, even Yana from the window.

"Where were you?" Keira asked.

"She said she had something to show me in the basement." My stomach tightened. Their suspicious gazes made me feel anxious — guilty, even — like I'd done something wrong. Even though I knew, logically, that I hadn't.

"What did she show you?" Taylor asked.

"Nothing." I shrugged. "At least, I didn't see anything. I just heard her moving boxes around, near the wall to the left."

"You heard? Where were *you*?" Keira asked.

How could — or should — I explain the hallucination?

"I went in the other direction, to the other side of the basement." I cleared my throat. "I thought someone was calling to me."

"Someone was calling you?" Taylor asked.

"Who?"

"No. I — I think I was just hallucinating."

"When did you go back upstairs?" Keira asked. It was like she and Taylor were suddenly detectives, studying my every twitch and blink.

"I . . ." I faltered. If I admitted I couldn't remember, what good would that do? It wasn't like I'd pushed Poppy outside. I knew I wouldn't do something like that, even while tripping. But would the others believe me? Would Wren?

"I fell asleep for a while on a couch," I said. "Then I woke up and went to my room."

"And was the door open?" Keira leaned forward. "You would've felt the cold, right?"

"I don't know. I don't think it was open."

"When are the police coming?" Wren asked suddenly, her voice flat.

"They'll be here as soon as they can," Taylor said soothingly. "The roads are closed, so they're sending people on snowmobiles."

"They'd better come soon," Keira muttered.

The late-afternoon light was already shifting, turning orange as the sun sunk in the sky.

The minutes and then hours ticked by. Chitra brought out cold cuts and snacks around three, but no one ate. Yana and Roza went to radio the police again and came back with identical scowls.

"They're not going to make it tonight." Roza gripped the back of a chair.

"What?" Keira cried.

"They had to rescue a family whose generator stopped. They have a baby." Roza's knuckles were white. "They said they'd come tomorrow morning."

"Baby trumps dead girl," Taylor said.

Wren stared at her in horror. Keira dropped her head into her arms with a moan.

Panic rose, breaking through the icy numbness. I jumped up and realized everyone was staring at me.

"I need to go take a bath." I held up a shaking hand as if for proof.

"I'll come up with you." Keira got to her feet. We left silently, walking side by side.

"Should we be doing something?" I burst out as we climbed the stairs. "I feel like we should be doing something. If she's out there —"

"Alex . . ." Keira pressed her warm hand to my shoulder. I looked over to find tear tracks shining on her cheeks. "If she's out there, she's long gone."

In my room, I climbed onto my bed, curled up into a fetal ball, and cried.

Eventually I got up and ran a hot bath. I lay comatose as rivulets of sweat ran down my face. I felt both exhausted and wide-awake. But it still hadn't fully sunk in. Just hours earlier a very alive Poppy had been pulling me along, determined to show me something. What had she said?

She's not who she claims to be.

Who on earth had she been talking about? Roza? Wren? Some figment of her imagination?

The questions felt solid, an iron bar I could cling to, to avoid dropping into a bottomless cavern of horror.

Maybe I could dig out a clue, something that would help.

So: Poppy had been tripping. People said outlandish things when they tripped. And, really, the only reason her words struck a sinister chord now was because she'd disappeared. Still, it was strange that she'd felt drawn to the basement, first sleepwalking, then on LSD.

Maybe it could've been any basement. Basements were symbolic. They held all the junk we didn't want to look at.

And it hadn't only been Poppy acting unusual. I'd not only imagined hearing Horace throwing a raucous party and Daphne fervently whispering in the basement — those hallucinations had been subtle enough. I'd also had what felt like very vivid sex with a demon.

Maybe it was this house. Maybe there was something here, some remnant from Daphne's time.

Maybe, by writing about it, I was opening up a channel to it. Some dark energy that still vibrated in the walls.

After my bath, I sat at my desk, wrapped in a robe and staring into space. Supernatural forces. Was that really where my mind was going?

But why not? As I'd told Taylor, I'd experienced the supernatural firsthand. Maybe it was up to me to ask the question.

"Hey." Taylor poked her head in my open door. "You'd better come here."

I followed her to Wren and Poppy's room, doom hovering in my chest. Wren and Keira were sitting on Poppy's bed, bent over her splayed-open suitcase. It felt gross and wrong, like an invasion.

"What are you doing?" I asked sharply.

Keira brought something over to me. "Look."

It was a New York State driver's license. For a second I expected to see Wren's face looking back. But instead it was Poppy. Her hair was different — dark brown and shoulder-length. But it was definitely her.

"Look at the name." Taylor stood over my shoulder.

"Zoe Canard." This didn't make sense. I looked up at Taylor, then Keira, who had settled back on the bed next to Wren. "What the hell?"

"She's not Poppy." Keira took the license. "Her name's Zoe Canard. And she lives in upstate New York. Way upstate. North of here."

"What — why?" I asked. The mystery was expanding. I felt a ripple of hysteria creep up my shoulder blades.

"Unclear." Taylor gestured to the suitcase. "We found it in an inner pocket. Credit cards, too, with the same name."

"You just happened to be searching her stuff?" I asked.

"I was looking for contact information," Wren said and coughed. "Her phone's locked. We need to get ahold of her family."

"Right." I sat heavily on the floor. My

brain turned this new fact around, fiddling with it like a Rubik's Cube. "Maybe Poppy was her pen name?"

Taylor rubbed her chin. "But then why wouldn't she use her real name with us?"

Wren stared into space, clutching a crumpled tissue in her lap. Her nose was red and raw, her skin pale. Beside her, Keira chewed her thumbnail, staring at the license.

"Did she tell you anything?" I asked. "Wren?"

She met my eyes. "No."

"Poppy was from Atlanta," Taylor said. "Born and raised. Remember? That's what she told us, anyway."

It didn't strike me until I was back in my room, my head spinning.

What Poppy had said to me on the stairs.

She's not who she claims to be.

Had Poppy — or Zoe, apparently — been speaking about herself?

CHAPTER 23

Dinnertime. I wasn't hungry, but someone said we needed to eat to keep up our strength, so I followed the group downstairs. Then the food smells hit and my stomach revved like a lawn mower. Roza's chair remained empty.

I ate mechanically, without tasting anything. My mind kept looping over this new piece of the riddle. So Poppy wasn't actually Poppy. Had she lied to get into the retreat? How on earth had she managed to do that?

Chitra came out to check on us. "Are you girls all right?" Dark bags hung under her eyes.

"Not really." Taylor sighed. We'd agreed to keep the info about Poppy between us, for now. We'd share it with the police, but we didn't know how Roza, Yana, or Chitra would react.

"When are the police coming tomorrow?"

Keira set down her fork.

"I think Roza said the morning?" Taylor watched her.

"Good," Keira said. "I'm leaving with them."

"Via snowmobile?" Taylor asked. "What about your stuff?"

"Yana can mail it. Or not. I don't care." She pushed her plate away. "I just want to get the hell out of here."

"Alex?"

I woke with a start. I was in bed, my e-reader on my chest. I'd been certain I wouldn't be able to sleep for hours. But apparently I'd passed out immediately.

Wren stood at the door. She'd turned my main light on.

"What's up?" I rubbed my eyes.

"I have to talk to you."

"Sure." I sat up, crossing my legs. The situation meant that we'd made an unspoken truce, that we'd set all our issues to the side. And I hated to admit it, but the circumstances — a disappearance, a likely death — were making our conflict seem almost trite.

"I wanted to show you something." Wren looked wan but better than she had earlier in the day. She plopped down on the bed, handing a book to me.

"The Knowing," I read from the cover. Underneath the author name — Soo-jin Park — were the words Advance Reader's Copy.

I recognized this book.

At work, there was a table near the elevators that held advance copies of the novels published by my company's literary wing. I'd seen this book in the pile maybe six months ago. After picking it up to read the back I'd put it down. I wasn't reading any novels at the time, as they only served to remind me of my own writer's block.

"Where'd you get this?" I asked.

"Just read the back." She watched as I did so.

Min-seo is visiting family in Busan when she meets a woman at a café who tells her about a small group in the mountains who have found a god. The woman tells her that this is not metaphorical: the god exists. She has seen him. An investigative journalist, Min-seo decides to track down this group to find out what's really going on. But what she discovers will change everything she thought she knew about life. In this thrilling debut, Soo-jin Park explores issues of family, friendship, and faith.

"It's her book," My chest ached like the wind had been knocked out of me. "The book Poppy — Zoe — was writing. Finding God in the cave." That's why the story had sounded familiar to me during our first writing group session, when we'd shared our book ideas.

"She's been copying it." Wren turned to the front page. "Changing the location and names. But most of it's word for word."

"But why? What does that mean?"

"That she's not a writer." Wren stared at me. "She's not supposed to be here."

"You think she lied to get in?" I asked. "That she used a fake name?"

"Maybe," Wren said. "But if her goal was to get in here . . . I mean, what are the odds that she'd win a spot that way? Out of thousands of applicants."

"So she didn't try to get in." I drummed my fingers on my leg. "She waited until the winners were picked and convinced one of them — the real Poppy — not to come?"

"That has to be it." Wren's eyes widened. "Right?"

"But how would Zoe know?" I asked. "They kept the winners a secret."

"Well, the winners weren't allowed to announce it on social media, but I'm sure they told some people. I mean, I told Evan. I had to tell my boss. So maybe Zoe found out through one of Poppy's connections."

"Okay." Adrenaline threaded through me. "So say Zoe hears that this girl she's somehow connected with got into Roza's retreat. She convinces Poppy to let her go in her place? Apart from the odds of this girl agreeing, how would it even be possible?"

"I don't know." Wren shrugged. "It's not like they asked us for ID to get in the door."

"Social media?"

Wren chewed on her lower lip. "Do you think Roza — or her team — are that thorough? Did they really look into the lives of the women they let in? You think they're that concerned about optics if they accepted almost all white girls?"

"True." I remembered my surprise the first day at seeing that Keira was the only woman of color in the group.

"And even if they did check social media, Poppy could've set her profile to private."

"Zoe clearly dyed her hair," I said. "So maybe the real Poppy's blond."

"Makes sense." Wren glanced up. "But what about the background check?"

"That's easy," I said. "If they did a background check on Poppy, they'd just find info on the actual Poppy."

"Damn. Yeah."

"You were close with her," I said. "And you didn't get a sense of *anything* weird?"

"Not at all." Wren shook her head, baffled. "She seemed totally normal."

I had a flash of being on the steps with Poppy — Zoe — last night. I'd asked why Poppy why she was there. And she'd told me; she'd given me an answer:

Proof . . . Of what she does. That she's not who she claims to be.

And then: *Over here. It's this wall.*

"We have to go downstairs." The words rushed out of my mouth.

Wren looked up from the book. "Why?"

"She was looking for something. She said, 'She's not who she claims to be.' For a second I wondered if she was talking about herself. But I don't think so, not in the third person like that. I think she scammed her way into the retreat to get proof of something. So when she said that, she must've been talking about someone else. Maybe Roza?"

"Wait." Wren's eyes narrowed. "You're just sharing this now?"

"But I told you guys that she was looking for something." Hadn't I? I tried to think

320

back, but the last fourteen hours were a blur.

"You didn't mention she was looking for proof of some identity con. That seems like important information."

A familiar irritation rankled me. "It's not like I'm keeping secrets. I'm trying to figure this all out as we go along too."

"Okay, look." She held up her hands. "Let's just go to the basement."

As Wren and I descended the steps, the immense incongruity struck me: after two weeks of being each other's nemeses, we were now a team, following clues like the Hardy Boys.

I never could've imagined it. Not in a million years.

I led Wren where Zoe had gone, off the stairs to the left. Winding through the ubiquitous junk, we reached boxes stacked high against a cinder block wall.

"I remember hearing her pushing boxes around." I moved my phone's light over the cardboard shapes. "Did someone put these back?"

"Maybe there's something in them?" Wren asked.

"But she mentioned the wall."

"The wall?" Wren sniffled. "This is ridiculous. She was on LSD. She was probably just saying things."

"Let's just move the boxes away from the wall and see. Maybe there's writing or something." I winced at the sharp scraping sound the boxes made against the cement floor. After a second, Wren joined me. Some of the towers were heavy and we had to disassemble them box by box. When we finished, we were both sweating. We'd formed a little aisle between the boxes and the cinder block wall, which was cold with some damp, wet spots. It was dark, nearly pitch-black, and Wren shone her phone to check: no writing.

"Nope," she said. "Nothing."

"I see that." Did I sense a hint of satisfaction in Wren's voice? That I hadn't been right?

"Where were you again?" Wren asked. "When this was all going on."

"I was at the other end of the basement."

"Doing what?"

"Nothing." I tried to calm my snappish tone. "I was wandering around hallucinating. I thought I was in a forest."

"Okay." Wren was pointing her light at the ground; her face in shadow. "And then?"

"What do you mean? That was it." Why was she questioning me like this, like I was

322

suddenly a suspect in Zoe's disappearance?

"You said you fell asleep down here. When did you go back upstairs?"

"I don't remember." I felt a pinprick of fear.

"I know you." Wren's voice was barely above a whisper. "There's something you're not telling me."

We were silent in a sudden standoff.

"Okay." I felt a burst of defiance. "I had sex with a demon, and then I passed out, and then I woke up in my bed. I don't remember coming back upstairs."

Her breath whooshed out. "Demon? What are you talking about?"

"It was just a hallucination. Like I said."

"So you were really out of it," she said.

"Of course I was." I bristled. "We were all out of it."

"True, but only one of us was down here with Poppy — I mean Zoe — when she went missing."

"You don't know that," I said. "I could've gone up before that happened. Either way, it's not like I had anything to do with it. It's not my fault she went outside." My cheeks burned.

"Well . . . I don't know. We can do really messed-up shit when we're wasted."

I glared at her. "Why don't you just say it?"

"Say what?" She had the audacity to sound confused.

"That — according to you — I'm an unstable psychopath."

She scoffed. "Alex —"

"Just stop. I know you told Roza you wanted to take out a restraining order against me."

"What are you talking about?"

"You're really going to deny it to me? That you said that?"

"Look, I don't know what you're talking about, but I don't have the energy to argue with you, okay?" She laughed, humorless. "Jesus Christ. We've been looking for a *body,* Alex. But again, we have to talk about you. How I've been so mean to you. How I've wronged you. It never ends."

"That's not true," I cried. "If you want to talk about acting like a victim —"

"I *don't.* That's actually the last thing I want to talk about." She raised her flashlight and I threw up my hands to shield my eyes. "I'm going upstairs." She stalked past me.

I listened to her make her way to the stairs, then run up the steps. I leaned my forehead against the cool concrete blocks, taking deep breaths, trying to quell the rage.

And as quickly as it had surged, it ebbed away. In its place was desolation, a dark well with no bottom.

Just twenty-four hours before, everything had been running along so smoothly. It hadn't been easy, scrambling to write a novel in close quarters with Wren. But everything made sense. The game was so straightforward.

And now . . . I didn't know what to believe. Could it really be true that Zoe was a frozen corpse, hidden somewhere under the snow? Could a fox or squirrel be running over her at this very minute?

I lifted my head. *Stop.* I couldn't think about —

Something clicked and popped out of the wall.

For a second I was stunned. Then I shone my phone on it and touched it. The cinder block I'd been leaning my forehead against had sprung loose. Not the entire block — just the front of it, opening on a hinge.

I touched the hinged covering: the side facing me was formed of the cement material, but it was only about an inch thick. A false front. The other side was smooth and felt like metal.

I opened it wider.

Beyond the false front the wall was metal.

A security code keypad sat in the middle of the square. I pressed a few of the tiny plastic numbers. They lit up in yellow. Then a tiny bulb on the upper corner of the keypad flashed red.

I started to close the false front, and it swung shut as if magnetic. For a second I panicked: What if it locked? But when I pressed against it, what looked like one of hundreds of cinder blocks comprising the wall, it sprang open again.

I leaned my phone against the cinder block column to mark it. With a burst of energy, I pushed the boxes farther back so that I had a clear view of this area of the wall. I turned off the phone's light, stepped back, and let my eyes adjust to the darkness.

At first, there was nothing. But then, slowly, they began to appear. They were hard to see, like stars in the night sky that disappear if you look at them directly. But by letting my vision blur, the lines came into focus.

There was light filtering in from the other side of the wall.

The keypad was in the middle of what looked like the outline of a door.

Wonder burst in my chest. A door meant that there was something behind it, some room we hadn't yet seen. Maybe the reason I hadn't noticed Zoe the night before was because she'd already found her way into this hidden chamber.

I have to show you something. I think I found it. Her voice came back to me. *Over here. It's this wall.*

Poppy had known about the secret room. And it looked like she'd gotten in — either by knowing the code, or some other means.

New questions arose, sending an icy chill up my spine.

If she'd gotten in — why hadn't she come out again?

Who had put the boxes back to hide her trail?

Who knew she was alive, and was pretending along with the rest of us that she was dead?

Okay. I had to stay calm. I had to figure this out one piece at a time. Pressing my ear to the wall, I called: "Hello?" No one answered.

I pressed on all the other cinder blocks nearby, knowing even as I did so that it was useless. There was only one way to open this hidden door, and for that one needed the code.

"What is going on?" I whispered, pressing a dusty hand to my mouth. I did another slow search around the wall, shining the light up and down.

In the deepest corner where the two adjoining walls met the ceiling, something blinked.

I gasped, my hand faltering, then forced the light up again. It was small and round, gleaming like the eye of a cat.

I pushed two heavy boxes into the corner, then heaved one on top of the other. They weren't terribly steady, but I held on to the rough walls as I climbed on top.

For a few seconds I just stared at the object. The lens wasn't much larger across than a dime, and it was trained in the direction of the hidden door. I'd never studied one close up before, but it was obvious what it was.

A security camera.

Chapter 24

Wren's door was closed and she didn't answer when I knocked. I tried the door-knob but it was locked. *Shit.* I felt a flash of frustration — I couldn't even text her in the Blackbriar dead zone — but forced it down.

I knocked louder and called her name, but gave up quickly. Wren was a heavy sleeper, and I didn't want to wake anyone else until I'd thought this through.

In bed, my mind jumped from thought to thought. I'd initially assumed someone was keeping Zoe in the secret room, but maybe that wasn't it at all. Maybe she was hiding.

And maybe this was just another fucked-up trick Roza was playing on us.

But could Roza really be capable of this? Hiring an actor to play one of the partici-pants, one who would disappear in order to stress us out and push us to greater writing heights?

I moaned, turning onto my side. Sixteen

days at Blackbriar and my sense of reality had been completely dismantled. If I were back in my Brooklyn apartment, I'd know if I was being unreasonable or if this level of duplicitousness was an actual possibility. Here, where Daphne's demoness paintings covered the walls and secret chambers lurked, it was impossible to tell.

And I had to wonder, too, if it wasn't wishful thinking. For Zoe to still be alive. For it not to be — here I forced myself to stay with the idea, no matter how uncomfortable — partially my fault for not noticing she'd gone outside.

I awoke suddenly. Golden ribbons of sunlight stretched from the windows to the floor, at odds with the dark thoughts that immediately filled my mind. Either Zoe was dead or Roza was unhinged. Fabulous options. I stretched, my hips and legs sore from the previous day's outdoor search. According to the clock on the nightstand, it was nearly nine.

As I got out of bed, I noticed a piece of paper that had been shoved under the door. It was handwritten in winding, cursive script:

Your presence is requested at a special emergency writing meeting. 9 am in the library. Refreshments will be served.

"Good morning, girls." Roza said the words gravely as we took our usual seats. She was dressed up, wearing a silky maroon jumpsuit that matched her hair and lipstick.

I'd scrambled to get ready, relieved that I hadn't slept right through the meeting. Wren and Taylor looked like they'd been up for a while. Now I cursed myself for not catching Wren earlier. I stared at her, trying to get her attention and transmit a thought: *I have to talk to you.* Wren would be able to tell me if my new theory was logical or not. She could be cold and calculating: exactly what I needed right now.

Footsteps thumped near the doorway and Keira strode in. She ignored Roza as she took a seat, tossing the end of her black scarf over her shoulder.

Roza watched Keira sympathetically. "Hard day yesterday, yes?"

"Where are the police?" Keira raised her head and stared straight at Roza. "I thought they were supposed to come this morning?"

"That's right." Roza smiled kindly. "I'll radio them again. I'm sure they'll be here soon enough."

"I packed my things." Keira's voice was

crisp. "I'm going to leave with them. I'll just take my backpack for now if they're on snowmobiles. Unless the roads have been cleared."

"Of course, dear." Roza looked down to stir her coffee.

"*Are* the roads cleared?" I studied Roza. If my new theory was right — if this was all planned — the police would never come, because they hadn't been contacted. But it couldn't take more than a day or two to clear the roads, and there were one or more cars in the garage for someone to drive to the nearest station. What excuse would Roza make then?

"Oh, no." Roza crossed her arms. "It usually takes quite a long time up here: a few days, at least. Our little house in the middle of nowhere isn't a priority."

Chitra swept in, bringing a tray of sweet-smelling pastries to the table.

"Even if that house has a missing person?" Keira raised an eyebrow. "Can we at least check the roads? And maybe snow-blow the driveway so we could drive out if and when they *are* cleared?"

"Well." Roza sighed. "Unfortunately, our snowblower is broken. We'll have to wait for the snow to melt a little before we can attempt that."

"You're in the middle of nowhere, in the middle of winter, and your snowblower is broken?" Keira cried.

"Yes." Something slipped in Roza's armor. A flash of irritation crossed her face. "You know, I'm doing the best I can."

"*Are* you?" Keira glared, brushing back her loose braids.

"K." Taylor reached out a hand, beseeching. "Let's listen to what Roza wants to tell us."

Keira shook her head, incredulous, but remained quiet.

"Thank you." Roza folded her hands. "I called you here because I wanted us to have a space to process before we move forward."

"Move forward?" Wren asked. She coughed, and I winced at the new sound of phlegm in her lungs. Examining her more closely, I saw that her nose was runny, her cheeks too red. This was the first time I'd seen Wren look sicker than she was acting.

"Yes." Roza nodded once. "With the retreat."

There was a beat of silence.

"What?" Keira said flatly.

"Tomorrow we will resume the workshop." Roza sipped her coffee. "Your new pages are due, as usual, by midnight tonight."

Keira let out a bark of shocked laughter. I

met Wren's eyes across the table and we shared the same incredulous look.

Roza raised a hand. "Keira, you are no longer bound to the timeline, since you're leaving. But for everyone else, we need to continue."

"But, Roza . . ." Wren's voice was husky, her eyes shining with tears. "Poppy is *dead.* We can't just go on like nothing happened. We haven't even talked to the police yet."

Lines creased Roza's forehead. "You think Poppy would've wanted us to just stop?"

"So you want us to just keep cranking out books for you as we wait for Poppy's body to be found?" Keira's voice was low.

Roza glared at her. "I don't even know why you're at this discussion. You weren't given an invitation."

"An invitation?" Keira's voice rose. "What, to this delightful tea party you're having? What planet do you live on?"

"That's enough!" Roza stood. "I've tried to put up with your attitude, I've tried to be understanding, but I've had it. Keira, you're done." She pointed to the door. "Please leave. You're no longer privy to this conversation."

Keira stared at the table. After a moment, she smiled slightly and nodded. She stood, facing Roza.

"If you think you're going to get away with this," Keira said, "you're not."

"Now." Roza's voice echoed in the cavernous space.

With a final glare, Keira left the room.

I wholeheartedly agreed with Keira, and I wished I could jump up and join her. But I had to remain in Roza's good graces if I had any hope of figuring out what was going on.

"Well." Roza sat back down. "I'm sorry you had to see that, girls."

"I mean . . ." Taylor cleared her throat. "She has a point."

"I know," Roza said. "I really do. But what happened to Poppy was an *accident.* No one could have predicted it. We did our best to find her. Now we need to wait for the authorities. And in the meantime . . ." She stared at each of us in turn. "You will all have to make a choice: whether to soldier on, even in the midst of such troubling circumstances. Or quit. Of course, you're free to leave with Keira if you'd like. I'm not going to keep you here. But I beg you to remember that I chose you for a reason. I saw a fire in you that now, more than ever, needs to be stoked. We're halfway through three groundbreaking novels. Novels that will become instant classics. Don't lose the momentum. Don't give up this opportunity."

Wren blew her nose. Taylor traced the purple flowers on her forearm. I tried to look thoughtful. This rallying pitch was exactly what I would've expected if my new theory was correct.

I clenched my hands on my lap. I still couldn't fully believe it was true. After all, how would it end? Would Chitra wheel in a giant cake on the last day for Zoe to jump out of? *Surprise!!!*

It was absurd. And yet . . . in the end, Roza wasn't doing anything illegal. If anything, it would bolster her reputation. One of us would get rich, all of us would get published, and we'd exclaim over this dark retreat in interviews, chatting about Roza's extreme tactics.

"I'm in." Taylor straightened. "If just to have something to do. I can't stand the waiting. Yesterday was pure hell."

Wren and I glanced at each other again. She looked exhausted and miserable. I widened my eyes slightly: *Follow my lead.*

"We can try." I attempted to sound sincere, though I knew there was no way I'd be able to sit down and write.

"Brilliant." Roza turned to Wren, one eyebrow raised.

With a last questioning look at me, Wren dipped her head. "Okay."

"Wonderful." A slow, easy smile spread over Roza's face. "Ladies, I knew you were warriors. We're going to continue our journey together despite the setbacks. And we *will* prevail. Yes?" She reached out and grabbed a pain au chocolat as she stood.

"And the police?" Wren asked. "You said you're going to radio them again?"

"Yes." Roza raised a finger. "I will do that right now."

I could hear the unspoken ending: *Before I forget.*

After Roza left, Taylor groaned and rubbed the top of her head, leaving blond tufts sticking up. I regarded her, then made up my mind.

"Guys, I think we should talk." I stood. "With Keira. Meet upstairs in ten?"

They agreed, watching with curiosity as I hurried to the hall.

Roza was wearing platform boots that day and her heels thudded against the rugs and runners. In socks, I followed like a silent ghost. She strode across the front hall, footsteps squeaking against the marble. She was humming faintly to herself.

The act of following caused fear to wrap around my throat. Not that I was afraid she'd catch me, necessarily: I could just say I had a question for her.

Maybe it was the horror of what I might hear.

She swept into the study, shutting the door behind her. I crept up to it and pressed my ear against the door.

Nothing.

I wondered, standing there, if perhaps the door was just thick and heavy enough to obscure any sounds. But then I heard Roza cough, clear as a bell. The wooden floor creaked as she walked across the room. She resumed humming. Maybe Roza needed a moment, but there was no reason it should take this long to radio the police.

Unless she wasn't planning to.

"You need help?"

I jumped. Yana, who'd snuck up on me in athletic shoes, stood with her hands on her hips. Today her tracksuit looked even tighter than usual, showing off her small, compact limbs. It struck me that she looked like a coach, maybe of girls' gymnastics, and one you definitely didn't want to mess with.

"I'm fine." I straightened, forcing a smile. "I just had a question for Roza."

Yana glared without answering. The door swung open.

"Oh, hello." Roza looked back and forth

338

between us. "All okay, ladies?" She closed the door behind her.

"She was waiting for you." Yana crossed her arms.

"Yes, dear?" Roza gazed at me, gracious but impatient.

"I — I just wanted to know what the police said. When they were coming. Just so I know." I willed my voice to sound light, trusting.

"Right." Her eyes softened. "They're going to get here as soon as they can. Likely this afternoon." To my surprise, she slipped an arm around my shoulders. "You're a very kind girl, Alex. I can see how much you care."

Coming from Roza, I didn't know if this was a compliment or an insult.

"I'll see you at dinner. Get to writing, okay?" She released me and walked away. Yana watched me a second longer before following her.

I pretended to be heading upstairs, pausing in the front hall and then doubling back.

I grabbed the office's doorknob. Roza hadn't used the radio to contact the police just now, which meant that I needed to. Even if this was some ruse Roza was pulling, I couldn't let it continue. Not with the possibility of death hanging over us. I could

339

put up with a lot, especially from someone I admired, but not this.

But when I tried to turn the knob, it wouldn't move.

The door was locked.

CHAPTER 25

Upstairs, I found the others waiting in Wren's room, all clustered on her bed. I closed the door firmly and settled next to Keira, who was lying back with her eyes closed.

I now had proof that something was definitely off. It was time to tell everyone, not just Wren. It wasn't fair to let them believe Zoe was dead, not if there was a chance she wasn't.

"What's going on?" Taylor played with her rabbit necklace.

"Roza didn't radio anyone." I clasped my hands together in my lap. "I waited outside the door and listened."

"Jesus," Keira muttered, covering her face.

"Are you sure?" Wren asked.

"One hundred percent sure." I heaved a sigh. "I also discovered something in the basement and now I have a theory. It's . . . kind of a lot. And I don't know if it's true.

341

But I feel like you guys need to hear it."

Keira sat up and Taylor waved a hand. "Theorize away, please."

As I told them about the secret keypad, the security camera, and my new suspicions about Zoe, I expected to see looks of disbelief. Instead, they listened intently.

After I finished, Taylor chewed at a thumbnail, staring into space. Wren's eyes stayed trained on me, horrified. Keira went to the window, leaning her forehead against the glass.

"That crazy bitch," she said in a conversational tone.

"So what do we do?" Taylor asked.

"You guys believe me?" I'd have expected relief, but instead I felt even more disturbed. The theory was hardening into actual possibility.

"Unfortunately, yes," Keira said.

"Poppy." Wren cleared her throat. "Zoe, I mean. If we find her, then all of this is over. Right?"

"If she's here, she's in that room." Keira plopped into the desk chair. "We searched the rest of the house, top to bottom."

"Guys." Taylor's voice was low. "I know how much we want Zoe to be alive. Is this our way of tricking ourselves into believing it?"

"No." Keira leaned forward. "This is our way of finding out the truth. If Zoe's out there in the woods, that's one thing. But if there's a chance she's alive, then we need to find out. After we radio the police, of course."

"The room's locked," I reminded her.

"I might be able to pick it." Keira jumped up. "Alex, come with? And bring your phone."

"I want to check that keycode." Taylor gestured at Wren. "Join me?"

"But the camera . . ." Wren squinted. "Won't whoever put it there see us?"

"We don't know who's looking . . . if it's Roza, someone else we've never seen, or no one at all. We don't even know if it's turned on." Taylor glanced at Keira, our new de facto leader. "If someone is watching, they probably already saw Alex. Right, K?"

She nodded. "I think it's worth it to try the keycode."

I'd left it wide open but hidden behind some boxes.

It wasn't until Keira and I were heading down the stairs that Taylor's words hit, making my whole body tingle with fear.

Someone else we've never seen.

We already knew there was at least one secret, hidden room at Blackbriar. Who was to say there weren't more? And who was to say they didn't contain multiple people we weren't aware of, spying on us like doctors watching their lab rats?

I forced myself to focus on the task at hand. Keira stopped in her room for bobby pins, and I tried to think up an excuse in case we ran into Yana. Thankfully, the halls were empty. At the door, Keira crouched down as I shone my phone light on the circular lock.

"Okay, let's see if I can still do this." Keira pulled out the bobby pins from her pocket.

"How did you learn?" I asked.

"Well . . ." She twisted one of the bobby pins, bending one end into a little hook. "I have a very curious niece who decided to lock herself in the bathroom at her second birthday party." She slipped the wavy side into the lock. "YouTube really saved the day."

"Wow."

A minute later, she turned the doorknob and it magically opened.

"There!" she cried.

"Amazing." I turned on the light.

The radio sat in the back corner on its own stand. It was the size of two stacked bricks, with tiny buttons and switches across the front.

"Okay." Keira flipped some switches. Nothing happened.

"It looks like it's dead. Shouldn't it be lit up in some way?" I bent and found the cord, which was plugged into an outlet.

"Something should be happening." She glanced up. "Hey, you should check the phone too. Maybe it's actually working."

I went to the white vintage rotary phone on the desk. I lifted the receiver and held it to my ear. There was nothing — less than nothing: a thick, silent deadness.

"Nope." I turned back to Keira.

She'd stiffened, the grooves of her shoulder blades showing through her tight black sweater.

"What?" I trotted to her side.

She'd turned the radio over. The bottom had been pried open, the insides removed. Torn wires lined the gaping plastic shell.

The reality of the situation took a second to hit.

There was no radio. No phone. No connection to the outside world.

Keira looked at me, and the same thought hovered between us: we were completely on our own.

We ran into Taylor and Wren in the kitchen.

"We saw the keypad," Taylor said. "Couldn't get in without the code, of course. Wren had the idea that we should try to figure out what's directly above it and see if there's a way in from upstairs."

"Did you radio the police?" Wren leaned tiredly against the kitchen island.

Keira glanced at me. "It's dead. Someone opened it up and ripped out the wires."

"What?" Taylor looked stricken as Wren gasped.

"So I think we can safely assume there's no police coming to save us." My intuition had been right. And it was clear we could no longer trust anything Roza said.

"What do we do?" Wren's voice sounded strangled.

"Well." Keira tapped her fingers against the marble countertop. "I'd say we should find Roza's car keys and just leave. But it's stayed cold the last few days; the snow hasn't melted. And whether or not the snowblower *is* actually broken, Roza's not going to let us find out."

"What about the snowmobile?" Wren said.

The three of us stared at her.

"Chitra said there's one in the garage." Wren shrugged.

"With keys?" Keira asked.

"I don't know."

346

"Whoa, hold on." Taylor raised her hands. "So, what do we think is happening here? Sure, Roza is fucking with us. But isn't this good news? That Zoe's actually alive?"

Keira scoffed. "Doesn't mean I want to wait around and see what happens next."

"What do you mean?" Taylor crossed her arms. "You think Roza is dangerous?"

"I don't know *what* she is." Keira shrugged. "But I'm done being a part of her game. I'm ready to go home."

"Hi, girls." Chitra entered the room, her expression grave, and I jumped guiltily.

"Hi." Taylor put on a sad smile. "How are you holding up?"

"Best as can be expected, under the circumstances." Chitra started filling up a teapot in the double sink. "Anyone fancy some tea? Maybe a snack?"

I studied her. If this was all a game, was Chitra in on it? She looked terrible: blotchy skin and reddened eyes. If she was acting, she was doing a damn good job.

"No, thanks," Wren said. "I'm not hungry."

"I'm going to heat up some chicken soup for you, love." Chitra sighed. "Wasn't good for you to be outside for so long yesterday — not with your cold."

"Thanks." Wren watched her, a hint of

longing in her expression.

We trudged to the library, which Taylor thought was directly over the secret room. Keira wanted to check out the keypad downstairs but agreed to wait until Chitra had left the kitchen.

Post–faux radio, we had to assume that everyone who worked for Roza was in on it.

"Here." Taylor stationed herself by the windows, then walked about twenty feet away from the glass. "I'd say this is where the false wall starts. Maybe a bit further. The basement — the whole house — is so huge, it's hard to tell."

"Did you read anything about a secret room when you were researching Daphne?" Keira asked me.

"No." I would've remembered.

"Let's pull up the rug here." Taylor dragged a heavy chair away from the window. "Maybe there's a trapdoor."

Keira and I helped with the chairs and Wren started pulling back one of the heavy oriental rugs. She was unable to do much until Taylor assisted, peeling it back and then hauling it further away like it weighed nothing. We stared down at a large expanse of polished wood floor. Taylor walked across it, then crouched and rapped on it with her knuckles.

"You okay?" I asked Wren, who was still breathing hard.

"I'm fine." Her cheeks were flushed.

"What about this?" Keira had walked to the left of the window about ten feet. She stood gazing up at three bookcases. They were pressed against a bulky pillar that jutted out from the wall.

"What if it's a passageway?" Keira asked.

"A vertical one?" Taylor studied it, hands on hips.

"Could be a ladder or something," I said.

"Maybe if you just pull out the right book, a door will swing open." Wren had flopped down on the wooden floor.

"There's hundreds of books on these shelves." Taylor studied them. "Might take a while."

"What's above this?" Keira pointed to the ceiling. "What's right over the library?"

"The west wing," I supplied. "Roza's room."

Keira smiled grimly. "Of course."

While Keira slipped down to the basement, the rest of us ate lunch quietly, lost in our own thoughts.

Keira quickly returned. As she sat down with a plate, I noticed that her energy was different: heightened, almost manic.

"Guys, I saw it." She spoke in a low voice. "Poppy *must* be in there. We have to figure out how to get in. One of us needs to search Roza's room."

"What?" Wren gawped as if Keira had suggested a ritual sacrifice.

"There has to be a way down there." She speared a tomato with gusto.

"But Roza's always in her room." Taylor looked intrigued. "Are you saying we stage an emergency or something so she comes out?"

"Well, we know that she'll be out of there tonight," Keira said. "For dinner."

"If she comes to dinner," I cautioned.

"She'll come to dinner." Keira rolled her eyes. "Roza likes her schedule. She's all about control."

"Speaking of which." I dropped my sandwich; my stomach was churning with nerves. "Is she really expecting us to write today?"

"Maybe we should try," Taylor said. "To keep up appearances."

Wren broke into a coughing fit. She was even paler now, verging on gray.

"You should go rest," I told her. "You don't look good."

"I'm fine."

Taylor rubbed her shoulder. "You just relax, okay? We'll be out of here soon enough."

"I just want to know what's happening." Wren lowered her head onto the table.

Keira stared at the table, lost in thought.

I sighed. "We all do."

"There *must* be more cameras," Keira said.

After putting Wren to bed, we'd regrouped in my room. Goose bumps stippled my arms and neck. I felt muddled and confused, unsure if we were taking our paranoia too far. This must be what a conspiracy theorist felt like: *It's bigger than you ever could've imagined!*

"They're tiny," Keira went on. "They can be like the head of a pin. You can put them anywhere. And you can literally buy them on Amazon." She surveyed the room. "If we found one in the basement, I'd guess there's more. A lot more."

"How do you know so much about them?" Taylor's asked.

"Well, I watch detective shows, spy shows, shows about psycho nannies, all that kind of thing. One day I just got curious about hidden cameras and looked it up." She pointed to my phone. "Can I use that?"

"Sure." I watched in a daze as she turned on the light, pointed it upwards, and ran it along the seam where the wall met the ceiling.

"What do they look like?" Taylor twisted her necklace around her finger. "What are we looking for?"

Keira shone the light under the bed. "Like I said, they can be just like a tiny black dot. Usually they have a small wire attached." She sat up. "Alex, you want to check the pictures?"

"Okay." I tugged down the nearest painting. Keira ran the light over it. The back of the heavy frame was covered in paper. Keira tore into it with her fingernails.

I held back my shock. Destroying Roza's property was making this even more real. But she'd left us no choice, had she? Keira and I examined more paintings as Taylor opened the drawers of the nightstand.

"Check the clock," Keira called to her, indicating the ornate wall clock that hung on the wall near the desk. "Look for little holes. It has to be able to see out." After Taylor inspected it, Keira placed it on the floor. Raising her boot high, she stomped. The clock rang out as if in pain. Keira sifted through the mass of pieces and broken glass.

Taylor watched, her face frozen in surprise. Our eyes met and I could almost hear her question: Were we going too far?

"Hey." Keira looked up at us. "Don't forget: Roza lied about calling the police. Poppy's missing. And we know there's at least one camera keeping watch. We have to figure out what the hell's going on."

"You're right." I turned to my dresser as Taylor went to the wardrobe.

An hour later my room was a disaster. We'd pulled everything off the walls, dumped out every drawer, searched the inner corners of every piece of furniture. Taylor had even stood on the back of the reading chair, Keira and I supporting her, and examined the chandelier.

We'd found nothing.

Tendrils of relief unfurled as I slumped on the floor, leaning against the bed. Taylor sat at the desk, her chin in her hand. Keira was going over the freestanding mirror a second time with her phone.

"It just doesn't make sense," she muttered.

"It makes perfect sense." Taylor rubbed her eyes. "We've gone off the rails."

"But the room in the basement?" I asked.

"I mean, who knows." Taylor gestured. "Maybe it's a temperature-controlled wine cellar. Maybe it's a panic room. Maybe it's a huge safe. There are a lot of possibilities."

"But she's lying about the police," I said.

"We know that."

"Who knows," Taylor said again, staring at nothing, her face slack. "Maybe the radio's *been* broken and Roza never got around to fixing it. Maybe she's waiting for the phone lines to be fixed so she can actually call. And lied to us in the meantime so we didn't panic."

Keira sat on the floor halfway between us, head on her knees.

A tidal wave of dread rose up. If it was true — if there was a reasonable explanation for everything — then that meant Poppy really was dead.

I closed my eyes and pressed my palms into my face, moaning. I felt too tired to cry. But the word echoed over and over in my mind: *Dead, dead, dead.* Poppy was *dead.* Regardless of her true name, her true self, I knew her flashing eyes, her quick laughter, her vibrant mind. The brief hope was slipping away, and in its place was helpless anguish and despair.

When I opened my eyes, Keira was staring at Taylor, an unreadable expression on her face. Maybe she, too, was in the midst of it: the realization that despite our minds spinning stories — because that's what our writer brains did — we couldn't bring Poppy back. That her body truly was out in the wilderness, frozen and fresh-looking, a Sleeping Beauty who would never awake.

But then Keira got to her feet. She motioned to Taylor. "Give me your necklace."

"What?" After a second, Taylor took it off.

Keira set the necklace on the desk and picked up a paperweight: a giant, sparkling chunk of amethyst. She raised it over her head and then brought it down. I jumped at the sharp bang.

"Jesus," Taylor muttered as I joined them at the desk. The rock had already put a huge dent in the rabbit's belly.

They're twenty-two-karat gold, so be gentle with them, Roza had told us during the first dinner at Blackbriar. I knew real gold was both heavy and soft; Mom had told me, showing me the few pieces her parents had left her from their jewelry store. No matter how bad it got financially, she'd never sell them.

Keira slammed the rock down again and again. Splinters flew up from the desk: this would not be fixable, put-back-able. Finally she stopped, breathing hard.

At first, all I could see was that the charm was now just a lump of gold, mangled beyond recognition. Then Keira picked it up and pulled something from it.

The rabbit's diamond eye hung out of its socket, connected by a tiny, hairlike wire.

CHAPTER 26

The decision of who should search Roza's room came down to Taylor and me.

Wren was too sick. Keira had offered, but Taylor thought she should try to mend things with Roza to keep her unsuspecting. Showing up to dinner would be a start.

We were sitting on my bed with Keira's phone in between us, loudly playing pop. It was hard to concentrate, but Keira said if there were other cameras around — which there almost certainly were, even if we hadn't been able to find them — we needed to cover up our conversation.

And if there were other cameras? If they'd caught us snooping in the basement, library, and office?

"Nothing has happened to us yet," Keira told us over the tinny, pounding bass. "I think there's a chance Roza hasn't been watching us that closely. And even if she has — she doesn't bring a phone to dinner.

So she won't know we're breaking into her room as it's happening. By the time she finds out, maybe we'll have found the secret room."

That's what it came down to, now. In the absence of truth, and in our inability to leave, we became hyperfocused on the one question we knew would give us an answer: a hidden room.

Taylor raised her hand to her chest, the fingers feeling for a necklace that was no longer there. Keira and I had buried our necklaces in the bottoms of our suitcases. But Taylor been wearing hers regularly; I could imagine she was the most disturbed.

Or: A new thought was taking root. What if she was in on all of this? What if she'd worn the necklace *because* she was supposed to transmit as much as she could to Roza?

Or: What if it was Keira? What if she was meant to shake things up on the retreat by arguing with Roza? Wasn't it suspicious that she'd known how to pick a lock and search for hidden cameras?

The new uncertainties were making me feel hot and prickly, like I had a full-body sunburn. But nothing was what it seemed in Blackbriar. For all I knew, Wren and I were the only ones who weren't a part of

358

this, some kind of sick Roza reality show.

A new determination took hold of me. Wren was down for the count. If anyone was going to figure this out, it had to be me.

"I'll go."

They both turned to me.

"I'll search Roza's room," I continued.

"Are you sure?" Taylor's brows furrowed.

"Yeah, I'm sure." I tried to smile. "Be sure to save me a plate."

Once we had a plan, Keira and Taylor returned to their rooms. We decided all of us should try to write — even Keira — to keep up appearances as much as possible. My new wariness extended to Keira and Taylor: I had to keep up appearances with them too.

And it hurt. I'd only been there a little over two and a half weeks, but I felt like I'd known Taylor and Keira much longer. I'd bonded with both of them. I thought I had, at least. The last few days had thrown everything into a new, ambiguous light.

I opened my laptop, not expecting much to happen. But as soon as I touched the keyboard, the words started to flow.

Two hours later, Taylor strolled into my room. "Hey! Ready for dinner?"

"I don't feel well." This was the plan: acting things out as much as possible, given the possibility of surveillance. "I feel kind of nauseous, actually."

"Sorry to hear." Taylor leaned on the edge of my desk and winked. "I'll let Roza know."

"Thanks." I forced a smile.

"Hey." Taylor reached down. "Where'd you get this? I was looking for it."

She picked up a tube of lip balm — the one I'd found in the basement.

"Oh." My mind raced. "It was in the dining room. Sorry. I forgot to give it back to you."

"No prob." She popped it open and ran it over her lips. "I get so dry in the winter."

I stared as she walked to the door.

She turned and smiled. "Feel better."

We'd agreed that I'd give them ten minutes to get settled at dinner, and in that time I stared out the window, calculating.

Had *Taylor* been with me that night? Was it possible that I hadn't just hallucinated a sexual encounter? Had we actually hooked up?

I thought of that moment on the bed, days before, when we'd been sharing the cheese plate. We'd shared those intense few seconds of eye contact. I'd felt something in that moment, some attraction, and it had scared the shit out of me, to the point where I'd pushed it from my mind. So maybe it wasn't out of the question to imagine that we'd been drawn to each other in our altered states.

But then, why hadn't she said anything? Had she been taking my lead? Had she been that out of it too?

There were also other possibilities. Taylor could've dropped the lip balm during the ghost story–telling game. Or she could've gone down there another time; there was no rule against exploring.

I heaved a sigh as I checked my phone and left the room. Too many unanswerable questions. And this was what happened here: more and more, the thick walls of practical reality crumbled down, leaving you stranded in a fog.

I half expected Roza's bloodred door to be locked, but it turned easily under my hand. The short hall was dark, but beyond, the lights were on. I'd been in here twice before for meetings with Roza, but it was different, going in alone. Now I felt nervous.

Concentrate. You don't have a lot of time.

We'd decided that I shouldn't stay in the room more than twenty minutes, in case

Roza got prickly about something and left dinner. They were going to do their best to keep her there, but they couldn't make promises. And there was no way to text and warn me if she left.

"Okay," I said to myself. My main goal was to find a passageway, as far-fetched as that seemed. And if there was one, it had to be off a wall without a window. Or the floor.

I inspected the sitting area first, spending what felt like a long time around the fireplace, pressing random stones, examining where it met the wall. I lifted up the oriental rug, but the floor appeared solid.

I was just putting the second chair back on top of the rug when the door creaked open. Horrified, I squatted down. I could tell by the cadence of the footsteps that it was Yana.

If she came into this part of the room, she'd see me.

Metallic fear rose in my throat. Somehow, Yana finding me was worse than Roza. Yana was a wild card. A vivid image arose in my mind: her spotting me, striding over, and lowering her hands to my throat with her usual blank expression.

She swerved right, striding into Roza's bedchamber, muttering to herself. When she sounded far enough away, I peeked over the chair. The nearest window had thick, red curtains. I tiptoed over and slipped behind them.

Yana reentered the sitting room and went straight to the fireplace. Empty wineglasses clanged together. I struggled to make out her indistinct words. They were in Russian.

Finally she left, slamming the door shut behind her.

I exhaled with relief and pulled out my phone. I'd already been in there for fifteen minutes; I needed to keep going. I went swiftly into the bedchamber. This part felt wrong, encroaching on Roza's personal space. I remembered the first night of the retreat: standing outside Roza's door, listening to her orgasm. She must've been loud if I could hear her all the way out in the hall.

Focus. I began the same process, working my way behind the bed, then around the side. As I peeked under the bed, scanning with my phone's flashlight, the question started to tug at me: *What are you* doing?

The question made me think of Mom, staring at me with a mixture of surprise and disdain. Her imagined perspective suddenly made me feel ridiculous.

You're looking for a secret passageway? How old are you, eight?

A frustrated sob caught in my throat. This

was crazy. The most likely scenario was that the secret room had a reasonable explanation. And even if there was another entrance to it, it could be anywhere.

When were you planning to stop this silly sleuthing and just ask Roza?

Mom was a realist; she'd rolled her eyes at the fantasy and sci-fi books I'd left scattered around the house. The few times I'd timidly given her one of my stories to read, she'd found pleasure in pointing out any improbabilities. *This would never happen.* I'd learned by age ten to keep my work to myself.

I stood in front of the huge double wardrobe that took up most of a wall. The doors were flung open, showcasing silks, lace, and knits in a rainbow of colors. A deep despair pulled at my gut. The problem with asking Roza is that it might rupture the fantasy. Maybe Keira, Taylor, and I had concocted a story to keep Poppy — Zoe, I had to remind myself — alive. Making her part of a villainous scheme, with Roza at the helm, was vastly preferable to the alternative.

I shoved Roza's clothes to the side and felt the walls and the back of the wardrobe. My fingers brushed against smooth wood. A new plan was forming. After this, I'd go directly to the dining room. It was time to bring this all out into the open, to give Roza a chance to dismantle our story. And if she did, we had to accept it. We had to acknowledge that Zoe was gone.

Mechanically, I moved to the next wardrobe. A line of fur coats awaited me, sleek and luxurious. I pushed two aside and felt for the back of the wardrobe.

I almost fell.

I righted myself, breathing hard. More carefully now, I extended my hand. Was I misjudging the distance?

But no. There was no back. And, more strangely, I could feel a cool breeze gently emanating from behind the furs.

With a shaking hand, I trained the light. Right behind the furs, there was a doorway, about two feet across and five feet high. Beyond, the passage stretched into darkness; I couldn't tell how far it extended.

I leaned against the wardrobe door, stunned.

"Okay," I said out loud. This was discombobulating. This was like half-believing in magic and then finding yourself hovering off the floor.

I'd been looking for a secret passageway; I'd found it.

And I wanted nothing more than to race back to my room and lock the door.

A powerful dread squeezed my ribs, so strong that I doubled over.

You can leave, I told myself. I could lie and say I hadn't found anything. That's what they were expecting to hear, anyway.

But of course that wasn't going to happen. Because I had to know.

I forced myself to stand.

And I wasn't a liar, anyway. Maybe I wasn't even a coward, even though I'd always been convinced, deep down, that I was.

I steeled myself. Pushing the furs aside, I stepped into the wardrobe.

CHAPTER 27

I half expected there to be nothing beyond the small doorway: just empty space that I would tumble down like Alice into the rabbit hole. But through the doorway stretched a wood-lined passage. It smelled like cedar, sharp and spicy.

The passageway went straight on for twenty feet or so, stopped by a far wall. There was also some kind of metal contraption at the end. I approached it, feeling dazed.

The metal thing was a spiral staircase that curled downwards out of view. I took a picture with my flash. Then I hesitated. I loved horror movies, but I had always blamed the protagonists — mostly women — for flagrantly disregarding signs of danger. Was I really going to do the same? Even as I wondered, I was already lowering myself down the creaky steps.

I tried to track it: I must be descending

through the high-ceilinged library, through that book-lined pillar. The wooden walls were tight around the rickety staircase and I tried to push away the swelling claustrophobia. My thighs started to cry out from the steep descent.

Finally I stepped onto a cement floor. It was freezing down there. *Should've grabbed one of those fur coats.* I held in an inappropriate giggle. This passage was lined in concrete. It ended fifteen feet ahead with a black metal door.

I walked over a small drain and started to shiver, unsure if it was from the cold or fear. The wooden passageway had felt friendlier, a mischievous secret, at least part of the human world. The concrete felt different: cold and cave-like, a place with drains in the floor to wash away blood.

Keep it together. I approached the door, noting another keypad on the wall next to it.

So that would be it, then. Relief poured over my shoulders. I didn't have the code. This was as far as I could go. I wouldn't have to see what horrors lay beyond.

But then I noticed: the door wasn't actually closed. It was slightly ajar, just an inch or two out of the frame. Light glowed from the other side. I gripped the knob and it swung towards me. It was too easy, wasn't it?

It didn't matter. I'd gone too far to stop now. A resigned inevitability arose inside me and I stepped through the door.

The light was so bright after the dark passageway that at first I had to cover my eyes, blinking to adjust. I was in a small room. Towards the right, rows of flat-screen monitors hung over a desk. It looked like the security office of a store or hotel. I crept closer. Small movements caught my eyes in the black-and-white tableaus: Chitra, moving from the fridge to the stove in the kitchen. The others shifting in the dining room, turning towards Taylor, who waved her arms theatrically. I leaned forward and stumbled, accidentally touching the screen. Sound filled the room.

"I'm serious!" Taylor's voice rang too loud in my ears. "Have you seen what a guy on meth does to himself? The last time I —"

I tapped the screen again and the sound went off. I scanned the other monitors, looking for Yana. I found her in what appeared to be her own quarters, lying motionless on her bed and staring at the ceiling.

Terror filled my throat as I found our rooms — and our bathrooms! — all nice and neat in a row. Roza had been watching us — even shower and take shits — this entire time. The cameras looked down from above; they must've been installed in the chandeliers and bathroom light fixtures.

Keira, Taylor, and I hadn't even thought to search my bathroom. We'd assumed Roza wouldn't have been that extreme.

I grabbed my phone and took pictures, trying to steady my shaking hands. I'd prepared myself for a game. For surveillance, even. But this went far beyond. There was no way Roza could spin this outside Blackbriar's walls.

I forced myself to scan the monitors once more, searching for a secret room containing Zoe. But I didn't see anyone else. Heart sinking, I turned.

And froze.

There was another desk across from the first. It displayed just one lonely monitor, smaller than the others. I crept closer, willing the image not to be what I was seeing.

The camera, filming from the upper corner, showed a small mattress and toilet in what looked like a large prison cell.

Something moved. It was Zoe, sitting up on the mattress. She wrapped her arms around her knees, staring at nothing.

Zoe! Zoe was alive! The sudden relief was

so powerful I felt dizzy. But even as the tears sprang to my eyes, the other, darker realization made me gulp down my joyful sob.

There *was* a secret room, and it was a dungeon.

"Okay." I straightened, scanning the room. I needed to get to her. At the far end of the surveillance room was another door. I ran to it, barely pausing before I pushed it open.

And there it was: a surprisingly spacious cell enclosed by iron bars. Zoe hadn't looked up when I opened the door.

"Are you okay?" I cried, pausing a millisecond to make sure the door would stay open, then raced to her. She lunged upwards, grabbing the bars. I grasped her hands, which were freezing. I could smell her: BO edged with a metallic fear.

"Alex." Her dark eyes bulged, her voice frantic. "Oh my god, help me. You have to get help." Her face was pale, smudged with dirt, and her blond hair was greasy. She wore the red Valentine's Day dress from the night she'd disappeared.

"What happened?" I gasped. "Did Roza do this?" I took a step back and scanned the bars, spotting yet another keypad.

"Alex." Her voice lowered, became even more determined. "You need to leave. Find the car keys and drive until you get service or until you reach the convent. Call the police. You have to —" Her eyes, intently focused on mine, flickered to my left shoulder.

"Watch out!" she cried but it was already too late.

Something lodged in the back of my neck, painful as a bee sting.

Instantly, without ceremony, everything went black.

CHAPTER 28

I awoke with a start.

This wasn't right. I wasn't in my bed, sunk into the plush mattress, ensconced in silken sheets. I was lying on top of a camping pallet, so thin I could feel the cold radiating up from the cement floor. I blinked against bright fluorescent lights. Slowly I sat up, a headache prodding behind my right eye.

The cloud started to clear. The last hour poured back in: Roza's room, the wardrobe, the passageway . . .

The dungeon.

Zoe was curled up on a yellow-stained duvet a few feet away.

"Hey." I cleared my throat. "Zoe?" She didn't move: Had she been drugged too? Slowly I dragged myself to my feet — the cold air was bracing, I could say that — and walked around the perimeter of the rectangular cell. The concrete ceiling was low and I had to stoop slightly. In the back corner was a camping toilet, emanating a sharp urine scent.

On the other side of the barred door, there was a small space where people could come in and hang out with those interned, a nice little foyer. In the upper corner of this area, the lens of the camera gleamed. Below was a square white speaker. Near the door there was an electrical outlet sticking out of the cement wall. At the far end of the space, across from the control room, another metal door was set into the wall. It had to be the hidden door that opened the basement.

"Alex." Zoe was sitting up. "Are you okay?"

"I think so." I didn't know if it was the aftereffects of whatever drug had been spit into my system, or if I was just in shock, but I felt completely numb. "I'm just . . . I'm taking it in. Did someone seriously knock me out with a syringe? Who did it?"

"I don't know." She rubbed her face, leaving a dirty smear. "They always wear a ski mask. I don't know if it's one person or more than one person. They're similar in size."

I pushed the horrifying image away. If I allowed my mind to linger, I would fall to the ground and curl up into a ball. I took a few deep breaths.

"Did they drug you too?" I sat gingerly on the duvet next to her.

"No, I just passed out. It's been happening more and more." She swept her greasy hair back. "Time has no meaning down here — they don't turn off the lights — so I've just been randomly falling asleep. I don't even know how many days I've been down here."

"Three," I said.

She nodded. "I thought it was longer. Time drags when you have nothing to do."

"Zoe." I paused. "Your real name is Zoe, right?"

"Yeah." She plopped her chin on her hand. The purple circles under her eyes verged on black. I had a flash of her the first day: animated, pretty, her voice taking up so much space. Now she looked pinched and thin.

"We thought you were dead," I told her. "We thought you'd wandered outside, asleep or tripping. The door was open and there were footsteps."

"Clever." Zoe cocked her head. "But no. I didn't go outside." She studied me. "How'd you find me?"

"I found the keypad. We realized there must be a room here. I searched Roza's room to see if there was a way down here . . ." I felt a flush of shame. "I thought you might actually be in on it, though. That it was some kind of game."

She snorted. "It might be a game to Roza, but it's sure as fuck not a game to me." Dirty and enraged, she looked like Poppy's profane twin sister.

"So who are you really?" I asked. "We found your ID. And the book you were copying."

She stared at me. "You didn't call the police?"

"We tried," I said. "Keira and I tried to use the radio, but it was broken. We realized there were cameras and we talked about leaving, but we didn't know how. Roza said the roads hadn't been cleared yet. Whether or not that was true, the driveway is still covered in like three feet of snow." The words rushed out like a confession. "And we found out there was a snowmobile, and we should've used it to get out, but again . . . we thought you might be in on it. We wanted to try to get into the secret room first. We didn't think . . ." I waved my arm around.

"That makes sense." She scratched at her bare leg, the anger and exasperation gone.

"So . . . what happened? Why did they lock you in here?"

Zoe tugged the duvet over her legs. "They caught me in the control room. I passed out in front of the monitors. I'm assuming they thought I knew too much."

"About Roza watching us?"

"Yeah. I haven't worked out if they know who I really am. If they do, there's no way they're letting me out. We have the same last name."

"The same last name as who?"

"My aunt." Zoe dropped her chin on her knees, looking exhausted. "Roza killed my aunt."

"Roza killed your aunt," I repeated. The words sounded absurd. "What? Why?"

"My aunt Lucy wrote *Lion's Rose*," Zoe said. "Roza stole it and published it as her own."

This stunned me. *Lion's Rose:* the novel about the gardener whose HIV had progressed into AIDS, and whose garden was keeping her alive.

"I knew about the book because Lucy had been working on it for years," Zoe went on. "Her good friend died of AIDs in the eighties; she got HIV from her husband, who was secretly sleeping with other men. Anyway, Lucy and I were really close, and I was a writer too, so she'd give me parts to read. She didn't show anyone else, just me. So when she died and her famous friend's new novel came out less than a year later and it was Lucy's book, I was the only one who even knew what had happened."

There were so many questions, but I managed to pin one down. "How did they know each other? Lucy and Roza."

"Lucy was the assistant of Roza's editor. I guess they just hit it off and Lucy showed Roza around when she was in New York. They were both in their twenties. At some point Lucy must've showed Roza her own work, and it was good enough to kill her for it."

I swallowed, my throat tight. "How did she kill her?"

"Roza made it look like she overdosed." Zoe's face was expressionless. "People believed it because she'd been an addict. But she'd been clean for years at that point. Sure, she got depressed sometimes. But she never would've used again."

"But how did Roza do that?" I asked. "Fake an overdose?"

"I don't know for sure." Zoe shrugged. "I assume Roza stayed over with her and just stuck a needle into her when she was sleeping. They found her alone in her apartment."

"Oh my god." It felt like we were talking

about a TV show. This couldn't be real.

"When the book came out I had a complete meltdown, as you can imagine. But I didn't have any proof. Lucy would always print out excerpts and I'd edit them and give them back to her. So when I went to my dad — Lucy was his sister — he acted like I was unhinged with grief. My friends believed me, but of course there was nothing they could do about it. We were freshmen in high school. Even my favorite teacher thought I was delusional. And then" — Zoe smiled, humorless — "I started emailing reporters. When they found out how old I was, they disappeared. Just some crazy teenager from Bumfuck, New York, trying to get attention."

"That's awful." My brain shuffled through this new information. Could Roza have actually murdered someone? It felt like too much. And who knew . . . Maybe Lucy had actually overdosed, and Zoe hadn't been able to accept it?

Then again, Zoe and I were trapped in Roza's dungeon right now. So perhaps I was the one having trouble accepting things.

"So I waited," Zoe went on. "I knew Roza would mess up at some point. Lucy had told me some weird things about her, especially towards the end, when she was starting to realize what kind of person Roza really was. She told me Roza had a personal assistant who was in love with her, obsessed with her." She shrugged. "Yana."

"Yana?" It was hard to imagine her, cold as she was, obsessed with anyone.

"And she told me about this too." Zoe waved an arm around. "Lucy visited when Roza bought Blackbriar. She didn't remodel it for a long time, but Roza showed her around the old mansion. She was really excited about the secret passage and the secret room. Apparently she joked about using it as a secret writing factory, forcing young girls to churn out her stories."

The words, shared in Zoe's flat voice, made me shiver.

"And so even though no one believed me, I didn't give up. I kept track of Roza, reading all her magazine interviews and articles at the library. There were a lot after *Lion's Rose* came out. No one had liked *Lady X,* but people loved *Lion's Rose.* And as she came out with more books — *Polar Star* and *Maiden Pink* — I knew there was no way she'd written them. I kept waiting for something, some news to break. But she kept getting away with it." Zoe sighed. "Ten years after Lucy died, Roza poured all this money into remodeling Blackbriar. I read all those articles too. And none of them mentioned the secret passage or room. Wouldn't that be something cool you'd want to show journalists? Roza kept it to herself." She picked at the duvet, her eyes faraway. "But it didn't matter. At that point I realized I had to move on. I could follow Roza's every move, but it wasn't going to change anything. I was in my mid-twenties, living at home with my dad. I'd squandered all this energy and focus for *years.* So I went back to school, got my degree, and tried to live a normal life. Got a job, got married, got divorced. That last one was rough, but overall things were pretty good. I never even thought about Roza anymore. Until . . ." The corners of her lips lifted. "I've never been a spiritual person. Not after Lucy died. But when I got that text, it made me reconsider. It was too much of a coincidence."

"What text?" I was fully immersed, picturing Zoe standing in a sun-filled kitchen picking up her phone.

"My friend's daughter, who was going to school in Atlanta, got into the retreat." Zoe stared at me, her eyes wide, as if she were learning the news again. "Can you believe it? And this was my close friend from *high school.* She knew all about Roza. And she wasn't about to let her daughter go. She wasn't going to let her daughter spend a month with a murderer. So then I had to decide what to do with this information. I knew an opportunity like this would never come up again. I had to go. If I could fool them into thinking I was Poppy, I would have a way into Blackbriar. I could snoop around, and I could find the secret room. I would find *something,* some evidence to show people who she really is: a con artist who has murdered at least one person and has been stealing people's books her entire career. I knew that if I could just get in, I'd be able to take her down."

Zoe was gripping the duvet tightly in her left fist, and now she released it. "So I convinced Poppy to let me go in her place. I paid her more than I could afford. I dyed my hair and tried to figure out how to dress and do my makeup like a twenty-eight-year-old PR girl from Atlanta. I got an unpublished book I could copy, from a friend who works in a bookstore. And I showed up." Zoe shrugged. "It worked. It was easier than I expected. Wren — all of you — believed me. I mean, who would turn down a chance to meet with the great Roza Vallo?"

We were both quiet. The story had left my head spinning.

"So Roza hasn't written any of her books,"

I finally said, my lips feeling numb.

"No. Except for *Lady X.*"

"But . . ." The idea wouldn't compute. "That can't be true. She wrote . . ."

"The only book she wrote was *Lady X,*" Zoe repeated. "The one that bombed. Everything else was from someone else. At one point I hired a forensic writing analyst, who confirmed it. Roza edited the books to make them sound more similar. But they were all written by different people."

"Even *Devil's Tongue?*" A sudden indignation swelled inside me. An outrage, a bait-and-switch at the heart of my very own writerly passion.

Zoe stared at me, confused. "It was written by Mila. Her friend who supposedly got sick. Roza poisoned her."

"Oh my god." I lowered my head into my hands, feeling suddenly nauseous.

"I thought you knew." Zoe sounded surprised. "Or at least had an inkling. You told that ghost story the first night. About the girl who killed her friend."

"I did?" I didn't remember, but then words started coming back to me distantly, as if from a dream. *Once upon a time there was a girl who had a best friend. They did everything together. They played together, they went to bookstores, they played pranks on their family. And then one day one of the girls was kind of a bitch to the other girl, and so the first girl decided to kill her . . .*

"I thought you had to at least be suspicious. And that you were pushing Roza to see how she'd react." Zoe blinked. "That's why I tried to drag you down to the basement with me when she drugged us. I know I wasn't being too articulate at the time."

"No. I had no idea." I hadn't even thought about the story afterwards; I'd been too upset after my scare in the basement. Had an unconscious part of me guessed? Had it been trying to send me a message I was too dull to hear?

"So the sleepwalking . . . that was faked?" It felt urgent to pin everything down.

"I thought it was a good excuse if anyone found me looking around." She smiled wanly. "I almost spilled everything to you right then. But I couldn't totally trust you. I thought maybe you were a friend of Roza's that she'd snuck into the retreat. But when Roza drugged us, my guard went down. I wasn't really in my right mind."

"Because of the LSD."

"Well, yes. And the Rohypnol."

"What?" I exclaimed. "We were roofied?"

"I'm almost certain." She rubbed her forehead. "I've done LSD before and it wasn't like that. I barely remember bringing you down here. I think I was alone when I found the keypad. I don't know how I remembered the code in that state."

"How did you know the code?" I asked.

"Lucy told me the password to Roza's safe in her New York apartment. She thought it was touching at first. It was the day Mila died." Her lips twisted. "Now we know how fucked-up it is."

"So it was the same password. And you got in."

"Yes. There." She pointed at the basement door. "I got in, walked past the cell, and went into the control room. I vaguely remember sitting on a chair and watching the monitors. Then I passed out. Woke up in here." She shivered, then wrapped her arms around each other. I slipped an arm around her shoulders.

"I'm going to die in here." She said the words in a flat monotone.

"No you're not." I responded automatically; my brain was still sifting through all these new facts.

She wiped at the tears that began running down her face.

"Zoe," I said. "Roza doesn't just kill people for no reason."

"She's a *psychopath*." Zoe sniffled. "And

she must know who I am by now."

"She doesn't. We found your ID, true, but we didn't tell her."

"She was watching," Zoe said firmly.

"Maybe she wasn't. Maybe she missed it."

"She's *always* watching," Zoe insisted. "Plus, she saw me get in here. How else would I know the code?"

"I don't know." I squeezed my eyes shut for a second. The questions felt too complex. "Maybe she didn't see that either. Maybe she thought they left the door open and you wandered in."

"She saw it. She saw everything. What do you think she's doing?" Zoe pulled back to look at me, incredulous. "She's not *writing*, Alex. This whole retreat was just a scheme to trap you all here and steal your books."

Horror ignited in my chest. The sentences broke apart and the words zinged around like a pinball machine: *Scheme. Trap. Steal.*

A creaking sound came from the door to the control room. Zoe and I both stiffened and clutched at each other as the door swung open.

But there was nowhere to hide.

CHAPTER 29

"What the hell." Keira came through first and hurried to the bars. "Are you guys okay?" Her voice was high and strangled sounding.

Taylor followed, eyes wide, taking in every detail. Behind her trailed Wren. With flushed cheeks and glassy eyes, Wren looked seriously ill.

"Guys." Zoe jumped up, her voice a desperate hiss. "You need to go get help. Like, right now." We pressed ourselves against the bars. I had the sudden image of us as puppies in a pet store, straining to be seen. *Pick me!*

"How?" Taylor joined Keira. She touched her chin with both hands, uncertainly, as if her head might tumble off at any second. "The radio's dead."

"Alex said there's a snowmobile." Zoe looked at me. "You need to take it and go get help."

Behind Keira, a stunned Wren muttered: "What the actual fuck?"

"What is this place?" Taylor backed up, looking up at the ceiling.

"Okay. Okay, okay, okay." Keira straightened her glasses with trembling hands. "I'll take the snowmobile. And if I can't find the keys, I'll walk."

"It's too far to walk," I said. "I think it was like fifteen or twenty miles to the convent."

Taylor backed up all the way to the door. Her confused expression was melting into something else. For a second I couldn't process it because it didn't make sense.

It was an undeniable look of contempt.

"Taylor," I said in warning. The others whipped towards her.

It happened so quickly. Taylor swiftly stepped backwards through the door and closed it. A click echoed.

"No." Keira ran to the door and twisted the knob. "It's locked! Taylor, open the door!"

Wren scrambled up to stand. Next to me, Zoe exhaled. I could smell the metallic tang of her breath. My heart thundered in my ears as I sank into a crouch.

The sound of static filled the air. Then

came Taylor's voice from the speaker on the wall.

"Holy shit." She sounded gleeful. "Your faces! I wish you could see them."

"Taylor?" Keira turned towards the white box. "What are you doing?"

"I've got to say, I'm impressed, Poppy." Taylor's voice was casual. "Zoe. Whoever you are. You're an even better actor than me."

Wren moaned, hands pressed to her mouth. Keira stared at Zoe and me, her dark eyes blank, her mouth gaping in astonishment. It was sinking in. I felt a flash of vertigo, another wall of reality crumbling.

"Taylor," Zoe called out, her voice now filled with her old friendliness. "Hey, girl, why don't you come back in here and we can talk about this?"

"Talk about what?" Taylor's voice lowered into a snarl. "How all of you are fucking cunts?"

That shut us up.

"You know," Taylor went on, her tone thoughtful. "I can't even tell who's the most annoying. Wren, you are so full of yourself, it's unbelievable. You truly think you're better than everyone else. Guess what? You're actually just a pointless influencer who's going to fade into obscurity the second you get a wrinkle. K, let's move on to you. You complain all the time. Like, *all* the time. You think everyone's out to get you because you're Black, even though you basically had way more opportunities than I did. It's ridiculous."

Keira was frozen, expressionless, staring at the speaker. I felt a flush of shock and indignation on her behalf just as Taylor said my own name.

"And, Alex . . . ugh. You're a mess." Her tone went high. *"I'm Alex, feel sorry for me. Everyone is so so mean to me! And I might be queer but I'm too much of a fucking baby to accept it. Or maybe I'm just pretending to be so I can play with people's minds."*

The words pounded at me like physical blows.

"It was really shitty what you did," Taylor went on. "Flirting with me one minute, running away from me the next. Throwing yourself at me in the basement, and then pretending like it never happened. Holy shit, dude. Get a fucking grip."

I remained mute, my hands clamped on the bars.

"But I'm not Wren, right?" Taylor sighed. "And honestly, I don't want to go anywhere *near* the fucking sadomasochistic mind games you two are playing with each other.

390

No thanks. If that's what happens after you hook up with someone, Al, then I'll consider myself lucky."

Taylor knew about me and Wren. When I'd only told Roza.

"Anyway," she said and chuckled. "Oh my *god*! It's such a relief not to have to pretend anymore. Y'all are just too fucking much."

"This is Roza's plan?" Keira asked. "For you to trap us in here like this?"

A snort. "Roza's plan was to kill you. It's not like this changes anything."

Wren gasped.

"Taylor." Keira cleared her throat. "What are you talking about?"

No response.

"No. You cannot disappear right now." Keira's voice rose to a shout. "Taylor!"

I sank to the ground. Keira's yells became distant and far-off.

No matter how many times Keira called her name, Taylor didn't respond.

Keira's initial reaction was to try to jimmy open the door. Wren stood behind her, pale and watchful.

"It won't work," Zoe said. She'd dragged the pallet over near the door and we both were sitting on it, watching. "It's a dead bolt."

I'd returned from whatever shocked, numbed place I'd fallen into. Now I was attempting to manage the desperate jolts of helplessness that sizzled in my chest.

"Okay." Keira exhaled with a huff and turned towards us. "Poppy or Zoe or whoever you are, you need to tell me exactly what is going on."

Wren and Keira settled on the floor as Zoe spoke. I found myself tuning out, drifting back to the revelation about Taylor. I was starting to match the images of the electric-orange demoness with Taylor's compact body. It hadn't been Lamia; instead, it had been Taylor's lips I'd kissed, Taylor's nipples I'd teased, Taylor's clit I'd tongued and sucked.

In another world, it could have been a momentous experience. Because I *had* connected with Taylor during our one-on-one conversations. There had been a true spark of attraction between us, even if I'd been too scared to handle it at the time. And if Roza hadn't drugged us, our basement hookup could've been a life-changing sexual experience. It could've showed me the truth, that it was time to admit to — to *celebrate* — the fact that I was attracted to certain women.

Unfortunately, that's not how things had

played out. And I was now locked in a dungeon, and my sexual partner was taunting us.

"I didn't know Taylor was a part of it." Zoe was wrapping up. "Maybe it was even her in the mask. I figured it was Yana. Or Chitra. They're all pretty small."

My stomach growled loudly. After all, I hadn't had dinner.

"How'd you guys get down here?" I asked, trying to distract myself.

"Roza said she was going to take the snowmobile and check if the roads had been cleared," Keira said. "And Taylor said we should look for you, since you hadn't come back. She found the passage in the wardrobe. Well, pretended to."

I pictured Taylor's surprised, excited face: *Guys, look*!

"What are we going to do?" Wren rasped and coughed.

"We'll figure it out." I had no idea where the soothing words came from. My stomach growled again.

"They've been feeding you?" I asked.

Zoe nodded. "The masked person came a few times to give me food and water."

"You haven't seen Roza?" Keira asked.

"Nope."

"We have to fight them." Speaking in a

low voice, Keira locked eyes with Wren. "Someone will come through that door eventually. And when they do, we have to take them down."

"How?" Wren clasped her hands together, looking miserable.

"I'm trying to remember what I learned in that self-defense workshop." Keira considered. "It was a long time ago."

"Go for the crotch." Zoe erupted in an incongruous giggle. "Usually the attacker is a guy, though."

"Eyes," I said. Wren and I had taken a class through work, years before. "And nose? Can't you push up with your palm and smash their nose?"

"Yes. Good." Keira touched Wren's shoulder. "It's going to be our only chance."

"Okay." Wren fished a disintegrating tissue from her pocket and blew her nose.

Despite Keira's confident words, a deep fear shone from the depths of her pupils. It chilled me. Keira had always been the calm one, even while picking the lock of the office or searching my room for cameras.

Now she looked terrified.

"We're going to get through this." I said the words slowly, like an incantation.

But the phrase sounded hollow, even to me.

394

■ ■ ■ ■

When the door did open three hours later, it happened so quickly that we failed to register it until it was closed again.

We leapt to our feet, a second too late. Someone had opened the door and launched water bottles into the space. They now rolled down the concrete floor, crackling.

Zoe muttered, clutching the bars.

Keira gathered them and set them against the wall. They gleamed, sweating with condensation from the cold. I swallowed, wincing at my raw, dry throat.

"When's the last time you drank anything?" I asked Zoe.

"A long time ago."

"We can't drink these." Keira uncapped one. "They're all open. Roza or Taylor or whoever must've put something in them."

"Roza's trying to drug us?" My empty stomach clenched. "Again?"

"Of course." Keira set the bottle down. "She needs to get Wren and me in there with you guys. I'll bet there are more roofies in here."

Wren moaned and slid back down to sit on the ground. Her cheeks were now a candy-apple pink, her eyes shiny with fever.

"How long can people survive without water?" I asked.

"Only a couple of days. Three days?" Keira cocked her head. "I think you're supposed to drink half a gallon every day. Like eight full glasses. Right?"

Zoe eyed the bottles. "I might have to drink one of those pretty soon."

"What if it's something lethal?" Keira asked. "What if they're trying to get rid of us? I mean, how do we expect this to end? We know too much. They're not going to let us go."

Wren started to cry quietly into her hands.

I stared. Wren had always been the brave one, the adventurous one. She'd talked our way into private parties teeming with models and celebrities. She'd snuck us into sold-out concerts through back doors and kitchens. She'd gone off on tattooed bikers and coked-up dealers and even drunk Jersey girls, throwing drinks in their faces when they took our barstools or stole the shots she ordered. And even the Jersey girls had stepped down, slinging insults, because they'd been able to sense what everyone else knew: you didn't fuck with Wren.

Seeing her crumble like this was making my head spin.

But maybe part of that was the hunger: it was shifting from a dull ache into a sharp need. Even worse, the water bottles had made me realize how thirsty I was. My lips felt cracked, my tongue fuzzy. I imagined cool water filling my mouth with an erotic longing, like a sudden rainstorm sinking into a dusty desert.

"So now what?" I asked.

Zoe broke the ensuing contemplative silence: "I'll do it."

"Do what?" Keira asked, suspicious. She'd placed an arm around Wren's shoulders. There had to be some kind of heat down here — after all, you couldn't see your breath — but it felt bitterly cold. Frigid air seeped between the threads of my thin sweater. And Zoe just wore a flimsy dress.

"I'll drink the water." Zoe motioned for a bottle. "You guys can see what happens to me."

"You really think that's a good idea?" I asked. Just a half hour before, she'd been crying about how she was going to die down here, and now she wanted to drink a high-risk beverage?

"They're not going to kill me with a water bottle." She shrugged. "That's not Roza's style."

"Either way, it's not happening." Keira

shook her head.

"They turned off the heat." Zoe rubbed her arms. "It's getting colder. It's all just going to get worse."

I heard a sharp clacking sound.

"What is that?" I asked.

"It's Wren." Keira bent her head down. "Her teeth."

"Sorry." Wren grimaced. "I'm really cold. And hot."

Keira felt Wren's forehead. "You're sweating."

"Fever," I said. "That's not good."

The speaker crackled and our faces swiveled.

"Good evening." It was Taylor, speaking with her English schoolteacher accent. "This is your tour guide, Mrs. Lillyputter, letting you know that your immersive experience comes with its own set of guidelines. Rule number one: In order *not* to die of thirst, you must drink the beverages provided. All of you. Please rest assured that these are perfectly safe and only include a few drops of a special ingredient to ensure the most quality rest on your first night."

Wren buried her head against Keira's shoulder, moaning.

"Rule number two," Taylor went on. "To ensure that our tenderest of guests remains alive, we highly recommend allowing us to provide her with medications, heaters, and blankets. In order for us to provide these, please see rule number one regarding drinking the provided beverages."

"Taylor." Keira's voice broke. "What the fuck is wrong with you?"

"Rule number three," Taylor went on, undeterred. "Once you are situated, you will have complete access to the hostess of the trip, the inimitable Roza Vallo. She will make herself available in the morning."

"Taylor," I called, just wanting to stop the psychotically exuberant voice. "Please, will you come in here and talk to us?"

"If you have any further questions or comments, please hold until the end of our tour, when a feedback card will be provided. Thank you and have a lovely day." Another electronic crackle, and she was gone.

"Okay, has she lost her mind?" I asked, infuriated. "Is this a psychotic break? Or has she been like this the whole time? Keira? You were close with her, right?"

"Sounds like you're the one who hooked up with her." Keira pressed her lips together. "Don't put this on me."

"I'm not. I just . . ." My cheeks warmed. "It happened when we were tripping. I mean . . . I guess there was some interest there. But . . ."

"It's okay." Zoe touched my arm. "She's a psychopath. Just like Roza. She can mimic human emotions well enough, but she doesn't feel them. She just sees it all as a game."

A game. A memory resurfaced.

"Wren," I said. "Taylor told me that she heard you telling Roza that you'd thought about getting a restraining order against me."

Wren shook her head. "I never said that."

"Well, she told *me* you didn't like my book." Keira snorted.

"That *I* didn't like it?" I asked. "I love it."

"She got me too," Zoe said. "She said Wren had told her I was like an annoying younger sister to her. Not that I really cared. No offense, Wren."

"So she was lying to all of us this whole time," I said. "Turning us against each other."

The maraca sound resumed: Wren's teeth were chattering again.

"We have to do something." Desperation rushed up through my throat. "She's really sick."

Zoe reached a hand through the bars. "Give me a bottle."

"No." I motioned to Keira. "Give me one.

I'll drink it."

"We *all* have to," Zoe said. "That's what Taylor said. Just let me go first to make sure it's okay."

"There's no time." I was almost shouting. "We've been down here for hours. Wren needs help now."

Keira moved away from Wren, who curled up on the cement floor. She handed bottles to us.

"Are you sure?" I was suddenly terrified of actually going through with it.

"You're right." Keira looked defeated. "Wren's really sick. We've been down here a long time. And I don't want someone's death on my conscience." She grabbed the other two bottles and sat back down. "And I think Zoe's right. Roza's not going to kill us. Yet." She touched Wren's back. "What do you think?"

Wren sat up and grabbed a bottle. We watched in silence as she drank deeply, drops running down the sides of her face. After it was empty, she lay back down.

Keira, Zoe, and I held the bottles. I felt two powerful and conflicting urges: to pour the water down my gullet immediately. And to hurl the bottle as far away as I could.

Zoe shuddered, either from cold or from fear.

"Bottoms up," she said, and twisted off the cap.

CHAPTER 30

I awoke to the smell of coffee. I stirred, comfortable in that safe, fuzzy place between sleep and wakefulness. For a second I thought I was in my apartment in Brooklyn and my roommate was brewing a batch in the kitchen.

But my bed was too hard. My eyes flipped open.

I was still in the dungeon.

Slowly I sat up, taking stock. It was much warmer, that was one thing. There were two space heaters on the other side of the bars, close enough that we could reach out and turn them up or down. I was on the folded-up duvet I'd passed out on. But the inside of the cell was now littered with pillows, comforters, and colorful wool blankets. Keira and Zoe slept back-to-back on a futon. Beyond, Wren slept on a twin mattress.

I stood shakily, nausea rising in my stomach. Fighting it down, I hurried over to the mattress, keeping my head low in the cave-like space. I distantly noted a new Japanese screen in front of the toilet. How nice.

Wren's face was hidden beneath a blanket and I pulled it back.

She wasn't breathing. Her face was pale and waxy: a death mask.

My heart stopped.

But then her eyelids fluttered and she exhaled. I pressed my hands into my eyes, taking a shaky breath. She was alive.

"Al?" She sat up, touching her forehead. Her diamond ring sparkled in the gloom. "What happened?"

"We all drank the water." I struggled to sound calm. "It knocked us all out."

"The water?" She swallowed. "Oh yeah."

"How are you feeling?"

"Okay. I don't think I have a fever any-more." She glanced beyond me.

"No." She jumped up unsteadily and then hurried to the door. It squealed as she pushed against it. "No!"

I followed her. "It's locked."

"What the fuck?" she whispered, staring at me.

"I know." I shrugged, feeling useless. And loopy. "Look, they made us coffee."

A large coffeemaker was on the other side

of the door, plugged into an extension cord, along with the heaters. Beside it were four stoneware mugs as well as individual creams and sugars.

Keira and Zoe stirred at the other end of the cell, on the futon.

"Guys." I straightened and slammed the top of my head into the concrete. I tried to ignore the pain as I ran over.

"Hey." Zoe smiled weakly. "We made it."

"How are you guys feeling?" I asked.

In response, Keira jumped up and ran to the toilet. She retched behind the screen.

"I'm okay." Zoe tucked a strand behind her ear. Her blond hair was now so greasy it looked dark. "Someone decorated, huh?"

"Yeah," I said. "Dungeon chic."

Zoe looked behind me. "How're you, Wren?"

"Physically, better." Wren collapsed on the futon next to Zoe. "Mentally . . . not great."

Zoe stood and went to the coffee machine. "Keira, you want coffee?"

Keira swore softly from behind the screen.

"We don't think this is drugged?" I approached and Zoe handed me a mug.

"Could be." Zoe shrugged. "But there's not a lot we can do about it." Without the young, energetic PR girl act, Zoe seemed like a completely different person: unruffled, purposeful. She must be in her early forties, and even though she didn't look it, she acted like it.

Keira rejoined us. "We're fucked, guys." She wiped at her mouth and accepted a mug from Zoe. "Now that we're all locked in here, we're officially fucked."

"Not yet." Zoe waved us in and spoke the words in a whisper: "We have to convince them to open the door of the cell."

"And how do we do that?" Keira's eyes were dull as she raised the coffee to her lips.

"Good morning!" Taylor's voice burst from the speaker. "Welcome to day two of Roza's retreat-within-a-retreat." The exaggerated English accent made me grit my teeth. "Because you all did such a wonderful job with yesterday's instructions, you have a treat coming. Yes, on top of the blankets and heaters and coffee. Stay tuned!"

Sometime later — fifteen minutes, forty-five? — the door creaked open. We were still on the futon. Barely speaking, we'd drifted off in our own thoughts as we waited for whatever came next. I struggled to make sense of what was happening, but my mind was filled with fog. Every so often I'd veer into another feeling: that this wasn't real.

That somehow I'd fallen into a dream I couldn't wake up from. That sense of unreality would touch on a deep, wretched panic. So I'd press my hands against the concrete floor to pull myself back. This *was* real. This was the present reality. But I couldn't stay with that information, either. The vague confusion would return, only to start the whole cycle over again.

Taylor's arrival was, in a strange way, a relief.

"Hi!" When she strolled through the door, she looked odd, and it took me a second to figure out why: she was dressed in Wren's clothes. Taylor was shorter than Wren, and the sleeves and ankles of the teal jumpsuit bunched. "Like my outfit?" She posed, hands on hips. "I hope it's okay, Wren. I didn't want your gorgeous designer pieces to go to waste."

Wren glared at her.

"Jeez." Taylor dropped her hand. "Look at the sourpuss faces on y'all. Aren't you happy that it's not ten degrees in here anymore? And that we gave you coffee?" She shook her head. "Talk about ungrateful."

Fury tightened like a fist in my chest. Taylor was as excited as she'd been the night of Valentine's Day. She was truly relishing this.

"You're lucky I'm not in charge." Taylor crossed her arms, considering. "This cell would look very different, let me tell you."

"Taylor." Wren's voice quavered. "Please, please let us out."

"You want me to let you out? Sure!" Taylor's cheerful grin widened. "Just guess the magic word."

A grinding sound came from the far end of the room. The metal door to the basement slowly swung inward.

"Chitra!" Wren jumped to her feet, knocking her head on the low ceiling. Keira grabbed my arm.

"Don't talk to her," Taylor commanded.

Chitra's shoulders hunched over as she shuffled in with a tray. She looked at least ten years older and fragile.

"Sit down," Taylor directed. Slowly, Wren settled back onto the futon, rubbing her head. Chitra refused to look at us as she set the tray in front of the door. Her eyes were red and raw.

The smell from the covered pot — some rich meat — was making me salivate. Besides the pot, the tray held four bowls, silverware, and a loaf of fresh bread. Taylor bent and touched something at the bottom of the door. A small section of it sprang outward towards her, swiveling like a doggie door. She pushed the tray through.

"Wait for it . . ." Taylor drew out the last word. "Go!"

Zoe ran to the tray, pulled off the pot's lid, and dished out the stew. My stomach twisted as I waited for my bowl; had I ever been this hungry before?

"Hold on," Taylor called to Chitra, who already had one hand on the door. "Don't you want to see them enjoy your culinary work?"

Zombie-like, Chitra turned back around.

"Chitra," I said in a normal tone, my mouth already full. Her eyes flicked to mine.

"I told you not to talk to her." Taylor's voice thundered in the confined space. "Do you want me to take away your food?"

"No." I looked down. "Sorry."

"Good." Taylor smiled and settled onto the floor, cross-legged. "Chits, you want to tell Alex how you fucked with her in the basement the first night?"

"What?" Wren asked.

"Roza told her to blow out *all* the candles, but apparently she disobeyed and left one burning for you." Taylor shook her head. "She's lucky the light went out on its own. It sounds like you were on the verge of seeing her."

Chitra stood still, head hanging.

"Why?" I asked. It was hard to divide my attention between Taylor and the food.

"Roza wanted to push you." Taylor chuckled. "You were clearly on the edge to begin with." She turned her head. "Okay, you can go."

Chitra slipped out and shut the door behind her. I chewed. It was strangely reassuring to find out that it hadn't just been my imagination. But it was nearly impossible to imagine sweet Chitra sneaking around like that.

"Eat up," Taylor said. "Roza wants you to be in a good mood when she comes down here."

I locked eyes with Zoe.

"When is that happening?" Zoe's voice was light.

"I don't know." Taylor smoothed back her hair. "Soon, I think."

So Taylor wasn't really in charge, despite the way she was acting: ordering us around, commanding Chitra to stay and go.

"You don't know?" I asked.

Taylor's eyes blazed. "Excuse me?"

I finished the second bowl and set it down. "I would've thought you'd know."

"I do know." Taylor was indignant.

"She's just making you do the dirty work." Zoe had picked up on my thoughts. "When did she hire you? How much does she pay you?"

"Roza doesn't pay me." Taylor scoffed. "She's my girlfriend."

There was a short, stunned silence.

"But," Wren's voice warbled. "You said your girlfriend's name was Kitty."

"That's my nickname for her." Taylor smirked.

I thought suddenly of my first night at Blackbriar, hearing the sounds of lovemaking coming from Roza's chambers.

It hadn't been her editor Ian at all. It had been Taylor.

Zoe recovered first. "So that's the reason Roza keeps you around." She grimaced. "Not because you're some lowly schoolteacher pretending to be a genius writer."

"You want genius?" Taylor stood and towered over us. "How about *Maiden Pink*? Ever hear of that? Well, guess who fucking wrote it?"

"Taylor." Another voice came through the loudspeaker. It was Yana's: monotonic, expressionless. "Come upstairs. Roza wants you."

Yana's calm voice was like an icicle pressed against my spine. Of course she was in on it too.

Taylor wore a disgusted sneer. "You four

411

act like you're such hot shit. But you're pathetic. Your books aren't even that good."

"*Taylor.*"

Taylor flinched at Yana's sharp tone. "Coming." With a final glare at us, she left through the basement.

I turned to Zoe. "You were right. Roza uses other people to write her books."

Zoe was licking the inside of her bowl. "Duh."

My stomach burbled from the meal and it was a toss-up as to whether the food would stay down. I peed behind the screen, gagging at the scent of my urine combining with Keira's bile, which lined the bowl. What happened when this camping toilet got full?

We sat on the futon like it was a boat in the middle of the ocean. Minutes passed, melting into hours.

And then, finally, the door opened. Roza strode in with Taylor close behind. We jumped to our feet, moving as if by magnetic force towards the bars.

"Hello, girls." Roza waited in the middle of the entryway. Taylor set down a stool and Roza settled herself on it like a regal queen visiting her prisoners. Her jasmine perfume wafted over us. "How's everyone feeling?"

Finally, Keira spoke for all of us: "Are you fucking serious right now?"

Taylor's expression was disturbingly anticipatory as she gently set down a heavy tote bag. Roza, on the other hand, looked slightly annoyed, as if we'd interrupted her plans for the day. She wore a chunky knit gray dress, red lipstick, and platform boots. Seeing her on the other side of the bars, the concrete wall behind her, she looked like she was ready to pose for some artsy magazine.

"I know you're upset." Roza held up a hand. "And I understand that. This wasn't how it was supposed to happen." Her gaze landed on Zoe. "But I didn't know we had an interloper in our midst."

"Roza?" Now Wren was using her calm, charming voice even though it was shakier than usual. "This is all a mistake. A total misunderstanding. If you let us out, we can talk about it."

"Wren, darling." Roza gazed at her with affection. "My beautiful bird. I wish that were the case. It was more fun playing with you all upstairs. This is going to be a bit more tedious. But *c'est la vie.* You all wanted — needed — to figure out the riddle. So here we are." She looked at Taylor, who picked up the tote bag and approached the bars.

"Back up, please," Taylor ordered. I noted the "please"; she was only using it because Roza was there. We retreated a few feet and sat. Taylor tossed in water bottles through the door. They rolled towards us. Zoe opened hers immediately, guzzling it down. I forced myself to take only a few sips. It was like liquid gold coating my throat, which had been made dryer by the coffee and salty stew.

"Now, girls," Roza went on. "I know that this is a surprise. But since we're here, let's try to make the best of it."

Keira scoffed. She'd left her bottle in front of her, untouched.

"You can be mad at me; that's fine." Roza folded her hands. "But you're entering a survival situation now."

"Survival?" Wren sounded panicky.

"Don't interrupt me." Roza's voice was suddenly cold.

I reached out and grasped Wren's hand.

"I don't like whining," Roza went on, her voice clipped. "Understood? Here's what's going to happen. You have two options. You can sit in this cell and die of thirst. It will only take a few days. We still have a week and a half left of this retreat, so no one will

414

miss you until it's too late."

"That's a lot of bodies, Roza," Zoe said. "How will you explain that?"

"Fire." Roza smiled, as if drifting into a happy reverie. "Fire takes all but the bones. You should know that, Alex. It happened to Daphne. All it would take is one candle on a desk, lighting a curtain on fire. Your whole wing would go up."

The cool words slammed into me like I'd walked into traffic. Horror was doing funny things to my body, causing my right foot to twitch, my arms to feel frozen in place.

"It would be a tragic event," Roza said, solemn. "We'd probably set up a new charity in your names. Something for other young female writers. That would be nice, wouldn't it?"

"What's the other option?" I asked. "You said there were two."

Roza grinned. "Good question." She again looked at Taylor, who opened the tote bag and pulled out an extension cord with a power strip. Taylor plugged it into the outlet near the door and slipped the end through the bars. We watched in stunned disbelief as she pulled open the small slot at the bottom of the door and slipped all our laptops and cords through.

"The other option is to write," Roza said.

"As long as you reach the word count each day, you'll be given water and meals. The count will be higher, since we've lost a couple of days due to all this nonsense. But I think you'll agree that there's not much else to do in here."

"And what happens at the end?" Zoe's voice quavered. "Another fire?"

Roza rubbed her chin. "Good question, Ms. Canard. So curious, just like Lucy."

I felt Zoe go rigid next to me.

"This is your fault, you know," Roza said to her. "I planned this retreat expecting we could all come to a peaceful agreement. I only needed one novel. I thought it could even be a team decision, picking the winner who gets published under their name, and the winner who gets published under mine. You must realize that if you give a book to me, I take care of you for the rest of your life. There are a lot of egos in the group, of course, and I figured it would take a little convincing. But, in the end, one of you would've agreed."

"What a great honor," Keira muttered.

Roza glared at her before continuing. "So this is all to say that I had high hopes that we could start and end with positive rein-forcement. That no one would have to get hurt. Unfortunately, Zoe ruined that for all

416

of you by bumbling into this space. Even then, I did everything I could to protect the rest of you by making you think she was dead. But you just couldn't let it go, could you?"

"So this was your plan B?" I asked, my voice cracking. "Locking us up?"

"Yes." Roza focused on me. "I always have a backup plan."

"Why would we do anything for you in here?" Keira scoffed. "If you're just going to kill us anyway?"

"Now, I didn't say that." Roza shifted on the stool. "My methods may be extreme, but they work. If you finish your novels in this setting, I can guarantee that they'll be magnificent. Zoe, I know you were copying that book, but I'm assuming you can still write, even if it's been a few decades. So I'll allow you to start something new. And we'll proceed with the original plan. I need only one book. I have plenty of money to share with everyone, and I know most of you need it. Of course, I'll need collateral to make sure you don't tell anyone what happened here. But cults do that kind of thing all the time. And besides" — she smirked — "who would believe you? There'd be no proof. Just a bunch of wannabe writers trying to get famous."

Wren shook her head. "I can't do it. I can't."

"Well, that's too bad." Roza raised a palm. "Because this is an all-or-nothing proposition. If one of you refuses, none of you get to drink or eat."

Wren covered her face with her hands.

"Fuck!" came the muffled cry.

"I know you hate me right now." Roza's voice was warm. "But eventually you'll thank me. You won't be able to hold out for very long, and you might as well start today instead of two days from now. Either way, it's going to be brilliant. Remember: 'What is to give light must endure burning.' "

"Are you . . . ?" Keira let out a startled bark of laughter. "Victor Frankl, huh? Love the irony."

Roza smiled softly. "I think I'm going to enjoy watching your process the most, Keira."

Zoe pulled her laptop onto her lap. The rest of us watched as she opened the screen.

"Good girl," Roza said approvingly. "Let's see, the word count is now six thousand per day. We'll bring down a printer and you'll print your pages by midnight. If any of you don't make the count, there will be no food or water the following day."

"Roza." My voice faltered. "How are we

supposed to write?"

Roza got to her feet and stretched. "I think you'll find it a great comfort, actually. The mind needs something to work on in this type of solitude. Otherwise it starts to tear itself apart. Any other questions?"

We were mute.

"Good." Roza fluttered her fingers. "Then get to work, my little chickadees. And remember: we're watching you. Don't get any ideas with all these cords."

My breath hitched in my throat.

"Wait," Wren called, her voice breaking. But Roza and Taylor were already leaving, closing the basement door firmly behind them.

Excerpt from *The Great Commission*

Daphne gripped the frigid bars, shivering with cold and disbelief. Her brain struggled to accept her new surroundings. It felt like she'd been dropped into a nightmare. After growing up in close, tepid quarters, she wasn't afraid of enclosed spaces. But she *was* frightened of silence. Blackbriar itself was a noiseless place, and she'd survived only by filling it with sound. Inviting Florence and Abigail over. Chatting with Martha in the kitchen. Even humming to her cat, Goldie. Down here there was no sound but her own breathing.

Horace had drugged her food and she'd woken up here. Martha must have helped; after all, she was the one who dropped off the tray in Daphne's new bedroom, the one she'd moved into to get away from Horace. They hadn't properly spoken in weeks. After he burned her paintings, she'd gone about the purification process more stealthily. But she'd still been too confident, too blithe. Expecting that his travels and his affair with the young maid Dina would keep him occupied. She'd understood that her refusal to act like a good and proper wife would provoke him. But she'd underestimated Horace: she hadn't suspected the dark, secret places he kept locked up in his manor and in his mind.

The chilly air pierced the blanket's thin fabric. She lay on her back and closed her eyes, wondering where Lamia was. Daphne had been communicating with her directly for the past few days. While Florence had left after the first commission, too disturbed to continue, Abigail had continued to help. She was supposed to come on Tuesday for the preparations. Daphne wondered what excuse Horace would give Abigail for her absence.

Save me, Lamia. Please save me.

Lamia's reply came from the black depths behind Daphne's closed eyes: *Save you from what?* She sounded surprisingly mild.

Horace. He's locked me down here.

So what?

So what? Daphne's brows furrowed. *How can we move forward if I can't get out?*

On the contrary, Lamia answered. *Now you will have even less distractions as you prepare.*

But how will I save your transmissions? The Great Commission —

Do not worry about that, Lamia interrupted. *Prepare yourself as we discussed.*

Daphne was silent and sullen.

This is part of the process, Lamia went on gently. *Do you trust me?*

Daphne replied grudgingly: *Of course.*

Then return to your practices.

With a sigh, Daphne sat up, crossing her legs. The heated rage towards Horace still coursed through her.

But she did trust Lamia. And she knew Lamia's power was much greater than her own. Or Horace's, for that matter. Soon she would channel it again, feeling it running through her veins like lightning.

She needed to be ready for it.

CHAPTER 31

A few hours later, at some indeterminate time, the basement door flew open and Taylor strolled in. She carried a round, large-faced clock that I recognized from the kitchen.

We'd pulled the futon and the twin mattress against the back wall, using pillows to make them both into daybeds we could sit on to work. Now we paused as Taylor set the clock on the floor against the back wall. It was nearly noon.

"Voilà." She straightened and brushed her hands together. "Remember, pages due at midnight. We're going to be turning off the lights from midnight to seven."

"When's lunch?" Keira asked, expressionless.

Taylor's eyes narrowed. "Well, that's presumptuous. You haven't turned in any pages yet."

"The toilet also needs to be emptied."

Keira gestured with her chin.

"What am I? Your fucking slave?"

Keira's hands curled in her lap. A grin spread across Taylor's face, as if she'd suddenly become aware of her choice of words.

"Hey," I said quickly. I felt annoyed, but we needed to use facetime with Taylor to figure out if we could manipulate her. "Taylor, did you seriously write *Maiden Pink*?"

"Yeah." Taylor leaned against the wall, crossing her arms.

"That relationship between the college student and her professor — was that you and Roza?" I leaned forward, widening my eyes with interest. Keira, Zoe, and Wren watched me.

"Not in real life. It was based on a fantasy I had. I wrote it to distract myself from dealing with snot-nosed little rich kids all day." She scoffed. "And I found an email address of hers and sent it. I never expected her to write back." The words tumbled out, eager to be heard. "It felt like a dream when she did. She asked if I wanted to meet her in New York. It was . . ." She sighed. "It made everything worth it, you know?"

"So how'd she brainwash you into letting her publish your book?" Keira asked.

Taylor just shrugged. "I mean, it was an

exchange. She said I could stay with her. And we were basically in love by that point."

"But wasn't that hard?" Zoe asked, earnest. "Seeing all the reviews and articles?"

"We were in love," Taylor repeated, over-enunciating. "I could see how hard it was for her, not being able to write. It's not like she didn't try. So I was happy to give that to her. Plus, how many people would have read it if it was my name on the cover? What were the chances of it getting published in the first place?"

The door opened and Yana stepped through in her pink tracksuit. While Taylor had become more lively, and Chitra had shut down, Yana looked exactly the same.

"Roza wants you upstairs," Yana told Taylor. She opened the door slot and pushed through plates of plastic-wrapped sandwiches.

"Cool." Taylor's chest puffed up slightly. "Later, losers."

I wondered if Yana had come down to stop Taylor from talking to us. And then I remembered what Zoe had told me when it had been just the two of us in the cell.

Roza had a personal assistant who was in love with her, obsessed with her. Yana.

"Yana," I said, the realization dawning. "You weren't just her assistant. You wrote

425

Polar Star, didn't you?"

She didn't answer, but two rosy dots appeared on her cheeks.

Zoe set down her laptop. "You did, didn't you?"

"It was beautiful," Wren said softly. Yana looked at her, something hungry in her eyes.

"It was my favorite," I added. "That relationship between the girl and her two aunts. How did you come up with that?"

Yana closed the slot and stood. "Just do what they say. Okay? No one gets hurt."

"Yeah, right," Keira murmured.

"Yana, can you help us?" Zoe asked. "We're really scared."

"Please help us," Wren echoed.

They were pushing her away; her eyes dropped to the floor.

"When did you meet Roza?" I asked, but it was too late. She turned and hurried out of the room.

Six thousand words was a lot, but by midnight when the lights switched off, we'd all printed out our pages and left them on the floor for Taylor to collect. Keira and Zoe collapsed on the futon, while Wren and I lay on the mattress. It was so dark I couldn't see her.

A dark, disturbing thought had begun

426

pulling at me sometime that evening, when I'd paused to hear the symphony of fingers clacking on keyboards. It had struck me that after the initial anger, we'd all pretty quickly agreed to the new plan. And yet again, Roza was getting exactly what she wanted from us.

"Wren," I whispered. She was turned away from me. "Are you sleeping?"

She rolled over. "Huh?"

"I was thinking . . ." I again felt that eerie, desperate vertigo of trying to parse out reality. "Do you think this is still part of the game?"

"What?" she whispered back.

"Roza could've lied to us. What if imprisoning us was part of the plan the whole time? What if . . ." I forced the words out. "What if Zoe or Keira is in on it?"

Wren scoffed. "That's nuts."

"But we know Chitra was part of this, messing with me in the basement. I never would've expected that from her."

"Chitra works for Roza. Zoe and Keira don't."

"Yeah." I rubbed my eyes, starting to feel relieved. "Maybe you're right."

After a moment, Wren whispered: "Zoe *did* lead us to the basement."

"She did." The thought made me shiver.

"And it was pretty dramatic. The sleepwalking, then when she was high . . ."

"And this whole story about her aunt, and how her friend's daughter got into the retreat?" Wren exhaled. "It's a lot."

"Yeah." The conversation was making me anxious. I rubbed at my tensed jaw.

"And what about Keira?" Wren asked. "She really knows how to pick locks? When you guys went to the office, maybe the door wasn't locked at all."

"Could they *all* be in on it?"

"I don't know." Wren shifted. "This is so fucked-up."

"I know."

"Does Roza really think she's going to get away with this?"

I opened and closed my mouth. I didn't have an answer. *Yes* seemed unlikely. But *no* meant a horrific end I couldn't currently deal with.

"We just need to go along with it for now," Wren finally whispered. "Maybe there will be a chance for us to get away."

"Okay." There was no other option.

"You can trust me." Her breath was warm on my face. "Maybe not anyone else. But you can trust me."

"Me too."

Eventually her exhales evened out as she

fell asleep. My mind continued to whir, the thoughts bouncing like pool balls around my skull.

Eventually, I drifted into sleep, but my dreams were filled with danger, something slithering through the dark towards me, getting closer with every breath.

CHAPTER 32

It happened the next night.

The day had gone much as the one before, a grotesque semblance of structure: coffee in the morning, sandwiches for lunch. We typed away in a line, ignoring each other's growing unwashed stench, pretending not to notice when someone inevitably had to pee or defecate. After Keira came back from behind the screen, muttering and clutching her stomach, Wren and I exchanged a look.

Could Keira really be a part of this? How much would one need to be paid to have diarrhea in a dungeon?

Then again, Roza had said it herself: we needed money. We weren't truly impoverished, especially not Wren. But how much did I have in my savings? Not more than two months' buffer. Not enough to quit a job I actively hated.

At seven that night, Taylor and Yana appeared.

"Good evening, ladies," Taylor crooned in a low voice as Yana passed a tray through the door.

"Why are there only three plates?" Keira's fingers remained over her keyboard, like a pianist waiting to begin. "Is this another fun game Roza wants us to play?"

"Actually," Taylor smugly replied, "it's the opposite. You've all been so diligent that Roza decided to restart one-on-one meetings. One of you will get to eat upstairs with her."

Wren and I glanced at each other wide-eyed, sharing the same thought.

The cell door would be opening. This was our chance to get away.

"Hmm." Taylor studied us. "Who should it be?"

I knew we all felt it: a desperation to get out of this confined space, to see something beyond concrete walls, to smell air not tinged with human waste.

"Zoe." Taylor grinned at her. "Roza likes your new work. Come on up."

"Sure." Zoe rose slowly, gripping her laptop.

"Leave your computer." Taylor pulled something out of her back pocket: handcuffs. "Come to the doorway and turn around. Everyone else: Stay by the wall."

I stared at Wren, realizing the limits of our psychic connection. What was the plan? Should we rush the door? If so, before or after Zoe was handcuffed? I could smell the fear on me, a sudden, sharp onion-like scent.

"Hurry up." Taylor sounded annoyed. "Or I'll pick someone else."

Zoe went to the door and turned as requested. She raised her eyebrows and mouthed: "Now."

Keira's body tensed next to mine.

It was time.

But then Taylor passed the handcuffs to Yana and pulled something out of the back waistband of her jeans.

It was black, sharp-edged. It looked familiar, a handgun I'd seen in countless shows and movies. Funny how I'd never considered it before — the sleek lines, the dull shine. But even as I studied it, a suspicion arose.

Could it be fake?

Keira exhaled. She shook her head, almost imperceptibly. The plan was off.

"All right." Taylor nodded at Yana. "No fucking around, ladies. Stay by the wall."

Yana raised her hand to the keypad. I counted six beeps. Something released and the door swung outward.

But then Zoe whirled around.

Wren's fall off the bar steps, the most horrifying moment of my life, had unfurled in slow motion. But this happened much too fast. All of a sudden Zoe was gripping Taylor's wrists, pointing the gun down at the floor. Keira launched herself towards them even as Yana froze. Then Yana grabbed at Keira, but Wren was now there, too, crouching and grabbing Yana's legs and sending her crashing to the floor.

How had they all moved so quickly? Shouts and grunts filled the air, and somehow over the din I could hear my own heaving breaths.

Move. But it felt like pushing through sludge to stand. I watched the violence like a play: Wren tussling with Yana on the ground, Zoe shaking Taylor's wrists to get her to drop the gun, Keira trying to pull Taylor into a headlock from behind.

One question kept repeating, like a running news ticker below the action:

Is this actually real?

"Alex!" Zoe shouted. But still I hesitated. Was the gun fake? Was Zoe acting? They'd tricked Wren, but would they trick me also?

Wren screamed. Yana had raked sharp nails across her face and now rivulets of blood ran down her cheek.

I stared at the smeared red. This was proof.

This was real.

I ran to the others, feeling clumsy and sluggish. I tried to block Yana, who'd left Wren howling on the ground, and I too grasped at Taylor's arms. Taylor's face was locked in a grim rictus, and it was red from Keira's grip around her neck. Together, Zoe and I twisted and shook Taylor's wrists and slowly her fingers began to unclamp. Zoe released one hand in order to grab for the butt of the gun. For a second it looked like she'd succeeded in taking it from Taylor and I glanced up at her in triumph.

But then Taylor managed to grasp the gun again, her arm moving swiftly upwards.

Zoe opened her mouth in a scream just as the gun exploded with a deafening *BOOM*.

Her brown eyes widened, warm and glowing in the fluorescent lights. Her lips made a ring as she flew backwards and crumpled to the floor.

"No!" Keira cried, releasing Taylor to run towards her. Wren was suddenly standing next to me, a hand clamped to her bleeding face. We stood there frozen, watching as Keira pressed her palms against Zoe's chest. The blood flowed out like a fountain, and though Zoe's lips moved, nothing came out.

For a few seconds, the only sounds were Zoe's gurgling gasps and Keira's encouraging words: "You're okay. Come on, you're okay." Keira looked up at us. "Help! We need help! Please!" Her face was shiny with tears.

I remained still, feeling nauseous from the metallic scent that filled the small space.

Taylor replied, but the words didn't penetrate until she repeated it more loudly. "I said, you guys have to get into the cell."

None of us moved. Then the safety clicked.

She trained the gun on Keira. "Now, Keira."

My awareness expanded. From my peripheral vision I saw Yana standing behind us, both hands pressed to her mouth.

Keira just gazed at Taylor. She wiped at her nose, leaving a streak of blood, and let out a sob. "Please, Taylor. We need help. We need an ambulance."

"She's gone, K." Taylor said the words almost tenderly. "Look."

Zoe's glassy, unseeing eyes were rolled up at the ceiling.

"Come on." Now Taylor's voice sounded ragged, almost pleading. "You have to listen to me. I don't want to shoot you. Go back inside."

"Okay." Keira closed Zoe's eyes, leaving two bloody dots on her eyelids. "Okay." She stood and stumbled back through the doorway. Wren and I silently followed. The sound of the gun going off still echoed in my ears, clouding out everything else, keeping it at bay.

"You stupid fools," Yana hissed, banging the door shut. Her perfect ponytail was mussed; a chunk of blond hair hung in her eyes.

"It's not my fault." Taylor watched us, solemn. "This is on you guys." Sighing, she stuck the gun into her waistband. She bent over Zoe's body and grabbed her underneath her arms. With a grunt, she dragged her towards the doorway to the basement. Yana picked up the handcuffs and stared at the blood.

"What a mess," she muttered.

CHAPTER 33

Keira poured water over Wren's wounds and pressed a piece of fabric from a pillowcase against them to stop the bleeding. Wren then pulled our mattress towards the far end of the cell and lay down, sobbing.

To my shock, Keira returned to her computer. She settled, picked it up, and started typing.

I sat next to her. Her fingers left maroon imprints against the keyboard.

"You'd better keep going." Keira's low words startled me. She paused and looked over. Her eyes were bright but slightly unfocused.

"But how . . ." She must be in shock right now. Was I also? I felt like a bag of wet concrete. I couldn't think, I couldn't feel. There was only one thing I knew, and the implications were darker than Roza, this dungeon, anything we'd faced.

"It's my fault." I pressed my face into my

437

hands, and stars danced across the inside of my eyelids. "I hesitated. I didn't know if . . . I wasn't sure . . . and now she's . . ." I couldn't finish the sentence.

Maybe someone more delusional than I could've decided that her death, too, was an especially realistic part of the game.

But I'd seen her lifeless eyes. I knew she was gone.

"Well." Keira sucked in her breath. "I don't know, Alex. I don't know what to tell you and I don't have the energy to try to make you feel better. Because . . ." Her eyes filled with fresh tears.

"I know. You don't have to." I wanted to thank her, strangely, for her honesty.

We both sat there for a minute, staring at the large red stain.

"They're never going to let us go," I said. "There's no point in writing."

"We need time." Keira wiped at her face. "And Roza needs a story. She's going to keep us alive until we finish. We have to use the time to figure out how to escape."

"But how?"

"I don't know." Keira shook her head. "*Fuck. I knew* something was wrong. I knew it. I should've left. But I couldn't. I thought this was my only chance."

"Your only chance?" I echoed.

"To get fucking published."

"But you're such a great writer."

"You think that matters?" She stared at me in disbelief. "You want to know how many books I've written? How many agents and editors have told me I'm so incredibly talented, but they're not quite the 'right person' for me? Or that I feel too 'niche,' or that my audience won't be 'wide' enough?"

"I'm sorry."

"Fuck." She moaned and dropped her head in her hands. "This is such a nightmare. This is . . ." She leaned forward, curling over her computer. I rubbed her back, my brain empty and floating. Beyond the bars, the dark stain looked like a comet, its tail whooshing through space.

The following day we were fed as usual, even though Wren and I hadn't finished our pages the day before. Yana brought us coffee, then a few hours later, sandwiches.

"You didn't make the word count." Yana stood at the bars, peering down at me with a questioning look. "And *she* didn't write at all?" Wren was still prone in the corner. I didn't know if she was sleeping or awake.

Sometime in the night, Yana must've come down and tried to clean up the blood. This morning it had been a big amorphous dark blob. Keira had typed all morning, though she'd been pausing for long periods of time. I was attempting, but it felt like the day before: like straining to get even a sentence on the page.

"I'm trying." I still felt empty, robotic. "It's hard. I'm sorry."

Yana glanced back at Keira and Wren, then left without another word.

At dinnertime Yana and Taylor both slipped through the doorway.

"Al." Taylor gestured to me, subdued. "Roza wants to talk to you."

"What?" I squinted at her. Despite her solemnity, she was wearing her LET ME LIVE sweatshirt. Was that on purpose? It couldn't be. Could it?

"Up." Taylor pulled the gun from her jeans. I scrambled back away from the bars.

"Look." Taylor held it up in the air. "I'm not going to use this if you behave. Got it? I shouldn't have had to use it in the first place. It's your own fucking fault for attacking me. That was dangerous."

Yana tossed handcuffs through the bars. They fell with a clank at my feet.

"K, put those on her," Taylor ordered.

Keira picked them up and snapped them on my wrists. They were cold and sharp. I felt a dull passivity seep through me.

"Okay. Al, you come here. K, turn around and press your hands on the wall."

Keira did so and I went to the door. Yana opened it and ushered me through, clanging it shut behind me.

"Good." Taylor's shoulders relaxed. "See? Not so hard. Now follow Yana."

Outside the cell, I straightened to my full height with a sigh of relief. I followed Yana out the door to the basement, where a path towards the stairs had been cleared. The plain, dusty space looked almost homey after days in the concrete cell. My knees ached as we went up the stairs.

At the doorway I slowed. Chitra was at the stove. She kept herself turned away, still as a statue. I felt like I was looking at a display, one of those life-size dioramas at the American Museum of Natural History: *Personal Chef for Famous Psychopath Prepares Dinner for the Writing Slaves.*

"Let's go." The cool nose of the gun prodded at my lower back. We went onwards. The floor beneath my thin socks was warm. The rugs in the hall were unbelievably plush. Up the marble stairs. Down the art-littered hall. And here was Roza's red door, closed. Yana knocked and opened it. She hung back, ushering me and Taylor through. She stayed behind, shutting us in.

I hadn't seen Roza since her announcement in the dungeon, only three days before, though it felt like weeks. When she saw me, she rose from the couch. "Hello, darling." She wore a ruby-red jumpsuit and her auburn hair was pulled back in a chignon. "Have a seat." She motioned to one of the chairs across from her.

I sat. This opulence felt wrong now, a gold crown on a rotting tooth.

"Taylor, dear." Roza looked behind me. "Please leave us."

"But, Roza . . . you need protection."

"Fine." Roza made the *Gimme* motion with her hand. "Leave it with me."

"Are you sure?" Taylor glanced at the gun. "I don't —"

"Leave it!" Roza bellowed, so loud the room seemed to vibrate.

I flinched. I'd never heard her yell before.

Taylor placed the gun in Roza's hand. She slunk out with a last glare at me.

"Finally." Roza set the gun on the arm of her chair and sighed. "Never work with fans, darling. They act much too familiar."

I shifted. My bound hands made the very act of sitting uncomfortable.

"Well?" Roza raised her eyebrows.

It felt like so much effort to speak. I finally roused a "Well, what?"

442

"You're barely writing." Roza crossed her legs. "So there must be something that you'd like to talk about."

I would've scoffed if I had the energy. "Zoe's dead, Roza."

"Yes. She attacked Taylor." Roza rolled her eyes. "It was a stupid thing to do."

"Stupid?" Anger flared up in me. "What do you call all this?"

One side of Roza's lips rose. "Good. Still a little bit of fire in you."

"Please, Roza." I shook my head, too exhausted to cry. "Please stop this."

She tapped her fingers against the gun. "Let me tell you a story, dear."

I moaned. "Stop with the stories."

"Just one more. I promise." She grasped her knee. "This is about me. You know, I always thought my life's purpose was to be a writer. I used to get good marks in English. And, of course, I read a lot. I just assumed I'd be a good writer, too. It was Mila who showed me my error. We started to write stories for each other, and it was immediately clear that she was much more talented. And if she was more talented, there were probably lots of others." She shrugged. "It was devastating. And it just didn't seem fair. It was only when Mila died that I realized my true calling."

"You *killed* Mila." I slumped back against the chair, ignoring the pain in my wrists.

"Well, yes."

"How?"

She smiled indulgently. "A plant called wolfsbane. I put it in her tea, a little at a time. The doctors just couldn't figure it out. As she declined, she scrambled to finish her magnum opus, this utterly bizarre story she'd come up with. She asked me to try to get it published so that her name would live on. I didn't think much of it, but my first year at university one of my professors became quite taken with me. When he found out I had a novel, he asked to see it, then connected me with some publishing contacts in New York. I was as shocked as anyone when they fell all over themselves for it. But then I realized." Roza raised a finger. "My role is not to create but to facilitate. To act as a kind of midwife to the books that fall into my lap. I edit them, you know. I put my own touch on them. That's why no one has even questioned me before."

"Fall into your lap?" I repeated. "Don't you mean: kill their authors?"

"Only two. With Mila, I wasn't thinking about the book, I just wanted her to suffer. With Lucy, it was different. I didn't love having to do that to her. But it was necessary. I'd tried one last time with *Lady X* — the critical response only cemented my true calling."

"Roza." I shook my head in disbelief. "This calling you're talking about . . . it's basically just being an editor. Do you realize that?"

"It's not, dear. Remember, I *have* an editor. This is more like tapping into a great force. It tells me what to do. There is some special alchemy that requires me to be the face of the books, some mythology that continues to grow around me. Thankfully, more and more have been offering up their works voluntarily."

"Right. Yana and Taylor. Why couldn't you have just gotten more books from them?"

"Well." Roza sighed, sitting back. "They've certainly tried. But it's as I suspected: most people only have one true masterpiece within them."

How had Roza found these women to surround herself with, women who would hand over their innermost creative cores? And remain attached, even after Roza found every new work of theirs untenable?

It sounded torturous. Perhaps Taylor hadn't always been a sociopath; maybe Roza had wrecked her mentally over time. Maybe Yana had once been vibrant and smiling.

"Did Chitra try to write something for you?" I asked.

"Of course not. She's simply my chef."

"Oh." That was even more depressing. "So she's just involved in all this for the money."

"Her daughter is terribly sick, dear. I cover her medical expenses."

I scoffed. "So it's worth it. Murder."

"Zoe's death was not planned," Roza said softly. "And, remember, she was never supposed to be here."

I stared at her. She was the very picture of health: glowing skin, sparkling emerald eyes. Had she become more attractive since we'd been imprisoned?

"You're enjoying this," I said.

"No." Roza closed her eyes. "I find violence rather crass. I would much rather discuss your manuscript, but we must have new pages in order to do that."

"Right."

Roza folded her hands on her lap. "So here's my proposal, dear. You continue writing. You convince Wren to keep writing. And if all three of you finish your novels, I will let you go. And I will let you take your books with you."

I laughed weakly. "Sure."

A knowing smile alighted her face. "I've been planning an escape for a while, you know. When you tap into something greater than you, the force I mentioned — well, you learn to follow it, like a scent in the wind. That's why I took the chance with you all. I knew my role as a facilitator of masterpieces was coming to an end. That this was the last book I would need. I'm realizing now that perhaps my last book has already been published: *Maiden Pink.*"

Taylor's book.

"So it's over?" I asked. "You're stopping, just like that?"

"Truthfully, I'm getting rather tired of the fame." She frowned. "I can't even walk down the street without people stopping me, wanting to take *selfies* with me. It's exhausting. Not to mention undignified."

"But . . ." This new information didn't compute. "If you're going to let us go anyway, why do we need to finish our books here? Why not release us right now?"

"Because" — her eyes glittered — "you *won't* finish them. You'll leave here and never want to think of them again. And even if you did return to them later, they wouldn't be what they are right now, with you writing from the very edge of a knife. They won't be truly great."

I opened my mouth and closed it.

In a strange way, I knew what she was saying.

"So." Her lips curled, as if she could read my thoughts. "You will stay, and you will finish. And you will live. All right?"

"But . . . wait. You said this part of your life is coming to an end. What do you mean by that?" I struggled to work it out. "What could the next part possibly be?"

"Don't worry yourself about that." She smiled softly. "I'll be just fine. Now, do we have a deal?"

After a few seconds, in which my mind settled on the truth, I nodded.

"Good." She grinned, and I could almost hear the unsaid, tacked on word: *Good girl.*

But it meant nothing to me. This conversation had made it clear.

I knew Roza believed what she'd told me: that a great unseen Force told her what to do. But even if she had a grand plan to disappear, I couldn't envision her unlocking our cell door and letting us go off with our novels. That was too generous, too kind. It seemed . . . un-Roza-like.

And there was one thing I *did* know about Roza, based on the works she'd chosen to nurture and launch into the world.

Roza abhorred a happy ending.

Excerpt from *The Great Commission*

Daphne stared with a mixture of shock and horror as Abigail — her sweet, supportive, innocent young friend — stepped through the doorway to the basement. Her face was as serene as an angel's. She carried a tray.

Still, Daphne held out hope as she flew to the bars. "Help me! The key . . ."

Abigail bent down, leaving the cold food within Daphne's reach. She then sat lightly on the stool that Dina had brought down to have a restful place from which to torture her.

"I'm afraid this is where you should be." Abigail watched Daphne with open curiosity, like a spectator at a freak show.

"What are you talking about?" Daphne sputtered, her hands squeezing into fists.

Abigail primly folded her hands in her lap. "At first it was all fun and games, Daph, but then . . . it took you over. You became obsessed. It wasn't healthy. And . . ." Her expression hardened. ". . . it wasn't real."

Wasn't real? Abigail had been there as Daphne wrote reams about things she didn't know, from people she'd never met. How could she experience those nights and think — what? That Daphne was making it all up?

"So you and Florence . . . ," Daphne started.

"Florence left a long time ago. That old cow." Abigail shook her head, disgusted but somehow pleased. It was the same look that came over Dina's face: a sudden joyful relief in taking off that veil of politeness, deference, kindness. That was the way of the world: if you were a woman, then you had a job to do, and that was to pretend to love everyone else walking all over your body, leaving imprints on your face. You were supposed to pretend to crave it, to beg for more. But down here in this dungeon . . . the normal rules didn't apply. Down here, women could be as honest as they wanted.

"We're trying to help you." Abigail leaned forward. Daphne could tell it gave her a deep thrill to look down on her this way.

And in truth, it was impressive. Daphne had always thought Abigail was the weak one. But it turned out she'd just been biding her time.

" 'We'?" Daphne asked, already knowing the answer.

"Well." Abigail smirked. "Of course I had to inform poor Horace of what was going on. Neither of us expected you to continue to be so bullheaded, not after he burned your paintings."

"Abigail." Daphne clutched the bars. "If you think this was fake, could you bring me paper? And pencils? There's no harm, is there, if it's just my delusions?"

"Daphne." Abigail tilted her head. "As soon as this damn storm passes, I promise that you'll get the assistance you need."

Abigail swearing — that might have been the most surprising part of all. Daphne pressed her lips together in a grim smile. And where was Abigail sleeping these nights? Was Horace another one of the poor lost sheep who needed her?

No matter. Daphne went to the dusty mattress and lay down, turning her face to the wall. She shouldn't have asked for the paper. Lamia would scoff to see her beg like that.

"Just another day or two." Abigail's voice drifted to her. "And this will all be over. We'll find a good place for you. A safe place."

Daphne knew exactly what kind of place Abigail spoke of: scowling nurses, straps on the beds, constant distant screams.

Abigail's skirts whispered against each other as she left. Daphne was hungry but too tired to make herself eat. Her whole body felt like it was stuffed with pebbles.

Keep up your strength. The words were strong, clear, as if spoken a mere foot or two away.

Daphne sat up. So Lamia was there after all.

You knew they would all betray you in the end. Lamia's voice was calm. *Now everything is laid bare. And when I show you the ultimate Truth, you must be ready.*

Daphne didn't trust herself to make a reply that wouldn't sound short-tempered. So instead she just went to the tray and started to eat.

CHAPTER 34

The next surprise occurred four days later. In the interim, the days melted into each other: write, eat, sleep, repeat. My scalp itched constantly and I wondered if I'd picked up fleas. I fell asleep at random times on the futon and dreamed that the sound of Wren's and Keira's typing was the thrumming of rain against a roof.

As Roza had predicted, my writing was the most vivid it had ever been. Scenes unfurled like flowers, one after the other. And as the possibility of escape seemed more and more remote, I clung to the book like a life jacket.

On Thursday afternoon, Taylor came in to collect Wren.

"You're up, princess." She tossed both the handcuffs and a wet rag through the bars.

Wren picked up the rag and gently wiped at her face, then her armpits. I never could've imagined seeing her like this:

greasy, hollow-eyed, almost feral looking. The deep scrapes on her cheek still looked raw and angry, despite the antibiotic ointment. There would certainly be scars.

But this was life now. I'd met with Roza alone for a second time the night before and had listened to her helpful feedback on Daphne and Lamia. Say what you would about Roza, she was an excellent editor. The thought made me want to start laughing and never stop.

"Don't let her know you've been crying," Taylor called as Wren threw back the rag. "It'll piss her off."

"Okay." Wren put her hands behind her back and I picked up the handcuffs. Keira watched both of us, forlorn. She'd spoken less and less, and she'd stopped talking about escape altogether. The meals had gotten smaller — maybe Chitra didn't have enough food — and it was making us even more listless.

Wren stood hunched in the low space, so different from her queenly, straight-backed posture. The knobs of her vertebrae stuck out of the back of her neck.

"It's okay," I whispered. I wanted to hug her, pull her to me like a child, but Taylor wouldn't like that. Handcuffed, Wren went to the door. Keira and I pressed our hands against the back wall, as was the rule, until we heard the iron door click shut.

Taylor whistled the Harlem Globetrotters tune as she waved Wren ahead of her into the basement. Keira and I went back to our laptops. A new anxiety fluttered around my chest: the fear of not having enough time to finish the novel. It was funny — wasn't it? — that the story had somehow become my main concern.

"Do you think they'll finish our books if we don't?" I asked suddenly.

Keira paused. "Yes." She went back to typing.

Twenty minutes later, Yana strode in. I wondered if she was going to grab Wren's computer — something Taylor had retrieved before for a one-on-one session. But instead she went quickly to the cell door and tapped in the code.

She pulled it open. "Come." She gestured and strode back to the doorway.

Keira and I stared at each other, shocked. Simultaneously, we jumped to our feet and hurried after her. We held hands, gripping each other tightly, as we followed Yana through the door, past the piles of boxes, and towards the back of the basement.

She stopped in front of the door that led up into the yard. The one that we'd thought

Zoe had sleepwalked right through. It seemed like that had happened years ago.

"Here." Yana pointed to a colorful pile of boots, snow pants, and fur coats.

Keira let go of me and grabbed a pair of red snow pants. I followed suit, shaking with bewilderment and adrenaline. Why would Yana do this? My boots were there in the pile, but the snow pants were too small and the coat was too big. No matter. I felt faint as Yana pulled open the door. The icy wind hit me in the face. The fresh air was sweet as ice cream and I gulped it in.

Tightly packed snow still covered the stairs, but Yana had etched some ruts so that we could climb out. She went first, leading us in her sneakers up the steps. The wind felt heavenly rushing over my itchy scalp. I breathed so deeply it made my lungs ache. Above, the sun was setting and a bloated moon shone bone-white in the sky.

Yana led us around the side of the house. The snow had melted from the storm but was still at least a foot deep, though dense and icy enough that we could walk on top of it. We crossed the uncleared drive and hurried to the garage.

Yana wrenched open the side door. Inside, two cars waited like sleeping, hulking creatures. Would we be able to drive out in the snow? I had a horrible vision of us stalled, the wheels spinning uselessly.

Then Yana pulled a plastic cover off something near the door.

The snowmobile.

"Here." Yana held up the keys, which glittered like jewelry. "You know how to ride?"

"Yes." Keira rushed towards it.

"Take these." Yana pulled hats and mittens out of her pockets and stuck them in my hands. She gave another set to Keira. "Go slow. The road was cleared but it might be slippery."

"Thank you, Yana." I stared at her, half-convinced Taylor would step out from behind her and laugh: another cruel game. But when Yana met my eyes, there was a determined set to her jaw.

"Just go." She slipped out the door and was gone.

"Oh, hell yes," Keira muttered, her voice tight with excitement. "Alex, help me pull it out."

"Yeah." I hurried behind the snowmobile, my foot kicking into something. It was a long object covered with a blanket. Something shiny peeked out. It took a second to process what I was seeing.

It was a silky, coiled chunk of Zoe's hair.

"Oh my god." My stomach dropped. I

hadn't even considered what they'd done with Zoe's body. But here it was, a frigid object, no different from a frozen chicken or a pizza.

"What?" Keira peered beyond me. She too stopped. Then she tugged at the handlebars. "Come on. We have to go."

We were able to pull the vehicle up and out onto the shelf of snow. Without hesitation, Keira jumped on and turned the key. The motor sounded like a bomb in the silence. I wanted to run back into the garage and hide.

Keira motioned behind her. "Get on."

I hesitated.

Keira whipped around. She wore a pink hat with a pom-pom — Yana's?

"I can't." The words were out before I could think them.

"Alex, come *on*," she cried. "We have to go *now.*"

"But . . ."

I knew as clear as if Lamia were whispering in my ear: *If you leave, Wren will die.*

The knowledge was heavy and solid, a peach pit in my gut. And though I wanted nothing more than to leap on the snowmobile and get as far away from here as possible . . . I couldn't leave her to be murdered.

"I have to help Wren," I called over the engine.

"Alex." Keira's voice sharpened to a fi ne point. "We need to go get help."

"I'm sorry. I have to stay." The front door to the house opened, the creak as clear as a gunshot.

"You go," I said. "Seriously, I'll be okay."

She gave me one last wide-eyed look of disbelief. Then, with an angry shake of her head, she gunned the engine and fl ew off, graceful in the waning light.

Heavy sadness pressed down on my shoulders, the top of my head. I knew what staying behind meant. I might never see Keira — or anyone — again.

Taylor had come out to the front porch: I heard her angry shouts. I turned and followed the trampled path back to the basement.

Roza would've expected me to leave Wren behind. She thought that she knew me, that we were similar in this way: the unending need to survive. Not just to survive, but to win.

And I had been that girl before, filled with so much fear and frustration that I'd physically harmed my best friend. But that was because I'd felt helpless. Like all I needed was a powerful, protective being to take care of me. Which was probably why I'd felt drawn to Wren and Roza in the fi rst place.

In the basement, I took a deep breath. The sadness faded and a delicate sense of peace settled on me, instead. It told me that the only way to get through this was to listen to myself. Rather, my body.

She would know what to do.

■ ■ ■ ■

PART FOUR:
THE ATTIC

■ ■ ■ ■

CHAPTER 35

I hurried back into the dungeon. The cell was empty; Wren must still be upstairs. Maybe I could find her in the commotion, hide, and make a plan.

But something kept me still. There was something I had to do first.

The cameras.

I ran into the control room, which they hadn't locked since we'd all been imprisoned. Scanning the monitors, I picked out Taylor, a tiny dark figure against the snow walking around the outside of the house. Roza, Chitra, and Yana were grouped in the front hall. Where was Wren? There — standing at the window in Roza's room. Her hands were still cuffed behind her back, making her look like she was a casual observer gazing outside.

How did one take down a surveillance system? I thought of smashing the monitors, but the equipment looked top-of-the-line. Roza probably had access on her phone.

I pulled the computer case from underneath the desk and unplugged it. The monitors went black. I quickly unscrewed the bolts and pulled off the plastic sides. Then I yanked out every wire I could. For good measure, I grabbed a pair of scissors and cut them in half.

I surveyed my handiwork. The blank screens made me suddenly afraid: What if Roza or Taylor was on her way here now? I dashed back to the basement and started up the stairs. The heavy coat was making me sweat. But at the thought of taking it off, something in me recoiled.

I was a wolf now. A wolf couldn't peel off her fur.

In the kitchen, the overhead lights blazed. Angry shouts came from outside. I slinked to the counter and pulled a knife from the butcher block, then crept through the hall. I peered in at the library; a fire roared in the fireplace, but the room was empty. I continued towards the front of the house.

"How could you let them go?"

A glimpse of Taylor in the front hall: she was training the gun on the grand staircase. Her short hair was mussed, her feet bare. I

464

inched closer, then crouched behind a statue.

Roza and Chitra stood a few steps behind Taylor, gazing in the same direction. Chitra's hands were at her mouth. She was shaking.

"Are you going to answer me?" Taylor shouted.

I could imagine Yana on the stairs, her impassive, unimpressed look.

"And now they're getting the police." Taylor's voice rose to a scream.

A sharp click made my chest seize.

"Taylor," Roza said sharply. "Stop. You're not going to shoot her."

"Why the fuck not?"

"Because I said so." Roza's voice was cold but not particularly fearful. I wondered what could possibly be going through her mind. Two of her prisoners had escaped. What were her options?

"Lock her in her room," Roza demanded. "Then take Wren back downstairs. Chitra? Could you please make me some tea?"

Chitra muttered an inaudible reply. I slipped back through the hall and into the library. I went to the furthest bookshelf and sat behind it. They thought I was gone. Unless they found me, I was safe.

After the confined cell, the mansion felt

luxuriously huge. It was a veritable play-ground to hide in.

Someone scurried down the hallway: Chitra, heading to the kitchen to make tea for her overlord. Soon Wren would be locked up in the cell. And unless I got the keycode, I wouldn't be able to get her out.

So I needed the keycode. The only person who would give it to me — hopefully, since I still didn't understand her motivations — was Yana. I'd have to break into her locked room.

There were too many people bustling around right now, too many variables. I would have to wait until night, when Taylor and Roza might be passed out from the stress of the day.

It's what Zoe had done too. Waited until we were all asleep in order to slip downstairs. And even then she pretended to be sleepwalking in case anyone saw her.

An image arose: the pale hank of hair on the garage floor . . .

I crumpled it up like a piece of paper. I couldn't think about that now. Keira was getting help. If I could break Wren out, we'd just have to hide until the police arrived.

A wave of exhaustion hit me. I needed to rest. I curled up and fell asleep.

I woke hours later, shockingly refreshed.

I folded my coat and snow pants and set them neatly behind the end of the bookcase. I needed to be more nimble for this next bit: breaking out Yana, then Wren. Gripping the knife, I crept out of the library, moonlight guiding my way. I entered the great hall, aware of Daphne's and Horace's painted eyes on me.

I slithered up the stairs, sensing the creaking and settling of the house. On the landing I went not to the left, to my former wing, nor right towards Roza's chambers. Instead I crept straight back, down a short hall with four closed doors.

There I paused. If I went into the wrong room — Chitra's, or maybe even Taylor's, if she had a long-term room in addition to the room she'd been staying in for the retreat — they might wake up. At the first door I turned the cold knob and took a few slow steps inside. The curtains were open and moonlight painted everything with a silver tinge.

I went stealthily over to the sleeping figure. I thought suddenly of a scene from my book: the horrific ghost standing over young Daphne in her bed.

Chitra's face looked young in sleep. Her first curled up under her chin as if she were pondering something. I felt a sudden, startling rush of affection for her. There was a framed picture on the nightstand and I picked it up. I could just make out two figures: the one on the left was Chitra, on the right was her daughter. I wondered what she was sick with. How Chitra must be so desperate to continue to protect Roza and Taylor.

If I wanted to, I could slip the knife right into her throat. Or I could hold a pillow over her face, pressing down with all my weight.

But even in this survival mode, I couldn't imagine actually doing it.

I crept out and softly closed the door.

The next door was locked. This was it. I tapped at the door with my finger. There was movement on the other side. A gentle tapping came at the bottom of the door. Two golden, U-shaped hair pins slid out onto the wooden floor.

This old trick. Had Yana been watching Keira and me, working at the door to the office? Or was this something she expected everyone to know?

I set down the knife and picked up the

pins. I heard Keira's voice, even though she was long gone. She must be at the convent, or maybe she was already at a police station, wrapped in one of those silver space blankets.

But it was harder without her there; it seemed to take hours. Finally, when the quality of the moonlight began to change, to fade, I heard a tiny popping sound. The doorknob turned.

Barely glancing at me, Yana slipped out and strode past, dressed in boots and a coat, carrying a tote bag. I picked up the knife and followed her down the stairs to the kitchen. In the gleaming rays of dawn, she grabbed items from the cupboards and stuffed them into the bag. Peanut butter. Soup.

She looked at me, finally. "Where is your coat?" Her eyes swept over me, her mouth tight, like a disapproving mother. She didn't blink at the knife in my hand.

"In the library."

"Get it." She returned to her task.

"Yana," I said, "we have to get Wren first."

"No time." She struggled to open the kitchen door to the backyard. It was blocked by that packed snow.

"I'm not leaving without her."

Yana gave up and went to the basement

steps. I followed her down. At the bottom she hurried to the back door.

"Wait." I grabbed her shoulder, hard. "Stop."

She turned, her pale face drawn, her sea-gray eyes dull. I wanted to ask her so much. What had happened between her and Roza? Why had she stayed on for so many years? When and why had she decided to help Keira and me? But there wasn't time.

"The snowmobile's gone," I said. "The cars will get stuck in the snow."

"I'll hide."

"In the woods?" My arm dropped. "You're going to freeze."

"Keira left, yes? To get help?"

"Yes."

"Then the police will come soon." She turned.

"The code," I said quickly. "What's the code to Wren's cell?"

She rattled off the numbers: 1-2-1-4-8-3.

I repeated it. Apparently, Mila had died on December 14, 1983.

"Hey," she called over her shoulder as I backed away. "I'll wait by the garage. Okay? If you don't come, I will leave." Before I could answer, she was gone.

I hurried through the doorway into the cell. The rancid smell of the overfilled toilet was even worse now that I'd spent a few hours away from it. At first glance I didn't see Wren and panic speared me. Had they moved her? Was she bound up like a mummy on the floor of Taylor's room?

But no. There she was. Just a slight bump on the mattress.

I typed the password into the panel. It flashed red. *Shit.*

I typed it again. A red flash and an annoyed beep. Wren stirred.

December 13th, right? Why wasn't it opening? Had Yana lied?

Wren sat up, rubbing her eyes. When she saw me, she flew to the door and grabbed the bars. "Get me out of here!" The angry scratches across her cheek moved with every word.

"I'm trying." I typed in the number again. Two loud beeps this time. Was it going to lock me out?

Wren was saying something but I said, clearly, "Shut up."

And she did. I waited, sinking back down into my body. I willed my mind blank.

December *14th.*

The panel flashed green and the door clicked. I pulled Wren out. As we hurried into the basement, my brain calculated. I couldn't take her outside. If I gave her my coat, then I — or both of us — would freeze to death. I opened the door. Wren waited behind me and cursed when I pushed her away from the frosty air.

"We're going to make it look like we left," I said.

BOOM.

A shot went off. We both jumped.

Another shot. Wren clung to me, sobbing into my shoulder. Someone was shouting in the kitchen.

I pulled us back into the dungeon, then into the surveillance room. The blank monitors reflected our movements. I opened the door to the tunnel, half expecting to see Roza looming like a vampire. But it was empty. We hurried up the rickety spiral staircase. I held the knife out in front of me, willing myself not to trip and fall onto it.

We burst out of the wardrobe. If Roza was there, in her room, she would see us.

But it was empty. I raced to the window. In the glowing light of dawn, dark figures moved on the wide expanse of the yard.

"No," I murmured weakly. Taylor, in her bright blue hat, was kneeling down by someone. Yana, facedown. Splotches of red stained the snow around her.

Taylor was calling in the direction of the

house. I stepped closer to the window and looked down. Roza and Chitra stood almost directly beneath.

Taylor bent over the body, and I held my breath. Maybe Yana was still alive. Maybe Taylor was tending to her.

But then Taylor grasped Yana's hands and began to drag her facedown towards the garage. This time the stains were beautiful watercolor strokes of salmon and rose against the pure white snow.

CHAPTER 36

Wren and I sat on the floor of Roza's wardrobe, clothes surrounding our heads like soft buffers against the world. The knife sat on my lap. I massaged my stiff fingers as I told Wren about the last twelve hours, ending with our need to hide until the police arrived. Wren said nothing, only gasping when I mentioned finding Zoe's body in the garage.

"They're going to look for me," Wren said when I finished. "They're not stupid."

"No," I agreed. "But they might be getting desperate. They know Keira's getting help."

"Then why did they kill Yana?" Wren's voice broke on the word "kill."

"I don't know. Roza told Taylor not to hurt Yana. Maybe she's losing control of her? In any case . . ." I tugged at my earlobe. "All we have to do is hide. And if they find us: fight."

"I don't know if I can fight anyone," she said in a low voice.

"Hey." I squeezed her leg. "Just think positively. We'll be okay." While Zoe's death had shattered me, Yana's had slid me into a deep calm. Maybe even acceptance. I would do everything I could to get us out of here, of course. But it might not necessarily be enough. We just had to wait and see.

We were quiet for a few minutes, staring at our hands.

"I'm sorry," I said finally.

"Me too." She fiddled with her engagement ring.

"No. I mean for what happened." It felt important to say this during our brief respite. "At the bar."

"Oh." She looked up at me. "That."

"I was so angry." I exhaled sour breath. "I didn't go in with the intention of hurting you, but I needed you to listen to me. And you just looked so disgusted . . . I might not have shoved you, but I did reach out and touch you. I knew you'd jerk away. I knew how close you were to the stairs."

"Stop." She shook her head. "We don't have to do this."

"I know. But I wanted to be honest with you. Finally."

She didn't respond. We sat in silence. I

realized how relieved I felt. Regardless of Wren's reaction, I'd done the thing I'd never thought I could do. I'd accepted responsibility.

Roza had tried at every turn to stoke my resentment. And it felt good to fight a larger-than-life villain. But it wasn't that simple. Wren and I were both fallible, imperfect, sometimes cruel people. Wren had hurt me throughout our friendship, but I'd allowed it, because then she was the Bad Witch, and I was the Good Witch.

"Listen." Wren broke into my thoughts. "I'm sorry too."

"Thanks for saying that."

"And it wasn't nothing," she went on in a rush. "What we did in bed. Being with you like that . . . it actually meant a lot to me. But I guess I was confused. Really confused. I'd never hooked up with a woman before. I know I said I did it with friends, but that wasn't true. But afterwards . . . It just felt easier to leave." Wren took my hand. The diamond scraped against my finger. "Though it made me feel really sad."

"I was sad too. And mad, obviously. Jesus." I smiled. "Talk about a breakup."

"Brutal." She was smiling, rueful. "I was a mess, truly. I got so depressed in the hospital. Of course I was scared for my hand, but

476

I also had this horrible fear that I could never be in a normal relationship. That I'd die alone."

"And then you met Evan." I said it lightly, but she withdrew her hand.

"Yeah, about Evan." She took a deep breath. "He actually dumped me a few weeks ago."

"What?" I felt stunned. "But the ring . . ."

"He wanted it back, and I told him to go fuck himself." She chuckled. "I don't wear it all the time, though. I guess I just wore it here because I wanted you to think . . . I don't know. To keep a barrier between us."

"Wow." The news made me feel disoriented.

"Well." Wren grinned. "Here's a silver lining: if we don't make it out alive, at least I won't have to go back on the dating apps."

I laughed and it came out as a sharp honk. Slapping my hand over my mouth, we both fell into sudden convulsive giggles.

Finally we calmed ourselves.

"Okay." Wren rubbed her eyes. "Not to change the subject, but I just thought of an idea." She paused. "Do you think Taylor might have more guns?"

I nodded, impressed. "I wouldn't be surprised."

"I think it's worth the risk to look."

"Me too."

"I just can't see you using that." She gestured to the knife in my lap.

"You don't think I could stab someone?" I cautiously pushed open the wardrobe door.

"Stab? No. Shove someone off a cliff? Clearly, yes."

I snorted but we managed to hold down more hysterical laughter as we crept to the entrance of Roza's room. We paused at the red door. No sounds. So we pushed it open and continued on, past the paintings and statues dotting the hall. At the landing, Wren moved towards our old wing but I grabbed her shoulder.

"Taylor lives here normally," I whispered. "Don't you think she probably has another room — a permanent room — down this hall?"

We froze as voices reared up from below.

"Well, go look then." Roza sounded exasperated. "Chitra, you —" But she turned and I couldn't make out more. We scuttled down the hallway, past Chitra's and Yana's rooms and into the third.

The curtains were open and the morning sun cast an unflinching light on the mess. It was like Taylor's other room, only ten times worse. Crumpled clothes were scattered on every available surface. Shoes took up most of the floor. There were books, journals, devices. Even some sparkling jewelry here and there, next to rotting apple cores and empty wineglasses.

By unspoken agreement, we went to opposite sides of the room and began to search. I set my knife on the floor and pulled open a trunk. Given the disarray, we didn't have to worry about being neat. I moved on to the dresser. On top was a tangle of jewelry. Funny, since she hadn't worn any of it, besides Roza's rabbit necklace.

Then I spotted it: a glass vial with dried purple flowers. The one she'd shown me what felt like eons before. I undid the chain, pulled the vial off, and slipped it into my bra.

"Oh, hello."

I froze at the sound of the familiar voice.

From the bed came a thump and a muttered expletive.

Taylor trained the gun on me from the doorway. Her face had a pinched quality and a smattering of acne covered her jawline. "Oh, Wre-en." Her voice was just as animated as ever. "Come out, come out, or your frenemy gets it." She gestured at me. "Drop that."

I'd grabbed the knife without even realizing it. I let it tumble to the floor.

"Come over here." Taylor motioned to her.

Wren's hands were in the air. She looked
like a fragile, startled deer.

"Now," Taylor said firmly. "Or I'll shoot
Alex in the leg."

Wren rushed to my side, pressing her hip
against mine.

"So Al stayed behind to save old Wren-
ster." Taylor scoffed. "You're more of a joke
than I thought, Al. Man, even after all she's
done to you, she *still* holds your balls."

I said nothing. *Survive until the police get
here.* If Taylor wanted to kill us, she could've
done so already.

"What did Roza tell you to do with us?" I
asked. Sure enough, there was a tiny tic near
Taylor's left eye. She didn't like being
reminded she wasn't in charge.

"Well, I thought it'd be a longer game of
hide-and-seek than this." Her lip curled.
"You guys really are pathetic. Just like Yana."

"Did Roza tell you to kill her?" I asked.
"Or was that your decision?"

"Shut up." Her eyelid twitched again. "I
will shoot you, Al."

"No you won't." I felt almost wild with
conviction. "Roza wouldn't like that."

"She wouldn't?"

480

"No." I glanced at Wren, who was staring at me with a horrified expression. "She told you to take us alive. To make us finish our books. Right?"

Taylor chuckled, settling back into her comfort zone. "I don't disagree with her. I know I've been talking shit, but I think they're both pretty good. Neck and neck at this point. Keira's was good, too, but I don't know if Roza would feel comfortable finishing it. You know, appropriation and all that."

"Why are you here?" I asked. "Shouldn't you be in Mexico by now?"

Taylor raised an eyebrow. "You think I should be running from the cops? Because Keira has escaped and alerted them, right?" Using her free hand, she pulled out her phone. "Let me show you something, ladies." She scrolled and held up the screen. For a second I struggled to make out what I was seeing. Then it organized, becoming clear.

It was Keira, splayed out on the snow. Shadows of tree branches fell across her body.

The dappled shadow wasn't just shadow, I saw now. It was also something darker, a liquid speckled on the snow.

"You thought this was all too quickly coming to an end." Taylor grinned. "But really, we're just getting started."

Excerpt from *The Great Commission*

In the doorway, Daphne froze.

The tiny Abigail crouched on top of Horace, a cat bestride a bear. Slowly, deliberately, Abigail turned and smiled at Daphne. The grin stretched too wide and the rows of blood-pinkened teeth gleamed.

Horace's expression was peaceful. It was incongruous: the way his stomach was slashed open, how his insides were now outside, like a purse carefully emptied of all its contents.

Daphne stumbled down the hall, her mouth yawning in horror. The hallway swayed around her like she was running across a rope bridge. She was in danger — had been since the moment she'd refused Lamia's order to kill Horace as a blood sacrifice. Daphne hated Horace in many ways but she hadn't wanted to murder him. Of course, she'd welcomed that brief surge of power as Lamia had entered her, filling her up. But even then, she'd very clearly thought: *No. I can't. I won't.* Daphne had felt Lamia's brief disgust as she'd left her body.

The Great Commission had all been leading up to this, and Daphne had failed.

And so Lamia had taken Abigail instead.

Daphne heard Abigail's guttural shrieks of laughter behind her. The one advantage she had was that Lamia thought she was weak. She believed Daphne had refused out of fear.

Here. Up on the landing.

Daphne gasped at the familiar voice that filled her head.

"Grace!" It was her beloved younger sister, who she'd been striving for so many years to reach. Daphne wanted to fall to her knees, to sob with joy.

Better not, Daph. She's right behind.

Daphne followed Grace's directions and raced up the stairs. She chanced a look back; Abigail slithered like a snake up the stairs.

God help me, Daphne thought, shivering with revulsion.

A familiar scoff from Grace. I'm *helping you. God be damned.*

Daphne hesitated on the landing.

Back here, Daphne.

Daphne ran towards the empty servants' quarters. There, in the back of the hall, a staircase was already lowering from the ceiling.

The attic. Daphne slowed. She'd always hated the attic.

Daphne could feel Grace watching with

impatience. *Go!*

With a sob, Daphne hurried up the steps.

CHAPTER 37

"You surprised me." Roza gulped from a juice glass full of wine. I guessed that, with Chitra otherwise occupied dragging Keira's body into the garage, Roza had had to forgo the tea.

Three frozen bodies: Zoe, Yana, Keira. The numbers just kept going up.

Taylor had readily explained on the way back down to the dungeon, after binding our wrists with belts from her closet. Apparently, Roza had emptied most of the gas from the snowmobile shortly after Zoe's escape attempt. Keira had barely made it out onto the road before the snowmobile died. She kept going on foot. Taylor quickly caught up with her and shot her in the back. Then she and Chitra hauled Keira and the snowmobile all the way back to the garage.

"I surprised you," I repeated dully. My head felt fluffy, numb, filled with stuffing. The same day that both Yana and Keira had been shot by Taylor, we'd been expected to keep writing.

I knew it was the penultimate day of the retreat: only 6,000 more words to go.

"I would never have guessed that you'd come back for Wren." Roza was curious. "What made you do that?"

"I didn't want her to die."

"You think she'd have done the same for you?" Roza asked.

"I don't know. Maybe." I considered. "Maybe not."

"I honestly can't decide if it's heroic or stupid." Roza poured more wine into her glass, then got up to shove a straw in my mouth. "Here, darling, have some." I obediently took a sip. My handcuffed wrists were completely numb.

"Well, it's a good twist." Roza set down the glass and picked up the sheath of papers. "In your story, I mean. I wasn't expecting Lamia to be the antagonist. Nor her sister Grace to pop up again. Did you know that was going to happen?"

"No."

She smiled, pleased. "You have a gift. It would be a shame to cut you off so early."

"What, you think I might have another masterpiece in me?" The sarcasm felt hollow, useless. Roza was no longer keeping up the pretense of letting us go. I knew exactly what she and Taylor would do when I wrote the last word. "Maybe you should keep me chained up and try to squeeze more books out of me."

"I'm considering it."

I stared at her. "What?"

"Not the chains. Look, I know you hate me now." She set down the papers with a sigh. "And you should. But I wonder how long that hatred would last." She rested her chin on her hand, studying me with her lizard-green eyes. "I really didn't have a lot of hope for you initially. You seemed so passive and weak. But then, when I found out you'd harmed Wren, I saw there was something there after all. And coming back for her — that's something too."

"Thanks?"

"So here's my proposition." She straightened. "You will survive the fire that will take everyone else. And you'll publish your book under your own name. We could probably get it out by spring." She mused, staring into the distance. "Again, I'll need collateral to make sure you keep your mouth shut. I'll need to record it. But I'll make it easy for you."

"You'll make what easy for me?"

"Killing Wren." She blinked.

I scoffed weakly.

"There are easy ways." Roza twisted back her hair into a low bun. "It doesn't need to be violent. Maybe just a quick needle in the neck."

"And then what?" The calm insanity of the plan faintly amused me. "We ride off into the sunset together?"

"I'm sure you'll need some time, and that's fine." She shrugged. "Maybe you'll want to grieve while touring Greece. Or rest for a year in Bali. Or process in one of those lovely treatment centers out west. I can arrange for any of those. As long as you don't tell anyone about our deal. Because if you do, I'll call you insane. And if that doesn't work, I'll leak the tape."

I tried to wrap my mind around the words. "But wouldn't that implicate you too?"

"It will be your word against mine, darling. I'll tell everyone I found out what you did and tried to help rehabilitate you. They might not like it, but they'll believe me."

"What about your plan to disappear?" My interest was faint. I didn't believe Roza's words, not really. Letting me rest in Bali? It was ludicrous.

"That's the thing about disappearing." She smiled. "You can do it at any time. I've been ready for the past three years. I have the new accounts, the new documents. If you have enough money, it's really not that difficult." She took a sip. "But maybe it's not quite time for me to make my exit. Not if you'd like to work together."

"Wow." I turned away, gazing out the window. "That's such an honor, Roza. Really."

"You'll need to decide by tomorrow. By the time you both finish your books."

"Gotcha." I bobbed my head. "Maybe I'll make a comparison chart. Pros versus cons."

She gave me a sympathetic glance. "I know this is a lot to take in, dear. And I will completely understand if you say no. I'll even promise that the end won't be unnecessarily painful for you. But . . ." She straightened and I did too. We were tied together now, via some deep synapse in the brain stem. ". . . I do hope you consider it. Especially given the alternative."

I lay on the mattress, staring up at a crack on the cement ceiling. Roza's words rattled around my brain. There was no possible way I could kill Wren. It was absurd.

Then again, when the needle was pressed against my own neck, would the survival instinct take over? Would my life necessitate the destruction of hers?

I rolled over on my side. It was almost nine at night and Wren was still writing, hunched over her laptop. We hadn't really spoken since our brief escape. Chitra was feeding us nearly nothing. We were already starting to die.

Had Roza given the same offer to Wren? Had she told her how special she was, how she wanted Wren to be her protégée? And if so, how had Wren replied?

The offerings on the table: money, power, prestige. All the things that I'd wanted so badly for so long. Things that I'd tasted with Wren and her fabulous lifestyle but had never fully swallowed.

And neither had she, really. No book deal. No fiancé. She'd needed Roza and the retreat just as much as I had.

Tomorrow would be the end. Tomorrow, all would be revealed.

And as we headed into the last day of the retreat, I reminded myself that I still had two secrets from Roza.

One was the tiny vial of wolfsbane in my bra, waiting under my right breast.

And the other was the end of the story.

The ending was really my only leverage, even if I didn't yet know how to use it. I lay on the futon, considering it, hovering between wakefulness and sleep. The ending glowed inside me, hidden like a small pearl. Sure, Roza could try to finish the novel herself. And she would, if it came to that. But it wouldn't be *the* ending. The one that already existed, buried underneath the surface, regardless of whether it was uncovered.

Only I had access to that.

Excerpt from *The Great Commission*

Daphne crouched behind a rocking chair, trembling like a newborn lamb. Her matted hair stuck to her sweaty face and she pushed it impatiently to the side.

The attic was huge, stuffed with furniture, boxes, and piles. It would take a while for Abigail — rather, Lamia — to find her. But she would. Daphne clutched a glass pitcher in her left hand; it was the only heavy object she'd been able to find. Abigail had turned on the lights, but they were a few bare bulbs, few and far between.

"Come out, come out," Abigail sang. "Daphne, why are you so afraid of me? Aren't we friends?" She cackled, a horrifying sound.

Focus. Grace's voice was fading in and out, and had been out for some time, but she suddenly came in sharp: *You need to kill her.*

And how do I do that, dear sister? Daphne gritted her teeth.

I don't know, but you don't have much time.

Daphne wanted to weep. How had she ended up in this nightmare?

Think of her weakness. Grace's voice waned again. *Where is she weak?*

493

Lamia *wasn't* weak. That was the problem. She was strong, too strong. She'd overpowered Daphne in her bed and it had terrified and pleasured her in equal measure.

Abigail was getting closer, her slow footsteps creaking against the wooden floor. Daphne cursed under her breath.

"He was the sacrifice." Abigail's voice was suddenly a low growl. "You are the Great Commission. Your body will be the doorway. Your blood will be the key. You will die but be reborn. My right hand. My lover. My daughter. I will teach you the new ways. You will die a mouse, but you will be reborn a god."

The boxes in front of Daphne were suddenly swept away as if by a giant's hand.

Daphne shrieked.

Lamia towered above her. Dried blood streaked her naked torso and breasts. She was too tall and Daphne realized she hovered nearly a foot off the floor.

Lamia's eyes glittered, red like rubies. She grinned.

"Boo," she said in Abigail's sweet voice.

CHAPTER 38

"Wake up, babies!" Taylor's voice cut through my sleep. I sat up slowly.

"Happy Last-Day-of-Retreat! You disgusting bitches get a special treat: a nice little bath." Taylor set down a small water-filled tub in front of the door slot and pushed it through, following it with a handful of shampoos and soaps.

Chitra stood close behind, holding a second tray. Her skin was drawn and pale, almost gray. Her dark eyes were like pebbles at the bottom of a murky pond. She was utterly unrecognizable from the cheerful chef of a few weeks ago.

Taylor, on the other hand, glowed with good health. She wore her LET ME LIVE sweatshirt and had artfully mussed her cropped hair.

"Wash up," she directed. "We're all going to have dinner upstairs."

My stomach growled, reminding me that

we hadn't been given any food all day. The clock on the floor said it was almost six. That morning, Taylor had shared via the speaker that Roza wanted us to wait to write the final scenes until that night. Maybe it was weakness from hunger, but Wren and I had managed to sleep through most of the day.

"Wash your hair near the drain," Taylor now ordered. "Chitra's going to bring down some more water for you to rinse with."

I took my clothes off carefully, keeping the glass vial wrapped in my bra. It felt almost sexual to lather up my greasy hair. I shampooed twice, a third time. Wren and I soaped ourselves up without shame. Taylor pushed through more things in baskets: fluffy white towels and a fresh change of our clothes.

"Hurry up, ladies." She snapped her fingers, scrolling through her phone. "We don't have all day."

Naked, I brought the fresh clothes towards the pile of dirty. Glancing back, I saw Taylor was still occupied. I hooked my bra and slipped the vial beneath my breast. Wren gently patted a white towel to her injured face, leaving traces of pink.

"No time for makeup or anything." Taylor made a face. "But at least you guys don't smell like shit anymore." She tossed in one set of handcuffs. "Wren, you cuff Alex. Then come to the bars and I'll cuff you."

She ushered us out like sheep. And we *were* like sheep. I felt so weak — from lack of food, the constant fear, and now this fun surprise — that it was all I could do to keep upright. Moving through the kitchen and hall, smelling clean, wearing clothes, reminded me of the early days. When all that mattered was winning the contest. When Wren had been my biggest threat.

Taylor directed us to the dining room. There, a table had been opulently set for five. Roza waited at the head, sipping from a glass of wine. Her eyes lit up and she stood, radiant in her long oxblood gown. "Hello, my beautiful darlings!" She grinned. "You look better than you have in a long time."

I wondered if Roza was in a good mood because this was almost over. Keeping people imprisoned must cause a lot of stress, even for her.

Taylor motioned for us to sit at the two furthest seats from Roza.

"No, dear." Roza patted the seats near her. "Let the guests sit by me."

With narrowed eyes, Taylor pulled out a chair for me, as Chitra did the same for

497

Wren. We were close enough to Roza that I briefly imagined sinking my teeth into her bare arm.

Chitra poured red wine into our glasses. Since I was still handcuffed, Taylor held the glass to my lips, purposefully pouring too much. I almost choked.

"Careful." Roza glared at Taylor. "And not too much. I need everyone clearheaded for our final game."

Wren and I locked eyes. Was she fucking kidding? Hadn't she tortured us enough?

Chitra carried in dishes and set them in front of us, a main course starring filet mignon.

"I thought we had to end with steak." Roza winked at me as she picked up her knife and fork.

Taylor fed me like a baby, and Chitra did the same for Wren. The rich food exploded in my mouth. I knew it'd make me sick later but I didn't care.

At one point I glanced up to find Chitra watching me. She mouthed something:

I'm sorry.

As I stared, she sadly turned back to Wren, slipping a forkful of peas past her lips.

Finally, Roza set down her silverware. Chitra started to stand, but Roza glared and she sat again.

"Well, girls. You made it to the end." Roza leaned forward to grab an open bottle of wine. She poured more into my glass, which was still almost full, until it nearly reached the rim. "Alex, I'll repeat that you really surprised me. That rarely happens."

"You're welcome." The food and wine were making me dizzy.

"And you." She turned to Wren. "You surprised me too. You're a very spoiled, childish girl, but you've been able to get through this as well."

Wren watched Roza, her face blank.

"Both of you were deeply hurt growing up." With a full glass, Roza sat back. "And you've spent the rest of your lives hurting others. Maybe you found an oasis in each other, but that doesn't mean it turned you into good and loving people, did it? You treated men terribly. You weren't nice to your so-called friends. You enjoyed a co-dependent, sadomasochistic relationship with each other that took only a moment of true connection to destroy. Wren, you shut down and treated Alex like she didn't exist. Alex, you physically harmed Wren and then fell into a hole of self-pity." She winked at me. "Not a bad story, actually."

I gazed back, impassive.

"Anyway." Roza crossed her arms. "I'm giving you girls the opportunity to finish this sordid tale. You've heard of the Oedipus conflict? The Elektra conflict? Basically, in order to grow, to evolve, you need to unconsciously kill your mother or father. We don't have your wretched parents here today, but no matter. You've mapped onto each other. And given that both of you are miserable, I'm giving you the chance to heal."

Dizziness swept over me again and I pressed my feet against the floor.

Focus. It was Daphne's voice, rising up from the depths of my mind. *Be still and focus.*

"How are you helping us heal?" Wren finally asked, her voice hoarse.

"You can't finish your stories," Roza went on, as if she hadn't heard. "Not without annihilating the other. I see that now." She slowly stood. "And maybe you need an example."

She looked back and forth between Chitra and Taylor. Chitra stared back warily while Taylor waited with barely contained enthusiasm.

"Chitra, dear," Roza said, her voice soft. "I'm going to need you to kill Taylor."

"What?" Chitra stuttered, going rigid.

"What?" Taylor chuckled.

"You have a knife right there." Roza nodded to the steak knife on Wren's plate. "And every second you wait, you're losing the element of surprise."

Taylor laughed again. "You think Chitra's going to commit an act of violence? She's too good, Roza."

Chitra appeared stunned, her lips slightly parted.

"No?" Roza swiveled her head. "Okay, then. Taylor, I'm going to need you to kill Chitra."

"Really?" Taylor rose immediately, clutching my greasy steak knife.

Chitra jumped up so fast, she knocked her chair over. Taylor stalked around the front of the table and Chitra turned, stumbled, then ran for the door.

I'd once watched blood fly from Wren's hand in a wide, perfect arc, gleaming in the bar's fairy lights. But this time the arc was much larger. As Taylor grabbed Chitra's hair, pulled her closer, and drew the knife across her throat, red sprayed out with the power of a fire hose, covering the doorway in a graceful curve.

With a strangled squawk, Chitra sank to the floor.

I realized I was half standing in my chair, mouth gaping.

Chitra's eyes fixed on me and she gasped like a fish as the red ran down her neck onto the floor, a deep vermillion color that reminded me of a beautiful nail polish I'd used before.

I smelled the now-familiar scent of pennies.

Breathing hard, Taylor walked back to the table. She pulled out her chair with a scraping sound and sat. Her eyes were wide, her cheeks dotted with red droplets.

"Whew!" she cried and laughed. "That was fucking crazy."

Wren sat frozen, dumb, staring into space.

"See?" Roza asked us gently. "Two cannot survive in the same space. Chitra was fading away anyway." She studied Chitra's crumpled body and the spreading pool like it was a not particularly interesting work of art. "But I'll support her daughter. I promised her that."

The hysterical words bubbled up: *Roza, this is madness. Roza, let us go.*

Shh, Daphne said. *Quiet now. Let her think you're seeing something new.*

So I looked down at my plate, studying the wet, pinkish tinges of the bloody steak Chitra had expertly prepared such a short time ago. I gave a slight nod.

"Good." Suddenly, joyously, Roza clapped

her hands. "Let's retire to the parlor, then, shall we? It's time for our final game."

CHAPTER 39

In front of the roaring fire, two dark lacquered tables awaited. They held our laptops as well as a stack of papers neatly arranged beside them. On the buffet table near the wall was a decanter of dark wine and a few wineglasses. The room was dim, lit only by candles on the mantel and the coffee table. What a nice tableau.

"Have a seat." Roza settled on the overstuffed couch facing the desks, about ten feet away. Taylor sat next to her, nearly bouncing with eagerness, like a kid at her first Broadway show.

I walked over to the farther desk and sat. Wren perched on her chair, shoulders hanging.

Red. Shiny. Pennies. The image of the growing scarlet pool made a helpless moan rise in my throat.

Stop. Daphne firmly shut the image away. Chitra's wide, pleading eyes became less distinct, then blurry, then were gone altogether. *Concentrate, Alex. You've seen the depths of her madness. If you don't focus, you're not going to make it.*

"Now." Roza folded her hands over her knee. "You are both very close to your endings. As you know from our meetings, you need two things: a resolution and a final scene. I think both could be done in three thousand words or less. But I leave that up to you."

The fire warmed my knees. My mind felt very still.

"So the final game," Roza went on, "is to finish those final scenes and print them out there." She indicated a printer on a side table near the sofa. "And then decide amongst yourselves who the winner will be."

"What?" Wren looked up and squinted back at me. "You mean, read . . ."

"No," Roza said. "I mean destroy. I know you're both squeamish about physical violence, so I'll allow the manuscripts to be proxies."

Taylor was grinning. I felt a bright flare of hate.

Good, Daphne said. *Use it to sharpen yourself.*

"So basically you want us to throw each other's manuscripts into the fire?" I asked.

"That's one way." Roza shrugged. "You can do whatever you want. Rip it to shreds. Eat it. Just get rid of it. There's no other copy."

The words pulled unexpectedly at my chest. So much time, so much energy . . . for it all to be destroyed.

"And" — Roza pulled out her phone — "to make sure you actually play, I'll be timing you both. Two hours. It's fast, but you can both make that time. If, at the end of it, no manuscript has been destroyed, then you will both die." She shrugged. "Either way works for me, really. But I do hope to continue working with one of you. You're both very talented."

Taylor's smile faltered. And I knew exactly what had happened in this strange, unhappy family. Yana had been first. Roza had seduced her young assistant, then groomed her, and eventually she'd taken her book. They'd been lovers: I knew that as surely as if I'd been told. When had it changed? When had Yana been demoted to housekeeper? Was it before or after Taylor had appeared, so excited, so anxious to please?

Chitra had been a part of it, too, but not in the same way. Chitra was a different game. Roza had pulled her in not with sex or validation but with her love for her

506

daughter. Roza had seen her weak spot and had known how to exploit it.

But Yana and Taylor: that had been the first competition. Yana had lost. Chitra's usefulness had faltered, and she'd been sacrificed to show us our real competitor.

Taylor.

Did Taylor realize what was happening? That Wren or I, whoever "won," was being called in to take her place?

It wouldn't be easy for her. Roza would make her suffer. It was all part of the game.

Wren was now shaking and crying weakly.

"Get her a blanket," Roza commanded. Taylor tossed a wool blanket on Wren's lap.

"And let's uncuff them," Roza said. "Wren? Keep it together, dear. It's time for you to write."

Stuffing her gun into her waistband, Taylor unlocked the handcuffs and tossed them onto the floor. I rubbed my raw wrists, opened and closed my numb, dead fingers.

As Taylor backed away, Wren glanced at me. Her eyes looked unfocused.

"Concentrate," I told her out loud.

She looked confused. And I understood. What for? What was the plan?

Something glinted in the dim room beyond Wren. The wine decanter on the buffet table.

Use it, Daphne said.

"Wait." I turned to Roza and motioned to the wine. "Is that for us? Can I have some?" I stood.

"Hey!" Taylor jumped up and trained the gun on me. "Sit the fuck down."

"It's okay, dear." Roza patted Taylor's hip. "Get her a glass."

"I can do it." I shook my hands and wiggled my fingers. "I need to do something before writing. Nervous energy, I guess."

"Understandable." Roza looked up at Taylor. "I'll allow it."

Taylor stayed standing as I went to the buffet table. I tried to ignore both her and the gun, which somehow felt more solid and real than any of us. If Taylor saw what I was doing, she'd use it to stop me, with or without Roza's approval.

I turned my back to her, grasping the decanter with my right hand and dipping my left hand down the loose neck of my sweater to pull out the glass vial from my bra. I poured a glass as I popped open the vial close to my chest. The top and the dried sprig fell to the table. I plucked the flowers, still palming the vial, and released them into the decanter as I set it down. I brushed the small top away and it fell between the buffet's surface and the wall.

508

I studied the decanter as I slipped the vial back into my bra. The wine was dark enough that you couldn't see the wolfsbane. That or it had already dissolved.

Well done, Daphne whispered, pleased.

"Hurry up, bitch," Taylor called.

I went back to the desk and took a sip of the wine. It was thick and bitter. There was nothing left to do now but hope they'd pour themselves a glass. I touched a key and flinched at the bright screen lighting up in the dim room.

"All right, ladies." Roza tapped at her phone. "Two hours starts now."

CHAPTER 40

Lamia hovered in the air, fixing Daphne in place with that blood-encrusted grin.

"Yes." Daphne stood, holding out her hands. "To become the Great Commission would be a magnificent honor. You said there was a ceremony? What materials do we need? Where should we do it?"

Lamia floated down a few inches. "We need fire."

"The parlor," Daphne said quickly. "Let us go to the parlor."

Abigail's face was beginning to slacken and slip like a wax mask. Behind it, Lamia's true visage was beginning to shine through. Daphne knew she didn't have much time.

"I know you are not yet convinced," Lamia said. "But you shall be. I know how much control others have wielded over you. How you have suffered. When you arise anew, you will have ultimate power."

And what did that mean? The power to kill? To serve Lamia? Daphne kept her thoughts pushed low, like seedlings in the dirt. Lamia could read her thoughts, if she wanted, but it seemed she was beyond caring about Daphne's reactions.

Hubris. Lamia thought she was invincible. That was her weakness.

Lamia was correct that Daphne had suffered.

But she had also survived. That meant that she, Daphne, had her own type of power.

My hands stilled over the keys and I stared into the fire. The word "power" filled my mind. It had never felt more alien, more unreachable, than this moment: writing at gunpoint. I thought of Chitra, her body crumpled on the dining room floor. Of Zoe, Yana, and Keira, frozen and stacked in the garage like logs.

I glanced at Wren, who was hunched over and typing furiously. She was scared, injured, pathetic. And yet, before, she'd held so much power over me. Even in her absence, she'd been an omnipotent phantom, haunting my every thought. I remembered how terrified I'd been on the subway ride to Ursula's book party, wondering if I would see her.

I thought of Wren as a child, locked in the closet, bruises peppering her arms and back.

I looked at Roza and Taylor — neither of whom had even glanced at the wine, unfortunately. Roza was now reading something on her phone, Taylor examining something on her gun — and a similar veil fell away. I saw both of them as younger versions of themselves, fresh girls slowly realizing that the world they'd been born into hadn't saved a place for them. Young Roza just missing the extreme horrors of the war, only to come upon them in the closet of her best friend's home. Adolescent Taylor existing in a space that hated girls so much that they decided to stop living. She'd had to shove her rage so far down for so long that it had festered in the dark.

And me. A young girl meeting a monster in the woods and knowing deep down that it heralded the end of something. That the hushed arguments and sharp looks and ominous energy at home meant it was all swiftly coming to an end.

Where did one's power lie in a world that stripped it from you, over and over again? How could we reclaim it when the dominant forces dangled it above our heads, shouting:

Only the strong survive? Was harming others the only way? Or was that a trick too?

Maybe the answer was even simpler than I could have imagined. Maybe the power had never really gone away. Maybe it still lived in me, in my guts, in my bones. Maybe all I had to do was see it.

Yes. Daphne's voice, solemn and proud, permeated my thoughts. *You've finally perceived the truth. Behind all this. Behind Roza. Behind yourself. You've reached the end.*

You're done.

I pushed my laptop away.

"I'm done." The words that came out were phlegmy and gruff.

"What'd she say?" Taylor asked faintly. Roza looked up from her phone.

I cleared my throat and turned to face them. "I'm done."

Wren stopped typing and stared at me, her eyes huge and frightened.

"You wrote for five minutes." Roza's eyes narrowed. "You can't be done."

I snorted. The sound startled me but then I laughed again, exuberant. The power of my resistance filled me, sparkling like a billion twinkling stars.

"Thank you, Roza," I said. "It took until now for me to understand."

"Alex." Wren's voice was low, filled with panic.

"Did it, dear?" Roza slammed her phone down. In the candlelight, her face looked slightly haggard.

"Yes. In a really fucked-up way, I think you saved me." My voice strengthened. "Before all of this, I was really just sleep-walking. I felt so numbed out. So unhappy. Hopeless." I took a deep breath. "But being here . . . you made me remember that I have this ability, to create whole *worlds* inside me."

"Um." Taylor glanced at Roza. "Is she serious right now?"

"For so long I let other people make me feel like that wasn't good enough," I said. "That, in order to be a real writer, I had to get some agent or publisher to believe in me. Until then it would just be a delusion. But that's bullshit. Because even if I never publish anything, I'm a writer." I paused to take a breath. "I'm a writer, and no one can take that away from me."

Roza just watched, one eyebrow raised.

"It's a rush," I went on. "And in some fucked-up way, I get it, Roza. You've gone to such great lengths to steal it from other people. But you'll never have this power."

She was smiling now.

"And so . . ." I stood and grabbed the back of the chair for support. Taylor jumped up but Roza put up a hand to stop her.

"I'm taking it with me. I'm done." I scooped up the stack of papers, strode to the fireplace, and threw them in.

Wren cried out but I just watched them burn. Peace alighted in my chest, gentle as a moth, as the pages crumpled and blackened. I could feel Daphne's ghostly presence beside me. She was beaming, as proud as a mother.

They could do whatever they wanted to my body, but they couldn't have my story.

"Oh, Alex." Roza rubbed her forehead. "You little fool. You didn't *really* think that was the only copy, did you?" She sounded amused. "Such a heroic act, though. And a speech! I'm glad you got that, dear. You deserve to go out on a high note." The mirth drained from her face as she turned to Taylor.

"Kill her."

CHAPTER 41

"Really?" Taylor seemed startled.

"Yes, really." Roza heaved a loud sigh. "I've given them too much leeway. I see that now. Anyway. Live and learn. Please take care of Alex. And then Wren will get to look at her best friend's body and decide how she wants to proceed."

"No!" Wren cried, her voice raw with anguish.

"Wait." My heart whirred in my chest, but still Daphne was soothing me. *Be calm. One last try.* I pointed at my glass of wine. "Can I make a final request?"

Roza hesitated. She wanted it over and done with, but she also had that pesky sense of curiosity. "What, dear?"

"A toast." Slowly, I reached out and picked up the glass. "To everything we've gone through together."

"Seriously?" Taylor's voice was shrill. "No fucking way."

And that refusal, combined with Roza's love for the dramatic, cemented it.

"What?" Roza asked crossly. "You have a busy schedule? Get me a glass. One for Wren too."

"This is so, so ridiculous." Taylor stuck the gun into her waistband. The three of us watched her pour the glasses at the buffet. She handed the first to Roza, set the second on Wren's desk, and kept the third.

"Happy now, Al?" As if in defiance, Taylor plopped onto the couch and took a large gulp.

"To Alex." Roza stood and raised her glass. "A truly talented young writer who has graced our world with her masterpiece. Well, most of it, anyway." She raised it to her lips.

Robotically, Wren did the same.

"Wren, don't," I murmured softly as Taylor took another drink.

Wren paused but Roza heard me. "What's going on?" She raised her glass and studied it. "Did you put something in this?"

"Wait, *what*?" Taylor's eyes widened.

It was then that I noticed something — someone — creeping towards us. At first I thought it was a trick of the candlelight, but then the shadow solidified, an indistinct but tangible figure crouched low to the ground.

It slunk closer, moving silently under the buffalo head.

I stared, stunned. Had I somehow called Daphne into being? Had my desperation brought her back to life?

Or had I accidentally inhaled some molecules from the wolfsbane earlier? Was I hallucinating like I had on Valentine's Day?

Taylor jumped up, training the gun on me. "Al, what the fuck did you do?"

"Here." Roza pulled something dripping from her glass. "It looks like . . ."

Taylor grabbed it. "Wolfsbane! But how did you . . ." She looked up, confounded. Daphne was getting closer, clutching something large and white. She was wearing a fur cloak and her hood covered her face.

I needed to distract them.

"Find this?" I reached into my sweater and pulled out the empty vial, wiggling it in the air. "Maybe you should keep dangerous substances locked up, T."

"Oh, shit. People die from this, Alex!" Taylor dove to the ground, dropping the gun, and stuck her finger into her throat. She started to retch.

Daphne was right behind the couch. Candlelight gleamed off her eyes and bared teeth.

"My goodness." Roza smirked. "Well, that

was unexpected. Bravo, dear. But I do hope you know it's nothing more than a small delay."

Daphne slipped over the back of the couch and stood on the cushions, rearing up to her full height. She had battled Lamia and won, but it clearly hadn't been easy. The fur cloak was matted and caked with blood. Her cracked lips pulled into a grim rictus as she raised the ceramic vase high.

The next second or two unfolded slowly, almost leisurely.

Roza started to turn just as Daphne jumped to the floor and brought the vase down on the crown of Taylor's head.

There came a shattering, jarring crash. Taylor was briefly outlined in a halo of white shards as the force drove her face to the ground.

When time returned to normal, Taylor's body lay prone. A spreading halo of red soaked into the rug.

There was something wrong with her skull. It was misshapen. Dented. Her blood-doused hair flattened into the concave valley.

Daphne stood above her, heaving.

Not Daphne. Keira.

She pulled down her hood and glanced at me, her breath ragged. It was the first time

I'd seen her without her glasses. In the midst of her reddened, cracking face, the skin around her eyes was a mottled purple, and the tip of her nose was a deep plum shade. Her eyes were filled with a determined fury.

Roza's mouth gaped open. She looked at the gun on the floor just as Keira bent and grabbed it.

Roza took off immediately, racing to the door. Keira ran after her. Wren and I followed.

Before, creeping around the house, sleeping in the library, I'd felt like an animal. But I hadn't felt like a predator.

Now, as the three of us chased Roza down the hall, all I wanted to do was rip off her limbs.

CHAPTER 42

Roza rounded the corner into the front hall. We tracked her up the grand staircase, over the landing, down the hall to her room. I jiggled the knob but the door was locked.

"Keira, you're alive!" I gasped in the pause.

Ignoring me, she shoved us back and aimed the gun below the doorknob. The sudden blast rang in my ears. She wrenched open the door and slipped inside. Wren and I followed, sharing a glance. Just another one of Keira's unexpected skills.

"The basement," I called in warning as we raced down the hallway to Roza's sitting room. She had to be hurrying down there to barricade herself within the thick cement walls. But in the sitting room we saw something that made us stop in our tracks.

A set of stairs hung down from the ceiling like an open jaw.

A door into the attic.

I laughed, feeling delirious at the new collision between my world and Daphne's. I pictured Daphne running up the attic steps, urged by her long-dead sister Grace, as Lamia followed close behind.

Who was I in this case? Was I still Daphne? Or had I become Lamia?

"Wait," Wren cried as Keira reached the stairs. "Can't we just leave her? Can't we just get out of here?"

"How?" Keira's voice was raspy; it was the first time she'd spoken.

"I don't know." Wren shook her head.

"No gas for the snowmobile." Keira ticked them off on her fingers. "Snow's too deep to drive. Too far to walk."

Close up, I could see that her ears were tinged with black.

"Oh my god." I reached out towards her but she jerked away.

"If we don't kill her, she's going to kill *us*," Keira hissed.

"You're right." I grabbed Wren's trembling shoulder, swallowing my own panic. "Okay?"

"Yeah." Wren shuddered but stood up straight.

Keira went up the steps first, pointing the gun in front of her. Her left shoulder hung oddly and she listed to the side. She smelled like the outdoors, fir-tinged and bitter.

I followed, and Wren came after me. As our eyes adjusted to the attic's dim light, I felt a pull of unease. Just like I'd imagined, it was filled with stuff: boxes, covered furniture, stacks of gilded frames. We passed by a pink velvet chair, uncovered and dusty, with a huge hole in the seat. Stuffing poured out like vomit.

Daphne's voice, instructing me on what to do, was gone. Now it was just the three of us, moving in a tight pack. We advanced slowly like soldiers sneaking through a forest. I scanned around us. Roza could be anywhere. This was too dangerous.

Wren gasped.

At the sound, Keira and I whipped around.

Backing away from us, Roza grasped Wren, pressing a hunting knife to her throat. Wren's eyes bulged and she whimpered in fear. For once, Roza's hair was mussed, her face shiny with sweat.

"Let her go," Keira growled, training the gun on Roza.

"No." Her voice was light but her jaw was tense. "No, I don't think so."

"Roza." Keira stepped forward and Roza moved back, dragging Wren.

"Well!" Roza managed a grin. "Another

twist: Keira returns from the Underworld! I knew Chitra was hiding something, slipping out of the house like that. Did she bring you food, blankets, maybe even heaters? You're a lucky girl. Although that frostbite's really going to take a toll on your looks." She sighed. "Stop squirming, darling."

The knife pressed a line into Wren's throat; blood smeared against metal and skin.

"Let her go." I was dizzy with sudden helplessness.

"Ladies, let's not waste time. There's no way you're going to allow me to kill her. So here's what we'll do." Roza's smile shifted into a grimace. "Keira, you're going to slide the gun to me. And then I'm going to lock you up downstairs so I can leave. How does that sound?"

Keira scoffed. "You think we can trust you?"

"You have my word. I know it's not much. But consider the alternative."

Wren cried out as a drop of blood weaved down her neck and pooled in her collarbone.

"Honestly, this isn't the worst way for me to go." Roza shrugged. "Prison always sounded boring, but death doesn't scare me. So you two decide. You can give up the gun. Or I'll slit your friend's throat and accept my death. Ten seconds." She started to count. "Ten, nine . . ."

Wren's eyes pleaded. I met Keira's gaze. Something wet oozed from the scaliest part of her face. *What should we do?*

I knew without a doubt that Roza would go through with it. After all, it was just part of the escalation: from poisonous flowers, to a needle in the arm, to a quick hard slash.

"One." Roza's arm lifted. Wren closed her eyes and swallowed.

"Stop!" I raised my hands. "We'll do it. Just stop."

"Alex, I'd like a word with you."

I paused at the doorway. Keira and Wren were already inside Yana's room. Wren sobbed on the floor while Keira kneeled beside her. Keira looked up and we locked eyes as Roza shut the door. She twisted the key and turned to me, gun casually aimed from her side.

In the attic, she'd picked up the gun and pressed it into Wren's back. She'd made us walk ahead of her, dropping the knife and warning us that she would have no problem shooting Wren if we tried to run. Keira and I had complied.

Now I watched Roza warily, unsure of

what she wanted.

"So." She smoothed back her hair. "Quite a wild ride it's been. Yes?"

She wanted to chat. I felt a sudden urge to burst out laughing in her face, but managed to keep it together. "It has."

"I want you to appreciate this." She nodded at the locked room. "I could very well have killed all of you. But . . ." She sighed, looking down. "I don't know. Maybe you've made me a little soft."

I stayed quiet, watching the gun in my peripheral vision. Could I grab it? I needed to keep her distracted.

"How are you going to get away?" I asked. "On foot?"

"Please, dear. You know I'm a planner." She smirked. "There's a full canister of gas for the snowmobile hidden in the garage." She gazed at me, then grinned. "Would you like to accompany me?"

For a horrible moment I thought she was serious, that she was going to force me to come with her.

She saw my expression and chuckled. "I'm just kidding, darling. I'm afraid our paths diverge at this point."

"Maybe you should stay." I managed to sound casual, like I was speaking to a friend at a dinner party that was winding down.

"You know that's not possible." She reached out and touched my arm. "The reason I wanted to speak with you is that I wanted you to know: despite it all, you did very well." Her expression was tender, almost motherly.

"Thank you." I concluded that if I even started to reach for the gun, she'd be able to shoot me in the belly.

"We could've had a wonderful time together. But you've made your choice." She pursed her lips. "Safety. Stability. And that sniveling idiot Wren."

Unexpectedly, the words made me want to defend myself. To tell her that I'd chosen not Wren but myself.

But it didn't matter. She wouldn't understand.

"Maybe you're right." I shrugged, exhaustion creeping up my spine.

"Anyway." She took a step back. "There's a flash drive on the desk in the office. In my ring dish. It contains all your books."

"Thank you." I forced a smile. "Wow, maybe you *are* getting soft."

Roza beamed at me. "You know what? I think you're going to have a long career. Jump-started by me and this crazy experience, of course. But long just the same. I'm looking forward to following it." She took a step closer. "Ciao, dear." As if it were the most natural thing in the world, she leaned in and pressed her lips to mine.

The kiss shocked me. I jerked away as she drew back.

She smiled, satisfied. Unlocking the door, she waved me in.

I joined Wren and Keira on the floor, listening to the click of the lock, then Roza's footsteps moving away.

"What did she want?" Keira asked, wary. Wren was curled up in a ball, possibly asleep.

"I don't know." My mind spun. "To say goodbye, I think?"

Keira nodded. "She liked you the most."

I felt an inappropriate flush of pleasure. As Keira and I searched Yana's room for bobby pins, I tried to push down the tangled mixture of rage, revulsion, and yearning.

If things had gone differently, if Zoe hadn't caused the house of cards to fall, maybe Roza *would* have convinced me to give her my book. Maybe the retreat would've ended differently. Maybe I could have convinced Roza that Taylor didn't need to die for me to take her place.

I imagined us boarding a plane together, seating ourselves in first class. Roza would smile at me and squeeze my hand. I'd squeeze back. We knew each other's darkest secrets, and that knowing would bond us more deeply than any other couple around us.

For a second, I felt the glee that would fill me as the plane took off, rushing us towards our new life together.

CHAPTER 43

Six Months Later

After the final battle with Lamia, Daphne slept for fifteen hours. Rising the next afternoon, she bathed and made herself a hearty breakfast. Then she crammed as much food as she could into one of Horace's packs. She dressed in his clothes, cinching the pants with a belt, feeling gloriously unencumbered by bustles and cage-like corsets. She topped off her outfit with his fur hunting cap. She stared at herself in his shaving mirror. Her blue eyes were bright, her cheeks rosy. She felt a flutter in her belly. Something — she didn't know what — awaited.

She left through the kitchen door, meeting the brilliance of the day. The sky shone in an unbroken cerulean glaze. The sun made the icy branches glitter. She took out her compass. The nunnery lay towards the east. It was many miles, but she felt certain she would reach it. They would take her in, shelter her, feed her. Cut off any blackened fingers or toes. And from there she would continue her recovery. She'd already picked a new name: Elizabeth. She was leaving her old self behind.

And who knew where she would end up?

Abigail's charred corpse lay in the basement. Perhaps it would be properly identified, perhaps not. Daphne knew Abigail had kept her spiritualist leanings from most of her family and friends. And while Daphne didn't like the idea of Abigail's family not having a body to bury, she couldn't see an alternative plan, not if she herself wanted to escape. Perhaps keeping Abigail from the bowels of hell had been enough.

Daphne breathed deeply, enjoying the crunch of snow beneath her feet. Soon the ice would melt. Green buds would burst from the trees. She would shed her heavy layers and swim naked in warm streams.

A chirping came from her right. A tiny chipmunk chattered at her from a nearby rock.

"Hello," Daphne said.

As if waiting for her permission, he bounded in front of her. Maybe he would be her new guide.

Perhaps he was her sister Grace incarnate, returning a second time to help.

Though . . . Grace had hated rodents. So perhaps not.

"Wait for me!" Daphne moved faster, pushing branches out of the way as she went deeper into the forest, towards a new life that was fast approaching.

The boughs swung as she passed them, then quivered, then were still.

I looked up, closing the book. "Thank you."

The applause was thunderous. It startled me — all loud, unexpected sounds continued to startle me — but I forced a wide grin.

"Thank you, Alex!" Tonya, my interviewer and another up-and-coming novelist, clasped my book to her chest. Dozens of Post-its peeked from the pages.

From the rows of the audience, what looked like dozens of hands shot up.

"So we're going to leave it at that." Tonya ignored the crowd. I nodded, relieved. I'd told them — "the team" — that I'd only read an excerpt at my launch event. I wouldn't answer questions from a moderator or audience members.

Because I knew they'd inevitably be about Roza.

"Enjoy the party, everyone!" Tonya cried. As we stood, she pulled me into a hug.

"I loved the book," she murmured into my ear.

"Thank you," I said.

"I heard you already sold the film rights?" She pulled back. "That's awesome. Now you can relax a little, huh?"

"I hope so."

The last six months had passed in a blur. The editorial team had wanted to fast-track the book. So I'd written the last few scenes, edited, rewritten, checked the copyedits, and approved the cover in a matter of weeks. I'd done everything they'd asked.

Except for the press.

"So tell me." Tonya took a step closer. "I heard you might be writing a book with the other two women about your experience. Is that true?"

Your experience. Such a delicate way to put it.

"Probably not." I shrugged. "But some film studios are interested in our story."

"Wow. That would make an *amazing* miniseries." She pressed a card in my hand. "I do script work. If you want any help — you know, from someone you trust — call me."

"Thanks." I tucked the card into my

pocket. I'd give it to Melody, my and Ursula's agent. But if we sold the rights, I didn't want anything to do with it. Whatever it turned into wouldn't capture what had actually happened. That was my story, one I didn't want to share with anyone.

Because, honestly, I was only just beginning to process it myself.

"Hey!" Ursula accosted me at the front of the room. "Our woman of the hour! Here." She handed me a plastic cup of champagne. "Cheers, babe."

"Cheers." I raised the cup but only took a tiny sip. Alcohol had been appealing to me less and less these days. All it did was make me feel woozy and give me a sharp headache. Which was a disappointment: I'd really been counting on it to help blur some of the nightmares and flashbacks. They'd been disturbing, though talking to my new therapist was helping.

"How are you feeling?" Ursula sounded breezy enough, but I could sense it in her eyes: that quiet concern from almost everyone I interacted with. I didn't know how to explain that I wasn't some broken thing. Despite the lingering aftereffects, I was stronger than they'd ever know. I was just reacclimating. This new life, this new self — I was still figuring out who I'd become.

"I'm okay," I said earnestly, and she smiled.

"Well, it looks great." She held up the book. The simple cover showed the title in thick white letters over one of Daphne's hall paintings. It had taken a lot of advocating on Melody's part — the editors had wanted a sexy image of a woman's naked back — but I liked how it had turned out.

Of course, I knew why it had been picked up and published so quickly. And that was the question: Would editors have been interested if not for the Roza-related back-story? I had no idea. Probably not.

But that was okay. It was good that people wanted to read my words, even if the interest didn't last forever.

And the money, for now, helped immeasurably.

"Hey."

I turned and there was Pete, my old colleague and friend and one-night stand, holding a glass of rosé. He held it out and we clinked.

"Classy, right?" I raised my eyebrows. "Free alcohol. Finally."

Ursula smoothly moved away, shooting me a coy look.

"Very hip." Pete gestured around the Brooklyn indie bookstore. It was one of the larger ones, though it still felt close and slightly too hot. Someone had just propped open the doors to let in the nighttime breeze.

"Thanks. You know me." I rolled my eyes.

"How are you?" Pete's brow wrinkled. He'd reached out via email once, I suddenly remembered, and I'd forgotten to respond. The shame began to creep up my spine. I hadn't treated him well. Sure, we'd both made the drunken decision to sleep together. But I was the one who had then immediately dropped the friendship.

Like Wren, actually.

"I'm okay. But, listen." I leaned closer. "I'm sorry about what happened between us. I acted really immaturely. I shouldn't have avoided you like that."

"Water under the bridge." He waved a hand. "I can't believe you even remember that, after what happened to you right after." He shook his head. "Man. I still can't fully wrap my head around what you went through."

"Me either." I smiled. "But thanks for saying that."

"Anyway." Pete hefted the book, clearly ready to move on to another topic. "This is great. I read it in, like, a day. Would you . . ." He looked a little embarrassed. "Would you sign it for me?"

"Of course." I pulled out a Sharpie from my dress pocket.

To Pete. Thanks for being such a good friend.

"I was also wondering." His cheeks reddened. "Can I — could we get lunch or something sometime? I mean, just as friends. Or . . . whatever." He looked tortured. Without thinking, I pulled him into a hug. When we separated, he looked relieved.

"I'd love to," I said sincerely. "But I'm actually moving to LA this weekend."

"This weekend?" His eyes widened. "Wow."

"Yeah." I heard Ursula's laughter and glanced over at her. "I just needed a change."

"Well, if you're ever back in New York . . ." He grinned.

I nodded. "I'll definitely hit you up. No whiskey shots, though."

"Alex! OMG." Wren's friend Craig, waiting behind Pete, became impatient. He swept in front of Pete and grabbed me in a hug, smelling of cigarette smoke and musky cologne. "Honey, the book is *fabulous.*" Ridhi appeared by his side in a hot-pink tank dress more appropriate for a Miami club.

I hadn't even considered my ex-friends would show up, but of course they were here. Where the action was.

"*So* fabulous," Ridhi seconded, diving straight in for her hug.

I smiled and chatted before noticing who was waiting behind them. Craig and Ridhi stopped in mid-sentence and parted to let Wren through.

"Hi, Al." She hugged me tightly as Ridhi and Craig respectfully retreated. "It's wonderful."

"Thanks." She was one of the first people I'd thanked in the acknowledgments, even though I'd seen little of her over the past six months. She'd actually reached out a lot, inviting me to A-list parties, fashion events, restaurant openings. It was almost like she was an ex trying to woo me back. But I hadn't gone. Things had changed too much. *I* had changed too much.

"You all packed up?" Wren held on to my arms, studying me like a proud parent. The scars on her face were only barely visible now, thanks to Manhattan's top dermatologist. She was dressed down, in loose jeans and a tank top. She'd started brushing her blunt bangs to the side, letting them grow out, and she wore a soft peach lipstick instead of her trademark red.

"Pretty much." I bobbed my head. "The movers are coming tomorrow. I'm making it an early night."

"Promise me you'll come back for my book party this fall?" She was smiling but her eyes filled with tears.

"Of course," I said vehemently. Tears sprang to my eyes with our shared knowledge that I probably wouldn't.

It had taken a literal massacre, but Wren and I were officially over.

"I'll miss you." This I said honestly, and we grabbed each other in a final hug.

Others were crowding in, wanting to talk to me, so Wren squeezed my arm and walked away. Craig and Ridhi trailed after her like baby chicks.

"Congrats!" My editor, Sheena, pulled me into a hug. "Enjoy tonight, lady." She grinned and winked, not noticing my shiny eyes. "Tomorrow we'll talk about what you're going to write next."

That night I lay on my couch, surrounded by moving boxes, and texted with Keira. She'd helped me find an apartment near her, meeting with the broker and showing it to me on FaceTime. She'd also grilled the building manager and had even negotiated the rent down a little bit. I had a lot more about self-advocacy to learn from her.

Between her and Ursula, I knew that the move would be okay. Like Daphne, I had no idea where I'd eventually end up. But right now something about the warmth and sunshine of LA was calling to me.

I texted with Zoe's dad today, Keira texted. I said we'd plan another call with him and M this month.

Perfect, thanks, I responded. Keira, Wren, and I had decided to start a nonprofit for young writers in Zoe's name, with the input of her father and boyfriend — whose name was Michael, not Jack, as she'd told us. I was only just beginning to be able to think about Zoe without a despairing, bottomless sorrow.

There was so much that wasn't fair. It wasn't fair that we'd survived, and Zoe, Yana, and Chitra hadn't. It wasn't fair that Chitra's daughter no longer had a mother. It wasn't fair that Zoe had spent much of her life tracking down a secret that would kill her. It also wasn't fair that her aunt Lucy hadn't made it to thirty, hadn't lived to write more books.

But it was how it had happened. It was something we were going to have to learn to live with.

BTW, your party looked so fun, Keira wrote. So many people!!

It was, I responded. And it had been. Strange, but fun.

You'll need to give me pointers. Her own book was coming out in two months. I hate being the center of attention.

I pictured her now, dressed in chic black loungewear, pulling at what was left of her ear — a new anxious tic I'd noticed over a FaceTime call. Half of her right ear had been removed due to the frostbite. Thankfully, after surgery and months of PT, her left shoulder and arm were working normally, though they were still weak.

I knew Keira was still working through the emotional scars. After all, she was the one who'd barely survived in a freezing garage. At the edge of death, she'd stopped Taylor, effectively saving us all. I couldn't comprehend the aftereffects. And: it wasn't my place to ask about them. All I could do was be available if and when she did want to talk. In the meantime, I was here for more lighthearted conversations.

Just say thanks and hug people, I typed. It's truly all you need to do!

I set down my phone and bit into a leftover chocolate cupcake. The party — and life overall — had retained a gloss of surrealism, which I'd been feeling ever since leaving Blackbriar. My therapist had called it PTSD. But I still wondered: How could the traumatic experiences feel more solid and real than my actual life?

I let myself be drawn back to those final, concrete hours at Blackbriar. Keira had managed to pick the door's lock and we found a first aid kit in the kitchen to tend to Keira's and Wren's wounds. Wren and I had made a makeshift sling for Keira's shoulder and arm. Thankfully, her nose and face had regained their normal color, though her ear remained black.

I'd made them both grilled cheese sandwiches while Keira recounted how she'd survived several days in the garage. How Chitra, unable to move the grievously injured Keira into the house, had brought her electric heaters, blankets, painkillers, and food. How she'd sat with Keira every night, changing her bandages, comforting her. Chitra had apparently been wanting to leave Roza for some time; she'd planned to quit after the retreat. But then everything had devolved into chaos. Horrified, she'd watched us getting imprisoned, then killed . . . and she'd decided to bide her time and get help at the first opportunity.

Chitra hadn't returned that last night. Keira felt she'd regained just enough strength to sneak back into Blackbriar. Knowing her body was on the brink of shutting down, she'd planned to get ahold of the gun — which she'd learned to shoot while visiting a friend in Wyoming — or die trying.

After the grilled cheese sandwiches, we'd passed out on the double beds in Wren's room. The next day, as if in support, the weather had warmed quickly, melting the snow enough that we could drive out in one of Roza's cars. We'd traveled just a few miles before Wren's phone got service. Stopped on the side of the road, Wren tried to explain the situation to the 911 dispatcher but kept breaking into peals of laughter. Keira and I laughed too, our wails wavering between hilarity and relieved sobs.

We'd returned to Blackbriar to wait for the police, bringing our suitcases downstairs, freshly showered and dressed. I grabbed the flash drive from the ring dish, just where Roza had said it would be. We avoided the parlor and dining room. Keira had taken the news about Chitra's murder in stride, but I wondered if she was just in shock.

Three police cars had arrived, sirens blaring, shortly thereafter.

"Did you find Roza?" Keira had called from the front porch as the cops ambled up the porch steps. They didn't tell us right away, but the answer was no.

We found out later that other cops were already questioning the closest neighbors, including the nuns. But there was no trace of her at the convent or anywhere else.

The lead detective — he asked us to call him Larry — told us it was impossible for Roza to disappear like that, on a snowmobile with one tank of gas, in such a remote area. Someone at a gas station or farmhouse would spot her somewhere, given that her face was plastered all over the news. The story was already out, exploding onto the internet.

Where in the world is Roza Vallo? There were even *Carmen Sandiego* memes, since Roza had once been photographed in profile in a red trench coat.

But despite some false alarms, no one saw her — or at least no one admitted to it. By this time her bank accounts were already emptied, the money presumably converted into crypto.

Larry, who turned out to be more open than I would've expected a detective to be, told us he thought it most likely that she'd frozen to death somewhere in the vast expanse of woods. He predicted her body would be found in the spring when the snow thawed.

It wasn't. But that didn't shake him. There were thousands of acres of forest out there. Someday a hunter would come across her bones.

I wasn't so sure.

After all this, I'd gone back to the Midwest. Even there, reporters found me. Mom would answer the phone — she still had a landline — and would hang up with a stony expression.

I appreciated her stoicism. She and Steve, her husband, hadn't asked me any questions, which was both odd and comforting. His kids were in college, so it was just the three of us. Mom took off work and made me cookies and tea and even Hungarian goulash when I requested it. We sat in the living room and watched the Game Show Network: old episodes of *Wheel of Fortune* and *The Price Is Right.* Every so often she'd squeeze my shoulder, as if reassuring herself that I was really there.

Ursula's agent Melody sent me a quick text, saying she was interested in seeing the novel I'd written at the retreat. She apologized if it was too soon.

Maybe it was, but I emailed her the novel anyway. The next day, she wanted to get on a call — her, me, and Sheena, a well-known editor.

Around this time, my boss Sharon had gone on the offensive, sending endless passive-aggressive emails with questions about my projects, hinting that my mental health leave would soon expire. When I signed the book deal, I was able to quit. I did so with a one-line email on the day my paid leave expired. Then I logged out of my work account forever.

My main focus was on getting out the book, along with twice-a-week therapy. My new therapist seemed somewhat concerned about the amount of work that fell on me, but it turned out that Sheena had barely any suggestions. I scanned the edits, the copyedits, the page proofs, watching my words get solidified into something permanent.

Now: it was done. The book was in existence, a separate object from me. Though it had never really been mine to begin with.

I took another bite of the cupcake and the frosting erupted with sweetness in my mouth. I opened up a dating app that I'd downloaded. I hadn't yet set up my profile. I kept telling myself I was going to settle into my new city first. But the thought of using it thrilled and terrified me in equal measure. Clicking *Everyone* when it asked what gender I was looking for.

Ding. I got another text and clicked on it, expecting it to be from Keira. But it was from a number I didn't recognize. The text was long: a block of green. My pulse quickened as I started to read.

Hi darling, I read your book and I wanted to reach out and let you know that I loved the ending. I have to feel some sliver of pride, since you never would've written this story if not for the retreat. I would love to tell you these things in person, but of course that is not possible. Feel free to show this message to the police, as momentarily I will be dropping this "burner" phone into the ocean. (What ocean? The detectives scratch their burly heads.) I do wish that you were here with me. But I understand that you needed to go home. Your life will be less exciting, but perhaps that stability is what you seek. Just know: that wildness still exists inside you. Please protect it, foster it, keep it safe. And who knows, maybe you will prove the impossible: that you hold more than one masterpiece inside you. Know that I will be following you, cheering the ferocious creature in you, for the rest of my days. Kisses. R.

I could barely breathe. I jumped up and went to the window, scanning the street, as if she might be there looking up at me.

For a second, reading her words, she'd been right here, brushing back her auburn hair and fixing me with her emerald gaze. I could even smell her, that whiff of jasmine.

I called Larry immediately. He didn't answer so I left a quick voicemail, distantly noting the calmness in my voice. (*He's thin, Roza, not burly.*) It felt urgent, but it wasn't, really.

She'd survived, yes. And she was gone.

I felt a shifting kaleidoscope of shock, outrage, and fear, mixed with other things, less appropriate things: elation that she'd taken the chance to reach out to me. Deep appreciation that she believed in me. An intense longing to speak with her. So many emotions that together formed a numbness, like all the colors of the rainbow combining into white.

I sat on the edge of the couch, staring into space. I looked without seeing at the half-eaten cupcake, the pink sprinkles covering the white plate.

Sheena's teasing voice came to me: *Tomorrow we'll talk about what you're going to write next.*

Finishing my book had been easy, the final

chapters flowing out like water, though I attributed that to Daphne's help. I didn't know if the connection between us was real or imagined, but something had happened in that final showdown with Roza. My therapist thought Daphne had been a coping mechanism, a calm voice that had risen from the depths of my unconscious to keep me sane on the verge of death. And that would make the most sense. But my therapist wasn't a writer: she didn't know how it felt to channel something from beyond. I wanted to respect that, and to respect Daphne.

Unfortunately, after finishing *The Great Commission,* I hadn't been able to think of any other book ideas. My open laptop continued to feel like a brick wall. The most frustrating part was that I could sense *something* behind it, something pulsing with aliveness, with potential. But I wasn't able to break through. It scared me, the thought that maybe the writer's block had come back for good.

Now the wall was down. Shapes began to form out of the darkness.

I sat back on the couch and pulled my laptop onto my thighs.

I imagined Roza at an outdoor café wearing oversized sunglasses, lips pursed as she read from a book open in front of her. Her hair was chopped short and dyed black and tendrils flicked at her chin. A waiter came up to her and set down a coffee. (Slovakia: tea? Vietnam: juice?) She was so engrossed that it took the clatter of the glass to make her jump, look up, smile.

Roza was a psychopathic murderer. I could never, *ever* forgive her for the horrific things she'd done.

And yet . . .

She'd led me like a light in the darkness, ever since I'd opened the first page of *Devil's Tongue.* At thirteen, I learned from Roza's stolen book that girls didn't have to be sweet little creatures, that they could in fact be angry and dark and sexual. She inspired me to start my own writing, scribbling in cheap notebooks as Mom and I sped from one town to the next. Years later, she welcomed me to Blackbriar. She urged me to stay. She showed me how I could take my deepest pain and use it to create something beautiful.

So. No one would ever know. No one *could* ever know.

But some small, secret part of me would keep writing for her.

Opening a new Google doc, I stared at the blank page.

Slowly, and then with increasing speed, I started to type.

ACKNOWLEDGMENTS

A community of outstanding people made *The Writing Retreat* possible.

Thank you to my agent Alexandra Machinist who "got" this book (and me) immediately. You were the perfect champion for it — and such a pleasure to work with, to boot! Thank you also to Sophie Baker and Cathryn Summerhayes for your enthusiastic and tireless work with the book's foreign rights.

Thank you to my editor, Emily Bestler, whose wise feedback and warm support throughout this first-time process were invaluable. Thanks to associate editor Lara Jones for being so utterly helpful and on top of things. Thanks also to the rest of the Atria team: my publisher Libby McGuire, associate publisher Dana Trocker; publicist Ariele Fredman, marketer Maudee Genao, cover designer Chelsea McGuckin, art director James Iacobelli, interior designer

Esther Paradelo, managing editor Paige Lytle, and assistant managing editor Iris Chen. What a dream to get to work with you all!

Thank you to Ariane Resnick at Salt and Sage Books for your sensitivity read; your notes were extraordinarily helpful and informative. Thanks for taking the time to point out some of my blind spots, which — as a white cis woman — are many.

Thank you to Megan Giddings for your critique of my first chapter via the Authors for Black Voices auction. I felt incredibly lucky to connect with an author whose work I so admire.

Thank you to Andi Bartz, who I'm fortunate enough to have as a sister, and Leah Konen, who is a sister within my chosen family. You have both been instrumental in inspiring and supporting me at every single stage, including the times I've felt like a failed writer and wanted to give up altogether. You're brilliant writers and all-around amazing people, and I feel honored to be a part of our little community. Thank you for reading and offering feedback on this and other books, as well as the general encouragement, recommendations, advice, and real talk. I'm so delighted to have you both in my life.

Thank you to the lovely and astute Amanda Leipold, Abbi Libers, and Cassie Schmitt for reading earlier drafts and offering your thoughtful feedback (and, really, not blinking an eye at the disturbing content!).

Thanks to those who have been cheering me on for literally decades at this point: Sarada, Chris Benigni, Phil Edwards, Krista LaFave, Shivani Tripathi, Jana Truax, and Jenny Zoltan. How blessed am I to have such smart, good-hearted, and hilarious people in my circle, starting from the early days of Chadbourne (and, in Jen's case, BCHS!).

Thank you to the postcollege friends who have also championed me through the years: Julie Eisen, thanks for reading my Philly-era stories and for your continued friendship, despite geographical distance. Rebecca (Booters) Liebmann-Smith: you're another chosen sister, and I'm so glad that I forcibly broke into your clique at work and later followed you into a much more fulfilling clinical social work career. Thanks to the original Brooklyn crew: Blaire Briody, Kate Dietrick, Kate Lord, and Thomas Sander. I'm so glad that we're still planning fabulous getaways despite our busy lives. Thanks to my NYC loves: Eve Blazo, Meghan Felice, Sky Koltun, Samantha Langdorf, Alex Mager, and Hollis Wansley. The dance parties, reality TV marathons, manicures, thrift trips, and spell-castings literally give me life.

Thank you to Rey González for showing me true love and acceptance, and for making me laugh so damn much. I'm truly lucky to have met you.

Thank you to my mental health support team, especially during the difficulties of the last few years. I have so much gratitude for my therapist Meghana Sawant: I wouldn't be where I am without you. Thanks again to Amanda Leipold, my unofficial spiritual advisor and fellow witch. Thanks to Daniel Ryan and Amanda Yates Garcia for helping me heal. Thanks to the incredible yoga teachers at HealHaus, and the whole team at Slope Wellness.

Thank you to my family, who has always encouraged my creativity, especially: Mom and Dad, Tom and Cathy, and Grandma Denes. Your excitement over this book means a lot to me.

ABOUT THE AUTHOR

Julia Bartz is a Brooklyn-based writer and practicing therapist. Her fiction writing has appeared in *The South Dakota Review, InDigest Magazine,* and more. *The Writing Retreat* is her first novel. Follow her on Twitter @JuliaBartz and Instagram at @JuliaBartz.